A Promise of Grace

Other Abingdon Books by Lynette Sowell

Tempest's Course, Quilts of Love Series

Seasons in Pinecraft Series
A Season of Change
A Path Made Plain
A Promise of Grace

A PROMISE OF
GRACE

LYNETTE SOWELL

Abingdon Press
Nashville

A Promise of Grace

Copyright © 2015 by Lynette Sowell

ISBN-13: 978-1-4267-5370-1

Published by Abingdon Press, 2222 Rosa L. Parks Blvd.,
P.O. Box 280988, Nashville, TN 37228-0988

www.abingdonpress.com

Macro Editor: Teri Wilhelms

Published in association with the MacGregor Literary Agency.

The poem "High Flight" by John Gillespie Magee Jr.
is in the Public Domain.

Library of Congress Cataloging-in-Publication Data

Sowell, Lynette.
  A promise of grace / Lynette Sowell.
     pages ; cm. — (Seasons in Pinecraft series ; 3)
  ISBN 978-1-4267-5370-1 (binding: soft back : alk. paper)
  I. Title.
  PS3619.O965P76 2015
  813'.6—dc23

                                              2014045851

Printed in the United States of America

1 2 3 4 5 6 7 8 9 10 / 20 19 18 17 16 15

In loving memory of
Dorothy Jean Davis, 1947–2013

Acknowledgments

Again, I must thank Sherry Gore, Katie Troyer, and the good people of Pinecraft for extending friendship to me and welcoming me to their world. Any inaccuracies in this story are mine. The Plain world has many variations, with Pinecraft being one of the most unique places of all. While the world of Pinecraft is different from mine in many ways, I've found a familiarity in Pinecraft that makes me miss it. I truly hope by the time this book finds its way to bookshelves and readers, I've found my way to Pinecraft yet again.

Remember ye not the former things, neither consider the things of old.

Behold, I will do a new thing; now it shall spring forth; shall ye not know it? I will even make a way in the wilderness, and rivers in the desert.
Isaiah 43:18-19 KJV

1

The minivan's air conditioner gave one last puff of cold air not long after Silas Fry drove across the Florida state line. Silas merely lowered the front windows without saying anything to the children.

How many more hours to Sarasota? Two? Three?

"I wish we were back in Mozambique." Lena sighed and fanned herself where she sat in the front passenger seat. She leaned toward the open window. Her sigh sounded as if her world had suddenly crumbled. At nearly nineteen, she tended to see life in extremes. And Belinda had been the one adept at handling her moodiness.

"Me too." Matthew's echo was born of always wanting to follow in Lena's trail.

"I know you do, I know." Silas forced his voice to come out around the lump in his throat. Africa, his home. Their home. It would never be the same without Belinda. None of them would be.

Despite what Belinda had done long, long ago, he'd loved his wife until the very end. Until the day a semi had plowed into the van in which she and some other ladies had been riding home from a quilt auction. And he'd loved for a long time after.

None of those who died had suffered, the families were told. Suffering was left for the rest of the families left behind, spouseless husbands, motherless children. For them, the wounds ran deep and healed slowly.

Silas filled his lungs with the fresh, humid air blowing into the van. "Your great-uncle said we'll have plenty of time to go to the beach after supper tonight."

The seashore. The ocean had been the one constant where they'd lived in Africa, not far from the coast in Mozambique. And, one big reason he'd chosen to move them all to Florida. In landlocked Ohio, the children had balked and he even found himself feeling a bit constricted, his only refuge in the air, flying a Cessna.

Life with Belinda as their hub had fallen apart. Somehow, with God's help, they'd find a way to put it back together again.

Someone had told him children were resilient.

Children?

He often needed to remind himself that Lena wasn't a child anymore; her studies had ended long ago, and she was planning to continue her education, not to become a teacher like her mother, but to be a medical assistant. She'd already completed her high school equivalency certificate and planned to enroll in college in Sarasota.

Matthew, not a child either, all of fourteen and idolizing his older sister with her take-charge view of the world. They'd already discussed his finishing school in Pinecraft at the Mennonite school after seeing where he compared to other students his age. He had a good eye for building and construction, as well as taking motors apart and putting them back together. Silas was proud of the young man's skills.

But Silas couldn't help thinking of both of them as children. He'd been there from the beginning, when their first cries rang out. He'd seen them grow and thrive, through first words and first stumbles, through the first days of "I can do it myself." Especially with Lena, who seemed to have come from her mother's womb sure of herself and the world.

Lena shifted, her tanned feet now tucked up in the corner between the door and the dashboard, her chin resting on her hand as she gazed at the palm trees they zipped past along the highway.

Silas cast a look in the rearview mirror. Matthew, wearing his favorite shirt Belinda had sewn with the help of an ancient sewing machine before they'd left Africa. Not long from now, the sleeves would be too short and the last of Belinda's lovingly sewn clothing would be ready to donate to someone else's growing child.

"I miss the beach and fishing," Matthew continued.

"We'll have plenty of time for it here."

"But you're going to work."

"I am. I need to earn money for us, just like other fathers do." He'd explained to Matthew before. Lena accepted and, truthfully, she was more concerned with her own studies. Maybe it was her way to cope. He understood, part of him wanting to be at the controls of a plane instead of a minivan towing a small trailer with all their worldly goods.

Silas relaxed his grip on the steering wheel and decelerated. He wasn't flying, doing what made his heart soar the most. God hadn't taken it away from him. He would fly again, soon enough.

The Aviation Fellowship friends—like family, after his and Belinda's serving more than a decade overseas—had sent them off with a generous check and the beginnings of setting up a household.

"One day, you'll be back, Silas," Levi Brubaker had told him before they left Ohio. "God has you called to missions."

"My mission is in Florida now, with my family."

"I understand. We'll be ready to have you back when the time is right."

A lump had swelled in Silas's throat as he'd cut ties with the ministry he'd poured himself into. What would he—they—do now? Life for his fellow missionaries and pilots would go on. They all promised to keep in touch, of course. But things had changed too much for Silas to continue to subject his family to more uncertainty.

Which is what they were doing right now, the van limping its way to Sarasota and the Amish and Mennonite village of Pinecraft, their new home.

And, where Rochelle Keim lived.

He'd thought of her several times over the years. Each time he'd pushed the thoughts away. Deliberately trying to discover how Rochelle fared wouldn't be good for anyone. Now, though, he wondered how she'd aged, if her brown eyes still were soft, expressive, warm, and kind. Her beautiful hair—

"Are you okay, Dad?"

He blinked and glanced at his daughter.

"Mostly. It's been a long trip."

"I wish we could have flown. I wish you still had a plane."

"Me too. But this has been a good way for you to see some of the United States you've never seen before."

Lena shrugged. "That's true." She paused. "The air conditioning's not working."

"No. It's not. I'll see about getting it fixed after we get settled."

God, we need a lot of things fixed.

He thought they'd been fine, as fine as they could be. Until losing Belinda. Had it been almost a year?

He always believed when you didn't know what to do, do the next obvious thing God expected of you. And so, he was. Being a father, providing for his family again, soon piloting for a small private airport that often needed pilots on call for short chartered flights. His one concession to the children had been moving to Florida, to the coast, to the small Plain village within a thriving city.

Whatever came next, he had no idea.

⁙

Of all days for the washer to break down, and her with a pile of laundry. Rochelle Keim hauled the laundry basket from her house to the van and plunked it into the back. Part of her *kapp* caught on the edge of the van's hatch, and the *kapp*, including hairpins, nearly slid off her head. *Ow.*

The village of Pinecraft had its own Laundromat, the only one Rochelle knew of with its own set of clotheslines—bring your own clothespins.

Betsy and Emma, her Amish nieces a couple of times removed, were busy with a morning of wedding planning. How Rochelle wished she could have joined them. But no, she said she'd take care of all the household laundry, including bedsheets, towels, and clothing. Afterward, she had one cleaning client to visit, Emma had her own clients to serve, and Betsy was needed back overseeing business at Pinecraft Pies and Pastry.

Rochelle tried not to sigh. The action wouldn't change anything. Some days, she was tired of cleaning up after other people, herself included.

She fetched two more baskets of laundry, one of them sopping, from the house, then slammed the van's hatch closed.

She had already placed a call to Henry Hostetler, one of Pinecraft's handymen and contractors extraordinaire, about checking the washing machine if he had a spare moment. But the older man was busy finishing replacing a roof but promised to stop by on the way home just before suppertime.

Rochelle drove through Pinecraft's sunny streets, giving the occasional three-wheeled adult cycles wide berth. Most people walked or bicycled the village's streets, nestled on both sides of Sarasota's busy Bahia Vista Avenue and flanked on one end by the meandering Phillippi Creek.

Thankfully, she tucked her van into one of the few parking spots. She wouldn't have to lug her laundry too far. An Old Order Amish woman, Rochelle couldn't recall her name at the moment, moved her tricycle with its little trailer out of the way. The woman waved and smiled, then mouthed a *gut* morning.

Rochelle returned the wave and smile. She reminded herself she was blessed to live in such a place as Pinecraft, where Amish and Mennonites of all orders and fellowships converged, most of them during the winter months. A few, like her, called the village home year-round. Right now, the place was what some might call the proverbial ghost town.

But she couldn't imagine herself living anywhere else. The only other home she'd known was Ohio, and she'd severed ties with that part of her life a long time ago. Her parents, formerly Amish, left their order when she was but a girl, and joined the Mennonite church.

Even her father didn't quite understand why she'd uprooted herself and moved to Florida when she was barely twenty.

"God will guide your path; don't be hasty," her father had said.

Rochelle smiled at her father's words as she tugged the first load of laundry from the back of the van. She'd used those same words when providing counsel to her younger Amish nieces. However, haste hadn't goaded her to leave her family in the Midwest.

With the age of forty growing closer, day by day, month by month, with half a lifetime of years behind her growing up in Ohio, she wondered if she'd have listened to herself when she was her nieces' ages of twenty and twenty-two.

"Good morning," said Nellie Bontrager, the owner of the three-wheeler and trailer. "I see you have a household's worth of laundry there."

"Washer's broken." Rochelle shrugged.

"Here. I'll get the other basket for you."

"Thanks." She also tried to shrug off the unsettled feeling she had after hearing the washing machine clunk to a halt, belt screeching.

She wasn't just tired of cleaning other people's messes. She was tired of cleaning.

Period.

At least today.

Nellie huffed as she trudged along to the nearest empty washing machine. "Good thing it's not washday."

"Good thing," Rochelle agreed. If it was Monday, wash day for many in the village, she'd have to wait her turn for an empty washer. She ought to be thankful the calendar read Tuesday. Instead, her agitation simmered inside her, as if she were an unhappy three-year-old.

Instead of stomping her foot, she sighed, and set the basket she carried on the floor. The clomping noise the basket made didn't quite mask her sigh.

"Is everything all right, Rochelle?" Nellie's expression didn't quite pierce Rochelle, but the older woman studying her was enough to make Rochelle stare at the sopping wet bedsheets and undergarments. She needed to get the detergent and bleach from the van.

"Yes. No. I—I'm not sure." She had to force the confession out. Rochelle never liked to be unsure of much. Uncertain decisions like choosing which flavor of pie to order at Yoder's Restaurant for dessert—now they were a nice uncertainty. No matter what the decision, the results would have a delicious outcome.

Of course, everything was all right—with her—other than the fact today she hated cleaning, and her, a professional cleaning woman.

"It's—it's the weddings. I shouldn't talk about it, because it's not my business." She'd already said too much.

"Is it Betsy and her tattooed baker?" Nellie shook her head and clicked her tongue.

"No, no. Betsy and Thaddeus are doing fine." Of course, a few still doubted Thaddeus's baptism into the Amish faith, despite his proving time, baptism, and settling once and for all into the Amish fellowship in Pinecraft.

"Ah, young Emma and Steven, then."

Rochelle nodded. "Emma is young." She didn't add that Emma had broken off her engagement last winter to Eli Troyer back in Ohio and chose to remain in Pinecraft with her older sister, Betsy, the two of them occupying Rochelle's spare bedroom. She didn't add Emma never seemed to be able to make up her mind on matters and sometimes it changed with the breeze.

Despite her seeming indecisiveness and the rumblings throughout the community, Emma had joined the Mennonite church and planned to marry Steven. Emma attended services with Rochelle regularly, but little things made Rochelle worry if the union between Steven and Emma ought to take place.

Rochelle could clean and organize, but the matters of a twenty-year-old young woman had Rochelle's hands tied. Perhaps it's why God had willed her no family of her own.

Although with Betsy's easygoing ways, Rochelle had wondered more than once what it would have been like to have a young woman like Betsy as a daughter. Emma, though, would have caused her to build up calluses on her knees over the years.

"I hear they'll be here today, likely, and are renting a home from John Stoltzfus," Nellie was saying.

"Oh, who'll be here today?"

"Silas Fry and his family."

"In Pinecraft?" Of course, Nellie meant Pinecraft. John Stoltzfus, an Amish man who lived in Lancaster County, Pennsylvania, owned property in the village and leased it with the help of Nellie's neighbors, a Mennonite couple who lived in Pinecraft.

"Yes, Pinecraft. You know his wife died almost a year ago. Tragic. The van accident."

"Yes, I remember." Rochelle nodded and kept her hands steady as she poured laundry detergent into the machine. She still remembered the day her sister had shared the news with her.

More than once, she'd prayed for Silas and his family, as she ought to. More than once, she'd poured out long-restrained tears about losing Belinda, her one-time best friend. However, she'd lost Belinda years and years ago, before the semi-truck ended her time on this earth.

⌒◦⌒

Rochelle, 19

"My grandmother's turning eighty," Belinda Miller announced. "Almost four times our age."

"You make it sound ancient." Rochelle shook her head and laughed from her place at the sink. A few more dishes to wash, then she and Belinda could leave to go shopping for ingredients for Estelle Miller's gigantic birthday cake.

"Well, eighty is ancient, almost. Momma says she looks great for her age, and Grandma says she doesn't care how she looks for her age, she's happy to still be here to keep Grandpa out of mischief."

"There, I'm done." Rochelle set the last plate in the dish drainer, then wiped her hands. Their fellowship would celebrate the birthday of the matriarch of the Miller family during the coming weekend, and both she and Belinda had volunteered to make the cake. Belinda had taken several cake decorating lessons at a local bakery supply shop, and she was eager to show off her skills.

Rochelle was just along for the ride on this one, she'd assured Belinda, who'd designed a three-tiered round cake, white frosting, and multicolored wildflowers made of sugar.

"Did I tell you John Hershberger is picking me up for the party?" Belinda's cheeks flushed.

"So, you two *are* courting! And you didn't tell me?" Rochelle threw the dishtowel at Belinda's head. "I knew you'd been giggling and looking at him at youth meetings for months now."

Belinda ducked. "No, silly. We're not courting. Yet. I'm sure we will be soon."

For the past few months, all Rochelle had heard was John Hershberger this and John Hershberger that. Rochelle had been tuning her best friend out, because her college studies had kept her busy. Too busy for many of the activities the young adults participated in at Hope Mennonite Church.

However, one meeting not long ago had captured her attention. A missionary group, visiting from overseas, told them all about the great need for workers. Teachers. Doctors. Nurses. Pilots.

At the word *nurse*, Rochelle's ears had perked up higher than the ears on her father's dog, Patches. She was already studying hard for her nursing degree at their local college.

"There is great need here in the United States for good nurses and nursing care, but all members of the medical field are needed in Africa, especially in developing countries and where the gospel isn't always welcome," the speaker had said.

"Anyway," Belinda continued, "John said his best friend, Silas Fry, is riding along with him. You should come, too. We can all ride to the party together."

Daring, riding together, just the four of them in a vehicle.

Rochelle adjusted her *kapp*, then smoothed her apron. "I know Silas Fry."

Well, knew him in a roundabout way. Silas was the kind of young man everyone noticed. The other young men all liked to be his friend. The other young women liked to smile at him, and the boldest struck up conversation. They'd grown up together and participated in the same youth group, but in the last couple of years, childhood friendships had changed into something different as couples began to pair off.

Rochelle had spoken to Silas recently, entirely by accident. She'd gone up to him, thinking he looked like her cousin from behind and called him by her cousin's name. He swung around, with laughter in his eyes and she felt a tug of awareness in their blueness reminding her of a happy summer sky.

"No, I'm not Levi," he'd said. "I hope you're not disappointed."

"No, I'm not." She choked out the three words as her face flamed all sorts of hot. Belinda would tease her, probably as much as she'd teased Belinda about her budding romance with John Hershberger.

But nothing was budding with Silas Fry. She'd tried to keep herself from noticing him, because other young women couldn't help but notice him. However, from this moment, she didn't think she'd ever succeed at pretending not to notice Silas Fry, ever again.

2

No sooner had Silas turned off the van's engine and unbuckled his seat belt did the self-appointed Pinecraft neighborhood welcoming committee arrive.

Lena sprang from the van while Matthew groaned his way out of the back seat and opened the side door. Silas wanted to do a bit of springing or groaning himself—exactly which one, he wasn't sure. Instead, he calmly pulled the keys from the ignition and left the vehicle to meet the Old Order Amish man standing in his driveway.

"You're Silas Fry," the man said, extending his hand. They shook. "I'm Aaron Lapp."

"Nice to meet you. My children, Lena and Matthew." Lena and Matthew joined Silas on his side of the van.

"I heard you were moving in. If you need anything, I'm either here at the house or at the park or having a cuppa over at Yoder's."

"Thank you."

"I let the others on the street know you were coming." Aaron glanced over his shoulder. "There's not much to do right now in the village, so we're grateful you're here to cause a bit of commotion."

Silas wasn't hoping to cause any kind of commotion, but the gleam in Aaron's eye made him smile. "I'm glad we're helping break up the monotony."

"We don't have a whole lot of young people here, not like you'd find back in Ohio. Leastwise, not until winter, anyway."

"I don't mind." Lena nodded. "I'm planning to start college later this summer, so I'll be busy."

"Ah, I see."

"Here we are, Aaron," said another Old Order *daadi*-type of fellow, the wisps of his long white beard drifting on the breeze. "The bus from Indiana is late."

A trio of older men joined the first two, while several gray-haired women in *kapps* bustled around them, murmuring about not to worry, they'd bring the Frys some supper, and did they have fresh linens on hand, and one of their grown children and family had stayed in the same apartment for an entire winter and found the space comfortable and easy to clean with its tiled floors, and they were sure Mr. Fry would find the place ideal for him and his children. Silas's head almost spun from the chatter.

The older men spoke to Matthew, assuring him more people his age would visit during the winter months, but there were a few Amish and Mennonite families with *kinner* his age who lived nearby, and likely they'd see each other at Sunday church meetings.

Silas nodded. "We're going to attend the Mennonite services at the local church."

"Ah, *gut* services. *Gut* people," said the man with the wispy white beard. "My wife always goes to their quilt show every year."

"Yes, yes, I do," said a matron with hair color almost matching her white head covering. "I just finished a quilt last week from one of the quilt tops I bought at this year's show. Do you quilt?" she asked, addressing Lena.

"No."

"Well, you should come to my home sometime, and we can all teach you."

"Ah, well, I don't—"

Silas cut Lena a warning look. His daughter's tongue had gotten her into trouble more than once in Ohio. Pinecraft might be a bit more liberal than some Plain communities, but still, respect always served someone well, no matter where they lived.

Lena sputtered. "I'm not good at hand quilting. I do sew clothing by machine, though, and can alter clothing by hand. But I'm afraid I'll be busy with classes this fall."

"She's going to be a medical assistant someday," Silas interjected.

The older women nodded. After more introductions and comparisons of family trees (everyone seemed to know Silas's Uncle Tobias, which didn't surprise Silas), the group all pitched in and soon had unloaded the contents of the van, along with the larger household items in the small rented trailer.

"We'll be back soon, with food," said the older matron, who'd introduced herself as Wanda Mullet. "You must all be hungry after a long trip."

Silas wanted to find the bed behind stacks of boxes in his room and collapse onto the crisp, freshly laundered sheets, but he knew bedtime would be a while in coming.

At last, the welcoming committee left them, and a large pan of chicken pot pie, a bowl of marinated vegetable salad, homemade cole slaw, a bag of rolls—from Yoder's market—and two pies, one apple and one peanut butter cream, covered Silas's kitchen counter.

"We know there's only three of you, but we couldn't agree on which pie to give you, so you get both," Wanda said before she left. "Besides, you can never have too much dessert."

The three of them ate, with Lena and Matthew holding a conversation about Lena's lack of quilting skills, and Matthew's wondering if he'd see a real live alligator in nearby Phillippi Creek.

The banter buoyed Silas's spirits and by the end of the meal, he found himself suggesting they take a walk through the village so they could see the neighborhood better and find Uncle Tobias and Aunt Frances's home. Uncle Tobias had had a root canal today; Aunt Frances a migraine. Otherwise, the pair would have stopped by the house already.

A walk would also be a fine chance to stretch their legs after being cooped up in the van for so long, as well as an opportunity to meet more of the people.

And maybe see Rochelle?

Of course, he'd see Rochelle. Maybe not today, or tomorrow. But sometime, somewhere here in Pinecraft's sunny streets. Or, maybe at church.

Silas knew he'd be walking headlong into the past when he saw Rochelle again. It had been more than twenty years since they'd spoken, when Lena was growing inside Belinda, after the swift wedding.

He never had the chance to explain to Rochelle, and after she left for Florida, he saw no need. Their lives had diverged. Until now.

"Dad?" Lena waved her fork. "Are you ready for pie?"

He looked down at his mostly eaten food. "No, not just yet. Maybe tonight, with a cup of coffee." The flavorful meal had brought back memories of eating at his grandmother's table.

Another reason to be here in Pinecraft. His children could see firsthand the myriad ways the Plain people lived, from Mennonites more liberal than they, with women who cut their hair short and wore pants or even shorts, to Old Order Amish who retained their Plain conservatism, although everyone in the village did have electricity.

In a few moments, the children had slipped their shoes back on, and they were strolling south down Graber toward busy four-lane Bahia Vista.

"I need to make an appointment with a counselor at the college soon," Lena announced when they reached the crosswalk. "They emailed me before we left Ohio and said for me to call as soon as we got to Sarasota."

"I remember. I don't think they literally meant as soon as we arrived."

"Well, you know what I mean. I need to sign up for financial aid and choose my classes."

"Of course, I know what you meant. Watch your tone." To some, Lena was merely opinionated. To others, she could sound downright rude.

Maybe it was his and Belinda's fault. They'd treated the children like small adults for years. The children had witnessed more than most American children, Lena born and raised overseas and Matthew born in Ohio during a furlough and spending his childhood outside the States. To most adults, Lena's directness, especially for a person her age, wasn't tolerated like it would be from someone years older.

"I'm sorry, Dad. I'm tired. It's all—so, so much." Lena bit her lip. They continued east now, toward the string of buildings on Bahia Vista bearing the Yoder's sign.

"Yes, a lot has happened. But we'll get everything done in time. I promise. I don't start work for another week. We'll go soon. But not today. Maybe tomorrow." He gazed up the street ahead of them. Big Olaf's Ice Cream Parlor lay just ahead. Now visiting the shop was one memory he enjoyed, when he'd step up to the counter, barely able to see over the top of it.

"They have everything we need right here," Matthew observed. "We never have to leave the neighborhood for anything."

Across the side street from Big Olaf's stood several buildings, one of which contained an open-air produce market.

"No, we probably wouldn't have to."

The tinny ringing of a small bell sounded as a three-wheeled cycle zipped past with a Mennonite woman on the seat.

"Wow." Matthew pointed. "A motorized bicycle. That looks fun."

"Tricycle," Lena said. "It has three wheels."

"I know. But it only has two pedals."

"That's the fastest way to get around Pinecraft. Your great-uncle will probably help you both get set up with a cycle of some kind, probably not motorized."

"I want to help him in his shop," Matthew said.

"We'll have to see if he needs help."

They strolled past the giant ice cream cone at Big Olaf's, and a delightful whiff of something warm drifted on the breeze as they rounded the corner of Kaufman.

"A pizza shop." Lena rubbed her stomach. "If we hadn't just eaten, I'd ask if we could stop for some."

"Another time. Maybe soon, you'll make some friends about your age in the village." Silas hoped so, even as he spoke the words. Lena's forays into friendships had been a bit awkward in Ohio; Matthew's as well at first. But Matthew seemed to slide right into a few friendships after those moments. Lena, however, he'd found once crying in the bedroom she shared with her cousin.

"I never seem to say the right thing, Dad." She'd sniffled and scrounged for a tissue, her *kapp* mussed, her hair springing wild in spite of the hairpins to hold it back.

"Give it time, Lena. You'll soon meet a good friend, I'm sure. Anyway, isn't Rachel a good friend?"

"Rachel is my cousin. She *has* to be my friend." Lena wiped her eyes and blew her nose. Now, however, she had no tears over her lack of friends. She'd said goodbye to her cousins and left Ohio with dry eyes.

"Maybe, I will meet a good friend. Maybe at the college, too." Her tone bore the sunny tones of hope. Silas also hoped the attitude, like sunny weather, would last. "Oh, look, a Laundromat. And all the tricycles with little trailers hitched to them."

Silas glanced at the street corner ahead of them. They'd strolled deeper into the neighborhood, but a few blocks from Pinecraft park, if his memories didn't fail him. Everything seemed so much—smaller—from when he was a small boy.

A van was pulling out of a wide driveway by the Laundromat, and as it did, its driver negotiated the vehicle deftly around a cluster of cycles.

The driver, a woman, glanced their way as the van crept onto the street.

Her eyes rounded in her face.

Silas had seen the expression before, the same expression she'd worn when he'd first truly noticed her.

Rochelle Keim.

⋘⋙

Silas, 21

He had never looked forward to an old woman's birthday party until now. Imagine, him, Silas Fry, counting the hours until he and John would head over to celebrate an eighty-year-old woman's birthday, along with Belinda and Rochelle.

Rochelle Keim.

He'd known her name since they were both youngsters, and with her quiet ways, she'd always blended into the background of life. However, ever since she'd mistaken him for Levi and they'd actually had a grown-up conversation, he hadn't been able to keep her out of his mind.

And, for the first time, he noticed all the tangible ways she thoughtfully gave her time and energy for others. It appealed to him a lot. Not to mention her expressive eyes, the sheen of her hair in the sunlight. Her soft laugh, like music. She didn't look skinny like a few of the other girls. Nope, she had curves there, somewhere.

Also, she didn't seem as impressed with him as some of the other young women did. This bothered him a bit and, yet, intrigued him. And, it was something he wanted to remedy. He *wanted* Rochelle Keim to admire him.

A honk sounded outside.

"That would be John," he told his mother as he rose from the living room chair.

"I don't know why you need to ride with him. We're going, too."

"Well, ah, we're taking Belinda and Rochelle Keim with us."

"I see. I haven't spoken to the Keims in a while. They've been busy with doctor's appointments and such."

"Yes, they have."

"Well, when you see Rochelle, let her know I'm praying for her mother."

"I will."

Honk!

He grabbed his jacket and headed out the front door. The front passenger seat was already occupied by Belinda. A space for him waited in the back. There was Rochelle, beside the empty space.

Silas opened the car's rear door and slid onto the back seat.

Rochelle smiled. "I can't wait until you see the birthday cake. It's magnificent."

As Silas returned the smile, he realized two things: He wanted to kiss Rochelle Keim, and he also wanted to marry her.

Rochelle parked the van in the driveway. She turned off the ignition, then clenched her hands into fists to keep them from trembling. But they'd trembled and shook all the way home. She breathed a prayer of thanks she hadn't careened into someone's mailbox on her route through the village.

A pair of bicycles were chained up in the carport. Good, the girls were home after their morning of shopping and wedding planning.

Rochelle wrangled the first of the baskets of laundry from the back of the van. This time, she'd have help unloading again. She maneuvered through the front door.

Winston barked a warning, but his barks ceased and his body commenced a side-to-side wiggle, his tail whipping back and forth. No matter how tired she felt, the red dachshund always managed to make her smile with his antics.

"We found the fabric!" Emma darted into the kitchen from the open living room. She waved a set of swatches dangling from a ring.

Rochelle set down the basket and reached for the samples. "Oh, they're lovely, and soft, almost silky. Which color have you chosen?"

"All of them."

"All?"

"We decided to go with rainbow colors for the attendants," Betsy announced, her cheeks flushed. She bit her lip.

"Rainbow colors. Huh." Yes, the tropical hues would be lovely for attendant dresses. However, she suspected from Betsy's expression her great-niece wanted something simpler.

"I like the aquamarine blue the best," Betsy said. "It reminds me of the Gulf waters."

"I think all-blue dresses aren't as nice as rainbow." Emma frowned. "In Ohio, we'd never be able to use these fabrics, so I want to use them here."

Rochelle almost gave her opinion, then reminded herself neither young woman had asked for an opinion. "If you two could help me, I have our laundry to bring in." At last, her hands had quit their trembling. However, her stomach felt as if she'd been out on Steven Hostetler's fishing charter boat for far too long.

"I'm sorry we stuck you with the laundry, *Aenti* Chelle," Betsy said as the three of them went outside.

"Don't worry about it. I know you both needed to find your fabrics and get them ordered, and we all have clients to see this afternoon. It works out better this way."

"I think it worked out *gut*, too." Emma got to the back of the van first and pulled out the smallest basket. "I hope you can get the washer repaired soon."

"Henry's going to stop by right before supper and look at it. He said it might be something as simple as replacing a belt."

The young women continued their chatter about wedding plans as they all unloaded the laundry baskets and set about sorting the garments to their owners.

Rochelle allowed herself to get swept up in their conversation, listening. Yes, forty years old might be looming closer, but inside, she felt the same almost-giddiness the young women shared about their upcoming double wedding day.

A double wedding day, here in Pinecraft, in the winter. Five hundred friends and family, maybe more, once all names were tallied.

It made sense, though, to have the ceremony here and not Ohio, with both women living in Sarasota now and their young men part of the village as well.

"Everything okay, *Aenti*?" Betsy frowned, folding a set of pillowcases.

"Yes." She nodded. Everything was okay. "I'm just a little distracted. But tell me more. Did you both decide on a cake?"

The young women exchanged glances. Betsy set her jaw, and her chin stuck out just a little.

"We're having two wedding cakes," Emma announced.

"Two cakes?"

Emma nodded. "I want cupcakes to match the color of the dresses."

"And I want an all-white cake, three stacked tiers, with white sugar flowers, and white piping," Betsy added. "We just couldn't decide on something together."

"Well, I think it's all right to have two cakes. I know there will be plenty of cake for everyone who wants some." Clearly, the sisters didn't agree on everything. Plain or not, all brides had their own opinions. "I think both ceremonies and the meal to follow will be beautiful."

"I hope so." Emma grabbed her stack of laundry. "I need to put all of this laundry away, and I want to get my afternoon work done early. Steven is picking me up for supper with his parents."

Then Emma toted her stack of laundry down the hallway. Seconds later, her door closed with a click.

"*Aenti* Chelle, are you sure you're all right? You said you were distracted, but you look more upset than anything else."

"Maybe I am upset, just a little. I've had a shock, but I'll be all right." She didn't want to say more. She hadn't even processed her feelings at seeing Silas Fry, even a glimpse, after nearly two decades.

The last time she'd seen him, she'd turned her back on him and walked away, willing the tears not to fall, willing her heart not to shatter. It had been her fault. May her great-nieces never know her kind of pain. Betsy had felt the sting of unrequited love before she met Thaddeus Zook. But this feeling? Rochelle hoped Betsy never knew it.

"Well, *Aenti*, if you need a listening ear, I'm here. You were there for me, with Thaddeus, and I'm thankful."

Rochelle smiled at Betsy. "Thank you. I'll remember and let you know if and when I do. But, for now, I'll hold onto this myself."

Did her sister, Jolene, know Silas was moving to Pinecraft? And if Jolene knew Silas was coming, wouldn't she have warned Rochelle?

She shook away the thoughts. Time for a quick lunch, then a busy afternoon of cleaning what her clients would only dirty again.

3

The inevitable Sunday service came around, and the final echo of voices raised in song fell silent in the sanctuary. All the while, from the first greeting until now, Rochelle's brain had tried to process that Silas and his family sat two rows behind her.

Yes, his elderly aunt and uncle, Frances and Tobias Fry, attended Pinecraft Mennonite Church as well, but they weren't part of any of Rochelle's past memories. They had never questioned Rochelle's sudden move to Pinecraft many years ago, but had welcomed her to the village.

Voices swirled around Rochelle as she stood, murmuring greetings to those sitting in front of her.

Emma plucked Rochelle's elbow. "*Aenti* Chelle, did you ever hear anything from Steven? He said we might go fishing today, but he didn't come to services this morning." Emma frowned.

The young couple's whirlwind courtship had been a surprise to many, except for Rochelle. Last fall, she'd seen things brewing between Henry Hostetler's nephew and her great-niece.

Whirlwind was a good word to describe Emma. Formerly Amish but now fellowshipping at the Mennonite church, she had recently gained her full membership status in the congregation.

Emma said, "I want to meet the new family, the Frys. The daughter looks like she's around my age. She looks nervous, too. I know I was glad to already know people when I first moved to Florida, and, of course, Betsy lived here already."

"You go on ahead. I . . . I need to speak to Natalie." Rochelle picked up her Bible, then touched her head covering. No, it wasn't lopsided, but sometimes she just had a lopsided feeling. Like now. She didn't *need* to speak to Natalie Miller. *Need* was too strong of a word. Every time she spoke with Natalie, she came away feeling encouraged. And right now she could use some encouragement. So maybe she did need to speak with her young friend.

"Rochelle, it's good to see you," said Natalie Miller, glowing with the first signs of new life inside of her.

"It's good to see you, too. How have you been feeling?"

"Very well. I want to eat everything not nailed down, but other than food cravings like red velvet whoopie pies at three a.m., I'm doing great." Natalie's eyes sparkled. "Part of me wants to get an ultrasound to find out boy or girl, but I'm going with what Jacob prefers and we'll be surprised."

"I know you're excited, either way." The younger woman's words made Rochelle smile. Only converted to Mennonite within the last couple of years, Natalie felt a bit freer than most in discussing personal matters such as pregnancy. Especially in church. Rochelle glanced around. Everyone else was taken up in their own discussions after the service.

Rochelle continued from her spot at the edge of the pew to the opposite end, then made her way along the side aisle and headed through another door into the foyer, then shot to the ladies room. While the family introduced themselves to the congregation, maybe she could stall long enough for Emma to meet and greet Silas's daughter, who looked so much like Belinda at the same age it made Rochelle stare.

She greeted a few people then spent an inordinate amount of time washing her hands in the ladies' room and checking the hairpins securing her head covering. There. That ought to be long enough.

She realized how silly she must look, sneaking around in the crowd and avoiding the Frys. It wasn't as if she were a teenager. Not anymore. Rochelle squared her shoulders and studied her face in the ladies' room mirror. Bright red spots covered her cheeks.

"Rochelle, are you feeling all right?" Her sister Jolene had entered the ladies' room. "Your face looks flushed, and I understand why."

"I'm okay." She glanced from the mirror to Jolene. "I wish you'd told me they were coming." She needed to get better at masking her feelings, with several people inquiring about her health lately.

Jolene stepped closer and lowered her voice. "I didn't know. I promise. I would have told you if I knew."

The bathroom door opened, so Rochelle kept her response simple. "Good. Well, I need to get going."

"We should have a family lunch again . . . soon."

"Soon."

They both greeted the woman who entered, then Rochelle scurried from the ladies room. She needed to quit hanging back, letting Silas's presence get to her like this. With him living in Pinecraft now, she needed to get used to it as soon as possible. When winter came, bringing the snowbirds from the north and the village population swelled, avoiding him would be easier and far less obvious until she could deal with whatever she was feeling once and for all.

Rochelle nearly collided with Silas and his family, who were talking to Emma and others in the foyer.

"Here she is now," Emma called out.

⟲⟳

Rochelle appeared at his side in the foyer, almost knocking into his elbow.

Her cheeks shot with red, the expression was just as endearing now as it once had been. Quickly, however, her expression smoothed itself over.

"Hello, Silas."

He'd forgotten how it felt when she said his name, and the inches between them shrank. "Rochelle . . ."

"Oh, so you know each other?" Emma glanced from Rochelle to Silas, then back again.

"When we were about your age," Rochelle said. "But it was a long time ago. Ah, welcome to Pinecraft. I'm afraid I don't know the names of your daughter and son."

"Lena." Wearing Belinda's smile, Silas's daughter stepped forward and shook hands with Rochelle.

"I'm Matthew." His son wore a lopsided grin and shook hands with Rochelle.

"It's nice to meet you both. Yes, I knew your parents a long time ago when we all lived in Ohio."

"Your mother and Rochelle were good friends." Silas found his voice again.

Lena's eyes narrowed a millisecond. "But we never saw you or heard of you when we were growing up and visited Ohio."

Rochelle now looked at him. Yes, the explanation was his to give.

"Well, right before your mother and I married—" his voice cracked.

"I moved to Florida. I don't often get back to Ohio. I did know your parents were serving as missionaries in Mozambique." She looked apologetic for the interruption. But she'd mercifully interjected when his voice failed him. So, she'd kept up with them, a little. "Then, life happened. I started my business here, and well, your parents and I . . . lost touch."

"I want to go back to Africa, someday," Lena said. "I miss it."

"I'm sure you do," Rochelle responded, warmly. "So, what brings all of you here to Pinecraft? We don't often get new, permanent residents under retirement age."

"I have a job, flying, a private charter pilot. I'm thinking of earning my commercial license after all." He didn't miss the blank expression on Rochelle's face at the words *commercial license.* "And Lena here is going to start college soon for nursing."

Rochelle opened her mouth, but Emma spoke first. "Oh, just like my *Aenti* Chelle. She's going to finish her studies this fall, or soon anyway."

Now Rochelle looked a tad cranky, but again smoothed over her expression. "Oh, Emma, I'd only mentioned it a week or so ago. I haven't decided yet, for sure."

Emma nodded. "Well, I think you need to. *Aenti* Chelle has only two more semesters, and then clinicals. You need to finish."

"But you have a business here?" Silas asked.

"I have a cleaning company. Keim Cleaning. I discovered when I moved here people in the good city of Sarasota will pay good money for a Mennonite or Amish woman to clean their homes. I learned the business from an Old Order woman who lives here in the village, and she helped me find my first clients. So the business sort of grew and grew, and I'm always looking for good workers."

"I know Lena wouldn't mind something part-time, especially with school coming up."

Lena nodded. "Yes, I'd like that. I applied at Yoder's and Der Dutchman, and they're not hiring right now."

"I imagine I can find a client or two for you. And I sometimes need substitutes. We'll talk again about it sometime soon."

"All right." Lena beamed. "Thank you. Thank you."

Seeing his daughter smile so widely made his heart hurt. At last, the sun seemed to be breaking through for his family after a year of stormy skies.

"I'm going to help my uncle in his bicycle shop," Matthew chimed in.

"Now, we haven't discussed it yet, and it's up to Uncle Tobias," Silas said.

"Ah, yes. Fry's Bicycle Shop. Your Uncle Tobias has more bicycles than anyone in the village, I think." Rochelle nodded, then glanced at Lena and her niece, chattering together.

"*Aenti* Chelle, may the Frys come to the house for lunch today?" Emma asked, the young women exchanging hopeful looks between each other.

"Well, uh . . ." Rochelle's cheeks bloomed a deep pink.

"We don't want to impose . . ." Silas shook his head. He didn't know who wanted to bolt from the foyer most at the moment, him or Rochelle. He cleared his throat.

Rochelle squared her shoulders, then nodded. "Yes, we have plenty to share for lunch today. But weren't you and some of the others supposed to go fishing with Steven?"

Emma shrugged, a gesture Silas had seen a few times from his own daughter. "I hoped we would. Maybe we will later this afternoon."

Silas cleared his throat. "Thank you, Rochelle and Emma, but maybe we'll come for lunch another day." Or maybe not. He didn't want to add to Rochelle's obvious discomfort. He had the distinct feeling young Emma Yoder was accustomed to getting her own way, most of the time anyway.

But again, seeing the smile blooming on Lena's face did his own heart good. So far, it seemed as though his daughter was settling into life in Pinecraft. However, they'd only been here for several days. Time would reveal more.

He glanced at Rochelle, who appeared less stiff than before his polite refusal of the lunch offer.

"All right. Another time then." She gave him a soft smile, although he could still see apprehension in her eyes.

He now had more questions. So she'd never become a nurse? She'd never made it overseas, either. At least not that he knew of.

Instead of silencing the questions he used to have about Rochelle, his mind now spun with more questions. Of course, he knew a big reason she'd left school, and it wasn't just him. He'd told her, years ago, he always wanted her to finish her education. No matter what had happened between them.

❧

Rochelle, 19

"What do you dream about, Rochelle Keim?"

No one had ever asked her, Rochelle Keim, the younger of the two Keim sisters, what she dreamed about. She'd been too busy helping in the household and, with her mother having cancer, helping act as caregiver as well. She'd gotten her driver's license, could change wound dressings quickly, reminded her mother about her various medicines, and held her mother's hand while the retching shook her dwindling frame. She'd been the driver for Momma's chemotherapy appointments, too.

The question, coming from Silas, made her glow inside.

"I—I dream about working overseas, as a nurse. Remember the missionaries who visited a few months ago? Their visit made me start praying and thinking about it. I want to make a difference in people's lives, people who have no hope and are hurting."

"I think you'll make a wonderful nurse." Silas leaned back on the porch swing. "How much longer do you have until your studies are done?"

"Four semesters or so. I've, ah, only taken a class here and there recently, with Momma being sick. But, I want to get there. Someday." Rochelle thought again about her mother. Her older sister, Jolene, had a toddler girl, and Rochelle knew Jolene couldn't devote as much time to caring for their mother. So, of course, Rochelle had to be the one. She hadn't told the family about her heart's decision to search for a possibility overseas.

Silas studied her face. "I believe you will. I know it's been hard with your mother's illness, but your whole family can pitch in and help with her. She's their family, too."

"I know. It's just easier if I take care of her." She wanted to explain how the Amish part of the family didn't acknowledge her parents, being shunned, and people at their home church . . .

It was easy to forget people with chronic illness.

"Easier for who? Them or you?"

Rochelle shook her head. "Silas—"

"Never mind." He smiled at her like he smiled at no one else. Ever since the first time he caught her attention, she noticed how he treated other people. Always kindly, warmly. But when he looked at her like this? Well, it was the kind of smile reserved for her alone. It made her insides warm—no, blazing hot if she would admit it to herself.

"Anyway," he continued. "I need help with a diagnosis. I have, uh, a lip lesion."

"Lip lesion?" She studied his mouth. "I don't see anything."

"Look more closely." He pointed at one corner. "It's right here." "Where?" She leaned a little closer, and her breath caught. She saw nothing.

But she was close enough for him to easily pull her to him and place his lips on hers.

The first kiss—ever—in her young life, and it was beautiful. The sweetest gesture, ever. But oh, how her insides shook. Her heart thudded.

"Silas?" Her throat croaked.

"Yes, Rochelle?"

"Is—is it better now?"

"Much better." He punctuated the phrase with another swift kiss.

4

The great-nieces' whispers in the kitchen drifted onto the lanai, where Rochelle sat sipping a sweet tea and listening to the soft breeze whistling in the palm trees. She closed her eyes. Florida, even in the summer with its humidity, had never lost its appeal. She thought of the coming fall season and plummeting temperatures up north. Dealing with humidity was far easier than digging out of a snowstorm.

Even Pinecraft's quietness in the summer didn't bother her.

However, with the Frys' arrival, the village began to hum, just a little.

"Well, *something* was going on with them. They *know* each other," came Emma's voice. The young woman had pouted, ever so slightly, over the fact that Steven wasn't meeting her immediately at the house after church, but brightened upon learning they would be going to a singing in the evening at his parents' neighbors' house.

"Leave it alone, Emma. If *Aenti* Chelle wants to tell us, she will. It's up to her." A sound of swishing fabric. Someone had risen from the kitchen table and pushed back a chair. The refrigerator door clicked open. "We're almost out of iced tea."

"Oh. Sorry. I meant to make more, but I forgot," Emma said. "Could you please pour me a glass also?"

"They'll be small servings. There's only enough for one glass."

Oops. Rochelle knew she probably ought to have started another pot brewing, but figured the girls would each be off to visit with friends or others. Without guilt, she took another sip of her tea. Let someone else take care of little details like keeping them all supplied with iced tea. She smiled.

"Never mind, then."

"Isn't Steven stopping by soon?"

"Yes, he's going to walk me to the singing."

And so went the exchange between the sisters, much as it did each Sunday afternoon. The subject of their late December wedding day didn't come up, for once. Rochelle exhaled softly. No controversy. Not today. Her likely not-so-hidden reaction to seeing Silas again, up close, and speaking to him, might have given them something else to consider besides the wedding.

Sweet girls, even Emma with her spirited demeanor. One day, her young enthusiasm would be more of an asset to her than now. So much about Emma reminded her of Belinda. Her personality claimed hold of a room, and you couldn't help but notice her.

The sound of footsteps grew louder. Rochelle glanced toward the doorway. Betsy stepped onto the tile floor. She held a glass of iced tea, half-full.

"So," Betsy said as she sank onto the closest cushioned chaise lounge. She tugged her hem into submission with her free hand before settling back on the chair.

"So."

"You. And Silas Fry. You knew each other. Or know each other."

"Knew. A long time ago. We were just kids. Young adults. A little younger than you are now. We, ah, grew up together in the church."

"I see. You told us as much at church today. But you've never mentioned him or his wife, Belinda, in all the time I've been here. And it sounds as though you were such good friends, too."

"Were is the correct word. And I don't know Silas Fry anymore, either. I haven't seen him since, well . . . before his daughter was born."

Betsy said nothing, but took a long sip of her tea. The ice clinked in the glass.

"So."

"You like that word today." Rochelle had to smile at Betsy.

"So this was before you moved here to Pinecraft then."

"Yes, it was." Rochelle swallowed more of her iced tea. She loved it, year-round. And the amount in her glass now dwindled. Betsy's quiet persistence should be rewarded. Of course, she wanted to know what had happened, not out of mere curiosity, but from loving concern. "Belinda was my best friend. Much like you and Miriam are close."

"When she died, last year, it must have been hard for you."

"It was. I never had the chance to make things right between us, at least on my part. I figured . . . Oh, I don't know why either of us never tried. Life happened, I suppose. It was easier to say nothing."

"I'm . . . I'm sorry. I can't imagine Miriam and I never keeping touch again."

"I thought I was going to marry Silas Fry one day, and Belinda marry someone else." The words ripped open a long-covered scab of memory. Surprisingly, though, Rochelle didn't feel anything. This should come as a relief to her. It was something she hadn't spoken of since leaving Ohio, and ever since she and Silas and Belinda had gone their separate ways.

Good. She watched surprise flicker across Betsy's face.

"Oh, *Aenti* Chelle, what happened?"

Rochelle took a deep breath.

"A lot. Like often happens in life. Yet, God took care of all of us. Silas, Belinda, me, too. Nothing that happened was anything we imagined. But I've realized everything has turned out all right. If things hadn't gone the way they did, I wouldn't have ended up here." She surveyed the lanai, the section of green yard outside, the palm trees lining the inlet of Phillippi Creek running mere yards from the edge of her lawn.

Yes, her life hadn't turned out as she'd imagined. Today, though, she finally felt a peace about the twists and turns. Even after her reaction to seeing Silas again.

But why, then, didn't her tone sound as convincing to her own ears?

◦◦◦

Silas, 21

Silas finally understood what the word *smitten* truly meant. Thinking of all the things that had happened after the grandmother's birthday party—several walks over the last few weeks, one night talking for hours on Rochelle's front porch with two kisses, plus one goodnight kiss following—he soared on the clouds higher than the small Cessna he was soon to fly solo.

Today, he could hardly concentrate at work. He'd caught himself staring vacantly at the computer monitor several times as the figures on the spreasheet ran together.

"I think I'm finally going to ask Belinda to marry me," John announced.

"You think?" Silas chuckled. "Are you sure?"

John's face flushed red. "Yes, I'm sure. I've never wanted anything more. I've prayed about it, and I know she's been praying, too."

"No worries. No need to get defensive. I'm glad you're sure." Silas held up his hands in surrender. "You just don't use words like *think* and *finally* when making one of the biggest decisions of your life. It's not like you *think* you're going to get around to cleaning out the shed or *finally* trimming the tree branches in the backyard."

"I love Belinda. I do. She's . . . amazing . . ." John's voice trailed off, and he looked out across the workshop.

Silas turned his focus back to the computer in front of him. He needed to finish entering the stack of invoices by the end of the day, so the accounts payable department could write checks to the suppliers.

"Now, this is more like it, friend. More enthusiasm." Now it was his turn to stare off into space and think once more of Rochelle. John's recent lack of exuberance where Belinda was concerned worried him a bit. John and Belinda had been courting each other for several months, and lately Silas had agreed to accompany them with Rochelle rounding out the group.

"So, you seem enthusiastic about Rochelle Keim," John said.

"Yes, yes I am." Silas wasn't embarrassed to admit it, not a bit. No one had captured his attention like she did, and the more he learned about her, the more he loved.

"What does she think about your idea of becoming a pilot?"

"She's excited about my solo flight. In fact, she's going to ride with my family to the airport and watch."

"Well, I'm happy for you."

"Thanks, John. It seems like things are looking bright for all four of us."

"Yes, thanks to God. I'm grateful for His provision, of sending me such a special woman, and sending a special woman to you, too."

Silas nodded. "You're right." He'd better get back to work, especially if he wanted to continue to have a job to help pay for more flying lessons.

<hr />

Sunday supper at his aunt and uncle's house, and it was only the five of them. Were it Christmas time, the number would likely be tripled or even four times that number. Today, though, Silas thanked God it was only him and the children, along with Aunt Frances and Uncle Tobias.

He sat on his uncle's front porch, watching the palm trees across the street sway in the breeze. Everyone in the village had probably settled down for an afternoon nap. He yawned. A nap sounded like a good idea to him, just as soon as Aunt Fran made sure the enchiladas were heated all the way through.

Thankfully, both he and Rochelle had managed to extricate themselves from Lena and Emma's finagling to share a Sunday meal together after church.

Rochelle's discomfort was as obvious as her attempts to keep a distance between them. Some might say the years between them were plenty distance enough. Until now, they had been.

He'd had his own reaction to seeing her again, up close.

The years had been kind to her, leaving only the faintest of lines around her eyes. Her skin, still smooth with a hint of color on her cheeks; her hair the same rich color he remembered with the first

few strands of silver. As her expressive eyes took in her surroundings, their expression had softened for a millisecond when she'd
seen him, then something had overcome the softness. A wariness.

But she'd made herself clear years ago. The memory still made
him feel like a failure. The old argument still wanted to spring to his
lips, but it served no purpose now.

"Dad? You coming?" Matthew tugged on his sleeve. "Uncle Tobias
wants to show us his shop."

"Sure, yes." He shifted to a standing position and stretched,
thumped his stomach, and yawned again. "My meal is still settling,
I think."

Matthew had developed an instant fascination with the bicycles
of Pinecraft. Instead of the buggies used in other parts of the country by the Amish, most everyone here, Plain or otherwise, used this
method to get around the village.

"Uncle Toby said I can get my own bicycle."

"Oh, he did?" Matthew's enthusiasm made Silas smile. Gone were
the boy's earlier stormy frowns about missing Africa. Referring to Silas's
aging uncle as Uncle "Toby" made him chuckle.

"What's so funny, Dad?" Matthew asked as they crossed the lawn,
then rounded the corner to Uncle Tobias's wide expanse of driveway
sloping down toward the large, covered workshop where a veritable
stable of bicycles and tricycles sat, waiting to be rented.

"I've never heard anyone refer to Uncle Tobias as Uncle 'Toby'
before."

"Well, he's not old. And Tobias sounds like an old name."

"There you are," Uncle Tobias stood at the door to a large shed.
He worked a key inside a padlock. "You ready to see the beauties
inside?"

"Yes, sir." Matthew craned his neck to look past his great-uncle.
"Do I get to pick mine out today?"

Tobias glanced at Silas. "As long as it's okay with your father."

"Well, Uncle Tobias, I think it's a good idea, but—"

"I won't take a penny for it. I know you, Matthew, and Lena
are getting up on your feet again." Tobias flipped on a light switch,
revealing rows of bicycles and tricycles. The scent of oil filled the air.

"However, I'm going to need help the rest of this summer and into the winter snowbird season, especially. I was thinking we could set a price for a bicycle, and Matthew here can work for it."

"Like a real job?" The eagerness in Matthew's voice raised its pitch ever so slightly.

"Like a real job. And once you've worked off the cost of the bicycle, I'll pay you a wage." Uncle Tobias led the way to a large worktable, covered with bicycle parts. Wheels, gearshifts, brakes, all jumbled together in an order only Tobias probably knew. "You look around, ask me whatever you'd like to know."

Matthew strode up and down the rows of bicycles, hopping astride one then another, stopping to look at one with a large basket on the back and some sort of a motor as well.

"Thanks, Uncle Tobias," Silas said. "This means a lot."

"Aw, it's nothing. Young Matthew's growing up, and I'm glad to get to know him. And you again. I'm glad you're here." Tobias moved from the work table to a desk, stacked with papers and an adding machine. "There are times I've been looking for an extra pair of hands around here. So you and the kids being here is an answer to a prayer."

"Good. Matthew can be a bit, ah, rough and tumble. He likes all kinds of gadgets and figuring out how things work. Pretty handy as a construction helper, too."

"I imagine you're pretty handy, too, being overseas for so many years."

"I can swing a hammer and use power tools, but I'm nowhere near being a craftsman. Small engine repair is more my thing. You get pretty adept at learning how to fix an engine or otherwise stay somewhere remote overnight."

"How about this one?" Matthew called out across the workshop. He beamed from his perch on a three-wheeled cycle with candy apple red paint and gleaming chrome handlebars.

"That's an excellent choice," Tobias said. "Retail cost, with all the features, right around three hundred dollars."

"Are you sure?" Silas tried to keep his voice low.

"Of course it's okay." Tobias took a tag from a stack on the desk and scribbled on it with a pen. "Here, Matthew. Peel the backing off this tag and stick it to the handlebar somewhere. Then we'll know which one is yours."

Matthew trotted across the workshop. His face bore Belinda's smile, his chin mirroring hers as he stuck it out in determination. "Thanks, Uncle Toby."

"You're welcome. It's nice of you to help an old man with his business."

"It's going to be fun." Matthew accepted the tag from Uncle Tobias and lost no time in affixing it to his bicycle. Matthew beamed.

Uncle Tobias joined Matthew among the bicycle rows, answering questions about this bike and another, and telling him about one of the greatly prized models of cycles, motor-operated contraptions.

Silas's gut reminded him tomorrow was Monday. First day of work. The small municipal airport was perhaps five miles or so away from Pinecraft, a comfortable distance. He would report there after dropping off Lena at Sarasota State College where she had appointments with Admissions and Financial Aid departments. He'd wanted to be there with her, but she insisted on handling it herself.

"Hey, Dad." Lena appeared in the doorway of the workshop. "Aunt Fran said everything's ready now."

"Good. I'm ready to eat." He glanced toward Tobias and Matthew. "You two ready?"

"Yes, sir!" Matthew grinned. "I don't think I've had enchiladas before."

"You have." Lena shot him an elder-sister look. "Lots of times."

"Well, I haven't had Aunt Fran's."

Tobias locked up the workshop, and the four of them strode across the lawn to the house.

Lena stepped beside Silas along the way.

"Oh, I don't need a ride to the college tomorrow," Lena announced. "I found a ride."

"Who?" Silas asked. This independence of Lena's was scaring him. Where did the little girl go who used to hang back beside her mother's skirt when thrust into unfamiliar situations?

"Emma's Aunt Rochelle is picking me up in the morning around nine. She's going to the college to register for classes, too."

No, he couldn't object. No need. But somehow, Rochelle had been convinced to give Lena a ride. However, Rochelle probably needed little convincing. Always ready to help someone if she could.

"All right, as long as she doesn't mind."

"No, Emma said her aunt didn't mind, especially since she's going anyway. I think I'm going to talk to her about a job, too, for after classes start."

"Good. Just don't bite off more than you can chew. I've heard college studies can be quite rigorous." Silas wanted to add, "Are you sure you don't need me there, too?" but didn't. He'd studied flying, but had never enrolled in a degree plan through a college.

Uncharted territory, for all of them.

Lord, help us.

He kicked his thoughts to the side. All Rochelle was doing was giving Lena a ride to the college. No big deal. People helped each other in the village, he'd been told. At the least, maybe he and Rochelle could be friends. It was a place to start.

5

Promptly at nine a.m., Rochelle pulled up in front of the Frys' rental home and waited. Yes, Emma had talked her into giving Lena a ride. The two had chatted for a while on Sunday afternoon. However, it didn't take any convincing for Rochelle to agree to give Lena a ride to the campus. It made perfectly good sense since Rochelle had business at the college anyway.

Forget butterflies in her stomach; she had a flock of seagulls beating their wings. Back to her studies, at last. With her sealed transcripts from Ohio in the portfolio beside her, she knew she was well armed.

Here came Lena, wearing a cape dress a shade of robin's egg blue, her head covering crisp and white in the morning sun. Her cheeks glowed.

"Good morning," Lena said as she hopped into the passenger seat. She clutched a manila folder. "Thanks for taking me to the college, too. Dad starts his job this morning, so he gets to go straight there."

"Not a problem." Rochelle put the van into gear and pulled away from the side of the street. "So, this is your first time attending college?"

"Yes, I was hoping to when . . . when we returned to Ohio from Africa. Before the accident." Lena fell silent. Rochelle glanced her way. The young woman stared out the window at the passing traffic.

"Ah, I see. Well, I'm glad you now have this chance. I'm new at Sarasota State also. I did tour the campus when I was making my final decision about returning to college." She stopped for a red light ahead. Sarasota bustled with its stop-and-go traffic.

"It's busy here. I like the city, a lot." Lena shifted positions on the seat. "So, you said you are returning to college. How long have you been gone?"

"Ah, about nineteen years or so."

"Wow, it's a long time."

"Yes, it is. It is . . ." Rochelle's seagulls began their incessant flapping again. "But, I'm going to finish. The advisor told me my credits are still good, but I have a few refresher courses to take, based on my unofficial transcripts. Today I'm bringing the official copies and planning my schedule."

"So why'd you stop going to college?"

"My mother passed away when I was about your age. It was . . . a hard time for me. Then, I decided to move to Florida. I ended up starting my business. And, so, here I am."

"Why didn't you go back to college?"

Rochelle shrugged. "I'm not sure, exactly."

Why hadn't she gone ahead and finished her education? Instead, she'd buried herself in building a business—and a successful one. But still . . .

"I'm glad for you, Miss Keim. I'm glad for both of us." Lena smiled. Her smile was so much like Belinda's it made Rochelle's heart hurt.

"Thank you. I'm glad, too."

They passed the rest of the trip in silence. All the while, thoughts swirled. Belinda's daughter. Yes, she could see her former best friend. The likeness was unmistakable.

She tried not to think about the fact that the young woman sitting beside her was also Silas's daughter. So quickly, Belinda had conceived after the wedding. So quickly, Silas had moved on. Truthfully, he'd always had a soft spot for Belinda. Part of her now wondered if it had been part of the problem that had blown up into a tumult after John's death.

Maybe, back then, he'd been having feelings for Belinda, too.

Stop it.

Rochelle shoved the idea aside internally, while on the outside she smiled and nodded at Lena exclaiming over the flamingos in the pond in the center of the park-like entrance to the college.

"I think I'm going to like it here," said Lena, to which Rochelle responded with a nod and another smile.

She shouldn't be turning the past over in her mind like she had been, ever since her first glimpse of Silas in the village. For almost a year, since first learning of Belinda's death, she'd avoided thoughts of Silas and what his life must be like. Daniel Troyer had distracted her last fall, but she'd learned from her mistake and wouldn't repeat it again.

Lena kept a chatter up about classes and activities now that they'd reached the parking lot. She talked of what it would be like to work in a lab and study more chemistry and biology and how good it would be, a number of semesters in the future, to finally see patients and care for them.

"I wonder if I can get some credits for helping."

"Helping?"

"There is a Mennonite medical clinic in the village where we lived, in Africa. I would volunteer and help there as often as I could," Lena said.

"What valuable experience." Rochelle maneuvered her van into an empty parking space.

"I think so. I knew then I wanted to learn how to help people get better, to figure out what their illness is, and help them stay well."

Rochelle wanted a bottle with a cork to gather some of Lena's enthusiasm. Where had her own disappeared to?

Suddenly, she felt old. When had it happened to her?

She tried not to sigh as she turned off the ignition. "Well, here we go." She smiled at Lena. Yes, the seagulls began flapping their wings once again. She could do this. She knew she could. It was time to finish what she'd started.

❧

Silas arrived home to a quiet house, earlier than he thought, not long after one o'clock. He'd given Matthew permission to bicycle over to Uncle Tobias's shop immediately after breakfast and right before Rochelle arrived to pick up Lena for the college.

He opened the refrigerator and pulled out a container of Aunt Fran's enchiladas she'd sent home with them last evening. Good stuff. He scooped a few onto a plate, then popped the plate in the microwave and watched it spin as it heated.

Tomorrow, he'd make a practice flight to get himself back into the swing of things, so to speak. He'd kept up his pilot's license while in Ohio. Life would have to go on, he knew, and having it constant in his life—the sky—helped immeasurably. That, and the children, of course.

The children.

He'd almost said no to Matthew's request to bicycle the few short blocks to Uncle Tobias's house. The boy was fourteen, almost on the brink of manhood. When he was fourteen, he was already doing plenty, not treated as if he were a six-year-old. And where they'd lived wasn't exactly the safest place.

"I just don't want anything to happen to him. Or Lena," Silas spoke aloud as the microwave beeped.

He and Belinda had drifted along, their life a series of ups and downs as they lived overseas. But never like this. Not this fear the hand of God would yank their worlds out from under them again.

Enough. He pulled the steaming enchiladas from the microwave, then winced as he set the hot ceramic plate on the counter.

He knew he'd protected them all as best he could. Even if it wasn't enough, he had no right to question God's ways.

As far as the heavens are above the earth, so God's ways are above man's ways, didn't the Scripture say?

And he'd seen firsthand, spending hundreds upon hundreds of hours above the earth.

"I don't understand, God. But I trust You still. Somehow." Yes, he'd loved Belinda. They'd built a good life together, worked as a team overseas, her teaching, him flying out on medical missions here and there, but always being grounded in the town beside the coast where they'd lived. Over a decade, fifteen years, they'd begun to see fruit from their work where once was poverty, disease super- stition, and hopelessness.

And now?

The missions board had said for him to take as long as he needed, then one day he could go back. Piloting short flights, here in the States, would do for now.

The front door banged open. "I'm home!" Lena's voice rang out. "Do we have some iced tea or lemonade?"

"I believe we do," Silas called toward the front of the house.

Another voice murmured something, too. Rochelle, something about being parched. Female laughter.

He saw Rochelle hesitate a fraction of a second before stepping into the kitchen.

"We're so talked out, Dad, we're practically hoarse." Lena strode to the kitchen table and set down a colorful folder, covered with a large blue "SSC."

"Ah, I see. Or, I hear." Both women chuckled.

Women. Yes, Lena was a woman, and he finally saw it despite the fact his mind balked over the idea yet again. She and Rochelle somehow had a camaraderie going on, as Lena pulled glasses from the cabinet.

"I think we should see where our classes overlap." Rochelle set her own folder, similar to Lena's, on the table. "If they do, you can ride in along with me instead of taking the bus."

"So," Silas said, grabbing his own glass from the cabinet, "I gather this morning's venture was successful."

Lena scooted past him and opened the refrigerator door. "Yes, it was. I'm glad I submitted paperwork before we got here. A lot easier to sign up once we got to the college. There were a few long lines, and I was worried I wouldn't get the classes I wanted to start with, but I did. Biology, a math class, advanced chemistry, and technical writing."

Silas shook his head. "Wow. You'll have quite a bit of homework, I imagine."

Lena poured some lemonade for herself and for Rochelle. "No more than I had when we were overseas."

"Well, those weren't college studies." He couldn't help the words, but Lena sometimes had an unrealistic viewpoint compared to the actual circumstances.

Rochelle glanced from him to Lena, then back to her folder.

"I know, but I'm going to work hard. You'll see." She smiled at him.

"I don't doubt it at all." His own smile wanted to spread across his face.

Lena studied his plate on the counter. "Oh, you're having lunch. We can move to the living room and sit there."

"No, it's fine. Please, stay in here." He spoke to Lena, but kept his focus on Rochelle, who looked up from the open folder in front of her.

"All right, then." Lena took the empty seat on the corner opposite Rochelle, while Silas settled onto the chair across the table from Rochelle.

Silas ate his first bite of enchiladas. Even better than they'd tasted yesterday.

"I have Biology on Monday, Wednesday, and Friday mornings, first thing," Lena said. "My lab is Tuesday morning."

"Okay. That's when I go in for Chemistry." Rochelle tapped a computer printout. "I've already taken Chemistry, but because I earned a C the first time, they suggested I take it again. It's been a while." Then, she caught Silas's eye.

"I'm glad you've restarted your studies," he managed to say.

"Thanks, Silas. I'm a little nervous about it, but it'll be good to finish."

He took another bite of enchiladas and nodded. Then swallowed. "I meant to say thanks again for giving Lena a ride today."

LYNETTE SOWELL

"Not a problem. I didn't mind one bit. So, you started your new job today. Piloting."

"Yes, I saw the airport, toured the office and the hangars. Tomorrow I get back in the air again." The thought sent a thrill through him. To feel the push of the engines, forcing against gravity and propelling him into the blue sky above. . .

"You look happy about it."

He nodded. "It's been a while, but it'll come right back to me."

"I still remember your first solo flight." A glimmer entered her eyes. "You were so . . . so . . . I don't know. As if you were Charles Lindbergh or someone like him. Or Chuck Yeager."

"You remembered all my bragging, what I said before my solo flight, about wanting to be like Lindbergh and Yeager?"

She nodded and laughed.

His own memory of the flight came back to him, and a laugh like he hadn't experienced in many months came out. "Then I finished the flight, got out of the cockpit and lost what breakfast I'd had all over the tarmac."

Her laughter joined his, while Lena gave them both a quizzical look. "Yuck," was all she said.

Yuck. But it was one of the greatest days of his life.

⁂

Rochelle, 19

The sun beat down from a bright blue sky, and winds were nearly calm. This, Silas told her, was a good thing.

"Oh, son," Jonas Fry said from the back seat, "are you sure about this?"

"Definitely. J. D. said I'm ready to solo, and I've logged more than enough hours." Silas grinned at Rochelle sitting beside him on the front seat of his vehicle. They'd nearly reached the small airport where Silas had been taking flying lessons.

Today, the day of the solo flight.

Silas's grin did little to quell the tremulousness in Rochelle's stomach. It was one thing to fly with an expert at the controls beside you, but to be in command of the small plane?

The what-ifs swirled around inside her head like autumn leaves in a whirlwind.

What if something went wrong? What if the engine gave out? What if a rogue crosswind caused the plane to spin out of control? What if one of the wheels or something broke off on landing?

Rochelle didn't voice these questions aloud. His parents likely had the same concerns. But to see the gleam in Silas's eye, the rush of adrenaline already making his breathing come a bit faster, she didn't dare squash his enthusiasm.

One day, they would fly out together on an adventure and change the world. He would fly them into a remote area, somewhere in desperate need of medical care and the gospel. She'd be at his side, helping in the clinic and ministering to the sick.

Oh, Silas hadn't mentioned courtship, specifically, but it was clear she had a special place in his heart. Any day now, too, she suspected he would speak to her father.

Yes, skies were sunny and blue today.

They passed through the chain-link gate of the airfield. Rochelle could see rows of small planes, single engine, some twin engine. Silas could rattle off specifications of this model and others. His plane today? A single-engine Cessna.

"And this is just the first one I've learned to fly," Silas said as he pulled into an empty parking spot. "After this, it's studying and training for my private pilot license. Well, along with IFR."

"IFR?" She was trying to pay attention to Silas's conversation, but her pulse kept pounding in her ears.

"Instrument flight rules. I can qualify to fly by instruments. I'll need it, for overseas flying."

His parents remained silent in the back seat, but after they left the car, his father spoke.

"We'll be praying for you, Silas."

"Thank you, Dad." At his words, the wind picked up a bit.

"Isn't it too windy to fly?" The question escaped before Rochelle considered whether she ought to ask.

Silas cast a glance to the windsock. "No, it's good." He scanned the area. "We're supposed to meet J. D. at the hangar."

The next minutes passed in a blur, as Silas introduced his instructor, J. D., to his parents and Rochelle, and J. D. led him over to a white Cessna with dark-blue detailing. The two men checked over the plane, nodding. Silas held a clipboard, making notes on whatever paper was clipped to it.

She could scarcely breathe when Silas climbed into the plane without J. D. The two of them talked through the open window of the plane. Then Silas glanced up across the tarmac at them, grinning as he did so.

"I can't believe it. Silas is going to fly on his own." Mrs. Fry shook her head. "Oh, my husband, I know we prayed for our son when he was young, but I know now we will pray all the more for him, the older he grows every day."

"How are you holding up, Rochelle?" Mr. Fry asked.

"I'm all right." Her words came out as a squeak. "I can't help but look, yet part of me wants to look away."

The three of them watched as the propeller began to turn, faster and faster as the engine's whine increased. Then the wheels began to roll as Silas maneuvered the plane away from the hangar and taxied toward the runway.

J. D., the flight instructor, sauntered in their direction, glancing toward Silas and the plane every few paces.

"Well, it's all up to him now." A grin spread across the older man's wrinkled face. "I tell ya, I've been teaching a long time, and this never gets old, watching a first solo flight."

"How long have you been teaching?" Rochelle managed to ask.

"About twenty-five years, right after I retired when I got home from 'Nam."

Ah. A military man. "How—how long is the flight going to be?" She had to keep talking, to keep her mind from thinking the worst. Even though Silas had told her at least three times this week what his solo flight involved.

"Three takeoffs, three landings. Not long."

Long enough.

There went the Cessna, shooting like a small white dart along the runway, then its nose tilted upward and Silas was zipping up into the sky.

Oh, dear Lord, please keep Silas safe. I love him, and I can't imagine my life without him.

The ominous silent prayer made her shiver, along with a puff of wind.

6

A week after classes began at the college, the fabric for the wedding dresses arrived, and Emma and Betsy asked Rochelle to accompany them to Frances Fry's house to see it. Rochelle would rather have put her feet up after a long day at work and enjoy a tall glass of iced tea on the lanai.

"But you have to come. We have a surprise for you," was all Betsy would say.

Emma looked as if she would pop from excitement, but said nothing.

"All right, I'll come, too."

"And no, it's not to give us a ride in the van. You know we don't mind walking or taking our bicycles," Emma blurted out.

Rochelle laughed. "I thought no such thing. So, the fabric is at Frances Fry's?"

"Yes, she called me today to let me know it's here. They were out of the shade I wanted, so it's taken longer. But it came in today on the Pioneer Trails bus from Indiana."

"So it did." The young women's enthusiasm pulled her along, and soon they were cycling their way through Pinecraft's streets, waving to the rare passerby on their route to the Frys' home.

"We should be back in plenty of time for supper." Betsy slowed her bicycle at the stop sign on the corner of Clarinda and Hacienda. They all stopped as a black buggy crossed in front of them.

The sound of a horse's neigh filled the air. But there was no horse pulling the buggy, slightly smaller yet longer than the traditional-size buggy used in places like Ohio or Indiana.

"What on earth—" Rochelle began, then glimpsed the driver. Silas, grinning at all of them, as he sat beside a bearded man— Tobias Fry.

"Hello!" the men called out, continuing on their way.

Rochelle laughed, then shook her head. "I imagine we'll hear all about this after we get to the Frys' house."

"Another buggy in Pinecraft." Betsy resumed pedaling. "I wonder if one day buggies will outnumber bicycles."

They continued chatting about the horseless buggy, and Emma, of course, speculated if Mr. Fry would let them each take a turn riding around the village.

A few more blocks and, after carefully crossing the bustling four lanes of Bahia Vista Street, they glided up to the Frys' wide driveway, which ended at a large utility barn of sorts. A few tricycles stood padlocked by the doorway.

They pedaled to the nearest set of empty bicycle stands at the end of the driveway where they stopped and locked their tricycles. Rochelle thought it a shame even in a place like Pinecraft, you still had to use a bike lock. But they were in the city, something she'd quit reminding herself of years ago. She simply locked her tricycle, locked her van, and locked her front door.

Betsy and Emma lost no time scaling the steps to the Frys' side door. Emma rapped her knuckles on the frame of the wooden screen door, squinting into the house as she did so.

Frances Fry bustled up to the door. "Come in, come in. I was so excited to see the bolts of fabric come off the bus, you don't know."

Rochelle pictured the bolts hopping down from the massive travel bus and searching for Frances, their way home, and laughed.

They followed Frances into the snug kitchen, where something delicious baked. Rochelle sniffed. Fresh bread.

Frances Fry stepped over to the kitchen table and opened a thick narrow rectangle, wrapped in plastic and bearing a shipping label of sorts. "Here 'tis. I already peeked. It's lovely fabric."

Betsy took the package from Frances and peeled back the open end to reveal a light turquoise blue. "Oh, yes, it is."

Emma reached out to touch the fabric. "Almost the color of the Gulf of Mexico water. Pretty."

Rochelle smiled at the young women. Maybe she'd never had the chance to plan her own wedding, but moments like this made up for it. Her heart swelled, and she ran her fingers over the fabric.

"I'm glad this finally arrived."

Frances nodded. "It was back-ordered, I was afraid it wouldn't arrive in time to get the dresses started."

"We bought enough to make you a dress, too, *Aenti* Chelle," Betsy announced. "That's our surprise."

"Me? But I'm not attending you at the wedding."

"*Nein*, but you have been here for us. You've helped both of us, and our *mamm* is happy you have helped us when she can't," Betsy said.

"This isn't traditional."

Frances shook her head. "We're in Pinecraft. Some things can be a bit nontraditional." She clapped her hands. "Now, I've heard from your mother, girls. The fabric arrived in Ohio for your attendants there, and she is helping see to their dresses."

Betsy hugged the bolts of fabric. "Oh, I hope this works. I'm trying not to fret. Perhaps we should have had the ceremony in Ohio."

"But then, Steven and I couldn't marry there," Emma pointed out.

They'd had this back-and-forth already. The sisters, one Mennonite and the other Amish, along with their betrothed, had somehow arranged for their bishop and pastor to agree to a same-day wedding celebration. Emma and Steven would wed first, married by their Mennonite pastor, then Betsy and Thaddeus would wed in a separate ceremony, married by their Amish bishop. Then both couples would celebrate with a large meal for all their guests.

Like Pinecraft, they somehow would make it work.

"Now, let's get measurements for the three of you." Frances motioned for them to follow. "We'll do this in the guest room, in case the menfolk come traipsing through the house."

"We saw the buggy," Rochelle said. "When did Tobias get it? Or did he build it?"

Frances waved her hands before closing the guest room door behind them all. "Oh, he built the contraption. He bought a used double-seat golf cart at an auction, and started from there. He's as excited as a little boy on the first day of summer. He can't wait until the snowbirds come for the winter. He'll be giving rides morning, noon, and night."

"I'm sure he will. The neighing horn was unexpected."

Frances chuckled. "When he found that horn in a mail order catalog, oh, mercy me, he went to the mailbox almost every day until it came in. . . . All right, who's first?"

"*Aenti* Chelle." Emma nudged Rochelle's elbow as Frances plucked a measuring tape from a nearby countertop, covered with stacks of fabric on both sides of a sewing machine.

"Come, come," Frances said.

Rochelle stepped up to allow the older seamstress to take her measurements. Frances measured and wrote, measured and wrote, until she'd completed everything she needed to size the dress.

"Thank you, Betsy and Emma. I never expected this."

"*Mamm* gave us the idea." Emma beamed.

Betsy and Emma then had their turns being measured.

"Ah, one day, two weddings. You girls are smart," Frances said. "Family and friends will only need to cook once for the wedding meal."

"That's what we thought. Also, right after Christmas, before New Year's, a lot of people will be in town anyway. And, no snow to deal with." Betsy stood up a little straighter, and Frances stretched the measuring tape from Betsy's waist down to her hemline.

"Well, providing no other issues with this fabric, I will have these ready in late November. I have a pile of sewing to do before then, but don't you worry, I'll get these dresses finished. Now, your mother is sewing everything else in Ohio?"

"Yes, *mamm* said she has measured our attendants, some of our cousins, and friends," Betsy said.

Rochelle glanced out the window as the women continued to chat about wedding plans. *Thank You, God, for helping these young women in this most exciting time of their lives.* There were the men, in the sideyard, talking beside the horseless buggy. What a clever, novel idea. Pinecraft was a Plain place, but you always prepared yourself for the unexpected. Like horseless buggies.

Silas looked up, his gaze traveling to the house where it landed on the window. No, Rochelle was sure he couldn't see her because of the brightness outside, but his intense expression almost made her believe he could.

⎯⎯

"Will you stay for supper, Silas?" Uncle Tobias asked. "Henry Hostetler is coming by, and if I know Frances, she'll invite the three young ladies inside to stay for supper, too."

"Well . . ." He pondered for a moment. Lena was working on a project with her lab partner and wouldn't be home until later, and Matthew was already here, working on a pair of bicycles or whatever odd jobs his uncle could find for him.

"It'll save you some cooking. And, Henry and I have an idea we'd like to run by you."

"Ah, no cooking, and an idea to boot. Sure, we'll stay." *And Rochelle is here.*

"Good. You know, until you and the kids came to town, we didn't realize how much we miss having the younger crowd around. Ours have long-gone and flown the nest."

"But they visit you sometimes, right?" He'd last seen his cousins at Belinda's funeral.

"They do. But it has been good to have someone around all the time. Young Matthew, he keeps me on my toes, for sure."

Some banging and clanking came from the direction of the bicycle workshop.

"I haven't seen Matthew jump into anything with as much enthusiasm, since, ah, I'm not sure."

"He's quite adept at mechanics. I showed him one of the electric motors, and we took it apart and put it together not long after lunchtime today."

"Hey, Dad." Matthew left the workshop. He clutched a rag and was wiping his grease-covered fingers. "I found a bike. I'm gonna fix it up and sell it."

"Or, you can rent it," Uncle Tobias said, clapping him on the back.

"That's great, Son." In the two months they'd been in Pinecraft, Matthew had changed, for the better it seemed. Now he didn't follow in his sister's shadow, but had found his own interests, namely bicycles and fishing.

"I might rent it to people, six dollars a day." Matthew nodded. "If someone rents it for two weeks, it's eighty-four dollars."

"You might not get six dollars, Matthew," Uncle Tobias said. "I only charge five per day, and Mr. Kaufman charges only four for his older tricycles."

Matthew's expression sank a little. "Oh, I see."

"But it's a good idea," Silas said. He didn't know much about running a business and looked to Uncle Tobias for more input.

"We can talk more at supper. Let's go wash up and get the rest of the grease off your hands." Uncle Tobias nodded toward the house, and the three of them headed inside.

Feminine laughter met his ears as they entered the kitchen, where four women sat at a square table with a sewing pattern spread out between them. Rochelle looked up, gave him a small smile, then looked back at the papers in front of her.

"So, I'll put some extra strips of ruching about the shoulders and hem—on Emma's and Rochelle's dresses, but not for yours, and only two pleats, Betsy." Aunt Frances jotted something on a note pad.

"That's right," Betsy said. "It was enough to convince them to let us have our weddings together. I don't want to make everything the same, especially our dresses, and especially something so fancy."

"I don't know why Bishop was so skeptical of the two ceremonies." Emma sighed. "I mean, we have the same family, even though our churches are different, and we see each other's church friends in the village. We're all together here, in one jumbled pile of Plainness."

Silas laughed and tried not to snort at young Emma's observation. Her pointed frankness reminded him of Belinda. There weren't a few smiles around the table, but Betsy appeared perplexed.

"It's so our out-of-town visitors won't feel uncomfortable," Betsy began.

"I understand," Rochelle said. "You're just trying to find a common ground. And I think you have, literally."

"Anyway, we have about ten or eleven weeks until your big day," Frances said. "I know everything will come together."

A kitchen timer beeped, and his aunt hopped up from her chair. "There's the pie. You all *are* staying for supper, aren't you?"

"I suppose we can. Betsy, Emma, do either of you have plans this evening?"

"I need to go by the bakery tonight," Betsy said.

"I don't have any plans. I was going to write a letter home," Emma responded.

"Why then, I suppose we can." Rochelle stood. "But Frances, let me help with something. You have pie, so I won't suggest dessert. What else can I help with?"

"I've made a cheeseburger casserole. If you'd like, maybe run to Yoder's Fresh Market and pick up something for a tossed salad. I have a few fixings and salad dressing I made earlier in the week, but not enough for all of us."

"All right, I can go."

"And if Silas likes, he can give Rochelle a ride in my buggy," Tobias interjected. "I know he's been wanting to give it a spin."

It was true. Silas *did* want to drive the glorified golf cart around, if only once. It would be fun. He shot a look at Rochelle, who stood.

"Only if you look both ways before we cross Bahia Vista."

⤜⥤

Rochelle climbed inside the buggy, and Silas took his place behind the wheel on the front seat next to her.

"I promise, I'll look both ways." His eyes twinkled. She hadn't been in this close proximity to him in, well, since way back when.

"I know you will. I was just teasing." She smiled back at him.

"Of course, you were." He turned the key and the motor puttered to life. "Well, here goes."

She knew the girls would be staring and she'd hear about this later. However, tonight this was a simple trip to Yoder's Market for fresh vegetables, just like she made twice a week from her home. Except never in a black horseless buggy and never with Silas Fry.

He steered the buggy down the driveway and out onto the street, pressing the button for the horn as he did so. A whinny rang out. Silas pressed the button again, and Rochelle laughed.

"Are you going to try it all the way to Yoder's?"

"Only if you keep asking me if I will."

She laughed again. Riding beside him was easy enough, pretending he was someone she'd recently met. A new friend. She focused on the houses they puttered past.

"I like hearing you laugh," Silas said.

"I like finding a reason to laugh." There'd been too many reasons to cry, and she was done with crying. Amazing, how changing one's mind-set and focus could improve someone's mood.

"Well, I'd like to give you plenty of reasons to laugh."

She didn't know how to respond, but didn't turn her head to meet his eyes. She only nodded. A woman was toting a bag along the path from her driveway to her home and waved. Vera Byler. Rochelle waved back.

"Who's that?" he asked.

"Vera Byler. She works at Betsy's bakery." She didn't add Vera might share the tidbit of news she'd seen Rochelle riding in Tobias Fry's horseless buggy with the new widower at church.

"Ah, Pinecraft Pies and Pastry. I've had some of their pie. Some of the best I've ever tasted."

"True. Between Betsy's shop and Yoder's, Pinecraft will never, ever have a shortage of sweet things to eat."

They zipped along, but now Silas slowed the buggy as they approached the Bahia Vista light.

"Wow, I can't say I've ever had to hit the brakes on a buggy before. Not like this." They stopped beside an older man astride a three-wheeled cycle; his beard drifted on the breeze.

"You've driven a real buggy? I thought your family's always been Mennonite?"

"We have." The light clicked green, and off they shot through the intersection. "This was at a distant cousin's, or second cousin's, farm. Old Order. Swartzentruber."

"I had no idea your family had ties to the Swartzentruber Amish." The Frys, connected to one of the most conservative Anabaptist groups. She couldn't remember seeing Swartzentruber Amish visiting Pinecraft, although there might have been one or two. No, Pinecraft was deemed far too worldly by most of their branch of the Plain people.

"Yup. I think I was ten or eleven at the time, and the older cousin let me drive the team. I was thrilled, scared to death of the horses. I don't remember why we were visiting them." Silas shrugged.

"Huh." She gripped the railing on the seat as they blipped up into the parking area at Yoder's, then crept over to a small area away from the cars, where Silas could tuck the buggy into the space.

"Yes, there's still a lot we don't know about each other." Silas set the parking brake, then climbed out of the buggy. He moved to the other side and extended his hand to help her from the seat.

"I'm sure you're right." Rochelle looked down at his hand. It was only a helpful gesture. No need to overthink it or anything else about their interaction.

A couple passed the buggy, glancing at its black square bulk, and smiled. Silas reached across Rochelle and pushed the horn button. Way too close for her comfort. As the "horse" neighed, Rochelle stared at her lap.

Silas straightened up and smiled at the couple's reaction to the horn.

Rochelle wiggled from the seat and took a step away from the buggy. "I guess we should see about the salad and scoot back to your aunt and uncle's."

"Guess so." He touched her arm. "Rochelle, I have an idea."

"What?"

"We have a lifetime behind us since we've seen each other last. We're two different people now. Would you, can we, just start from this point on, as friends?" All joking had fled his expression. "Rather than drag all of it out, and look at it again?"

Rochelle raised her chin and made herself look him straight in the eye. "I think it's an excellent idea. Friends."

"Good." He nodded, and they continued on their way toward the bins of produce.

❧

Rochelle, 19

The medicine hadn't worked this time. Rochelle could see it on her mother's face, despite the bravery she also saw. God wasn't answering their prayers. Other mothers, other women had beat uterine cancer.

Uterine cancer. Harsh words to describe a disease claiming the part of her mother that had sheltered and helped nurture Rochelle and her sister as they grew inside her.

When did one give up praying? When did she surrender to the knowledge that not too far from now, she'd be standing at her mother's graveside, no matter what well-meaning friends said.

"Just keep believing."

"Things will turn around."

"God will take care of her."

"God will make sure His will is done."

Rochelle didn't want God's will to be her spending the rest of her life without her mother. Someday, she wanted to sit at her parents' kitchen table and tell her mother she would be getting married. Then someday, tell her mother she was carrying her first child.

In the bottom of her soul, though, she knew those things wouldn't happen, no matter what well-meaning people said.

"Silas is coming up the porch steps," her mother said, from her comfortable perch in the easy chair. Rochelle's father had arranged the chair just so, in order for her mother to be able to see activities outdoors.

Silas, the one constant in her life, a bright spot. He made her laugh on days when she didn't feel like laughing at all.

Thank You, God, for someone like Silas.

7

Silas managed to stuff himself with a slab of Aunt Fran's cheese-burger casserole and a generous pile of Rochelle's tossed salad. He stared at his empty plate.

"Aunt Fran and Rochelle, I'll stop trying to learn how to cook if I can eat this well every night."

"Silas, you can always come here for supper every night if you'd like. You know you're welcome," said Aunt Fran. She picked up his empty plate. "I'll pull out the pie after we get the table cleared and the coffee brewed."

"Oh, I can take care of my plate." He moved to stand.

"No. Let me fuss over you. It's been a while since I've had anyone to fuss over."

"You can fuss over me," said Uncle Tobias. "I don't mind."

Rochelle came in through the side door. "The girls are on their way home; Emma, to write her letter, and Betsy needs to get up at four for the bakery."

"I promise, we won't keep you too long," Uncle Tobias said. "If you're not comfortable cycling home at twilight, we can strap your bike to the buggy and get you home safely."

"Thanks. I think I can manage fine riding my bike."

"Coffee's almost ready," Aunt Fran said from the kitchen. Rochelle joined her at the counter, where the women pulled cups from the cabinet.

From where he sat, Henry Hostetler placed a three-ring binder on the table. The older man's reputation preceded him. A widowed Mennonite man and self-employed contractor and fixture in the village, he reminded Silas of his own father with his strong yet quiet ways.

"Now, I'm glad you're here, Silas. And Rochelle. I'm not sure if you knew or not, Rochelle might, but earlier this past summer a few of us formed the Pinecraft Heritage Committee."

Silas glanced at Rochelle.

"Yes, I've heard about the committee."

"Well, we're looking to enlarge the committee. At our most recent meeting, we realized all we have are some old-timers in the group. There's nothing wrong with old-timers, but . . ."

"With age, comes wisdom," Silas said.

"Between the five of us, we have plenty, if you go by age. We add up to almost three hundred years of life experience. But what we don't have is younger people's perspective." Henry glanced up; Aunt Fran set a mug of coffee in front of Henry and Uncle Tobias, while Rochelle settled onto the seat next to Silas.

"We've been talking, and we want to invite you to join the group. Both of you." Uncle Tobias smiled at Aunt Fran. "Thank you, dear."

"Both of us?" Rochelle asked. "But I'm a . . ."

Silas knew she was going to say "a woman," but he didn't see why it should matter.

"We know," said Uncle Tobias. "But you're a businesswoman. You've also lived here, year-round, for nigh on twenty years. You have an excellent reputation in the village and plenty of good common sense."

"I can see you inviting Rochelle, but I'm a newcomer." Silas took a sip of his coffee. "I've only visited here a handful of times, and those visits were when I was a child."

"We know," said Henry. "Sometimes it takes an outsider's perspective for people to see where they need to improve. I can't tell you how many people don't realize their home needs sprucing up on the outside until someone sees it with what they call 'fresh eyes.'"

"I understand what you mean by fresh eyes."

"Me too," Rochelle said. "But part of what's special about Pinecraft is its Plainness. We don't have hotels, we don't have condominiums. Just simple homes and a few duplex apartments. We're not glitzy and developed like a resort. Or there's the other extreme, if we have outsiders, they won't understand. Some outsiders might expect things to be like they are at home in Ohio or Pennsylvania. No offense meant, Silas."

"None taken. Anyway, I've lived outside of the United States for more than a decade. So I'm about as outside as they come."

The men chuckled, and the women smiled at his words.

"Right you are," said Henry. "And you're a reminder of why we in Pinecraft do what we do. As a missionary pilot, you and everyone you worked with have directly benefited from the fund-raising we've done. I know the biggest fund-raiser is the Haiti Benefit Auction in January, but we don't just support work in Haiti. Our committee can head up raising funds for other areas in need. Even here in Sarasota."

Silas nodded. "I see."

"Cream and sugar, right here," Aunt Fran said as she set the sugar bowl and container of half-and-half on the table.

Rochelle doctored her coffee, pouring from the tiny pitcher and scooping some sugar. "What does the committee do? I know they headed up the park mural project. The mural has made a beautiful difference in the park."

"We're going to do several things such as organize community activities, one per quarter. Sometimes we'll do a benefit, like a fish fry or a haystack supper, and we'll have the village vote on who the benefit will be for. Not to take anything away from the churches who do those things, of course," Henry said.

"Cornhole tournaments, bocce tournaments, volleyball, too. We could have a 'field day' in the winter time for all of those, even shuffleboard, and sell food and give out prizes to the winners," Uncle

Tobias said. "Something for the old and the young to spend time together."

Aunt Fran set five plates of pie on the table, along with a small tub of vanilla ice cream. Silas's mouth watered: apple pie. Aunt Fran paused, propping her hand on her hip. "If you ask me, which you haven't, I say the idea is just so a bunch of you can keep busy and keep us organized. Sometimes we get too caught up in the organizing; it takes the fun out of things."

"Now, Francie—" Uncle Tobias began.

"No, I understand what you mean, Frances," Rochelle said. "We've done a good job in the village, keeping things Plain, as they should be, while . . . adapting as needed. I don't know if *adapting* is the right word."

"I don't mean we should put a television in everyone's home. Certainly *not*," Uncle Tobias said. "I think I can count on one hand the people I know in the village who own a television set or admit to it. It's not what I mean."

"The city of Sarasota has taken notice of us," Henry said. "With the media coverage over the past few years, and millions of people who saw a story on television, on the *Today* show, well, I imagine we'll have a new influx of people wanting to visit the village."

"So we think if we have a Heritage Committee in place, it would look better for us as a community." Tobias dolloped a scoop of vanilla ice cream onto his still-warm pie.

Silas took his own bite of pie and let his taste buds dance a little jig before speaking again. "What will I have to do, as part of this committee? I typically have two flights per week, and occasionally an overnight, depending on the airport schedule."

"We meet once per month. At the first meeting of each quarter, we plan for three, then six months out. The rest of the quarter's meetings are devoted to looking ahead to the next activity and planning, while evaluating how we did with the most recent activity," said Henry.

"Phineas Beachy is donating his time to help us with the legal paperwork to form a 501(c)(3) nonprofit," Uncle Tobias said.

"Who else is on the committee, besides both of you?" Rochelle asked.

"Bishop Smucker from the Old Order church, Samuel Byler—one of our deacons at the Mennonite fellowship—Rochelle, you know Sam—and Gerald Beachy, Phin's grandfather." Henry set down his fork and stared at the pie on his plate. "This is mighty good pie."

Rochelle nodded slowly. "I . . . I believe I'll need some time to think and pray about this. I like what you're doing, but I wouldn't want my presence to be a hindrance. Thank you for inviting me. I'm honored you did."

Silas understood her reluctance. A woman's role varied, sometimes greatly, among the Plain people. He'd heard of some of those distant cousins of his, forbidding their women to even speak in public, or question anything, or offer an opinion. And then there were people like him—he'd always treated Belinda as his equal in many ways in their marriage, although she always deferred to him as the leader and final decision maker for matters within their marriage and family—a revolutionary concept among some of those more advanced in years in their home fellowship back in Ohio.

Rochelle stifled a yawn. "I'm sorry. It's been a full day."

The clock chimed eight; darkness had fallen outside.

"Look at the time. I'd say they've rolled up the sidewalks, except our street doesn't have any," quipped Uncle Tobias. "We didn't mean to keep you so late, either of you."

Only it wasn't late. Silas smiled.

"Thank you, Francie, for such a delicious supper and dessert," Henry said. "Silas and Rochelle. You can let me know at church, or if you see me out and about, when you've decided. No hurry. But if you could decide soon, before our October meeting . . ."

"Yes, I will let you know by then." Rochelle stood as well. "Thank you, Frances and Tobias, for the supper."

"I'll be sure to let the girls know when I get started on their dresses. And yours, too."

"Well, Rochelle, let's get your bike strapped to the back of the buggy. No way I'm letting you bicycle home in the dark," Uncle Tobias said.

❧

Rochelle had two voice mails waiting when she checked her phone. She'd left it at the house while the three of them went for their dress measurements at the Frys' and completely put the phone out of her mind during supper and the chat that followed.

Two of her cleaning clients called, one wanting to reschedule her service instead of having it tomorrow and another one leaving a cryptic message, something about the quality of service they'd received lately. It didn't bode well, and she tried not to let worry claim her thoughts as she toweled her hair dry after a hot shower. People rescheduled sometimes. No problem. But quality? Rarely did she ever get a call about a quality concern.

The girls waited in the living room for her, and the fact she'd been on not one but *two* rides with Silas in the buggy today would be the topic of their bedtime conversation. Rochelle wasn't sure if she was up for any grilling tonight. There was nothing to grill her about. But still, people sometimes talked. Like Vera Byler. What would Vera say, too, when she heard Rochelle and Silas had been tapped to join the Heritage Committee?

Likely, the woman already did know.

"Ah, Lord, why can't life be a little simpler?" Rochelle said aloud. She worked some leave-in conditioner through the length of her hair, thankful for a product to keep her hair from snarling into little knots at the nape of her neck

You'd think in an Amish-Mennonite community, life *would* be simpler. Ah, but throw people and their idiosyncrasies into the mix and all kinds of complications happened.

Of course, Rochelle had jumped into plenty of complications herself, with choosing to go back to school. Some things were worth the complication.

She entered the hallway to find Winston waiting to give her a four-footed escort to the kitchen, where she found the great-nieces making grilled cheese sandwiches.

"After the meal we had at the Frys?" she asked, teasing. But nothing like melted cheese, especially cheese from Holmes County.

"I'll make one for you, too," said Betsy with a grin.

"Thanks." She turned on the kettle. "Just a half sandwich, though. And I think I'll have a cup of tea as well."

"What is it, *Aenti* Chelle? Is there anything wrong?"

She shook her head. "No. I'm going to miss both of you after you're married. It will be a lot quieter around here."

"Do we make too much noise?" Emma asked.

"Not at all. It's been . . . *nice* . . . having someone else in the house."

"Well, we're thankful you've let us live with you." Betsy surprised Rochelle with a hug. "Most everyone in our families was sure we'd both gone on *Rumspringa*, moving in with you."

"I did!" Emma said. "I'm not afraid to admit it."

Betsy rolled her eyes. "You never went *Rumspringa*, silly *kind*."

"I'm not a silly child." Emma flipped a freshly toasted sandwich onto a waiting paper plate.

"Now, *this* is what I was talking about." Rochelle laughed. She'd never realized how quiet her home had been until she'd let Betsy move in with her nearly two years ago.

"So, how was the horseless buggy ride, *Aenti*?" Betsy asked.

"You mean, horseless buggy *rides*," Emma interjected.

"They were fine. No mishaps. Nobody ran over any curbs or pedestrians, and we managed to avoid larger vehicles both times."

"I think the Frys were trying to be matchmakers."

"Hmm." Rochelle went to fetch a mug from the cabinet. "I don't need a matchmaker. Or, a match right now, either."

"I think he likes you," Emma said.

"Of course he does. Who wouldn't like our *Aenti* Chelle?" Betsy sliced more cheese.

Rochelle laughed again, shaking her head. "Silas and I are friends. We agreed to start a friendship. He's a good man, and he's had a lot happen in his life in the last year. During the toughest times in our lives, we appreciate our friends and family more than ever. So, I'm glad he is where he is."

"Friends is good." Emma put another sandwich on the griddle. "Steven and I started as friends, and then, it was like we both woke up one day and noticed each other and . . ." She leaned on the counter, staring at the backsplash.

"I knew right away I liked Thaddeus Zook. As soon as I saw him at a haystack supper and he asked me about ganache. Flirted, like the *Englisch* say. Of course, back then I didn't imagine what would happen." Betsy smiled, then sighed.

"Girls, your stories of inspiration and romance warm my heart. Thank you for being so encouraging, but Silas and I . . ." She shook her head. Too much back there, even though they'd both agreed it had been left behind them.

⁓⁓

Rochelle, 19

Rochelle knew this day would come, despite everyone's pleading and prayers. Her mother's body was worn, spent and empty like a shell.

"I can't. Talk. Much more." Her mother's voice came as a bare whisper.

"Shh, Momma. It's okay. We've . . ." Rochelle swallowed around a lump before continuing. "We've already said everything we need to say. I know you're tired. It's all right. You . . . you've been such an example to us all. I only pray I'm half the woman you've been."

No one had told her how unimaginably hard this saying good-bye would be. Oh, but what a gift. To say good-bye, until they saw each other again. What sights Momma would soon see. Her own parents, grandparents. The baby sister Momma had lost when she was six years old.

"Don't . . . don't let unforgiveness hold you back. Life can turn out different than we plan, or expect. God's hand will always be there. Don't . . ." Momma began coughing, the spasms shaking her body. A few tears streamed down her face.

"I . . . I won't. I promise." From here in the back of the house, she could hear the front door slam. It would be Jolene, her husband, and the baby.

"We're here." Jolene bustled into the room. "When is the hospice nurse coming back?"

"Soon." Rochelle rose from the chair tucked beside Momma's bed. "Soon."

Soon, the nurse would return. Another dose of morphine for Momma. This dose likely would sedate her even further, to block out the numbing pain.

How long? Another few days, a week at most?

She ought to have known Momma's burst of energy last week was a sign the end was near. She hadn't believed the nurse. None of them had. Even Father seemed more chipper and talked about plans for Christmas time, how they'd all go to Pinecraft for a nice, long vacation. Nobody tried to tell him otherwise.

As Jolene and her husband talked to Momma in low tones, Rochelle fled the bedroom. Air. She needed air.

Rochelle stopped on the porch and leaned on the railing. A car passed at the end of the lane and continued along its way. The rest of the world continued, too.

But everyone only had one mother, and when the mother soon wouldn't be around anymore, the thought should make the earth screech to a halt on its axis.

Except it didn't.

The world kept spinning, cars kept driving, people kept on about life as usual.

"Oh, Momma, what will we do without you?" Rochelle choked out the words. A familiar figure appeared, rounding the fence and passing by the mailbox.

Silas.

How could her heart sing while it was breaking at the same time? And yet, it did.

She left the porch and met him on the lane.

Silas enveloped her in his arms, and she didn't care who might see them from the house.

"How is she?" he spoke into her ear.

"Slipping away." A sob found its way out of her mouth, and she leaned against him.

He rubbed the back of her hair, and, for once, she wished she wasn't wearing her *kapp* and her hair was down.

"I wish I could make it better. I wish I could fix it for you."

"Only God can, and I don't understand why He won't." She regretted the words, but they held truth for her. God could, but wouldn't.

8

"I apologize for having to call and tell you this . . ." Mrs. Gentile said. "I've been your client for several years, and there's never been an issue until now."

"No apology needed, Mrs. Gentile." Already, the first pinpricks of a headache began in Rochelle's temples, and it was only eight-thirty in the morning. She knew who cleaned Mrs. Gentile's townhouse, and she didn't look forward to the conversation she'd soon have with the young woman who did.

"I had to remop the kitchen. And the lanai wasn't even swept. The bathroom shower enclosure hasn't been touched in several weeks, at least, judging by the buildup on the glass. Like I said, I've never had an issue until now."

"You said the shower enclosure hasn't been touched in several weeks?"

"No, I don't believe it has."

Rochelle inhaled instead of sighing. "I'll send Emma today along with a list of everything she needs to redo. This is inexcusable."

"Thank you. I've debated about saying anything, but my husband insisted I do so."

"Of course. I'm glad you called. In fact, I'll take one week off this month's bill."

"Oh, thank you again."

"You're welcome."

Rochelle ended the call. In nearly twenty years of working in the cleaning business, she'd never had something come up quite like this. Misunderstandings and clarifications of what clients expected for services, yes. Those were easily ironed out.

But substandard work?

She ought to have known, Emma being distracted and being Emma, things might start to slip.

Where was she now? Rochelle stood up from her spot at the computer.

She found Emma in her bedroom, folding laundry.

"Emma, Mrs. Gentile gave me a call last night while I was out, but we finally spoke this morning."

Emma looked up from her place at the foot of the bed. A stack of undergarments and stockings sat side by side.

"Oh, is everything all right?"

"Not exactly. Unfortunately, she hasn't been pleased."

Patches of red shot into Emma's cheeks, in sharp contrast to the white of her head covering. "What did she say? What didn't please her?"

"A number of things. I'm going to give you a list, and today, if you could, please go over to her home and take care of them."

Emma's face glowed redder. "Yes, *Aenti* Chelle. But I know I did everything I usually do, the last time I was there. I know I did."

Who was Rochelle to believe? Of course, she wanted to keep her customers pleased. And she had never doubted Emma being truthful before.

"It may well be, but I've not had anyone this displeased in recent memory, probably ever. Anyway, I'll get the checklist for you." Were those tears in Emma's eyes?

Emma said nothing more, so Rochelle went over to the bed and sat down on a free spot. "It's all right. We'll just make sure Mrs. Gentile is happy and go on from here. I had a lot to learn when I first started cleaning, working with Leah Graber. She was at least seventy years old, if she was a day, and was no-nonsense. But she taught me the business. During the first week when I followed her from house to house and tried to learn, I wasn't sure I'd last."

The young woman nodded, but continued to be silent.

Then, she whispered, "But I had plans. Today is my day without any homes to clean."

"I'm sure you'll be done, quick as a whistle," Rochelle tried to state it as brightly as she could.

"I'm sure I will. *Danke, Aenti* Chelle."

All right. Rochelle decided to leave Emma with her thoughts. At first she'd had her doubts earlier in the year if Emma could handle the clients, when Emma took over the remainder of Betsy's clients when Betsy's shop kept her increasingly busy. Emma preferred needlework and quilting to cleaning, something she'd made clear when first accepting the full-time job.

But when living in Pinecraft year-round, a woman had to do what was available to make ends meet, and Emma needed to learn she wasn't on vacation. And for many Amish or Mennonite women, available work meant waiting tables, cooking, taking in sewing or alteration work, or, in Rochelle's case and other women like her, cleaning houses.

Rochelle left Emma's room, but not before she glimpsed a tear on the young woman's cheek. There was nothing Rochelle could do to make Emma feel better, short of going to Mrs. Gentile's house and taking care of the home herself. However, she wasn't about to do so.

She shook off the same feeling she'd had when seeing Silas for the first time in the summer, the feeling of being tired of cleaning up other people's homes—and messes.

Today, yes, she had classes—and she was due to pick up Lena in fifteen minutes. Rochelle bustled through the kitchen, packing her tote bag, ensuring she had her textbooks in order along with her notepad and enough pens.

Maybe the feeling of being tired of cleaning would pass. The Scriptures spoke of contentment. She ought to work on it, being content and thankful for what she had. After all, this is what she'd chosen for herself, and God had blessed her.

She called out a good-bye to Emma and heard no response, so went on her way.

 ❧

Silas entered the airport office; the airport business manager had called this morning saying he had a different type of contracted flight available for Silas, should he want it.

Jeremy Stiles, manager, and a pilot himself, was sitting at his desk. "Mr. Fry, I'm glad you could make it in. I know it's short notice."

"It's all right. Flying is what I'm here for. So, you said something about a new flight?"

The older man nodded. "We have a local client who needs an afternoon hop up to Atlanta. However, it's an overnight trip because of the air traffic. Can't get the return flight back until tomorrow morning."

"Afternoon flight, when?"

"Today."

Silas paused before responding. Yes, this is what he wanted. But overnight, at such short notice? If he said no, he might lose future opportunities. The private piloting industry was competitive enough. All Jeremy had to do was pick up the phone and he'd have someone else to step in.

"I'll do it."

"Your overnight accommodations and meals will be paid for by the client, of course. The plane's in hangar two. Nothing you haven't flown before."

"What time is preflight?"

"Two. In the air at three, at the gate in Atlanta by four-thirty, the latest. Destination's Fulton, not Hartsfield."

"All right." He accepted a file folder from Jeremy with more details. "I'll get started on this."

Silas left the office by the side door and went down the steps and out to the tarmac, where two hangars stood, housing private planes. The maintenance hangar lay a farther distance away.

He inhaled the scent of fuel and oil when he entered the hangar. There stood the gleaming turboprop described in his folder. Not a sleek Learjet; he wasn't qualified for those. But this Cheyenne would give them a nice ride and a little bit of elbow room.

And, he didn't need a copilot and could run the controls himself. He climbed up the drop-down steps and entered the plane.

Nice cockpit, seats for two, but for this flight he didn't have a copilot.

"Mr. Fry, I presume?" A voice came from the doorway side of the plane, and a man wearing a business suit stepped inside.

"Yes, sir."

"Ted Kingsley. Jeremy said you'd be out here."

They shook hands. The man's brow furrowed as he leaned over to see the cockpit; dark circles made shadows under his eyes.

"I apologize for the short notice. My young son is sick; he's been taken by medical air transport to Atlanta. His mother is with him, but I wanted to get up there tonight, as soon as possible. How long before we can leave?"

"We're in the flight plan for three. I'll see if they can squeeze us in sooner, but I'll be making my preflight checks no later than two."

"All right."

"What's wrong with your son?"

"He's waiting for a heart transplant, and they've told us a heart will be available tomorrow morning."

Silas's gut tightened. "Well, I'll be praying for him and your family."

"Thank you. It's been . . . a long road. He's only seven." Mr. Kingsley straightened to a standing position. "I'll let you get back to your work."

Silas nodded. "We'll be ready to get you up there soon."

Mr. Kingsley left, and Silas continued his instrument check. Then he stopped. He needed to see if Matthew could stay with his uncle and aunt this evening. Lena would be studying at home. Of course, he'd have to get back to the house himself to get a change of clothes and some toiletries.

An overnight trip. Not in his plans, but trips like this reminded him of why he liked to fly. It was almost like a medical mission. He started to grin as he continued checking the plane over, as well as the flight plan.

⁂

Today, Rochelle had helped dissect a sheep in Anatomy and Physiology. Her stomach felt queasy all the way home, and even Lena commented she looked a tad green when they met in the student center commons. The ride home felt bumpier than usual.

"I'm glad it's over." She pulled into Silas's driveway.

"I thought it was interesting. I'm almost thinking of changing my major to biology." Lena's phone chimed from her backpack. "Oh, it's Dad."

She pulled it from the front pocket, and took the call. "Hey Dad . . . yes, I just got home. . . . Oh, you are? Well, that's good. . . . Overnight? Okay, yes . . . I'll go there for supper . . . yes, I'll keep my phone charged." She pushed a button on the phone.

"Is everything okay?"

"Dad has an overnight trip, flying someone to Atlanta. His first overnight trip since we've been here. I think he's nervous."

"About flying?"

"No. To leave us. He would never say so. Ever since my mother . . . it's like I'm ten years old again and Matthew is only four. And we're not."

"I'm sure every parent feels the same." Although she had no frame of reference, not having children herself. So how could she say?

"We'll be fine."

"And so will he, I'm sure."

"Well, thanks, Rochelle. I still want to call you Miss Keim."

"Whatever you're comfortable with."

"Can I call you Chelle sometimes, like Emma and Betsy do?"

"Of course. It's fine with me." She smiled as Lena nodded, then left the van.

Rochelle continued on her way home. Silas. Overnight, away from Pinecraft. Funny, she'd miss him being away, just for a night. She'd grown accustomed to him being around. Even not seeing him, it was nice to know he was there, somewhere in the village.

Once arriving home, she found Betsy in the living room, her feet up on an ottoman and looking like a thundercloud.

"Betsy, what is it?" Rochelle set her tote bag on the kitchen table and glanced toward the living area.

"Emma, is what."

"Emma?"

"I think she ought to be the one to tell you."

"Where is she? Is she home?" Rochelle hoped Emma followed through on her visit to the Gentiles' house to clean.

"Oh, she's home all right."

Emma came from the hallway, clutching an apron, a burgundy print. "See? This is the apron we have to wear." When she saw Rochelle, she froze. "*Aenti* Chelle."

"Hello." Rochelle stared at the apron. "What is it?"

"Ah, my new apron. I got hired at Der Dutchman, as a waitress. I start in two weeks."

"Two weeks."

"Um, I was going to talk to you . . . and let you know I'm not going to work for Keim Cleaning anymore. In two weeks. I've heard, when giving notice at a job, it's good manners to give two weeks' notice."

A number of things shot into Rochelle's brain at that moment, and none of them she deemed appropriate to say to a young, care-free—no, care*less*—Mennonite woman.

"Yes, so it is good manners," was all she could manage to say. "I'm . . . I need to study. I'll be in my room for a while." Rochelle snatched up her tote bag and headed down the hall.

"*Aenti* Chelle—"

"Emma, *hush*," was the last thing Rochelle heard before closing her bedroom door behind her.

Rochelle, 19

Momma left them peacefully and went on to the world beyond this one, while Rochelle's world crumbled. Despite knowing what would happen, nothing truly prepared her for it. Dad simply went to his work shed after the funeral home took her momma away.

The house felt empty after the funeral, despite being filled with friends from church and a few Amish family members who decided to overlook the shunning for one day.

Silas stayed close by her, not saying much of anything, at first.

"Here, eat something." He gave her a plate crammed full of food, most of which she didn't care for.

"No, I can't."

"You need to eat something."

Right now, she didn't care about eating. She wanted to tell everyone to go, to let them be while they figured out what to do next.

"I'll eat later." Rochelle tried not to sigh. "I pulled out of my semester classes. The professors are going to give me withdrawn status on the courses."

"But the semester is already half over . . ."

"I . . . I can't deal with classes right now." She shook her head. "Maybe in the spring semester. I'm not sure."

"You need to keep busy."

Rochelle set the plate on the kitchen counter. "Silas, *please*. Please stop telling me what I need."

"I'm only trying to help you."

He had no idea everything he'd suggested didn't help. Nothing helped right now. Nothing would. Not for a long time, she knew.

"Of course, you're trying to help."

"Then let me."

"I appreciate your efforts. I do. But please don't get offended when I tell you what you're suggesting isn't helping me."

Silas raised his hands in surrender. "Never mind. I'll . . . I'll go talk to some of the others. You know where I'll be."

Rochelle wondered if it would be rude to retreat to her bedroom while everyone visited. If her father could hibernate in his workshop, surely she could go to her room.

She watched as Silas walked from the kitchen.

Later, she'd call him and talk. But not right now. Right now, she felt all talked out.

࿔

Rochelle had wandered through the thrift store with Emma and Betsy as they searched for plain glass vases for the wedding flowers to cover the tables at the reception.

They shared a common shopping cart and pushed it up and down the aisles. They weren't hard to miss, with one of the wheels rattling.

She stopped at a shelf of all kinds of plaques and pictures, assembled in a jumble. The image of a jet plane, with a swirl of jetstream behind it, caught her attention. Blue sky served as the background for the wall plaque, no larger than a piece of notebook paper.

The poem's words made her arms bumpy with gooseflesh.

High Flight

Oh! I have slipped the surly bonds of earth,
And danced the skies on laughter-silvered wings;
Sunward I've climbed, and joined the tumbling mirth
Of sun-split clouds,—and done a hundred things
You have not dreamed of—Wheeled and soared and swung
High in the sunlit silence. Hov'ring there
I've chased the shouting wind along, and flung
My eager craft through footless halls of air . . .
Up, up the long, delirious, burning blue
I've topped the wind-swept heights with easy grace
Where never lark or even eagle flew—
And, while with silent lifting mind I've trod
The high untrespassed sanctity of space,
Put out my hand, and touched the face of God.

—*John Gillespie Magee Jr.*

This was Silas. She ought to buy it and put it away for him as a Christmas gift. However, thoughts of a Christmas gift for him would be presumptuous.

He would understand the message of the plaque itself, of course, though maybe none of the others would. She clutched the plaque as tightly as she dared, then set it back on the shelf. No. It was silly. Poetry on a plaque. Maybe she ought to buy him a Scripture plaque instead. Or not buy him anything at all.

But the words . . . so beautiful.

Time to quit worrying what others would think when they saw it. The plaque was meant for Silas.

She snatched it from the shelf as if it might get away from her, then marched to the counter before she changed her mind again.

"Ah, this is a good one," said the clerk, an older man, older than her Amish *Aenti* Sarah. "You know the poem?" He studied her *kapp* and plain dress.

"No, it's the first time I've read it. This is a present, for a friend, who's a pilot."

"The man who wrote this was in the Royal Canadian Air Force. He was born in China, to missionary parents." He ran a scanner over the price tag. "I was Air Force, back in the day, so I know the story of the poem."

"Oh, how interesting. The person this is for, he's been a missionary pilot before. Or is."

"Well, I think he'll like this one just fine, then." The old man paused. "John Magee, though, he died young. At nineteen. In flight."

Rochelle almost canceled the transaction right then and there, with Emma and Betsy now standing beside her, looking over her shoulder at the plaque. Neither would understand about her buying a poem for Silas, but she wouldn't let it deter her either.

"Five dollars, even," the man said.

She fished a bill from her wallet and gave it to the man.

Died young, at nineteen. She tried not to shudder at the thought.

9

When he and Belinda lived in Africa, Silas had made overnight trips, some over several nights, at least once a month. Tonight, however, he found himself in a midrange hotel near Fulton County Airport on the west side of Atlanta.

The lights and traffic from nearby I-20 glittered not far from his window. A billboard proclaimed Six Flags amusement park lay only two exits away.

He'd been back in the United States more than a year now, and it still often struck him how "much" there was to the country. Every store didn't have just one type of ketchup; there had to be a minimum of five or six. Same thing for things like laundry soap, toilet paper, and more.

The first trip back to an American grocery store after being out of the country for three years, Belinda had frozen in place in the middle of the paper products aisle.

"There's too many things," was all she could say, trying not to burst into tears. Then they made a joke of it, she relaxed, and they went on their way.

Even now the memory made him chuckle and shake his head.

No wonder some of the most conservative Plain people gave warnings about visiting, let alone living, in Pinecraft. Smack dab in the middle of the outside world, far from the simple farms and rolling hills and fields of Pennsylvania or the Midwest.

Silas's phone rang on the dresser, where he'd laid his wallet and keys.

Uncle Tobias.

"Hello, Silas. This is Tobias. You're in Atlanta?"

"Yes, sir. I'm at the hotel now. Getting ready to eat a late supper." The hotel had a nice-looking restaurant, fancier than anything he was accustomed to. "Is everything all right?"

"Oh, yes. Everything's fine. Matthew is working on his homework, and Lena is here as well, studying, too."

"Good. Thanks again. I'm sorry I sprung this on you and Aunt Fran at the last minute."

"Not a problem. This will save me from eating so many leftovers."

"Did she hear you?" Silas joked.

"Yes, and I'm getting the stink eye. Anyway, I called to remind you about what Henry and I asked you about the Pinecraft Heritage Committee. I was going to wait, but figured I ought to call you while I'm thinking about it. Our meeting is in two weeks, and our next big fund-raiser is in three. It would be nice to have you on board before then, if you're willing."

Oh, yes, the committee. He'd thought about it, to be sure. He was honored they'd asked him, if a bit puzzled at first.

"One thing I should ask is, how long of a commitment is this? A year or so?"

"We don't have terms for anyone, not yet. We're still drafting bylaws or guidelines. I think, to begin with, we'd be thankful to have you for as long as you'd like to be on the committee."

"All right. I tell you what. I'll give you my decision tomorrow, when I get home."

"I'm not trying to rush you."

"I know. But I'll have plenty of time to think it over and pray about it tonight."

"Well, stop by when you get home. I'll be working in the shop."

"Will do."

He ended the call and set the phone back on the dresser.

If Belinda were here, she'd be someone he'd discuss it with. He valued her insight and opinion, and now he missed it again acutely.

If Belinda were here, they'd be in Africa, three of them, anyway, with Lena beginning her university studies stateside.

Lately, he wanted to find something to *do*. He'd spent the last year having people hold him and the children up and support them. Yes, they'd needed it, much as he never asked anyone for help.

Maybe serving on this committee would be a way to give back to the people who'd done so much for him. They'd cooked for him, cleaned their old rental from top to bottom, showed up to pack up when he announced they were moving to Florida. Countless prayers were offered for them.

And tonight, he realized, while he missed Belinda—part of him would always miss her, with all the years they shared—he wished Rochelle could have been here on this adventure.

Nothing improper of course, but she deserved some fun, when most of her time was taken by her job and now her studies.

⌒◦⌒

Things always looked better in the morning. Rochelle poured herself a cup of coffee, picked up her Bible, and went to the lanai for some quiet time. She was rewarded by seeing the first glow of daybreak come up over the palm trees.

Yes, things did look better in the morning. After a brief discussion with Emma last evening, Rochelle's initial irritation at Emma's giving notice had faded quite a bit.

She didn't want to employ someone who didn't truly want to clean homes. There were times when people had to work at something they didn't particularly enjoy, but needed the earnings. Such was life.

Rochelle picked up where she'd left off reading the day before yesterday. She found her bookmark, in Psalm 16.

"The lines are fallen unto me in pleasant places; yea, I have a goodly heritage. I will bless the Lord, who hath given me counsel: my reins also

instruct me in the night seasons. I have set the Lᴏʀᴅ always before me: because he is at my right hand, I shall not be moved."

Despite the ups and downs of Keim Cleaning, yes, the Lord had cared for her and given her wisdom and showed her the way.

One temperamental formerly Amish young woman wouldn't derail her business.

Still, the sensation that Keim Cleaning wasn't for her either wouldn't leave her alone.

"What do you want me to do, Lord?" she prayed aloud, softly. "One day, I know I'm going to finish my nursing studies. Maybe not as quickly as I'd thought at first. But they will be finished. Should I just close the business down? Surely someone else could, or would, be interested in running it."

Yet it wouldn't be for a long time. She could sell the business before she finished her studies, then live on some of the money while she completed her nursing program.

Either way, God would guide her, and the right answer would come.

Rochelle sipped her coffee. There went a heron, taking flight from the narrow creek bank, an inlet of Phillippi Creek, behind her home.

"Thank You for this beautiful place, Lord, and that I get to live here."

She closed her eyes in silent prayer, and then she knew.

Yes, she'd agree to join the Heritage Committee. She wanted to keep Pinecraft Plain and honor the traditions and ways making Pinecraft village what it is. Some of the old-timers didn't have the energy to keep up with planning, and since living in the village for so long, Rochelle herself had seen the transformation for some of the others who'd been the age she was now, when she first moved to the village.

People like Henry Hostetler, even Vera Byler.

If someone younger *didn't* step up, who would?

"*Aenti* Chelle?" Emma stood in the doorway. She'd already dressed, in a cape dress a vivid shade of coral and a starched white prayer covering.

"Good morning, Emma."

"I'm sorry. I should have told you sooner I wasn't happy cleaning houses anymore."

"You should have, yes, but don't worry, I'll find someone else."

"I didn't want to disappoint you."

"Dear girl, you're not disappointing me by being honest. If you'll be happier waiting tables at Der Dutchman, it is perfectly fine with me. I didn't expect to need to find another cleaner right now, but I'll make do. It's not the first time someone has given me notice and left."

Emma came onto the lanai. "All right. I don't mind cleaning so much. But every day. And some people are *so* messy. Like pigs. And some have acted as if it's my fault because they can't keep things clean."

"Oh. I wish you'd told me."

"It only happened once or twice."

"Well, I'm glad you did find a job. You'll like it there, I'm sure."

"So what are you going to do?"

"Like I said, I'll find someone else to take the clients. It will all be *fine*."

The young woman nodded, then left the lanai.

Rochelle bit her lip. She hadn't needed to call the Yoders in Ohio, not about Emma or Betsy, but she had a feeling there was something wrong with Emma, something Emma still wouldn't share.

Would Nora Yoder, Betsy and Emma's *mamm*, be able to help? But then, if she had a daughter of her own, she'd like to know if something was troubling her, no matter what her age.

She had the number to the phone shanty and could leave a message. It was still early, and who knew when Nora or someone else in the Yoder household would go to the shanty to check the voice mail?

Rochelle glanced toward the doorway leading to the kitchen. Better to move a discreet distance away, in case ears were listening. She placed her Bible on the small table between the chaise longues and stood.

She entered the slice of green she called her backyard and ambled over to the edge of the creek bank, not five yards away.

When she dialed, the phone immediately clicked over to the voice mailbox.

"We are Jedediah and Nora Yoder. Please leave us a message and we will return your call. Thank you and *danke*." Jedediah's voice had the lilt of an accent Rochelle was accustomed to her in her Amish relatives.

"Good morning, Jedediah and Nora. This is Rochelle Keim in Pinecraft. Please call me when you have the chance. I am leaving for the day, but I will be home tonight after supper. Thank you." She left her phone number, then pushed the end button on her phone. Did her voice shake a little? No, she sounded much as she would have, were she calling a housecleaning client.

Anyway, perhaps Nora would assume Rochelle was calling about wedding plans. And Nora might have some advice on how to handle Emma. Few people would understand a young woman better than her mother.

A pang of old grief rippled through her. *Oh, Momma.*

❧

Silas, 21

Silas wondered how many times Rochelle would push him away. It was as if she'd retreated into her grief, inside a locked room where no one else was welcome.

Finally, he decided to stop at the Keims' house and invite himself for supper and not take no for an answer.

He held a fresh bunch of flowers while he approached the familiar home as he had dozens of times before. The family's two vehicles sat in the driveway, Mr. Keim's pickup truck and Rochelle's sensible sedan she drove back and forth to college. When she was enrolled.

Mr. Keim had assured him he was welcome "anytime," the older man said.

Rochelle answered the door. Smoky circles made smudges under her eyes, but she had a smile for him. "Silas."

She tugged his hand and pulled him inside the house. Something smelled like cheddar cheese and beef. "I'm inviting myself for supper." He held up the flowers.

"Thank you. We just threw out the last of the wilted ones. These are beautiful." She held them up to her nose and inhaled, closing her eyes.

"I've . . . I've missed you."

"I've missed you, too." She turned, leading him toward the kitchen, where she found a vase for the flowers.

"I don't know what to say." He might as well be completely honest. He had no idea of how to help her, and his own helplessness shouted in his ears that he wasn't quite good enough.

"Then, don't say anything. Just be here."

"Are you resting all right? You look tired."

Rochelle shrugged. "I think the last couple of years have caught up with me. I've spent so much time between caring for Momma and keeping up with my classes, I just don't know what to do right now."

They visited during and after supper, had dessert and coffee. But Rochelle seemed distant to him, and he left not long after finishing one cup of coffee and a slice of cake.

10

Rochelle's phone rang at seven the next morning, a call from the Yoders.

"Rochelle, this is Nora Yoder. I received your message yesterday afternoon, but the phone shanty was busy and then it was too dark for me to stay. I came back this morning to call. I hope this isn't too early for you."

"No, not too early at all. Thank you for calling me back."

"I still have four more attendant dresses to finish for the wedding, but I should have them completed in plenty of time. My husband and I will be arriving in Pinecraft on the eighteenth."

"Good. I haven't spoken lately to Frances Fry, the seamstress here, but she's only sewing three dresses, not eight, as you and your friends are sewing."

"I am so thankful, both my *dochders* marrying, the same day. And I am thankful for everything you have done for them."

"I'm glad to. I, ah, I've been wondering. About Emma . . ."

"Is something wrong with Emma?"

"I'm not sure. She wasn't happy working for me. It was the cleaning. She quit—she gave me notice, yes, but I didn't know something was wrong."

"Emma was always my one more interested in fun than work. Oh, she's a *gut* cleaner, when she does clean. I admit I was surprised when she said she decided to work for you. I thought it was a phase, and then she would return to Ohio."

"I did too, at first. Maybe it was a long phase." At Rochelle's words, they both chuckled. "But she doesn't seem . . . settled, I guess is the right word."

"She always was the one flitting like a butterfly, after this thing, then another."

"How did you manage her?"

"Much prayer, and attempts to reason with her, to help her seek out the wisest solution."

"So, pretty much what I've been trying to do as well."

"Count the days, Rochelle. Less than sixty days and she will be her husband's responsibility. And, speaking of which, I have written the announcement for Betsy's wedding to run in *The Budget*, in December. I also mentioned Emma, as they're sisters and I don't want family or friends to be surprised by two ceremonies on one day."

"Good. I was going to ask about the family coming for the wedding. Nora, I know you have a full day ahead of you, so I will let you go now. Thanks again for calling me."

"You're welcome. And next time you speak to both of my *dochders*, please remind them I would like a call, or letter, from them as well."

"I will."

৵৶

Silas arrived back in Pinecraft after his return from Atlanta the next morning and headed straight for Uncle Tobias's house. The village's atmosphere embraced him. While it was a thrill to be at the controls of a plane again, it seemed like he'd been away from Pinecraft for days.

He tried not to yawn as he pulled into his uncle's driveway. The hotel, while nicer than any he'd ever stayed in before, had a mattress leaving him stiff and achy. After his flight home in the Cheyenne, he was ready to take a couple of pain relief pills and take a nap.

The sound of the van's engine drew Uncle Tobias from his work-shop. The older man's face broke into a smile while he approached the van.

"I'm back." Silas left the van and stretched.

"So I see." Uncle Tobias looked as expectant as a dog waiting for a snack. "Well?"

"Well."

"The Heritage Committee. You said you'd let me know your deci-sion. Will you come, give us some younger blood and ideas?"

"Yes, I will." His uncle's eagerness made him grin. "I'll do my best to give good input. But, you know, our move here might not be permanent."

"It's not?"

"My lease is for a year, yes . . . but I thought you should know. In case you want someone who'll be here year-round."

Tobias's shoulders sagged a bit. "I appreciate that. Well, Fran and I are pleased to have you around for as long as it may be. All of you."

"Thank you. My parents . . . they didn't understand why I didn't want to stay in Ohio. But I couldn't. Too many reminders. You know?" Maybe Uncle Tobias didn't know.

"I imagine it's true, but no, I don't know. Your father is more understanding of why, but a mother, now, she always likes having her brood close by." He squinted in the direction of the house. "Fran does. She's been as happy as Christmastime with Matthew and Lena around."

Sometimes, Silas realized, his journey wasn't about him. Maybe God did have a hand in sending him to Pinecraft. Or gave Silas the nudge even in the midst of the numbing sensation of loss.

"Well, I'm glad she is."

"So, what was it like, flying again?"

"Felt like I never left, felt like the first time I soloed, sort of. It came back to me right away."

Another vehicle pulled up into the driveway behind Silas's van. Henry Hostetler, the Mennonite with the tropical shirts. Today's was sky blue.

"How do," Henry said, tugging on his suspenders as he approached. "You about ready?"

"Ready?"

"We're having a quick committee meeting this afternoon at Betsy's bakery. Around four o'clock or so. Rochelle has clients this afternoon and doesn't think she'll be able to make it."

"Yes, I'll be there." He was free; no more flights until Friday, a quick hop to Miami and back, a business lunch.

❧

Silas opened the door of Pinecraft Pies and Pastry, and the scent of apples and cinnamon embraced him, pulling him inside. Henry Hostetler was there, along with Uncle Tobias, the Amish bishop, and Samuel Byler.

"Good to see you," Henry said. He nodded at an empty chair. "Get yourself some coffee and something sweet, and we'll get started."

Silas helped himself to the coffee—the sign said it was for donations, so he put a dollar bill in the jar. Then he went to the counter, where Betsy Yoder stood.

"Hello, Mr. Fry. How may I help you?" She kept her hands clasped in front of her.

He studied the case, and his mouth began to water. Dutch apple pie, fresh from the oven, the sign read. Special of the day.

"I'll take a slice of the special."

"Warmed, with vanilla ice cream on the side?"

"Well, sure, if you insist."

"I don't insist, but I do recommend." She smiled at him as she reached for a plate.

"All right, then."

She dished up a slice of pie, then disappeared for a moment through a Dutch door, into what he figured was the kitchen, then reemerged not thirty seconds later with the pie and an accompanying scoop of ice cream.

He'd never been to the shop, not since moving to Pinecraft, and his waistline thanked him.

Silas returned to the table, where Henry stood beside an easel with a chart propped up on it. The others waited while he sat down. They'd already eaten half their desserts.

Uncle Tobias was polishing off a chocolate fried pie. "So, you see, here's our list of things to do for our first event, a fish fry. We already have many of the tasks accomplished. But we're still haggling back and forth on a fair price to charge for the plates."

"Remind me again, what the proceeds will go toward?" Silas took a bite of pie along with a taste of vanilla ice cream.

"This is our initial fund-raiser, and we're using it to pay for operating expenses for the next events."

"I say we should use part of the money to fix the pavilion roof," said Bishop Smucker. "I would like to show people we are not only taking their money, but they see something with their own eyes, how we care for the village."

"Does anyone know when the roof was last repaired?" Silas asked. "Also, do we know how much it will cost to fix it?"

"I would have to get up there and look," Henry said. "But I would be willing to do it for the cost of materials."

"How much should we charge for the plates? This seems to be the big question," Uncle Tobias said.

"Did the foundation have to buy any of the food or plates?" Silas asked.

"No, those are all being donated. The fish, too. Several hundred pounds of catfish from someone who wishes to be anonymous." Samuel Byler studied his empty coffee cup.

"How about we ask for eight dollars a plate, but people can donate the change if they'd like?" Silas suggested. "If people can only afford eight dollars, then so be it, and if others can do more, they're welcome to."

"I had the same idea." Henry nodded.

The bell over the front door clanged, and in came Rochelle, her cheeks flushed. Did the flush deepen when she glanced at him?

"Hello. I finished earlier than I thought I would." She served herself a cup of coffee and joined them at the table.

Henry scooted over to make room for her, while Silas fetched her an empty chair from an unoccupied table.

"We've just started," Henry said.

Rochelle nodded. "What is the menu for the fish fry, besides fish, if I might ask?"

The men exchanged glances.

"Potato salad . . . and beans," Bishop Smucker said.

"Do you have a dessert planned?"

"Ah, no . . . we didn't get that far yet."

"And the fish fry is in . . . ?"

"Two weeks."

Rochelle's eyes widened. "You don't have dessert planned, and you only have potato salad and beans for the side items. What about bread or rolls?"

Samuel huffed. "We don't need bread."

Bishop Smucker coughed. "Maybe nobody *needs* bread. But bread and butter are good to eat on the side."

"So, we need to get butter pats now, too?" Samuel frowned.

"We are planning to feed at least seven hundred. It's a lot of butter pats." Bishop Smucker nodded.

Silas shook his head. "Does the foundation have any money to spend?" He shouldn't have asked. Of course, they'd try to spend as little money as possible. But sometimes, spending a little money was necessary.

Henry stood up and moved over to the easel. He took out a marker. "Friends, we need to remember why we're doing this. We're going to make a difference in the community and show the village we care, and they'll get behind us. Maybe we won't agree on butter pats and such, but to me, butter pats are a minor thing. Even if there's over seven hundred of them."

"I agree," Bishop Smucker said.

"Excuse me for a moment." Rochelle glanced at Silas. "I believe I need a dessert."

Rochelle went to the counter and bought a chocolate fried pie, then returned to the table.

"Do we have flyers prepared?" Silas ventured to ask. The men were well intentioned, but the meeting's direction had careened along a rabbit trail.

"No." Henry added *flyers* to the to-do list. "We hadn't quite decided on a price yet, so we had to hold off on printing the flyers. But we plan to print at least one hundred, for people to post. Also, we need someone to post flyers on light poles in the village and at the post office."

"We should vote on a price." Bishop Smucker looked at Silas. "I like Mr. Fry's idea. Eight dollars, for this fund-raiser, and if anyone chooses to donate the change, all the better."

"Let's take a vote," Henry said. The vote passed, five to one, with Samuel Byler casting the lone dissenting vote.

"I'll note we approved the price for the catfish supper," said Uncle Tobias, who evidently was acting as the group's note keeper.

It had taken them nearly half an hour with this roundabout discussion. Silas hoped the rest of the meeting would go more quickly.

He glanced at Rochelle, who seemed to be savoring every bite of her fried pie. Then again, more time with Rochelle wasn't such a bad thing.

Two hours later, twilight had descended on Pinecraft, but the foundation committee had come up with a price for the meal, a full menu, wording for the flyers, and somehow Rochelle found herself in charge of securing desserts to go with the more than seven hundred catfish plates they planned to sell.

Seven hundred desserts? She'd participated in haystack suppers before through the church, but nothing as large as this. And to pull it together in two weeks.

She helped herself to a large cup of coffee and apologized to Betsy for them staying so long at the shop. Betsy was wiping down the counters before closing for the evening.

"I don't mind, *Aenti* Chelle. I think the men bought two desserts apiece." Betsy, ever cheerful, grinned as she cleaned.

Silas lingered in the background after the other men left for home, their wives likely having to keep supper warm for them tonight.

"Walk you home?" he asked her when she picked up her tote bag on the nearest chair.

"I took my bicycle."

"I see. Well, I can walk fast."

She laughed as they left the bakery. Night fell, and temperatures dropped slightly. "If you want to keep up. I suppose I can pedal slowly."

"How are you going to drink coffee on the way home?" He studied the covered foam cup she held.

"I can ride with one hand. I learned how when I was eight." She couldn't resist a little bit of sass.

"Very funny."

She did hand him her coffee as she took her seat on the bicycle, then accepted the cup back from him. "So, what did you think of the meeting tonight?"

"I think we're going to have an interesting time."

"Interesting is right. But I like what they're doing. If we sell out, we'll have plenty of money to fix the pavilion roof." She pushed off with her foot, steering with her free hand, and inched along the street.

"I agree. What are you going to suggest for dessert?"

"Cupcakes. They're portable, fast, and easy to carry. We won't need a dessert plate for them, either."

"I can see if Aunt Frances can make some."

"Oh, would you? I don't know if I have money I can give people for supplies, but if a few ladies each make four dozen, we'll end up with plenty."

Streetlights illuminated their way home. The streets were nearly deserted. The main vacation season in Pinecraft hadn't begun yet, but wasn't far off. A trio of dark figures a block away made Rochelle freeze.

She kept going, listening to Silas talk about the flyer wording, how he was going to type it on the computer, print it out, and bring a copy of the file to the printers who volunteered their services.

Rochelle paused under the streetlight. The figures drew closer. They weren't Amish or Mennonite. Some young men in regular street clothes. One bounced a basketball. People visited the park, as it was open to the public. Nobody restricted anyone from coming in. Even a homeless person slept in the park here and there.

"Are you all right?" Silas asked.

She nodded, not trusting her voice at the moment. Years ago, when everything changed for them, it had been another walk home, but with two other people who were no longer with them, both gone before their time.

"I'm . . ." *Breathe, Rochelle. Breathe.* The young men didn't want to hurt her or anyone. Just some locals, heading to play basketball, a pickup game, she'd heard them called.

Her hand clutching the handlebar went numb, along with the rest of her. She hadn't felt this way in years. Maybe it was because Silas stood beside her.

He placed his hand on hers. "It's all right, Rochelle."

The young men, talking and laughing, paid the two of them no mind as they passed by on the opposite side of the street.

She didn't let herself look over her shoulder at them, but forced herself to keep moving forward in the direction of home and safety.

⚬⚬

Rochelle, 19

Twilight had come as the four of them walked along, feeling the first chill of fall in the air. John and Belinda, Silas and Rochelle, couples together. They'd picked apples and laughed and talked, then John's grandmother had fed them all an early supper. A perfect afternoon.

"What will you make with our apples?" Silas asked Rochelle, tightening the grip on the bushel basket they carried between them.

"Pie, of course. Maybe some fried pies." She smiled at him. "Our" apples, he'd said.

"I'm going to make apple bread," Belinda said as she shared a grin of her own with John.

"If you don't burn it this time." John's gentle taunt made them all laugh.

She could do this for the rest of her life, spend happy afternoons like this with Silas. And John and Belinda. She realized for the past few hours, she hadn't thought of her mother at all.

Part of her felt a bit guilty about letting her mother slip from her mind. She did miss her mother, but it felt so *good* for life to be normal again, if only for a few hours.

A vehicle approached, then slowed to a crawl, a dark four-door sedan.

"Hey, looking good, ladies. Love that walk!" a gravelly male voice called out.

Rochelle's spine stiffened and she stopped on the roadside, as did Belinda. Silas and John stopped as well.

The car sped off.

"What is wrong with people?" Belinda said, her voice high-pitched.

"They're mean, is what." John gave a little tug on the basket. "C'mon, not much farther. Then you can get to apple peeling.",

"Bossy man." Belinda spoke the words gently, and smiled at him.

Rochelle's heart pounded, but she forced her feet along. The sooner they arrived home, the better. For some reason, the tree-lined road felt darker, and not for the reason of the lengthening shadows.

They continued along as the road grew dark, with the fields beyond still holding a golden glow of leftover light.

A roar made them look up. The same car, with the same loud-mouthed man. No, there were two. Another one in the passenger seat.

It screeched to a halt. A man leapt from the passenger side.

He held a baseball bat.

Frame by frame, the next sequences seared themselves into Rochelle's memory forever.

John and Silas, releasing their hold on the bushels they helped carry.

Someone shouting for wallets and money and rings.

"Wait, please," from John.

Profanity, slamming into each of them like a fist.

"No—" A strangling word from Belinda.

She pulled away from the man who'd grabbed her by the *kapp*.

The swinging of the baseball bat.

Screams. Rochelle's throat hurt. She sank to the ground. *God, please—*

She felt the pavement, pricking through the fabric of her dress and biting her knees. Then the sounds of more profanity, guttural laughter, and screams. The sound of something cracking.

John, slumped to the road, looking at Rochelle with his big brown eyes, blood streaming from his forehead and covering the pavement. "Help."

"Do something! Silas!" She screamed, looking up at Silas, who faced the men down. "Help him."

Do something, Silas, the strange male voices mocked her.

Silas only stood there as the pair drove off into the descending night.

An apple rolled toward John, whose eyes stared up at nothing as Belinda crawled to him, clamping her hand onto his skull, as his blood streamed between her fingers.

No, no, no.

11

Since the evening walking home from the Heritage Committee meeting last week, Rochelle hadn't seen Silas except at church. But thinking about her reaction to seeing a group of young men simply heading to play basketball in the park still rattled her a bit. She hadn't had such a tremor of panic in years. She'd seen young people in the park plenty of times, young men who weren't Plain.

Why did the sensation of almost paralyzing fear come upon her the other evening? After witnessing John's death, it had taken time for Rochelle to walk outside alone again, and she used to avoid the practice. Even now, she occasionally felt the need to glance over her shoulder, although in the village she felt relatively safe. When she spoke with Beatrice, her pastor's wife, about what happened, her friend believed Silas being there brought back the feeling of the night John died. It made sense.

Today, a sunny day told her she ought to be upbeat and excited about the fish fry, and so she dug up some enthusiasm for the event. Caring for the park's pavilion was a worthy cause, and today's meal would show the community, and the city as well, the villagers cared for the park.

She found the last parking spot at the park, thankful she'd gone early enough. Of course, parking on site meant she'd likely be one of the last to leave. She came alone today; Betsy had the bakery, and

Emma was working a shift at Der Dutchman, but promised to meet her at the park for a plate. Rochelle told the young women ahead of time she'd purchase plates for all three of them.

The men had set up a trio of fryers. Several large jugs of cooking oil stood nearby, along with propane tanks for fuel to keep the oil in the fryers hot. A wide expanse of large foil pans were arranged on a series of tables beneath the trees dripping with Spanish moss.

"I've got the cupcakes, at least three hundred," she called out to Henry Hostetler as she approached. "Do we have a table ready for the desserts?"

"Right over here." Henry stood at a far table, where already someone had dropped off several trays of cupcakes. A few pans of some type of dessert, crowned with mounds of whipped cream, lay next to them.

"Good. A few of the women who agreed to bring desserts said they'd drop them off here early." Rochelle surveyed the desserts. "I'll get my cupcakes and Beatrice's from the back of my van."

"I'll give you a hand," Silas said.

She smiled. She hadn't seen him when she arrived and wondered when he'd arrive at the park.

"How are you doing?" He glanced at her as she opened the rear hatch of her van.

"Doing well. Busy. And looking forward to today, also." She picked up a tray of cupcakes and handed them to Silas.

"These look good. Can I have one?"

"Only if you buy a supper plate," she teased.

"Doesn't the Bible say something about not muzzling the ox while it treads the grain? After all, I'm carrying these to the table for you."

"Okay, ox, have a cupcake."

"You just called me an ox." He feigned shock.

"You were the one bringing up Scripture." At her words, they both laughed.

They used to laugh a lot, like this, long ago.

Rochelle led the way to the dessert table and placed her tray of cupcakes beside the other desserts. "I think there's plenty, good thing."

She glanced toward the fryers. Henry and Samuel and Tobias clustered around a large cooler.

"Plenty of catfish, too." Silas followed her gaze.

"So, where are Lena and Matthew?"

"Lena is studying, and Matthew is coming with his aunt soon. Should be here any moment."

Was it her imagination, or did Silas suddenly seem nervous?

She'd gotten over her nerves about being around him, reminding herself to live in the present despite the past trying to roar into her ears from time to time.

They headed back to the van for one more trip.

"How are you, Rochelle?"

"You asked me already." She reached for another tray of cupcakes.

"No. The other night, on the way home. When we saw those young men, heading to the park. You froze."

"Yes. I did. It had been a long time since I'd remembered how it felt . . ."

"I know what you mean. I used to wake up, from having nightmares about what happened." Silas frowned.

She wasn't going to have this conversation with him now, but supposed they needed to, since the last conversation they'd had about John was a disaster.

"I . . . I didn't know. I'm . . . I'm sorry." She smiled at Nellie Bontrager, who glided up on her tricycle. Nellie had promised to help serve potato salad and beans.

"I don't know why God allowed it."

"I always wish I knew." She bit her lip. But she'd come to a calm acceptance now over the tragedy. She didn't like the idea, but her screaming at God hadn't helped years ago.

"We failed each other, and I'm sorry about it."

We failed each other?

She couldn't think of how she'd failed Silas, after what happened to John. She'd been racked with grief already over her mother.

"Well, it was all a long time ago, Silas." She tried not to shrug, because she wasn't trying to shrug off the pain or the history. "I think it best if we move forward from here."

Wherever that was.

"Hoo-eee, those cupcakes look mighty delicious." Henry snapped his suspenders and reached for a cupcake.

"Not you, too. Next thing you know, everyone will want one. And we haven't even started serving yet." Rochelle scolded him, but smiled as she did so. He'd worked wonders on fixing her washing machine, and the handyman definitely deserved a cupcake or two.

Henry grinned and picked up one with white frosting and multicolor sprinkles. "I need a bit of sugar before we get started. I see a line is beginning to form."

Rochelle looked past the split-rail fence at the edge of the park. A small group had clustered together and stood watching the setup.

She kept her smile in place when she saw Silas staring at her. Normally life flowed for her here in Pinecraft. With her business, church, her friends, and the variety of activities in the village, she knew what to expect. Silas had upended things when he'd pulled into the village, with his minivan and trailer.

Her mother always said God knew what was going to happen. Sometimes, Rochelle wished He'd give her a bit of notice ahead of time.

⁂

Silas hadn't intended on getting Rochelle's dander up, but it happened. The other night, he'd been concerned about her, although she'd regained her composure after the moment of panic while walking home.

Years ago, with his brashness of youth and his pride, he'd let her down. She'd hurt him, too, with her words later on. He'd learned you couldn't take back words any more than you could put toothpaste back in the tube.

"Well, you ready?" Henry said beside him. He licked his fingers after downing the cupcake he'd snagged from Rochelle in two bites.

"I think so." He had never participated in a fish fry, not at this scale, anyway. An elderly Mennonite woman and her husband stood by the cooler of fish fillets, ready to apply the breading and crumbs. They would then pass a tray of breaded fish to Silas and Henry, who'd put the fish in a basket and immerse the fillets in the hot oil. After timing the fish to cook for a few minutes, the men would pull the baskets, then put the fish to drain, after which the servers would put the fish on plates, and so on.

The line officially opened for business, with volunteers collecting donations and the workers preparing the plates. Men wearing suspenders, women in all different sorts of *kapps*, as well as people in regular street clothes, from toddlers to the old, passed through the line.

"You settled in pretty well?" Henry asked.

"I think so. My children enjoy it here, so I'm thankful for some sense of normal life."

"You've had a lot of changes in your life."

"Yes. It seems life is all about change. Not changes I'd have chosen, either."

"It would be nice if we could pick and choose, wouldn't it?"

"Yes, sir, it would."

"So you're a pilot?"

"Yes, I made my first solo flight not long after my twenty-first birthday. I knew God had a purpose for me flying, as nontraditional an occupation as it is."

"I bet Pinecraft is quiet compared to where you've been, maybe a bit boring."

"Quiet, yes. Boring, no." He let himself glance down the line to where Rochelle was handing out cupcakes and serving up desserts.

At last, there was a lull in the line, so Silas went to get two bottled waters, one for him and one for Henry. Rochelle was picking up a bottle of water herself.

"What a crowd." He pulled two bottles from the large steel bucket of ice.

"Yes. It's been a blur."

"Ah, I was wondering . . . how would you like to go for a flight?"

Rochelle paused. "A flight?"

"Yes. I'm making a trip to Atlanta, flying my clients, Mr. And Mrs. Kingsley. Their son had a heart transplant recently, so they've been going back and forth. Mr. Kingsley said if I ever wanted to bring a friend, I could. So, consider yourself invited."

He could see a spark ignite in her eyes at the offer. "Oh, I'd love to take a flight. But . . ."

"It won't cost you anything, except keeping me company on the flight back to Sarasota the same day." He decided to strike out and shoot for the moon. "We could have supper there, downtown, before flying home."

Pink shot to her cheeks as she glanced around the park area.

"I'd love to. As long as my schedule cooperates."

Silas wanted to let out a whoop, but restrained himself. "We fly out a week from Thursday. We'll leave late morning, be in the air a couple of hours, then have time to spend downtown before flying back to Sarasota after supper."

She nodded. "Yes, I can do it then." Her smile warmed his heart.

12

*R*ochelle met Silas at the small private airport at the appointed time. Her stomach turned over on itself, flipped right-side up, then flipped over again. She didn't think she'd feel this way without even lifting off the ground yet.

The plan was simple, she reminded herself. Fly with Mr. and Mrs. Kingsley to Atlanta. She and Silas would then have supper out somewhere special, then he would fly her and Mr. Kingsley back to Sarasota while Mrs. Kingsley remained in Atlanta with the couple's son, recovering from a heart transplant.

Emma and Betsy exclaimed over the fun she'd have.

"I've always wanted to fly," Emma said.

"Make sure you order a special dessert at supper so you can tell me about it," Betsy said.

Rochelle concentrated on the idea of an elegant dessert. Silas told her they'd have supper at La Boheme in Atlanta, a legendary restaurant. He'd made reservations, too.

Was this what some would call a date? He called it a belated birthday present, as hers was in March and he hadn't arrived in Sarasota yet.

"It's only right we go. I'd always wanted to take you flying," Silas had admitted.

She locked her van and carried her tote bag with her, heading toward the area marked "Office," where Silas said he would meet her before they went to the tarmac to board the plane.

She pulled open the door and stepped into the quiet bustle. Silas stood by the counter and greeted her first with a grin.

"You ready?"

She nodded. "I'm nervous."

"You'll never forget this. I still remember the first time I ever went up in a plane. An old crop duster biplane, open cockpit, back in Ohio." Silas picked up a clipboard and a pen. "Follow me, Miss Keim. The Kingsleys will be meeting us in about an hour, and right after we're cleared, we'll take to the skies."

Rochelle followed Silas out a side door, then down a set of steps and along a short sidewalk, through a gate and onto the airfield. Several planes stood lined up side by side on the tarmac.

A light breeze came from the south. Not cool, but enough to make the gooseflesh pop up on her arms. She rubbed them and tried not to shiver.

They continued along to what looked like a small jet. It gleamed white in the morning sun and had a set of propellers.

"Here's the Cheyenne." Silas unlatched the door, opened it, and a set of steps unfolded. "Make yourself comfortable while I start my preflight checks."

She was about to get onto a plane. And Silas Fry would be the pilot. Well, she'd never imagined anything like this happening. Not even in a dream.

And supper to follow, with Silas? Just the two of them.

Just friends.

But she hadn't heard of Silas flying any other friends anywhere else, just them.

Stop thinking so much and enjoy *yourself.*

Rochelle climbed up the steps, and ducked her head a smidge so she didn't bonk it on the doorway.

Two pairs of seats at the front of the plane sat back to back. Beyond the first pair, she glimpsed a control panel and wide front window. Two more pairs of seats toward the back, with a table of sorts between them.

At the rear of the plane, a small flat-panel television had been bolted to a panel running floor to ceiling. To the right of the panel was a compartment, likely for carry-on bags.

She maneuvered herself into the nearest seat. When the Kingsleys arrived, she'd move to the rear of the plane, or wherever was most convenient for them.

"Okay," Silas said. He angled his body so he could slip through the space between the front seats. "Need to make some checks here, then I'll go over the outside of the plane."

Rochelle nodded.

"You nervous?" He stopped his forward movement, placing his hand on her arm.

"A little. No, a lot."

"I'll take good care of you. I always check and double-check. The weather is perfect for flying today. And God is always watching us, keeping us in His care. If we didn't have the knowledge of Him, how frightening life would be."

"Sometimes it is, even with the knowledge."

Silas paused for a moment. "I'd have to agree with you."

"Anyway, I don't want to keep you from your checks." She stared at his hand on her arm, then tapped her tote bag. "I brought some studying to do."

"Studying? You'll be studying? Don't forget to enjoy the view." He removed his hand and continued into the cockpit area.

"Oh, I won't." She ought to have brought a camera. Wait, her phone had a camera. But wasn't there some rule about not using phones during flights? She knew that much. She'd have to ask. When Silas wasn't busy, of course.

She moved toward the back of the plane, where the table was, then pulled out her book and her notes, then immersed herself in Florida state law and standard care practices for patients.

A pair of voices outside, one male, one female, pulled her out of her notes. She couldn't quite make them out from where she sat, but she'd meet the Kingsleys soon enough. Rochelle glanced at the clock on her phone. Almost time to leave. Her stomach quavered as footsteps sounded on the steps outside.

A woman entered the cabin first. "Hello, you must be Rochelle Keim. I'm Amanda Kingsley."

"Nice to meet you, Amanda. And thank you for letting me ride along." She almost admitted she'd never flown before, but thought better of it. She didn't want to think about how wealthy these people must be, to own a plane like this and have it at their disposal.

"Our pleasure," Amanda said. "Oh, this is my husband, Ted."

Rochelle shook hands with both of them. "Silas tells me your son has been in the hospital."

"Yes," Amanda said. "He had a heart transplant about three weeks ago and if we get good news today, we might be bringing him home to Florida in one more week."

"Oh, how wonderful for your family. I'm happy for you."

"Thanks, we're so grateful. We're also thankful we found your Silas, too. Our regular pilot had a family emergency of his own to see to recently, so Silas has been a true godsend for us." Amanda smiled at her husband. "Imagine, a Mennonite pilot!"

"Have you ever been up in a Cheyenne?" Ted asked.

"No, this is actually the first time I've ever been in a plane."

The couple looked at her as though she'd just said she could turn herself invisible.

"Imagine." Amanda shook her head. "You must be incredibly excited."

"Yes, and nervous, too."

"Nothing to be nervous about," Mr. Kingsley said. "This Cheyenne is in tip-top working order. So much more convenient to travel with. She also has a lot of kick to her."

Rochelle nodded. This couple reminded her of some of her housecleaning clients. Warm, kind, and wealthy.

"I see you're a student."

"Yes, I'm in nursing school, finishing my degree program the semester after next, Lord willing."

"Wonderful. I admire nurses. I don't know if I'd have the stomach to do what some of them must do." Amanda frowned, then her expression brightened. "But the nurses taking care of our Benjamin are truly gifts from God. When you see a little one, your little one, lying in a bed, so helpless . . . and you know you don't have the skills to help him." She pulled a tissue from her leather bag and dabbed at her eyes. "Pardon me."

Mr. Kingsley reached across the aisle and squeezed his wife's hand. "You have wonderful skills, my love. Once we bring Benjamin home, he'll do even better. Nothing like sleeping in your own bed."

"It hardly seems like weeks, more like years." Amanda focused on the floor, then snapped her attention back to Rochelle. "Now, please, make yourself comfortable. There's a bathroom in the back, behind the panel, if you should need it on the way."

Rochelle's face flamed. "Thank you."

"The mini fridge under the table there has some bottled water, and I think some sodas, too."

Rochelle nodded. "Again, thank you for letting me come along today."

"Well, it's no trouble at all. Silas thinks so highly of you, we suggested he ought to invite you to come along, have supper out with him."

Oh. So, the idea hadn't quite been his. Not that he'd have asked her to come along after fishing for an invitation from the Kingsleys. Still, her face burned.

Silas climbed back into the plane. "Almost ready. One more check outside, and I'll close the door, then we'll be on our way once the tower clears us."

Ten minutes later, true to his word, Silas had closed the door, sealing them inside the plane.

"Ladies, Mr. Kingsley, please buckle up and I'll let you know when we've hit our cruising altitude. Good weather and visibility. There might be a little chop as we ascend, but once it's over, we'll have smooth sailing until Fulton County."

Rochelle took a seat in the back, facing forward, so she was looking at the backs of the Kingsleys' seats as they faced forward.

A whining noise began, then a buzz and hum as the propellers began to turn. The noise filled the cabin.

"Rochelle," Amanda, turning in her seat, called out above the sounds. "Do you want some gum?"

"Gum?"

"Chewing gum . . . it'll help pop your ears when we go up." She waved a stick of gum.

Rochelle slipped out of her seat belt, grabbed the stick of gum as the plane began to roll forward. "Thanks." She skittered backward and plopped onto the leather seat.

After fumbling with the gum, then her seat belt, Rochelle watched the buildings pass by the window as Silas taxied the plane to the runway, covered with all sorts of different colored strips and lights and symbols.

In the background, below the engine's roar, she could hear Silas's voice as he communicated with the tower. Then, gravity held her back in her seat as the engine's thrust took hold and the plane shot down the runway, faster, faster, with fence and parking lot and tarmac flashing by.

A bump and a jolt, then they were airborne.

She clutched the armrests.

Oh, Lord, I can see down on the treetops and palm trees.

It all grew smaller and smaller. She chewed more vigorously as her ears began a curious pop-pop-pop. She leaned on the armrest closest to the window. There was the parking lot. The top of her van.

She scanned the horizon. Miles away, the shimmering Gulf of Mexico.

So beautiful.

Lord, we're so small. What tiny creatures we are, from heaven's viewpoint. What is man, that Thou art mindful of him?

She tried not to think of the thousands of feet of empty air between them and the ground. She was *flying*! Rochelle couldn't help but grin.

⚜

A perfect flight to Atlanta. Just like last time, the Kingsleys hired a vehicle to take them to the hospital, but first dropped Silas and Rochelle off in the bustling downtown area of Peachtree Center.

"We'll send the car to pick you up and return you to the airfield," Ted said. "In two hours. Or, stay as long as you like."

"Thank you." Silas made a note of the time. Right around four now, then a pickup around six would have them back to the airport before seven. An evening flight home to Sarasota.

Rochelle's face glowed. She exited the rear of the vehicle after saying good-bye to Mrs. Kingsley. Then she looked at Silas, expectantly. "This is all so . . . so *big*."

He shut the car's door, and it glided away from the curb. "Isn't it?"

What had he thought, reserving a table at a swank downtown restaurant for them? It seemed like a good idea at the time, to make their brief stop in Atlanta special.

"Look at these buildings." Rochelle tilted her head back to study the buildings which rose up high on either side of them. And a shopping center.

"Something else, huh?" Silas shook his head. "We can walk around after supper, if you'd like to."

Rochelle nodded. "Yes." And then, her stomach growled. "Sorry."

He laughed. "Well, our reservation is at four-fifteen. There's La Boheme, a few doors down."

"I can't wait."

Silas wanted to offer her his arm or take her hand. But he reminded himself this was friendship, making up for lost time. And if Belinda were here, he wouldn't be thinking of holding Rochelle's hand or offering her his arm.

He did, however, open the door for her, and she passed into the restaurant's softly lit reception area.

A hostess clad in black and white stood at a wooden desk. "You have a reservation?"

"Yes, it should be under Fry. Silas Fry."

The woman scanned the listings in front of her, then frowned. "I'm sorry. What time was it for?"

"Four-fifteen, an early seating." He'd called last week, after inviting Rochelle and making the suggestion of supper in the city.

The hostess lifted her computer pad and turned it so he could see the listing. "I'm finding nothing under Fry. We did have a server error last week and lost a few entries. I can fit you in around seven-thirty."

"I'm sorry, it won't work. We'll be leaving the city before seven."

"I apologize. Perhaps another evening?"

"Perhaps." He didn't look at Rochelle's face. A simple supper, and now they had no plans to be anywhere.

They left the restaurant and stepped onto the sidewalk. Silas squinted from the brightness. "Well, take heart, I will find us a place to eat supper."

"I'm sure you will." Rochelle continued to take in her surroundings. A tall, glittering building stood not far away. "I wonder what that building is."

"A hotel, maybe? I don't know."

"I don't mind walking somewhere, to stretch my legs."

They ambled north, along Peachtree Street.

"We could always go to the mall." He glanced at her and grinned.

"You flew me to Atlanta to go to a *mall*?" She laughed aloud.

Yes, she could still catch his jokes.

"No, of course not." He studied the sensible sweater she wore over her short-sleeved cape dress. "Are you warm enough? It'll be a bit chilly later, since we're so much farther north."

"Yes, I'll be fine. We'll be indoors most of the time anyway."

He stopped there on the sidewalk. A few other pedestrians passed them by, one or two giving a curious look at Rochelle's *kapp*.

"All right, I have a confession to make."

"What?" Her eyes sparkled. She was expecting another joke.

"I have no idea where we are, or what's nearby. I only chose La Boheme because Ted suggested it."

"We can stop at the next restaurant we see. Maybe they can let us look at a menu."

Silas liked to plan. In Africa, plans and timetables often got upended. Life in the States could, too. This time, though, he'd wanted this to be special for Rochelle. Right now, his plan had collapsed, except for his flight plan to take off at seven forty-five tonight.

"Sounds good." His own stomach had begun rumbling as well. What a duet they made, when hungry.

Crossing to the next block, they saw a sign hanging from a historic building on the corner: *Mama's Kitchen: Comfort Food.*

"Let's go here," Rochelle said, placing her hand on Silas's arm. The touch made him break his stride for a second.

"Comfort food. Sounds good." He led her to the door where they stopped and perused the menu taped to the glass. He'd budgeted plenty for supper for two in a city, and these prices would leave him some money to spare.

"Meatloaf, fried chicken, beans and cornbread, and more," she read aloud. "And dessert, chocolate cake, peach cobbler, or strawberry shortcake. I think I might want one of each."

"Me too." He held open the door for her. "Shall we?"

"We shall." She stepped into the restaurant ahead of him.

All the while, it seemed to him as if the years dripped away and vanished like morning dew.

13

*A*fter supper, which they ended up not being able to finish because of the generous portions, Rochelle and Silas took a short stroll around the block, and past the edge of Olympic Park. She had never seen anything like it before; they had just enough time before twilight descended to enjoy a few more sights.

Rochelle carried the doggie bag of leftovers. The restaurant had an insulated disposable bag, and the server assured her the food would keep warm for hours until they arrived home. All the way to Sarasota, even.

When their server, a sweet mother of four named Angelica, heard they were visiting from Florida, she exclaimed about the Amish restaurant with the pies.

"I saw it on a travel show once, the guy ate a whole pie, I think," she said, nodding.

"It's the place. Our homes aren't too far from the restaurant."

"Oh. You're not together? I thought you were . . . ah, a couple."

Rochelle wanted a cushion to crawl under and hide. "No, no." Her face burned, but she kept her composure. Of course, someone would assume they were married, seeing them together.

A half-grin grew on one side of Silas's face and transformed into a full smile after the waitress took their check.

But he said nothing until he found his phone and checked the time. "We have about thirty minutes to stretch our legs some more and walk off some of the dessert before the car arrives."

"It feels like we just arrived," she said.

"It does, doesn't it?"

So now, they found themselves strolling back toward the Mall at Peachtree, discussing the buildings and how busy the city was, as well as the best parts of the meal tonight.

"The food reminded me of Pinecraft. Comforting," Rochelle observed. "I have to admit I'm glad the other fancy-pants place lost our reservation."

"I am, too." He glanced down at her arm.

Was he going to try to hold her hand? She had a flashback to the old courting days.

No, it was in the past. The present couldn't be built on former heartache and heartbreak. This wouldn't do.

Although Rochelle realized part of her wouldn't mind traveling the road ahead of them and seeing what happened with Silas.

Yet, she didn't know how long he'd be in Pinecraft. She knew she would likely go, someday, for a mission trip at the least. But the sunny neighborhood was her home. Silas's home lay on another continent.

"Are you sure you don't want to go to the mall?" he asked. "We could grab a coffee."

"I'm fine. I drank so much water with supper, I think I could float."

He chuckled. "That's my Chelle, telling it like it is."

My Chelle.

She chose to ignore the "my." Only the nieces called her Chelle.

"Thank you for the lovely birthday present. I never expected to get a chance to fly, and the supper was fun. I can tell my friends how I went to Atlanta for supper one evening and then back to Pinecraft again."

"You're welcome. Aren't you glad you flew?"

"Yes, I am. It's good preparation for the future."

"The future?"

"I'm going to apply to a medical missions board and go overseas for some short-term projects after I earn my RN."

"But your business . . ."

"I'm thinking of selling the business." She shrugged. The idea simultaneously thrilled and frightened her. To no longer be responsible for other people's messes. To be somewhere else besides Pinecraft, if for a short time, say one or two years.

"Selling," he repeated. "I think, one day, I'll be back piloting for missions. But piloting right now for the Kingsleys, which is almost like missions work. Yes, they've probably got more money than I'd know what to do with, but even they have needs."

"I noticed that. I hope and pray their little boy is able to go home, soon. What will you do when they don't need you to fly them anywhere?"

"I'm sure I'll get a contract with someone else."

A few more minutes, and they stood at the place where the hired car had picked them up, and right on time, the car returned again, this time without the Kingsleys.

They arrived back at the airport, and twilight had come and gone. Rochelle hadn't considered the probability of them flying home in the dark. She swallowed hard as she stepped up into the plane while Silas proceeded to make his preflight checks once again.

The interior of the plane was dimly lit, and Rochelle tried not to yawn. She shifted on the supple leather seat. She wouldn't be able to study much on the way home.

Her phone buzzed. Emma, always the one to phone more quickly than Betsy.

"*Aenti* Chelle, how was your first flight and supper?"

"Very good, it's all been wonderful. I'm a little tired, though. We had a nice walk downtown. You'd not believe the size of the buildings. I've seen skyscrapers in pictures, but never in person."

"I can't wait until you're home again. It feels like you've been gone a week."

Rochelle had to laugh. "It's only been an afternoon."

Silas pounded up the steps and entered the cabin. The look on his face made her pause.

"Emma, I'll be home soon. I'll let you know everything."

"*Gut.* I'm looking forward to it."

The look on Silas's face, however, made Rochelle's stomach give a flutter. "What is it, Silas?"

"One of the gauges isn't working properly. The maintenance man on duty tonight pulled the gauge and is testing it for me, to see if it's the real problem. If it is, we need to replace it."

"Can we still fly tonight?"

"I'm not sure. If we need a replacement part, then we have to wait until morning. If not, we might not be able to get out of here until tomorrow morning, anyway, if we lose our place in the flight lineup."

"Tomorrow morning," she repeated. "But . . . where will we sleep?" Surely not on the plane. And, of course, not in a shared room or space of any kind. Rochelle wanted to scurry down the steps and go into the airport terminal.

"I've let Mr. Kingsley know of the problem, and he's prepared to put us up overnight here in Atlanta. We won't be stuck here on the tarmac."

"A hotel?" Rochelle shook her head. She'd rather sleep in the terminal and use her sweater as a makeshift blanket and her tote bag as a pillow.

"Not together, of course. He's prepared to book separate rooms for us."

Rochelle tried not to shudder. What would people say, about her and Silas remaining in Atlanta overnight? It wasn't like it was their fault. Silas needed to stay to fix the plane. She wouldn't impose by asking about a commercial flight to Sarasota, either, even if she could afford the cost. Driving the hundreds of miles overnight was impractical.

She wanted to call the nieces, but knew Emma would spin into a tizzy once she heard the news and be full of questions Rochelle couldn't answer right now.

Today had been a sweet time, her and Silas together, just the two of them. It had been easy to pretend he was only a new friend.

Now, though, she wasn't sure how much longer she could keep up pretending.

⁂

Silas regretted being the bearer of bad news and causing a crease to appear in Rochelle's forehead. However, he couldn't think of any way around the two of them having to stay in Atlanta tonight.

Even if he could find a flight to Sarasota for Rochelle this evening, it would be expensive and he knew she didn't want to be any trouble to the Kingsleys. Even if the gauge issue was resolved tonight, they'd lost their spot in the flight lineup. So here they were.

Ted had understood about the mechanical issue with the gauge.

"Better safe than sorry," he said. "Find a mechanic, get the part, figure it out. Have them bill me."

But the maintenance staff was tied up with another plane, a commercial flight, and Silas had to wait his turn. And if a part was needed, they likely couldn't get it until the morning. Unless they had a gauge waiting around the hangar somewhere.

He left Rochelle fretting in the cabin, after trying to assure her he was doing everything he could. He had to see to the plane first.

Smitty, the on-duty mechanic this evening, approached. He wiped his hands on a greasy rag. "We can get another gauge and replace it, but not until first thing in the morning. Sorry you're stuck here instead of in Florida."

"It's not your fault. Not the first time I've had an unplanned overnight stop. What time in the morning?"

"Morning shift comes in around seven. We put the order in, gauge should be here first thing." Smitty squinted at the plane. "It's the best we can do tonight."

"I understand. I'll be back here around seven and file another plan for noon tomorrow. It ought to be enough time to get the gauge tested, then get ready to fly."

"Sounds like a good idea. We'll see you back here in the morning."

Silas shook hands with the man, then paused at the bottom of the plane's steps when his phone warbled. Ted Kingsley.

"Hello, sir."

"I've booked a pair of rooms for you at Hospitality Suites, same place you stayed in last time. I'm sending a cab for you, whenever you're ready. I'd be staying there as well, but I want to spend time with Amanda and Benjamin tonight."

"I understand. I'll reimburse you for the expense of Rochelle's room."

"Nonsense. This wasn't your fault. Call me when you have a status tomorrow, and I'll let you know when we need to be picked up next week."

"I will. Have a good evening."

"You too, Silas."

Rochelle looked up at him expectantly when he entered the cabin. "So?"

"We're definitely staying the night. Mr. Kingsley has reserved two rooms for us at a hotel down the road, and he's sending a cab to take us there. I've stayed there before. It's nice. Free breakfast, too."

She wrapped the strap of her tote bag around one finger. "How . . . how kind of him. Truly, to pay for rooms for us."

He wanted to ease her discomfort, but didn't have a clue on how to do it. "We'll head straight back to Sarasota as soon as this issue is taken care of. I can keep in touch with you by phone, so you don't have to wait here in the morning while they work on the plane."

"No, I don't mind. Whenever you leave in the morning, I'll wait in the terminal. Or office."

He opened his mouth to suggest she think of tonight like an adventure, but figured it wouldn't help much. "Well, we do have leftovers to snack on tonight. And there's always vending machines at the hotel."

Rochelle nodded, her frown deepening. "I . . . I should call my nieces, let them know. I have a morning client. I need to figure something out. Betsy has the shop, and Emma has another client at the same time . . ." She clamped her mouth shut. "I'm sorry. I'm just thinking out loud."

"It's all right. You weren't expecting to be stranded, and I know you have a business to run."

Silas didn't add how he understood she lived by a schedule. He'd learned years ago sometimes the schedule needed tossing out the proverbial window. He'd ended up stranded in much worse places, like in a remote village. A one-night stay turned into a week of wearing the same clothes while waiting on a part delivery. But this was the first time he'd ever been stranded anywhere with Rochelle Keim.

⟷

You're a certifiable big baby, reacting like this to being stranded. Of course, when she'd spoken to Betsy, her great-niece's tone registered nothing but shock at the idea her *Aenti* Chelle found herself stuck in Atlanta, hundreds of miles away from Sarasota.

"*Ach*, sometimes it's better just to keep one's feet on the ground, I think," Betsy said. "I'm glad you had a nice time, though."

Rochelle reassured her, of course, she and Silas had separate rooms. A tongue or two might wag, but surely nothing serious could come of this unfortunate delay in returning home.

Nothing romantic was going on with Silas, despite his aunt and uncle's and other well-meaning friends' subtle efforts to urge them to spend time with each other. The whole idea of courtship felt different now, especially with him a widower and her, well, her current age. Neither were starry-eyed youngsters.

She shook her head at the idea of Silas's parents or someone else being a chaperone for them. She was careful not to ride in a car alone with him, and the open-air horseless buggy rides didn't count. What did the "appearance of evil" mean, anyway? Was it evil that they were stranded overnight in a strange city and stayed at the same lodging?

It would have been silly for them to stay at two separate hotels, and how could she have even asked Silas to ask Mr. Kingsley, who graciously paid for not just Silas's, but her hotel room?

No, this was overreacting. Like a little child.

She waited in the lobby of a lovely hotel, with marble floors and expensive-looking furniture. Silas stood at the mahogany reception desk. He nodded as he signed some papers and the woman behind the desk gave him the key cards for the rooms.

Then he turned and crossed the lobby to join her.

"Here's your key. I only got one for each room." He clutched a pair of small plastic bags. "And, here's a bag with toothpaste, toothbrush, toiletries."

"Thanks."

He led her toward a set of elevators and punched a button. "She put us in adjoining rooms on the top floor, facing downtown for the view."

The elevator dinged and the doors slid open. Rochelle stepped inside, ahead of Silas. As each minute passed, she felt like a country bumpkin even though she'd been a city girl her entire adult life. Pinecraft had a coziness and she'd nestled herself inside it as much as possible, except for visiting clients and an occasional trip to a flea market or to the beach.

"You're awfully quiet," Silas observed as the elevator glided up to the tenth floor.

"I'm a little tired, I guess." She smiled and clutched her tote bag a little more tightly. "Emma is trying to find someone to help with a client tomorrow morning. Betsy can't. And I'm here, of course."

"What about Lena? Maybe she could do it. I don't think she has class tomorrow."

"Oh, I hadn't thought of asking her. Do you think she would?"

"I'm almost sure she will."

The elevator stopped, then the bell chimed as the doors slid open. Rochelle stepped from the elevator.

"Which room again?" She glanced at the tiny envelope—marked 1015—then at the tiny brass wall signs covered with numbers.

"I'm in 1017."

They went in the direction the arrow pointed until they reached a pair of doors, side by side. A suite.

"I imagine there's an inner door separating the rooms."

"I imagine." She slid her card into the lock. "Well, what time do you plan to head to the airport in the morning."

"Seven. It's early, but I want to get the part ordered and installed ASAP."

"I'll be ready. Good night, Silas."

"Good night," he replied as she entered the room and let the door click shut behind her.

Someone had left a single light burning in the corner of the room, where a comfortable-looking easy chair and ottoman sat. A massive king-size bed took up a good portion of the opposite wall adjoining the inner door Silas had just mentioned.

Rochelle tossed her tote bag and the sundries bag on the bed and strode to the large door leading outside. She had a small balcony, it turned out, along with a sparkling view of downtown, miles away.

The night had a bit of a chill to it, so Rochelle turned on the room's heater. She missed Florida and its warmth.

Strangely, after the doziness she felt while waiting inside the plane's cabin, now she knew sleep would be a while in coming. And the two of them, having to be up and out early in the morning.

A cup of tea should do the trick, and Rochelle set about brewing a cup. Her phone rang, again. She ought to turn it off tonight, to save what remained of the battery.

Emma.

"Hello, Emma."

"*Aenti* Chelle, I found someone to take the Baxters tomorrow. Lena said she could do it."

"Oh, good. Silas mentioned the possibility a few minutes ago, but I was waiting to see if you found someone first."

"Everyone is shocked you're having to stay overnight. The house is too quiet without you, *aenti*."

Everyone is shocked. Did Emma tell *everyone* in the village she and Silas were stuck in Atlanta overnight?

"Ah, I'm glad you miss me. But, Emma, who did you tell?"

"Vera Byler, for one. I asked if she or Patience could help, but she said they couldn't."

Rochelle bit her lip. "Well, I'm glad this all worked out. I'm making a cup of tea right now, and then I'm going to turn my phone off to save the battery. In case you call me and wonder why I don't pick up."

"All right. Good night, *Aenti* Chelle."

Rochelle tried not to groan as she turned the phone off. She set the alarm clock for five-thirty, then saw to her cup of tea. Now she knew she'd have a time trying to sleep. What would Vera Byler have to say about Rochelle's unplanned overnight trip?

☙

Rochelle, 19

Belinda shed no tears at John's funeral. Hundreds from their community turned out for the service, including many strangers. Rochelle sat beside her best friend, and the two clenched hands during the service.

After the service's closing, they all went to the town's civic center, as the church's fellowship hall had been deemed too small for the hundreds of Mennonites from the community who stayed for the potluck meal. Everyone understood how things were done. Rochelle suspected the Hershbergers would eat well for days to come.

Nobody sent meals or much comfort for Belinda. If she were John's wife, the story would be entirely different.

Rochelle didn't tell her friend this. Instead, they went through the food line together. A quiet murmur filled the church hall.

"I guess I should eat." Belinda stared at her plate, full of the most comforting food, all suggested by Rochelle.

Rochelle swallowed the bite she'd been chewing. "Try something. The broccoli cheese casserole is especially good."

"John always said cheese can make almost anything better." A smile quirked one corner of Belinda's mouth. She picked up her fork.

This made Rochelle smile, too. It sounded like something John would have said.

Someone pulled the chair out beside her. "Hello." Silas nodded at both of them. "How are you managing, Belinda?"

She nodded, then swallowed. "I'm managing."

"Good." He glanced at Rochelle, then back at the woman across from him. "You know, Rochelle and I are both here for you. And we'll always be here for you."

"Right." Rochelle found her voice again. "We're here."

Belinda nodded slowly. "Thank you. Thank you both." She scanned the room, her gaze falling on John's parents. "John's parents have been wonderful. But, it's not like I was their daughter-in-law or anything. Not yet. I . . . I was hoping to be. One day." Her face blushed.

"Oh, Belinda." Rochelle reached across the table and squeezed her friend's hand. A single tear slid down Belinda's cheek. She pulled free of Rochelle's hand and swept the tear away.

The three of them took their time through the rest of the subdued meal.

Heaven might be rejoicing at welcoming John Hershberger into the Kingdom, but here on earth, the rest of them ached with a pain that would be slow to heal.

14

Silas brewed himself a cup of decaf. He decided to spend a few minutes outside on the balcony. The last time he'd stayed here, it wasn't in a room with a view like this. He might as well enjoy it for a few moments before turning in.

He slid open the glass door and stepped onto the balcony. Steam rose from his cup of coffee and blew away.

A figure stood nearly six feet away, beside the railing for the balcony next to his.

"Rochelle."

"Oh, Silas. I thought I'd have a cup of tea. I don't feel like I can sleep right now."

"Me, either." He held up his cup of coffee. "Decaf here, though."

She faced the city lights. "Well, I'm glad we're not camping out on chairs inside the airport."

"Same here. Anyway, the airport is closing soon. It's not likely we could have stayed there."

Rochelle nodded slowly. Even after all these years, he could read her face. It shouldn't surprise him. Although they had a lifetime of years between them, in some ways she still appeared to be the same vibrant young woman he'd once known.

Despite her saying she wasn't that person anymore.

The same went for him.

The more he'd seen Rochelle since living in Pinecraft, the more he remembered what it was like being with her.

Seeing the admiration on her face made him want to go out and conquer the world, or at least share the gospel with it.

Which was why, at the bitter end long ago, her disappointment in him hurt worse than anything he'd ever felt or imagined.

His grandfather used to warn him, "Silas, beware the guise of pride in accomplishments. It's not our accomplishments, nor praise from men, that give us our true meaning."

Oh, yes, as a pilot, he'd savored the knowledge he was at the controls of a machine carrying people hundreds of miles in the space of a few hours, soaring thousands of feet above the earth.

Not many people could do so.

Rochelle kept sipping her tea, watching the world below pass them by.

He wanted to break the silence, but didn't want to say anything that would create more awkwardness between them.

"Rochelle, I know we're not exactly the same people we were years ago. I was so full of myself."

"And I was so stubborn." A smile quirked the corners of her mouth. "Okay, I may be still a little stubborn. And controlling. I like my schedule, you know."

He had to laugh. "Yes, stubborn and scheduling."

"But no, I don't think you were full of yourself. Confident, enthusiastic. All the young men wanted to be like you, and all the young women wanted you to like them."

"And I chose you . . ."

"Yes, you chose me . . ." Rochelle's voice quavered a moment, and she cleared her throat. "And I tossed it aside. What was I thinking? I know what I was thinking. I was young. I just *knew* the world had to be a certain way. I just *knew* you would have known, or should have known, exactly what to do, when John—"

"Stop."

"No, I won't. We should have had this conversation a long time ago. Like, right after it all happened. I should have tried to talk to you . . ."

"I didn't make it easy on you, though. I was angry, myself. Angry you'd hold it against me."

"We were a couple of children." She turned to face him. The lights from the parking lot below cast a glow on her face. "Looking back . . . well, maybe it's not such a good idea to look back."

Silas nodded. "I have to say, I agree with you."

Her face bore a worried wrinkle on her forehead.

"What is it? What else is wrong? Is it being stuck here?"

"Yes and no. The room is beautiful and comfortable. I'm sure I'll rest well, once I do rest. But Emma happened to tell Vera Byler you and I are staying in Atlanta tonight. In a hotel."

"Ah, I see." It irked him someone might construe something more than was actually there. Yes, he felt . . . *something* . . . for Rochelle. But he wasn't about to dishonor God or her by stepping into an area he oughtn't.

"I just don't want there to be any, ah, repercussions over this. Sometimes, well, people have more time on their hands to criticize others or think the worst of them." Rochelle shrugged. "But then, nothing may come of this."

"Well, we'll have to pray so. Will speaking to the pastor help, to let him know, if he hears anything?"

"I think so. I've attended there for almost twenty years. He and his wife are kind, caring people who try to believe the best of others."

"Just wait and see what happens after we get back to Sarasota. Not borrowing any trouble."

"No time to borrow trouble, I have enough to think of right now, with classes, running a business, not to mention two brides-to-be under one roof."

"Now, the last one, I can't imagine." He shook his head.

Rochelle gave a soft chuckle. "It's funny sometimes. Emma most of all. Having a spirited young adult around can be an up-and-down experience."

"I know what you mean. Lena has her mother's fire and her d—" Silas stopped himself. "She's compassionate. She's a big champion of what they call the underdog."

"I . . . I missed Belinda. But, before I knew it, years had passed, and then, well . . ."

"I understand you not writing. I know she missed you, too." The memories tugged at Silas's heart. Maybe getting stranded tonight, without the distractions of everyday life pulling at them, had been a blessing.

"I never imagined life turning out like it did."

"Nor did I. I know she wrote you, at least once. Maybe the post office didn't forward the mail for whatever reason or it got lost."

Rochelle faced him again. "She did? I . . . I wish I'd known." He wasn't certain if he glimpsed a brightness in her eyes. Or maybe it was just the lamplight.

"No going back, is there?"

"No. It's just as well, though. I ought to take the advice I gave Betsy once, to take some time and see what God has in store for the future, and not give the past any more attention than it deserves."

Silas took another swallow of coffee before continuing. "Excellent advice."

Rochelle glanced at her cup. "Well, I think I'm going to turn in now."

"Be ready early. You know, you can call the front desk and tell them what time you'd like wake-up call, in case you sleep through the alarm."

"Good idea. Good night, Silas."

"Good night." He watched her leave her side of the balcony.

～♋～

Rochelle, 19

She tried to speak to Belinda several times after John's funeral, but Belinda retreated into a shell and wouldn't come out.

Belinda would leave the Sunday morning church service imme-diately, and she stopped going to the youth meetings. Rochelle made herself go anyway, but felt as if she were on the fringes of the group, especially with Silas keeping a distance from her after the last rough conversation they'd had.

No, it hadn't been her fiancé who'd died. But she'd been there, seen and heard it all. Violence had touched their lives in a real way and had taken one of them.

She didn't know which was worse, losing her mother so painfully, so slowly, or losing John in the space of an evening. She did know they, the living, had the painful task of trying to put the pieces of life back together again.

Again, today as with other Sundays, she found herself walking to Belinda's house, over the back fields and through a small grove of resolute maple trees punctuating the spot between the properties.

When she and Belinda were girls, this space had been their meeting spot. As family obligations and growing up brought more responsibilities, they hadn't met here in years.

Sometimes children had it best, living in worlds of blissful ignorance.

She approached the Millers' house. A pair of cars stood in the driveway. Company? Perhaps she was intruding. But the Millers had always welcomed her to their home without a phone call first.

Rochelle took the simple wooden plank front steps, then marched up to the front door and rang the bell.

Mrs. Miller opened the door. "Why Rochelle, it's so good to see you. Please, come in."

"Thanks." She stepped into the family's parlor. "I'm just here to see Belinda, if it's okay. I won't stay long."

"You are welcome. We've already eaten and are only visiting now. But she's up in her room." Mrs. Miller took a step closer. "She needs a friend right now, no matter how much she says she doesn't want anybody around."

"I know she does. It's why I'm here."

"You've been through a lot, too, dear. How are you?"

"I'm . . . I'm managing." She forced a smile. Nobody asked her how she was handling this. "But then, I didn't lose someone I loved. I can't imagine . . ." Right now, the distance between her and Silas could have been a canyon.

"I know, but you've still suffered a loss, too." Mrs. Miller glanced at the stairs. "I don't know what I can do. I've tried, but . . ."

"I understand."

"Yes, you do." The older woman smiled at her.

Rochelle took the stairs and found her way to Belinda's room. She knocked on the closed wooden door. "Belinda?"

"Come on in."

She opened the door, found Belinda sitting on the wide ledge serving as a window seat. She still wore her church dress and had her knees tucked up to her chest. She wore her hair down, with her *kapp* and hair pins scattered on her bureau.

"Hey," Rochelle said. "I tried to catch you after church today, but I was busy talking to Naomi."

"I know. We . . . came straight home. Mother had a roast in the oven, and she didn't want it to dry out. And company came."

Rochelle nodded, and took a seat on the bed. "The youth group is planning a Christmas party. We're all supposed to bring a gag gift for the silly gift exchange." They'd always looked forward to the fun tradition every year.

"Right, not much longer now, and everyone will be celebrating."

Rochelle nodded. "My niece is practicing her one line for the Christmas pageant nonstop. Every time I see her, she tries her part out on me. I think I have it memorized, too."

Belinda gave a soft laugh. "Little ones are persistent at that age."

"For the silly gift exchange, I'm taking an umbrella I bought on sale at the dollar store. It's black, covered with yellow duckies. I got another one, too. Blue, covered with pink elephants . . . if you wanted to use it for your gift. If you want to come, too."

She waited. They'd always done thoughtful things for each other. See a sale, buy two. It's what they did.

Belinda turned her face to the window. "I'm not going. I can't. Everyone acts like things are all 'normal' again, and I should just carry on as usual. But I can't. Even for an umbrella with pink elephants."

"No, Belinda, I know things aren't normal again."

"I just. Can't. Do it. My life isn't ever going to be the same. I wish you, and my parents, and everyone else would just . . . leave me alone."

"I'm sorry. My heart is broken, too. I want to help—"

"Then let me be." Belinda faced her again. Dashed fresh tears from her face. "Let me be. Your heart isn't broken like mine is."

Rochelle leapt to her feet. "All right. I'm sorry. I'll . . . I'll leave you alone. I'll always be your friend, Belinda. Friends to the end, remember?"

Belinda said nothing.

Her own tears pricking her eyes, Rochelle left her friend's bedroom and closed the door behind her softly.

Belinda didn't want her help; didn't want the comfort of friendship.

Rochelle would listen to her friend, and let her be. When Belinda was ready, Rochelle would be there.

❧

By the time Rochelle pulled into her driveway in Pinecraft at nearly one the following afternoon, her eyelids felt like sandpaper on her eyes. The nice hotel's mattress had all the give of plywood and dreams plagued her sleep. All because of being in a strange bed in a strange city. She'd also conked out while gazing out the plane window at the world below.

She yawned. A bright yellow bicycle stood chained at their bicycle rack at the corner of the garage. Lena's bicycle. She owed the young woman a big thank-you for seeing to her client this morning.

"I'm home, everyone," Rochelle announced as she entered her home.

"*Aenti* Chelle!" Emma called out. "We're so glad you're back."

When Rochelle stepped into the kitchen, she noticed brightly colored magazine pages covered the top of the kitchen table. Flower arrangements and cake designs, ripped from bridal magazines.

"Oh, my," was all she managed to say. "You bought bridal magazines?"

"Why not? I might be Mennonite, but I like pretty things for weddings, especially flowers."

Betsy rolled her eyes. "I came home for lunch, and she had the whole table covered, so I sat at the breakfast bar. Emma's—"

"I'm picking out the flowers I want to have for the wedding tables."

"I thought you chose flowers, pink carnations."

"I changed my mind." Emma's face glowed as she scurried around the table. "Lena likes the flowers, too, don't you, Lena?"

"I like white lilies the best," Lena said. "They were my mother's favorite."

Rochelle studied the page. "Yes, it's a beautiful arrangement."

"What kind is your favorite, *Aenti* Chelle?" Emma shone her brightness in Rochelle's direction.

She might have thought about flowers once upon a long, long time ago. But now?

"I like these. Hibiscus, in orange, red, and pink." The riot of color expressed what she loved best about Florida. "By the way, Lena, thank you so much for helping with the Baxters' this morning. I wasn't sure what I'd do."

"Oh, it wasn't a problem." Lena and Emma exchanged glances. "I was wondering . . . I know you are still looking for someone to take Emma's clients."

"I did get a few names, but I was thinking of splitting up the clients because none of the ladies interested in the cleaning job can be available for all the clients' time." The idea was a headache for her, because it meant more employees to track instead of just one.

"Because I can take them all. Emma and I figured it out."

"Oh, you did?" Rochelle glanced at Emma. Yes, Steven would have his hands full with this one.

"We did," Emma announced. "She can visit each one of the clients, no problem."

"Ah, I see." Rochelle set her tote bag on the counter. "I appreciate it, but I'll have to let you know, Lena."

Emma's lack of tact earned her a glare from her older sister.

"Well, I need to get back to the bakery." Betsy stood, then tossed her paper plate in the trash. "*Aenti* Sarah has a doctor's appointment this afternoon, so I told her she could leave early." Then she left and Rochelle stood, staring at the cluttered tabletop.

"Emma, the time will come when you'll have to make a decision once and for all." She wanted to add it might be better to focus on the upcoming marriage instead of the wedding so much, but decided not to.

"I know. I'm looking forward to the day. I want everyone to remember it, and I want to remember it as well."

Rochelle sank onto the nearest empty chair. "Of course you will, and everyone who attends will remember it. People who care the most about you and Steven will be there."

"But not everyone will be." Emma spoke the words as if to the papers scattered on the table.

"What do you mean?"

"You know, a goodly part of the family won't come to the wedding. Because I'm not Amish anymore. I'm Mennonite. For Steven."

"Dear, you shouldn't have done it for him, but because you believed this is what *Gotte* has for you. This worries me a little. You went through your proving, and you knew what you were doing." Rochelle glanced at Lena, who had concern etched on her face.

"No, I don't mean I did it just for him. But I stayed here; being Mennonite in Pinecraft makes more sense to me."

"Staying here didn't mean you had to become Mennonite. Look at Betsy—she and Thaddeus are in the Old Order church here."

"*Yah*, and I don't want to do everything Betsy does."

"Anyway, about those people who aren't attending your wedding. You can't . . . you can't keep changing your mind to please everyone. If you believe, in the bottom of your heart, this is the path *Gotte* has for you, then follow it. All the pretty flowers in the world can't help you convince yourself."

Emma's shoulders sank. "Oh, *Aenti* Chelle."

"Perhaps you should call your *mamm*. I know she misses you and is looking forward to seeing you soon."

"I think I will." She nodded and glanced at her friend. "I'm sorry, Lena."

"It's all right. I'm sure you're nervous, too. I know I would be."

A knock sounded on the front door. "Hello? Emma?"

"Steven!" Emma's face brightened. "We're here. Come on in."

The front door clicked and soon Steven entered the kitchen. "Hey, Aunt Chelle." A boyish grin covered the young man's face. Had he grown even more since the last time she'd seen him? It hadn't been so long. His eyes sparkled when looking at Emma, who blushed.

"Hello, Steven."

He joined Emma at the table. "What's all this?"

"Flowers and cake." Emma sported a saucy grin. "Guess which flowers I chose?"

Steven surveyed the table. "Ah, well . . ." He cast a glance at Lena, who shrugged and gave him a grin of her own. The tips of his ears turned pink. "I, uh, thought you picked out flowers and cake already."

"I did, but I'm not sure."

He reached out and touched the page nearest his hand. "This one."

Good choice. The multicolored flowers had similar hues to the dress colors Emma had selected for her attendants. It made sense to Rochelle, as well.

"No. It's too much color. Think more simple."

He touched a photo of white lilies. "I like these a lot."

"They're my favorite, too," Lena interjected.

Emma shook her head. "Yes, they're pretty. But I chose these." She picked up a photo of a white carnation and fern arrangement. "People can take them home, and they'll last for a long time. And, they're easier to get."

"So," Rochelle said, "this must mean you've decided on flowers once and for all?" Never mind Emma had chosen pink carnations to begin with and, after all this to-do on the kitchen table, had changed her mind to white.

"Once and for all." But she focused on the page of lilies Steven had just touched. "I think."

Rochelle tried not to groan. "Your *mamm* will be here before long."

"I am looking forward to her coming." She waved the page with her chosen flowers on it. "She's going to be so surprised about how much I have done. And, she's going to have the dresses with her."

"Ah, I wanted to invite everybody out on the boat, on Sunday after service and supper," Steven said. "I know everyone has been busy, but I hope you can come. And, ah, Lena, your dad and brother are welcome to come, as well."

"Thank you," Lena said, her cheeks tinged with pink. "I'll speak to my dad and see if he'd like to go."

Emma said, "Now, if we can get Betsy to come and Thaddeus, it would be perfect."

"I won't have enough room for them. Sorry, Emma." Steven looked apologetic. "Not enough life jackets. You know I only have six. With you and me, Aunt Chelle, Lena, her dad and brother, these are all I can take on the boat."

Emma frowned, but didn't say more.

Rochelle couldn't recall the last time she'd headed away from the shore, let alone visited the beach. She wasn't in a hurry to spend an afternoon in close quarters with Silas. Anyway, she knew she needed to study for the final weeks of the semester. "I'd love to go out on the boat, Steven. Thank you. But I should stay home and study."

15

*R*ochelle, 19

Ever since the night on Parsnip Road, nothing had been the same.

With her mother, Rochelle had a chance to say good-bye.

With John, none of them had a chance.

The sudden loss, added to grief for Momma, gave Rochelle a physical ache that gnawed at her daily. Why didn't somebody *do* something? Why didn't God do something?

She didn't know why she'd called out for Silas to help. He'd been in as much shock over the attack as she. But he was big. He was strong. He was a man.

Yes, Anabaptists believed in nonviolence, nonresistance. Somehow, it included being attacked and robbed.

It wasn't about the money. The men, high on something, had only wanted money for more drugs.

All they'd gotten in the attack was fifteen dollars, the ten from John's wallet and the measly five from Silas. They'd both pled guilty and would soon be sentenced. Maybe in fifteen years or so, they'd be out with good behavior, only serving half the time of the sentences, or so everyone had heard.

But Belinda would never grow old with her John. Or raise a family with him. John, so quiet, warm, and kind, content to let Belinda sparkle in her own way.

The thought hurt Rochelle.

She sat, rocking on the porch swing while the chicken baked and the bread rose. Dad, out in his workshop, was crafting more furniture. It was his way of coping. And hers was keeping track of the house. It was neat as the proverbial pin, save for her parents' bedroom. Dad told her he'd tend to it himself, along with her mother's things. And so she'd let him.

Here came Silas up the lane. He'd been putting in extra hours at work, and she hadn't seen him but at church. He'd been pulling away from her, it seemed. But then, she could understand. Dad had done the same thing with Momma.

"Silas." She walked out to meet him at the bottom of the porch steps. "How have you been?"

"Okay." He shrugged and gave her a half-smile. "It's been busy at work."

She nodded. "I've been busy, too."

He didn't step forward to hug her, but instead stuffed his hands in his pockets. "My mother was looking for her casserole dish. The white one with the blue flowers. I thought I'd stop by to see if it was here."

"Oh." Rochelle backpedaled. "I'll, ah, check."

He followed her up the stairs and waited on the porch while she went inside. The screen door slammed shut behind her.

Casserole dish? He stopped by only for a *casserole dish*?

Rochelle stomped into the kitchen, her eyes stinging. She'd missed him, craved the sound of his voice and the warmth of his arms, and he'd come walking to their house for a stupid casserole dish?

She yanked open cabinet doors, shuffled pots and dishes—how on earth did they accumulate so many—until she found the one Silas had asked about.

Part of her wanted to smash the dish and its glass lid on the kitchen tiles and watch it shatter into a million splintered pieces. But it would solve nothing. It might feel good, though.

But the gesture would provide no lasting relief.

Instead, Rochelle squared her shoulders and carried the casserole dish outside.

"Here. Please, tell you mother thank-you again for us."

"I will." His gaze narrowed. "Are you all right?"

"No, I'm not all right. Why would I be all right?"

She turned on her heel and slammed the front door behind her.

⁂

Silas, 21

More than once in the past, Silas had heard his father comment about not understanding women and their ways. Even now, Silas understood what his father had meant.

He was bone-tired, body, soul, and spirit, and all he was doing was picking up a casserole dish of his mother's. A forty-hour-plus workweek, and Silas looked forward to the weekend. Rochelle's reaction to a simple request for a casserole dish baffled him.

Yes, Rochelle had lost her mother, grieved her still. They all did. Losing John, the fresher wound still throbbed in Silas's own heart. His best friend since they were five years old and now nothing.

Okay, maybe his question wasn't the wisest. Of course, none of them were all right, right now.

But right at the moment, he wanted to know what else was bothering Rochelle and if he could help.

He set the casserole dish on the porch swing, then yanked open the front door. No, he was careful not to be too many places alone with Rochelle. Not to borrow trouble or set tongues wagging. Because tongues would wag, even if their activity was perfectly chaste.

"Now, hang on a second—"

He stomped into the house, letting the front door bang behind him.

Rochelle whirled to face him. "What?"

"Why are you so, so—" He couldn't find the word. Her lovely brow was furrowed into an angry curl. Some of her hair had escaped her *kapp* and hung on her shoulder.

"So what? Angry?" She folded her arms across her chest. "Why wouldn't I be angry?"

"Over a dish?"

"It's not just the dish."

"What is it, then?"

"Why, Silas?" She sobbed.

"Why, what?" He wanted to understand, but it was as if Rochelle had become fluent in another language."

"*Why didn't you do something?*"

"Do something?"

"That night. With John." She clamped her hand over her mouth.

"What was I supposed to do?" His words came out in a growl. "There were two of them. One had a bat. And he used it."

"But you—just—" Rochelle hiccupped.

"Just?"

"*Just stood there, staring!*" The words came out in a screech he'd never heard from Rochelle before.

"You know, I wonder myself sometimes." Now his own voice roared in his ears. "Why didn't I use my superpowers? Why didn't I make them stop? Like it was up to me. Like it was up to any of us."

"Stop mocking me."

"I'm not mocking you." He reached for her, pulled her into his arms. He'd missed her so.

Her arms went around him in response, and they were kissing. Her curves, even through her modest cape dress, molded against him. His hand slid up her waist, as if of its own accord.

"Oh, my Chelle, I've missed you."

Then she wriggled from his arms. "No. Stop." She gasped, her own voice shaking as she trembled, rubbing her arms with her hands. "If you think a kiss is going to make everything all right, it's not."

"Rochelle Keim."

"What's going on here?" Her father stood behind them in the kitchen doorway. Silas hadn't heard the back door open.

"Nothing." Rochelle's voice held a ragged tone. "Silas picked up his mother's casserole dish, and he's leaving."

"Chelle—"

"Good-bye, Silas."

He didn't care if he let the screen door slam when he left.

❦

Sunday came, with gray skies in the morning and a light sprinkle of rain.

Rochelle should have guessed the day would carry a similar mood. Her *kapp* wouldn't stay straight; the increased humidity made her hair more unruly. She'd woken up with a crick in her neck. Still, she went to morning service and let the hymns and teaching buoy her spirits.

After the service ended, Beatrice, the pastor's wife, approached as soon as the last sounds of voices raised in the final hymn drifted away.

"Rochelle . . ." Beatrice smiled, but she glanced side to side.

"Hello, Bea." Something twitched in the pit of her stomach.

"Ah, Marvin asked me to speak with you . . . privately."

"I see."

"Oh, it won't take long. I promise." Again, the kind smile, but eyes filled with concern.

"Well, right away then."

Bea touched her elbow. "Come, let's go to a vacant classroom where it's quiet."

They left the sanctuary and continued down the side hall, Bea slipping into the nearest classroom.

Rochelle closed the door behind them. "Bea, what is it?"

It had to be the Atlanta trip.

"Let's sit, for a moment."

Rochelle joined Bea at the long rectangular table in the center of the room. *Relax. It could be nothing. Surely, you'll be able to explain yourself.*

"Marvin asked me to speak to you because someone has come forward to us, with an, ah, issue."

"Issue? Why didn't they talk to me if there was an 'issue,' as you call it?" She hated sounding defensive. She didn't intend to, but there it was.

Bea leaned forward, placing her hand on top of one of Rochelle's. "It's going to be all right. First of all, I've known you for years. You've been faithful here in the fellowship and as an unmarried woman, you've lived your life without reproach."

"Thank you." Rochelle shifted on the chair. She pulled her hands onto her lap. "So . . ."

"Marvin was told you flew to Atlanta with Silas Fry and spent the night with him there, then returned to Sarasota the next day."

Rochelle clenched her hands together. This was absolutely ridiculous. It was also a situation she'd worried about, then put out of her mind. Until a few moments ago.

"And now, you're giving me . . . and Silas, the chance to explain ourselves." She shook her head. Yes, Bea said she'd lived a life without reproach. "I . . . I find it rather silly we should have to explain. But if it makes you happy, I will."

"It's not about making me, or Marvin, happy . . ." Bea frowned.

"First, we didn't go there alone. He was flying a client. Then there was a mechanical problem with the plane, and we couldn't return at night as planned. So his client paid for *two* rooms for both of us near the airport. The next morning, we returned to the airport, the part was installed, and we came straight home." She wanted to tell Bea, a longtime friend, about the lovely supper out, and how different Atlanta was, and how much fun—although a bit nerve-racking—flying for the first time had been.

"I know. Of course, you did. But I—Marv—wanted to hear it from you. I believe you."

"Do I even get to know who brought this 'issue' to your attention?" No, she wasn't a child caught with her hands in the cookie jar. She was a nearly forty-year-old woman who valued her reputation.

"They preferred we didn't say."

"It had to be Vera Byler." She wouldn't be the first in the village to tangle with the effects of Vera's tongue wagging. Nor would she be the last.

The sheepish look on Bea's face told Rochelle she'd guessed right. "Now, I hope you don't think less of her. I did tell her it would be best if she addressed you directly, but she seemed nervous to do so."

I'll bet she was nervous. Only she didn't bet. Why did Vera feel she had to give her input, voice her opinion?

"She, ah, mentioned something about avoiding every appearance of evil. Especially as an example to the younger unmarried people."

"I would mention to her, then, to read First Corinthians thirteen, about how love always believes the best, charity thinketh no evil." Rochelle's cheeks flamed. She wanted to bolt from the room, head straight home, and close the shame behind her.

Which was ridiculous. She had nothing to be ashamed about. Others might not understand her sensation of shame, especially those outside the church.

Yes, she agreed with Bea. Women like her were looked to as an example, and so far, she thought she'd done a good job over the years.

She couldn't deny, though, the evening on the hotel balcony, how her heart had raced. As if the years had rewound themselves and she and Silas were half their age. But then, she'd reminded herself of the lifetime of years between them.

"You're right, Rochelle, you're right."

"I would like to sit down and talk with her, with you present, and if Marv thinks it is appropriate. And with Silas not quite finished with his proving time and awaiting his full membership in the church here . . . I don't like what she's trying to say."

Bea looked hesitant. "I think we should all sit down. I have to ask, what are your feelings about Silas?"

"You're not just my pastor's wife, you're my friend. I care for Silas. I don't . . . I don't know what's going to happen, or if anything should." Rochelle shook her head. "I don't . . . I don't want either of us to feel as if we should 'pick up where we left off' years ago."

Bea nodded slowly. Rochelle had never told Beatrice the whole story about Silas. She'd kept him and his memory at bay for a long time, even with his aunt and uncle attending the same church. After a while, it had been easy to think of him as someone she used to know.

"I'll talk to Vera, see if she'll meet with you. I'll also encourage her *not* to speak to anyone else about this."

Like that would happen. Rochelle tried not to roll her eyes, although it might feel good if she did so.

Lord, help us. Help me.

One of the things she loved about Pinecraft was its closeness. But this—this hurt.

"Thank you, Bea."

Both women stood, and Bea stopped her before they left the classroom.

"Pray. It's going to be all right. We're part of the family of God, and with all family, things can come up like this. God's grace will be all over the situation. You'll see."

Rochelle only nodded, then went out. She gave a smile to a few who greeted her. Air. She needed air.

She found herself standing at the van door, and leaned her head on the window. The sun chose just then to break out from the clouds. Yes, this too shall pass. She hoped it would do so quickly.

"Are you all right?" Silas stood beside her.

Rochelle turned to face him and put on a smile. "I will be. Did . . . did Pastor talk to you?"

He nodded, then scanned the parking lot. Families made their way to vehicles, some to bicycles.

"You were right. But don't worry, we'll get this sorted out." His jaw tightened for a moment. "Anyway. People know you. They know how you are. Even if they don't know me quite as well. I'm sure my aunt and uncle will hear about what was said."

"Not much we can do, is there? Sort of like trying to get tooth-paste back into the tube." A faint headache prickled her forehead.

"You're right." Silas looked thoughtful for a moment. "I guess the fishing trip or boat ride is on? Or not?"

"Steven will make the call. I think it depends on the waves or something. I'm glad the sun's coming out." She squinted at him. She'd left her sunglasses inside the van. "But, I've decided not to go out on the boat today."

"Oh, I see. Too bad. I know Matthew's looking forward to it."

"I hope you all have a good time. Maybe, next time I'll go." She unlocked the van door. Maybe he'd take the cue this was time for him to find his family, and go enjoy their afternoon.

If it were the six of them on the boat, who knows what might be said? This was ridiculous. She needed an aspirin, and then a few moments to lie down.

Silas, still concerned, yet cheerful. The quality was somewhat unsettling to her, worrywart that she was. But such a quality was, oh, so endearing.

༄

Rochelle, 19

Four weeks since the confrontation with Silas. Four weeks since the blistering kiss, which even now sometimes woke her from sleep with its memory. Rochelle had seen him at church, but it was all. Meanwhile, she kept the house immaculate and helped her father put an ad in the local paper to sell his handmade furniture. When he wasn't working at the mill, he would be out in his workshop.

Jolene had begged Rochelle to let her help, but Rochelle assured her older sister no help was needed. They were both finding their own routine, and besides, Jolene had her own household to care for.

The first snowfall had come to Ohio and blanketed the barren fields with white. Somehow, the whiteness helped by covering all dead and barren with a fresh coat of purity. But Rochelle knew what was underneath.

Even in the church cemetery, where her mother's simple head-stone stood beside others, snow covered up the mound that would one day smooth over and sprout green grass. As would John Hershberger's, along with the others.

The Sunday after Thanksgiving meant a fellowship lunch, and although Rochelle didn't have the heart for it, she still prepared a dish on her and her father's behalf, and they both attended.

Her father stood in the hall as he spoke with Viola Brubaker, a cousin of their minister's wife who'd come to visit her family for the weekend. Widowed herself, her snappy, blue eyes twinkled.

Then, her father chuckled. She hadn't heard the sound in months. Rochelle smiled. Momma had only been gone not quite six months, but still, she didn't begrudge her father the happiness.

Rochelle glanced around the church hall for Belinda. At last, her best friend seemed less a shadow of herself. Six weeks since they'd lost John, and they all missed him with an ache not going away anytime soon.

"Have you seen Belinda?" she asked Belinda's mother, who was in the kitchen, restocking a pan with fried chicken.

"No, I haven't."

Rochelle slipped silently into the hallway off the fellowship hall. Empty. She paused. Low voices, coming from one of the Sunday school classrooms.

Silas. Belinda.

"It's going to be okay," Silas said in soothing tones. "I promise. It will be."

"I don't know what to do. If only John were here—"

"I know. But I'm here."

"Oh, Silas. But Rochelle—"

"I'll talk to her. We'll work it out."

What? Rochelle tiptoed closer to the classroom, its door open. She ought to walk right in. Belinda, her best friend since, well, forever. And Silas, the man who she'd thought had claimed her heart.

She plucked up her courage most of the way, enough to slide her head around the doorframe and get a view inside.

Belinda, leaning against Silas, her arms wrapped around him as he held her, her eyes closed.

Rochelle whirled back into the hallway. Walk in and confront them both, or go?

She didn't trust her words just then, so she skittered silently back into the kitchen, wiping tears from her cheeks. No, now that she thought about it, Silas didn't need to talk to her. His actions spoke plenty.

Silas, 21

"You need to talk to Rochelle, Silas." His mother chided him at breakfast on Monday morning. "Are you sure you two can't work things out?"

"It's impossible, Mom." He took a swig of orange juice. "I've tried. I think it's all been too much for her. Losing her mother, and now everything with John. She blames me partly, and I kind of see her point."

More than once, he wished he'd tried to confront those thugs in the road who'd attacked them. Because he hadn't acted, things unfolded like they did.

"Son, I truly believe you and Rochelle were intended to be together," his father said. "This falling out, it's temporary. I'm sure."

"Nothing's changed. But Belinda and I, well, we've been talking more since the funeral. More than we ever have." Was it possible to love two women? He'd never thought so, but Rochelle had effectively slammed the door on him and had since her own mother's death.

He thought of Belinda. They'd both grieved losing John, but grieved together. It had bonded them.

And yesterday, after talking to her in the Sunday school room, it became crystal clear what he needed to do.

He smiled at his parents. "As a matter of fact, I proposed to Belinda yesterday during the Sunday fellowship meal, and she accepted."

"I can't help but think you're making a big mistake."

"Mom, I've never been more sure of anything in my life." Yesterday at church had changed everything.

16

Silas relished the tug of the breeze on his clothing as Steven Hostetler's boat pulled away from the dock. Almost as good as flying.

With the morning showers and clouds behind them, and a good meal inside their stomachs, who wouldn't be in a good mood? .

Even after the questions posed by Pastor this morning, privately and quickly after the service.

He'd hoped Rochelle had been wrong about loose lips and suspicious minds. But, here came someone casting a stain upon the sweet time he'd had with Rochelle.

Not romantic. Well, maybe a little bit.

The boat bobbed and salty spray struck their faces. The young women squealed. Despite his sober thoughts, Silas grinned and laughed.

Matthew's face glowed from where he sat, beside the older friend of his uncle's, Henry Hostetler. The older man had left his black brimmed hat in his vehicle and his white hair and beard blew in the breeze.

Casting all your cares upon him, for he careth for you . . .

And so, Silas did. For now, he'd enjoy the great afternoon.

"I hope we catch a lot of fish, Dad!" Matthew shouted across to him above the motor's roar.

"Me too. You ready to clean 'em later?"

"Yes, sir!"

Silas laughed again, this time at Matthew's enthusiasm. He'd see if the same enthusiasm showed up later when it was time to clean the fish.

They continued on for several minutes on the water, today glowing a shade of greenish-blue, even brighter than when they first arrived at the marina where Steven kept his boat.

Silas glanced back at the young man, piloting them over the waves. Good, stable kid. Still Plain, although driving a not-Plain boat. Steven had impressed him when he shared his calendar for the winter.

Dolphin watch, for some passengers. A few Old Order men, brothers and sons, were chartering the boat for a family fishing trip. Then one day a week, Steven donated free boat trips to whatever vacationer signed up first.

Steven explained to him earlier that during Pinecraft's down time in the summer, he still managed to keep busy with vacationer charters.

The boat's roar quieted to a low rumble as they bobbed to a stop on the water.

"Okay, we'll see how we do at this spot." Steven hopped from his seat and moved on steady feet to where he cast off the anchor.

Silas stood and found his balance, before heading over to the trio of fishing poles they'd brought with them, courtesy of Uncle Tobias. The three of them were capable fishermen, with Lena possessing a good hand at working the rod and reel to haul in many a fish.

"You fish much in Africa?" Steven asked them.

"As often as we could. It depended a lot on my schedule," Silas said.

"When Dad wasn't there, sometimes our mom would bring us in the morning, before lessons."

Lena nodded. "Those were the best days."

Silas didn't flinch at the silent *ping* needling his heart. Those days were gone, and he'd always miss them. The four of them had built a good family. So far, the three of them were doing . . . better.

They spent the next few moments in a flurry of baiting hooks and debating over the best places to stand at the boat. From the corner of Silas's eye, he could see Steven and Emma working on her fishing rod, her making faces at the bait.

Steven caught Silas's eye and rolled his own eyes.

Henry moved to stand beside Silas. "Good to get out on the water today, huh?"

"Yes, sir. Definitely. This is one of the main reasons I wanted to move us to Florida."

"I can understand." Henry cast his line, and the hooked bait flew out over the rippling water. Satisfied with the cast, he set his reel. "Ohio and Indiana aren't short on water. But you won't find many doing this in November."

"No, you're right."

"So, about a certain plane trip and one person's words about it . . . don't let the words of one person affect your view of the rest of us."

The guy didn't beat around a bush, but plowed straight through.

"Huh. No, I wasn't planning on it. Women—well, not just women, but men too—can have a habit of talking about things not concerning them or are borne out of a critical spirit more than genuine concern about someone's spiritual well-being."

"Well said." Henry tugged on his line.

Silas finally cast his own line, felt the *plop* of the bait and hook as it struck the water, then sank.

"I like the village. It feels safe, comfortable. We're in the city, but we have our place. Of course, being minutes from the water helps, too, like I said before." He felt a gentle tug on the line. Fish? He waited . . . no, probably a current.

"Your uncle and aunt have been good friends of mine for years," Henry said, tugging on his own line. "I can't remember when I've seen them so happy. You being here has helped."

"Good. I'm glad. Before coming here, I only met them a few times, years ago."

"Being half a world away, your family sure missed you."

"I want to go back . . . someday, when the time's right. For now, though, Pinecraft is home for us. Unique."

"Yup, it's unique. A blend, mishmash of the Plain. Nowhere else like it." Henry glanced his way. "Just so you know, things are a little different here than in Ohio."

"I'm used to different. My whole adult life has been different."

"Dad, I don't think I want to go back to Africa," Matthew said. "I missed it, but I like being here. I have more friends."

Silas nodded. "We have time to talk about this." He knew he'd been called to missions, as had Belinda. But their children, maybe God had different paths for them, callings of their own.

A tug on the line made it whir on the reel. Silas snapped his attention back to the line.

"Got a bite?" Henry stared at the pole, bending in an arc.

"Think so." Silas pulled back, turned the handle on the reel.

"You've got one, Dad!" Matthew called out beside him.

The tip of the rod snapped back, the rod straightened. The line fell slack. Silas reeled it in until he reached the free end, now empty of hook and bait.

"Something got a free snack." He moved over to the tackle box to find another hook, a larger one than last time.

"Aw, Dad." Matthew shook his head. "Almost."

"Far from almost." Silas tied another hook on the line. "I didn't even get to see what it was."

Back to the side of the boat, Silas cast his line again, with a new hook and fresh bait. "C'mon, you, whatever you are, try it again. Just try."

Matthew shouted beside him as the fishing rod bent. His son's reel whined, and Matthew gritted his teeth and cranked the wheel.

"Need a hand?" Silas asked.

"No. I . . . can do it." Matthew kept reeling in the line. His brow creased, he leaned back.

He ended up hauling in a good-size mullet, without help. The fish flopped on the deck. The young women cheered, and the men clapped Matthew on the back.

"First fish!" Matthew held it up, triumphantly.

Silas grinned. Yes, his son was his own person, on the brink of adulthood. For so long, Silas had only thought of his and Belinda's calling. He needed to prepare himself for his children's paths diverging.

Even Lena, who glowed as she chattered with Emma and Steven. One day, he'd be alone.

❧

Rochelle, 19

"Well, I've come to a decision," Rochelle's father announced at breakfast, the Saturday after Thanksgiving.

"What's that?"

"I'm selling the house."

"Selling?" Rochelle tried not to let her voice squeak. "When?"

"I'm putting it on the market in January."

"January." It seemed she was only capable of one word at a time, right at this moment. "Why?"

"This is too much house for you and for me." He waved his piece of toast in the air. "I'm going to buy a small condo. I should be able to get a good price for the house, workshop, and acreage. Don't worry. Both you and Jolene will get a share."

"A share." Rochelle shook her head. "But I'm not worried about that."

"Consider it getting your inheritance early."

"Inheritance." Was something wrong with her father? "Dad, are you feeling all right?"

"I'm feeling fine. I should be around to get old and ornery."

"Good, I'm relieved to hear it." She dabbed at her home fries. "Well, you'll be glad to know I'm thinking about going back to school. It's time, I think."

"Good, good. Your mother . . . your mother would be happy, if she knew. Always wanted you to finish nursing school. Me too."

"I'm going to sign up after New Year's. I might not get the pick of the classes I want, but I'll start somewhere."

"Now, I hope you don't think I'm overstepping, but I think you and the Fry boy ought to work things out."

"It won't happen. He's marrying Belinda, remember?" The words tasted bitter on her tongue.

"They're not married yet."

Rochelle shook her head. "It's too late."

ᴄᴇᴅ

After Sunday supper and a short nap, Rochelle woke to an empty house. Emma had gone fishing with the group. Betsy left a note saying she and Thaddeus had walked to *Aenti* Sarah's house where the family was gathered, visiting the spry Old Order octogenarian.

Before Rochelle went to lie down, Betsy had invited her to come along, too, but she politely refused.

With the headache now gone, Rochelle got up and paced the house. Today, a day of rest. Yes, she'd napped. No business today, either, she thought as she looked at her darkened computer screen.

She didn't recall the last time she'd simply taken a stroll through the village. The earlier conversation with Bea wiggled itself to the front of her mind.

Rochelle let her hair down, brushed it, put it back up again, then pinned on a fresh *kapp*. Time for a walk, to remind her of why she loved this village and not to let one sour apple spoil it for her.

The streets, nearly empty, were still damp from the rains earlier, with some shallow puddles at the street corners.

Rochelle's steps took her along to Graber and toward the home of her former employer, Leah.

Not far now, and she caught sight of Leah's house, a square cinderblock cottage, painted dove gray with white trim. A few hibiscus plants bloomed in front of the porch, where a lone figure sat in one of a pair of rocking chairs.

"Well, if I don't say, it's Rochelle Keim," called out the figure. Leah. White hair with a *kapp* to match, and still wearing her black dress and white apron she'd worn to service that morning.

"Leah." Rochelle found herself grinning at the sight of the woman.

"Come up here, sit a while. I'll get us some lemonade."

Of course, Rochelle had to comply. If not for Leah, Rochelle wouldn't have learned the ins and outs of the cleaning business.

"How are you?" Rochelle asked as she stepped up onto the porch and joined the elderly woman.

"I'm doing as well as *Gotte* wills me today. And, how are you?"

"Very well, thank you."

"Wait here a moment, and I'll get us some lemonade. Made fresh yesterday, from lemons in the backyard."

A few minutes later Leah emerged from her house. She carried a small tray on which perched a pair of glasses and a plate of short-bread cookies.

"Here. Wet your whistle." Leah set the tray on a table between the pair of rocking chairs.

"Thank you." Rochelle reached for a glass with one hand and a cookie with the other.

"I haven't seen you in a while." Leah's eyes sparkled. "You're still in business?"

"Yes, ma'am, I am. It's going very well." Rochelle took a sip of the tart lemonade and savored the accompanying sweetness.

"I heard young Emma has given you fits."

Rochelle chuckled. "She's young. I think she is happier now at Der Dutchman, waiting tables. I have a new helper now. Lena Fry."

"Ah, the missionary pilot's *dochder*."

"Right."

"So tragic, losing her *mamm*."

"I agree. Belinda and I were good friends once."

"You were the same age when you lost your own *mudder*."

"Yes, I was. And I ended up here." Rochelle nibbled on the cookie. Buttery, a perfect mild flavor to offset the lemonade. "I'm back in college now, finishing my nursing studies."

"At last. I thought you might have started sooner; I'm glad you are. You do a good job of taking care of so many people. I thought you would stop cleaning houses before now."

"It was a good way to make a living. Well, you know." Rochelle smiled at her own words.

"*Yah*, and I'm as proud of you as I would be of one of my grand-daughters. And what, no husband in your life? Nobody?"

"No. Not since the last time we spoke." Which had been far too long ago. Months and months. Was their conversation in Yoder's? She wanted to add, "Not really." She wouldn't even mention the Daniel Troyer disaster of last fall.

"These young people," Leah observed as a gaggle of young Amish women strolled by, chattering and giggling. "They move so quickly. Don't stop and think."

"Ha. I'm well aware. I've had two under my roof for almost two years now. But I love having them."

"They don't think about the future. Only now. Or if they have thought of the future, it's silly things." Leah shook her head.

Rochelle nodded. Emma's preoccupation with wedding details. Of course, if she were the one getting married, details would be important to her, too. But she wouldn't continually change her mind.

"Come, would you like to see my birds?" Leah set down her glass.

"Birds?"

"In the back yard. For some reason, they think my yard is the best of them all."

Rochelle followed Leah into the cottage, through the living room and kitchen, and then out a screen door.

They stepped out onto a patio, which had a picnic table. But beyond the picnic table stood a tall pole, topped with a large wooden birdhouse. The pole also had perches, one or two feet long, sticking out from the sides.

"Look up." And Leah pointed.

Parrots, at least a dozen of them, perched like emerald jewels on the birdhouse and preened in the sunshine.

"Oh, I've never seen so many of them, all in one place like this before. Even at the zoo."

A few of them called out to each other. One flapped its wings and squawked at another.

"They all of a sudden just appeared here. One or two, and then more."

Leah went to the small wooden shed in the corner of the yard and emerged with a large sack sagging on the bottom. Rochelle joined her and reached for the bag.

"Here, I can carry this." She had no idea how on earth the older woman managed to lug the sack of sunflower seeds from the shed.

"I couldn't help but start feeding them. So now, they wait for me." Leah chuckled.

At the women's approach, several of the birds took flight, landing a safer distance away to perch on the nearest electrical wires.

Leah reached for a lever, and as the pole glided down, the remainder of the birds flew to a nearby tree, but still kept watch as she and Rochelle filled the feeder.

"Do they talk to you at all?"

"I taught one to say 'pretty bird,' but I suspect he'll be shy today." Leah worked the lever, and the pole raised up to its original height.

"They're beautiful. How much do they eat?"

"Oh, I go through one bag of these seeds in a week. Friends help buy the seeds." Leah looked thoughtful for a moment, as if she wanted to say more.

"I'm sorry I haven't come by more." She could use the "I'm busy" reason, but Leah had always been a short walk away.

"Don't you mind about it. I've kept busy myself. I'm going to have another yard sale next weekend, getting rid of a few things. No matter how simple I've tried to keep my home, I keep finding little doodads in every corner, it seems."

Rochelle nodded. "I understand."

They watched the birds for a few more minutes, laughing as some of the birds would scramble for the seeds, a few of which sprayed from the ledge of the birdhouse and landed on the yard.

"Oh, speaking of things. Since you're here, I have something to give you. Follow me."

Rochelle followed Leah into the cottage, where they paused in the living room and stopped at a cardboard box on the coffee table.

"A few things I've gone through, and you stopping by today reminded me." Leah rummaged in the box and pulled out another, smaller box, carved from some type of wood and inlaid with a lighter wood in the shape of a cross.

"It's pretty," Rochelle said.

"I want you to have it. Do you remember the box?"

"I'm not sure."

"It was always on my kitchen table, years ago."

Yes, she remembered it now. Whenever Leah would distribute paychecks, she'd sit at the table and the box, no bigger than a shoe-box, would sit in the middle of it. Leah always tucked papers and mail in the box.

"I remember it now."

"I want you to have it." Leah handed the box to Rochelle.

"Thank you." She appreciated the kind gesture.

"Now, let's finish our lemonade. But I think the ice in the glasses has melted."

They returned to the porch, where Rochelle polished off the rest of her lemonade, as well as another glass, while Leah updated her on the family.

"And someday, I know my home here will belong to someone else." Leah frowned. "I only hope they keep it in the family."

"I hope so, too." As the older villagers went to their eternal reward, who would be left to care for the homes that had sheltered many a family during the holidays, and for some villagers like her, year-round?

Rochelle shivered. One day, who would have her home?

And, would she end up alone, like Leah?

After her third glass of lemonade, Rochelle bade Leah good-bye, promising to visit again. She would. Leah had been like a *mamm* to her those first months here in Pinecraft.

Rochelle strolled home, carrying her gift from Leah under one arm. When she walked up the driveway, she could already hear Emma's voice drifting out the front screen door.

"I'm so mad at that Steven, I could just—just—*spit!*"

Ah, so the girls were home.

⋙

Rochelle, 19

Word got around about the Keim place, and the old house had sold right after New Year's, along with the acreage, just as Dad had said it would. The red block letters of the SOLD label covered the agent's sign in the immense front yard.

"Are you sure, Dad? This is what you're supposed to do?"

Her father gave a slow nod. "I've prayed long and I've prayed hard. This is the best thing, for all of us. Whatever you choose to do with the money is up to you. Donate, save, invest. . . . It's too late to back out now, anyway."

He'd never mentioned investing before.

Rochelle bit back the words that wanted to come: "I don't need anything except to be right here."

"You're welcome to stay with me at my new place."

New place.

Momma would have flipped if she'd known Dad was selling his section of the family's property, along with the house. No one in the family ventured to buy out his share, either.

The old saying "When God closes a door, He opens a window" came to mind. Not quite scriptural, but Rochelle understood it. Every door had slammed on her, beginning with Momma passing away.

Her nursing studies had floundered, her relationship with Silas had soured and so had her friendship with Belinda. And then, there was the upcoming wedding, the announcement of which still made Rochelle's head reel.

Another snowstorm had come the night before, and she stared out at the fields covered with a fresh blanket of snow.

"I'm going to Pinecraft, too, for Christmas. My cousin has a room, said I was welcome to come."

Pinecraft, in Florida. Vacation spot for families and old people. She'd been a few times and enjoyed the volleyball and trips to the beach. But ever since Momma had taken sick, the trips had stopped.

"Dad, do you think Cousin Herb would have room for me, too?"

17

Silas's nose burned, as did his cheeks and the back of his neck after spending an afternoon on the waters. He sat on the back patio, cleaning fish with Matthew while Lena was in her room, studying.

Well, she'd told him she was studying.

All the way home from the marina, Lena had remained quiet as a stone in the front seat beside him, other than to comment about not forgetting sunscreen the next time they went fishing.

"I'm glad we finally made the time to go fishing." Silas added a fillet to the growing stack on the plate. Not enough for a large-scale fish fry, but enough for the three of them to stuff themselves with tonight and tomorrow night, too.

"I'd fish every day if I could." Matthew kept scaling the fish in front of him.

"I think it's relaxing. I'd forgotten how much."

"I don't think Lena and Emma and Steven were relaxed."

"What do you mean?"

"I think Steven likes Lena."

"Well, they're friends."

"Aw, Dad. Of course they are. But I think he likes her especially."

"Huh." When did his son start noticing things like this? "But he's engaged to Emma, you know. They're getting married in five weeks, or some time soon." He ought to scold the young man for saying such things, and he ought to mind his own business.

"I know. Lena says all Emma does is talk about the wedding."

"Ah, I see." But he didn't see.

The subject turned away from Lena and over to boats and fishing and whether or not Silas might buy them their own boat someday. They kept cleaning fish until they transformed the stack of whole mullet into fillets.

As soon as they'd finished, Lena ambled from the house, her cheeks red. "I have a headache. I tried studying, but it was useless."

"A day of rest today, including studies," Silas reminded her.

She nodded, flopping onto the nearest empty patio chair. She glanced at Matthew, then to Silas.

"Are we cooking these tonight? I don't mind preparing them."

"Yes, maybe half."

"Oh. Emma said there's a concert tonight, in the park, at seven. A bluegrass band from Pennsylvania is playing. I might go." Lena fanned herself with her hand.

"But you have a headache."

"I'll take something for it. Do we have any aspirin?"

"We should." He studied her face. She didn't quite meet his eyes.

Matthew picked up the bowl of fish bones and innards. "I'm going to throw out this stuff."

"Not in the kitchen can." Silas recalled the scent from the last time they'd cleaned some fish.

"Nope. I'll bag 'em and stick the bag in the big trash can outside."

"Good." Silas glanced back to Lena. "Now, if you could tell me what's going on? You've been quiet."

"I'm . . . I'm not sure. Emma . . . well, she was starting to get on my nerves today. Wedding this, and that." Lena wrinkled her nose.

"Hmm . . . I think someday, you'll understand from her perspective."

"No. Not like that. Steven . . ." Lena shook her head and stared at her tanned forearms.

"Steven?"

"He acted like she was getting on his nerves, too." She gave a small smile in his direction. "I like Steven. He's . . . nice. Smart, too. He knows so much about the fish and their habitat . . . I mean, he sounds like he could teach my biology class."

A pink hue deepened on her cheeks.

"Huh." This kind of talk made him fidget in his chair. If it had seemed strange to hear Matthew saying he thought Steven liked Lena, it was even worse to see the confirmation written on Lena's face.

Not good.

Not good at all, with a wedding less than two months away.

"So, Emma must be getting nervous with the wedding count-down. I know your mother was excited, nervous too. It was all she talked about, the closer the day drew near."

He remembered Belinda's excitement about their wedding, although they didn't have a long engagement.

With their grief still raw over John, some doubted their haste to the altar. At the time, Silas had been never more sure of anything. In his young adult mind, he needed to act, to do something. To right a wrong in the best way he knew how.

Silas, 21

Silas wanted to tell Rochelle himself about him and Belinda. It wouldn't be fair if she heard it from someone else, even though they hadn't spoken since the days just after John's funeral. After the meal, her demeanor had closed off from him, and he couldn't coax a smile from her, no matter how much he tried. However, it hadn't been a day for smiles of any kind.

The Lord would heal their loss in time, at least take away most of its pain. Or so Silas hoped and prayed. He and Belinda, together, now would honor John's memory.

He convinced himself true love would come in time, he hoped. Belinda had her own beauty, more obvious than Rochelle's. She was quick to speak up and not quite as careful with her words as Rochelle.

But Rochelle's recent turnaround had cooled his resolve.

Maybe his mother had been right. Maybe he ought to wait, give things some time.

He picked up the telephone, calling himself a coward as he punched in Rochelle's number.

She answered on the first ring. "Silas."

"Hello. Ah, um, how are you?"

"Doing well. Ready for Christmas to be over with for this year."

"I understand." Silence filled the line.

"So, how are you?"

"Doing well . . ." He wasn't sure how to continue. "Look, I think you ought to know, you deserve to know before anyone else. It might seem like things are happening fast, but . . ."

"You and Belinda are getting married, aren't you?"

"Ah, well, yes. Soon."

"Are you sure this is what you want?" Her voice sounded even.

"It's not always about what we want, Rochelle."

"What do you mean? What's happened to us?"

"There hasn't been an us, not for a while. I . . . I feel like a failure with you. And with Belinda, ah, I don't." This was coming out all wrong and getting worse by each passing second. Yes, things had happened quickly with Belinda. All the time the four of them had spent together, and Rochelle with her grief, then all of them losing John—it had all boiled into a mess.

"Well, I pray God's blessings upon your marriage. I hope . . . I hope you get the plane you always wanted."

He wanted to say, "We can all still be friends," but those words didn't sound right to his ears.

More silence.

"Anyway, Silas, thanks for calling. Um, Dad and I are going to Florida for Christmas. I'm glad he wants to do something besides work in his shop. And, well, the house sold, too. So, I'm not sure where I'll be after this."

"Wow, it's a lot to happen all at once."

"We've had a lot happen, all at once. Good-bye, Silas."

"Bye?" He spoke to a dial tone.

18

Rochelle stepped into the house, bracing herself for what would come next.

Had she and Belinda been so dramatic at the same age?

Maybe she ought to ask Jolene. Her older sister always seemed to be shaking her head over Rochelle when they were younger.

Likely it had to do with their age difference. Rochelle, the youngest, had likely been a bit spoiled, as she now considered herself from an older perspective.

Much like Emma now pacing the kitchen, while Betsy poured some water into the coffeepot.

"*Aenti* Chelle, I'm glad you're home." Emma paused. She leaned on the breakfast bar.

Rochelle crossed from the kitchen and into the living area. She placed the box from Leah on the coffee table before returning to the kitchen.

"Why?"

"Why do women do things like this?"

"Like what?"

"Lena is my friend. But . . ."

"But?"

"She and Steven were getting along well today."

"Aren't you glad your friend and your future husband get along well?"

"Not like this." Emma began pacing again. Then she stopped. "Oh, I shouldn't have said anything."

"Well, have you talked to Lena about it? I'm always willing to listen to you, but I'm not sure I'm the best person to solve this problem."

"No." Emma frowned. "Maybe I'm just a little . . . I don't know."

"As far as Lena's feelings, I'd ask her." Rochelle stepped forward. "But what's troubling you?"

"Cold feet." Betsy took down three mugs from the cabinet. "I'm nervous about getting married, too."

Their *mamm* would be here next week, along with their father. Rochelle helped herself to a cup of coffee. Wasn't there still some pie left from earlier today? She uncovered the remainders of the blueberry pie. Betsy had brought one home from the bakery last evening, her contribution to the Sunday meal.

"This is one of the biggest decisions of both your lives," she said aloud. She pulled out some forks and found paper plates. "There's bound to be some nerves. You've both made some choices in the past that weren't easy to make, I'm sure. Emma, I know it hasn't been easy for you, living here, as much as you've enjoyed the, ah, freer atmosphere than back in Ohio."

Emma nodded. "I . . . I love Steven. I do feel free when I'm with him. He makes me feel special, and I know we'll take *gut* care of each other. I love it here in Florida, too. Even if it does get a little boring in the village during the summertime."

Rochelle glanced at Betsy as the three of them gathered at the table. Betsy nodded, but didn't say more.

"Sometimes when we pray and ask for God's direction, it doesn't mean the answer will be an easy one to understand or carry out. Even if it's an answer we're looking for."

"*Ya,*" Betsy said. "When I last spoke with my *mamm,* she said a few of the other *aentis* and *oncles* aren't coming to Emma's wedding after all. Because Emma left the *Ordnung.* But they are coming to my ceremony because I stayed. Sometimes, it doesn't seem fair."

Rochelle tried not to sigh about the family dynamics. She knew this was how it worked, those who left their orders, even to join the Mennonites, sometimes being shunned. Thankfully in Emma's case, this hadn't happened. The decision was made by some of the family members, not dictated by their church. Thankfully, Emma belonged to a less restrictive group. Yet, because Betsy stayed in the family's order and was marrying Thaddeus Zook, she had the family's full blessing.

"I wish I could help," Rochelle said. "But I know there won't be any changing their minds. Not likely."

"I know." Emma stared at her piece of pie. "But you *are* a help, *Aenti* Chelle. You are." She gave them a weak smile. "And soon, I'm going to be Mrs. Steven Hostetler."

"Yes, you will be. Soon. But, if you have any worries, you should also talk to Lena. She seems like a good friend to you. I know what it's like to have lost a good friend. Sometimes, not talking about something bothering you is the worst thing you can do."

Silas had to grin as the Cessna shot through the blue skies. Far below, the Gulf waters glittered and gleamed. This afternoon's short flight—just for fun—mirrored the exhilaration of his first solo flight.

What a blessing to be doing what he loved most again.

"Tower Fruitland, this is Cessna fifty-two Charlie requesting clearance for landing."

"Roger that, Cessna fifty-two Charlie. Runway two clear, southern approach when ready."

"Tower Fruitland, Cessna fifty-two Charlie banking south."

"Roger, the wind is from the south, so a fast descent."

"Thank you, Tower Fruitland."

As always, the minutes spent in the air seemed like a blink in his eye. He slowed the engine, held the control steady, and kept the nose straight.

With a familiar bump, the Cessna's wheels hit the runway. The pull of the engine slowed as the plane gradually ground to a halt, and Silas taxied toward the hangar.

He glanced toward the parking lot. A black Land Rover stood in the VIP parking. Ted Kingsley.

Another piloting contract for him?

But Ted usually called or had his assistant contact him.

The plane's single propeller swung slower and slower as the engine shut down. Silas performed his postflight checks and shut-downs from the cockpit.

Ted arrived at the plane by the time Silas had climbed out.

"Mr. Kingsley." Silas shook hands with his sometime employer.

"Silas. It's been a while."

"Yes, sir. How's the family?"

"They're doing well. We're glad to have our son home again. An adjustment, but no more appointments until a follow-up with the surgeon right before Christmas."

"It's good to hear. I've been praying for his recovery."

"Thank you. Say, the reason I'm here is not just to book you for the flight on the twenty-third. I assume you'll be available then? I know it's close to Christmas, but we'll be back by Christmas Eve."

"Yes, I'll be available. If you give me the time, I'll be glad to handle everything from there."

"Good. Also, I have a job proposition for you."

"A job."

"Not contract work. It turns out, my other pilot isn't able to come back. And I want someone on my payroll permanently."

"Oh, I see." A permanent job? Of course, the idea appealed to him.

"No need to say yes or no just yet. I'll have my office send you a detailed proposal about what I have in mind. You're steady, safe. The family likes you. And, if you're looking to get commercial training, I'd be willing to help. We have a larger jet for Kingsley Holdings for transatlantic flights for our staff."

Flying a larger jet? Transatlantic?

"Wow, this is a great opportunity."

"I thought you'd say as much. Well, I'll see you in a few weeks. The trip to Atlanta is in-and-out, shoot for a day trip. Unlike last time."

"How's the Cheyenne?"

"In tip-top working order, as far as I know. I've had her in the shop for a thorough going-over."

Silas nodded. "Well, thank you, and yes, I'll see you on the twenty-third."

"Good. You'll have the offer in your e-mail by the end of the day, so make sure you look for it. You can let me know your decision by the twenty-third."

"I sure will. Thank you."

Then Mr. Kingsley turned on his heel and strode off in the direction of the parking lot.

Silas pondered the offer. A real job. Not contract work, no more trying to drum up support on furloughs spent traveling to churches in the Midwest, only to return to South Africa and do the same thing over again several years later.

God, I've been so tired. Is this the relief I've been looking for?

He'd been praying about what to do next. He knew from the first day arriving in Pinecraft he wouldn't make the village a permanent home. Yet he'd grown attached to the place, to spending time with Uncle Tobias and Aunt Fran. And seeing Rochelle regularly, even if things were a bit shaky between them.

Did the job mean leaving Pinecraft?

He'd find out soon enough.

He arrived home to an empty house, with Matthew and Lena still in classes. As he stepped into the kitchen, he realized he'd forgotten to change the wall calendar to the current month, and here it was, Thanksgiving week. At Sunday supper, Aunt Fran had asked if he could bring some bottles of pop along with paper cups for the whole assembled family to use.

Silas flipped the calendar to November.

Belinda would have remembered the detail. Now, Silas could keep track of plenty of things, but not calendars and such.

"We're doing all right, though, even without a flipped calendar." Silas said the words aloud to no one in particular. He found a scrap of paper and wrote a shopping list to include two-liter bottles of soda pop, paper cups, and toilet paper. They were about fresh out of note paper, too. Belinda would have seen to it all.

Enough. He figured he'd get some laundry done before the kids got home for the afternoon and then see if they wanted to walk to Village Pizza for supper. The atmosphere in Pinecraft, the closer it came to Thanksgiving and winter, took on an almost electric quality.

A knock sounded at the door. He'd left the inner solid door open to allow a warm breeze to drift through the screen door.

"Hello, hello." Uncle Tobias said.

"Come on in. I just got home," Silas called out to the front of the house.

The screen door banged, and Tobias joined him in the dining area.

"Thought you might be home. Not sure if the children were yet, though."

"No. Matthew should be home any moment from school. Lena will arrive later, closer to five."

"Good, good. I wanted to speak to you before Matthew arrived."

"Is everything okay?"

"Yes, sure is. I'm getting closer to my high season at the shop. I know he's been helping me a couple of afternoons when his homework is done. But, I'm going to need extra help, with all these buses from out of town bringing more snowbirds."

"I'm sure he'd be happy to work at the shop. He loves being over at your house."

"And we enjoy having him there." A frown flickered across Uncle Silas's face. "Now, Silas, I hope I'm not overstepping, but . . ."

"No, what is it?"

"Matthew and I talk a lot while we work. Mostly he talks, and I let 'im. I forgot what it was to have a youngster around, all the chatter."

Silas laughed. "He even talks in his sleep sometimes."

"What has me a bit worried is Matthew. Because he's worried."

"Worried? About what?"

"Leaving Sarasota. He tells me over and over again, he never wants to leave."

Silas heaved a sigh. "He mentioned it to me once, not long ago. He was never happy in Ohio. Mom and Dad . . ."

"Your parents did the best they could. But there's no beach in Ohio, no life like what you're used to."

"The thing is, Uncle Tobias, the man I've been flying for, well, he told me today he wants to offer me a job. A permanent one."

"Oh, I see. Well, I know there have been nights you didn't come home. Like the one time you were stuck in Atlanta because of mechanical problems."

"I'm not sure the job will keep me here in Sarasota. I'm pretty sure the family has at least one other residence besides their home here in Florida. He mentioned New York once. I didn't think anything more about it because I never imagined he'd offer me a job."

"So is this offer in writing?"

"It will be. He's going to have his office send me an offer by e-mail, by the end of the day today."

"What do you think you're going to do?"

"If the job keeps me here, in Sarasota, so be it. But if I have to leave—" The option didn't sit well with him.

"Your children are grown; well, one is, the other nearly."

"I know. I've reminded myself of it a lot. I don't like the idea of us spread all over. Lena off, with her studies. Matthew, already alone so much if he's not at your home." Silas shook his head.

"Change is never easy."

"No, it's not. If things would only change the way I see fit."

Uncle Tobias pulled off his cap, rubbed the top of his head, and chuckled. "If you were God, then?"

"No." He smiled. As if anyone could control the future, how life unfolded. He hadn't seen this coming. Not at all.

19

"This is one of the most ridiculous things I've ever done," Rochelle muttered under her breath as she scaled the front steps to the church.

Despite her words, the seagulls in her stomach had transformed into pelicans.

She reminded herself she was going in to meet with two of her favorite people in the world, her pastor and his wife. Silas would be there, and the thought warmed her a bit. She'd missed him, while keeping up with her studies along with her clients. He'd been off flying hither and yon.

And, the reason for tonight's meeting was supposedly going to be present tonight, Vera Byler.

It had been weeks since the fateful trip to Atlanta, and they finally had an evening when they could all meet and "discuss" the issue.

Rochelle also reminded herself she had shown up at this meeting to help make some peace. If it made Vera feel better for them all to sit down and talk, so be it.

"Hi, I'm glad you came," Bea said as Rochelle stepped into the foyer. "We're going to chat in one of the classrooms. It shouldn't take long."

Bea led her to the room where they'd spoken on the Sunday morning after the Atlanta trip. Her husband sat at the head of the table, with Vera and her husband on to the right of him, Silas to the left, then an empty chair. Bea took the vacant chair at the foot of the table, opposite her husband.

This wasn't as if she were Amish, called before the elders for some transgression she'd committed and needed to be reminded to repent.

Rochelle pulled the lone empty chair away from the table and took a seat.

"This is it; you're the only ones here," said Pastor Marv. "We should begin with prayer."

She didn't cast a glance at Silas beside her, but she sensed his presence. She bowed her head as Pastor asked for God's blessing upon their meeting, as well as a spirit of unity, peace, and love.

Yes, she could agree with all three of those.

"The reason we're here tonight is to mediate, Bea and I," said Pastor. "I know you've expressed concerns, Vera, but the way you handled this wasn't exactly biblical."

Vera gasped. "Well—"

"Vera, let the man speak," her husband said. "It's not your turn whenever you decide."

She said nothing more, but stared at the table.

"If you did have a true issue with Rochelle and Silas's actions, you ought to have gone to Rochelle privately." Pastor Marv's tone was gentle. "Did you?"

"No, Pastor, I didn't."

Rochelle kept silent. How many people did Vera talk to about this? But then, Emma had. She suspected, however, Emma only had the motive to find someone to clean the houses Rochelle couldn't.

She glanced at Silas, whose expression remained even, but his eyes warmed when her gaze met his.

Yes, it would be okay. She'd prayed about her feelings, especially regarding Vera. Sometimes, she wanted to give busybodies a piece of her mind.

And yes, she knew an overnight trip out of town wasn't a good example. However, it was out of her control.

"Vera," she said aloud. "I know at first, hearing something like this didn't sound good. Or appropriate. But I'm your sister in the Lord. You've known me for years. I would never . . ."

"And I would never put Rochelle in a position to compromise her reputation, either," Silas finished.

"Well, you two . . . have a *history*."

Rochelle sat up straighter in the chair. "Silas and I . . . it was a long time ago. Our lives went in different directions. The trip to Atlanta was a . . . a . . ."

"I made her a promise I'd take her flying someday. The overnight stay was not planned."

Why were they explaining themselves, yet again? She glanced at Pastor Marv and Bea.

Vera's husband studied his wife's face, then looked around the table.

Rochelle continued. "Vera, I'm sorry you believed our trip might have turned into something, ah, inappropriate. I would have never said yes to the trip were it an overnight trip. Besides not having the time, I consider it inappropriate to go on an overnight trip with an unmarried man. No matter if we stay in separate rooms. The fact is, and you're right, people . . . talk.

"I can't control what anyone thinks of me, or my actions. But I do know I have a clean conscience before God. I also know the Scriptures do speak of love always rejoicing in the truth. The truth is, Vera, nothing inappropriate occurred during our trip. You should be happy to know this."

At the end of her speech, she found her pulse racing. She kept her hands firmly in her lap. Hopefully, no one could tell they shook.

"I'm . . . I'm sorry." Vera bit her lip before continuing. "I was wrong to think the worst. I didn't truly believe you would have done anything . . . inappropriate. You're right, Rochelle. I've known you for many years. I would be . . . shocked . . . if I learned you ever did. And Silas, I don't know you well. But Samuel speaks highly of you, especially after the meetings with the Heritage Committee." She hung her head.

"And . . . I should have spoken to you myself and shared my concern. I was wrong to go to anyone else." Her shoulders drooped. "Please, forgive me. This is a bad habit I have, to speak or think about anyone like this. Especially if I know it's not true."

Rochelle's heart went out to the woman.

She's lonely. She thinks she doesn't matter as much anymore and craves attention.

"I forgive you, Vera. Any one of us can make wrong assumptions about people."

Bea nodded. "So true. It's a natural thing, to feel excited we might have some special knowledge about someone else, something no one else knows."

Vera sighed. "You're right."

Silas cleared his throat. "Ah, I know I'm nearly at the end of my proving time. Pastor, will this affect my future membership in the church?"

Pastor locked eyes with Vera's husband. An elder, of course. Rochelle kept her mouth closed. She said she'd forgiven Vera. She did. She'd work on it.

But no, it wouldn't be fair if this "story" about Silas and her jeopardized his full membership in the Sarasota Mennonite fellowship.

Pastor shook his head. "No, Silas. You've been faithful here, ever since arriving in Pinecraft. Your family, at least your uncle and aunt, have been longtime members here. And of course, your many years of ministry overseas count for a lot."

Some might not understand their ways of proving, but Rochelle appreciated it. People, no matter what they said, sometimes didn't live up to what they professed to believe. Fellowship meant security, community, but it also meant accountability.

"Good. I'm glad. Thank you, Pastor Marvin." Silas's grin made her think of the grin he used to wear years ago.

She couldn't help but grin herself.

After a little light conversation, the mood in the room lifted, and the three couples prayed together.

Rochelle recalled some trouble Vera had tried to cause last winter for Betsy. Maybe this had been Vera's lesson, once and for all.

They left the church building, and the lightened sensation continued.

Silas walked with her to her bicycle.

"Feel better now?" he asked.

"Much better. I was dreading this meeting. I was hoping they'd say never mind and cancel the meeting."

"This meeting was probably more for Vera's benefit than anyone else's." Silas gazed over her shoulder.

She turned. The Bylers were walking to their vehicle. "Maybe."

"We have a *history*," he said.

"History is something that once was," Rochelle countered.

"Rochelle . . . do you, would you consider, possibly . . ."

What was he asking her? Their road had taken more twists and turns and had a dead end. She had no idea what the future held, wasn't sure if she wanted to wonder.

"Would you come to Uncle Tobias's for dessert, Thanksgiving night? Maybe we could . . . go for a walk, too, afterward?"

She exhaled. Dessert and a walk she could handle. After all, they'd narrowly escaped scandal with their other trip. "Yes. I think I'd like to."

They said good-bye, and she hopped onto her bicycle. No, she wasn't twenty anymore, but she might as well be.

She waved before pushing off and gliding along the street in the gathering twilight. Passing by Pinecraft Park, she recalled the girls mentioning a concert in the park, as well as some volleyball, so she slowed her bicycle to see if she could find them.

≈≈≈

The week continued and here came Thanksgiving day. Silas could only think about how he'd invited Rochelle for dessert and a walk.

The family meal had ended, with his parents, Uncle Tobias, Aunt Fran, Lena, Matthew, along with the rest of the Fry clan clustered in various spots around the house. A cold front had come through, causing temperatures to dip down and bring a chill to the Florida air.

He glanced toward the front door. His stomach still felt stuffed to the brim, but he'd find room somehow for a piece of Aunt Fran's pie and maybe a bite of her blueberry delight.

"You expecting someone?" Uncle Tobias asked.

"Yes. I think so, if she decides to come." Should he have offered to stop by her house and escort her here for dessert? Maybe it would have been a better idea.

"Rochelle is coming for dessert," Lena said, nodding her head. "She mentioned it Tuesday, on the way home after classes."

She'd mentioned dessert. Good. Or so he hoped.

"Ah, Rochelle Keim." His mother gave him a knowing look. But she said no more.

Way back when, his parents hadn't understood their parting of the ways. Looking back, he didn't understand it either. Youth, in its rashness, often made life-altering decisions merely because they seemed like good ideas at the time.

He wouldn't have decided what he did had she not pushed him away.

Of course, he could have been more persistent and less stubborn.

Was it worth the venture now, to spend more time with Rochelle and see what happened?

A brisk knock sounded on the door. *Rochelle.*

He should have walked to her home, met her there, and headed off on the walk before stopping for dessert here.

Silas strode to the door, ignoring his mother who'd stood up and moved in the same direction. Suddenly, he was twenty-one again, with clammy palms.

"R—Rochelle."

"Happy Thanksgiving." She smiled at him, and touched her *kapp.* A few stray hairs floated on the light breeze. She tugged her navy blue cardigan a little tighter.

"Dessert or a walk first?"

"We can walk first. I think I overdid it a bit at dinner." Rochelle touched her stomach.

He joined her outside, and they headed off along the front walk. Delightful smells came from neighboring homes, and a few neighbors sat on their porches. They waved, and both he and Rochelle responded in kind.

"The neighborhood sure is quiet today," Rochelle observed. "Yesterday, did you see how crowded it was? I had a hard time getting down the street, for all the cars."

"What for? What was all the crowding about?"

"Yoder's, pie pickup, day before Thanksgiving."

"Ah. I wasn't sure what was going on."

Rochelle nodded. "Everyone lined up to get their pie orders. I don't know how many thousand they prepared for this Thanksgiving, but it was a lot."

"Speaking of preparation, what did you make for dinner?"

"Not much. I made mashed potatoes and a sweet potato casserole. I had clients to visit all the way up until five last evening. A few special requests before the holiday today."

"You amaze me, Rochelle Keim."

"What do you mean?" Her face colored.

"You're busy making other people's homes clean and orderly places. Lena is impressed. Thank you, by the way, for letting her work as a substitute cleaner."

"She's good. And you're welcome. You and Belinda . . . I'm sure she was proud of Lena."

"Yes, she was." Silas said, "About Lena . . ." He stopped himself. This wasn't the time to bring up the subject of the quick wedding so long ago, then Lena's swift arrival.

"What about Lena?"

"Ah, never mind." They reached the Bahia Vista light, the street surprisingly busy for a holiday.

He did realize he ought to tell her about the job offer, the details of which he'd kept a lid on while he pondered and prayed.

An unusual-looking vehicle approached from across the street and stopped at the red light. A black buggy, like Uncle Tobias's only larger, had the appearance of a traditional Amish buggy, but had seating for six instead of four.

"Would you look at that? Another horseless buggy." He smiled.

"They seem to be popping up all over the place." Rochelle shook her head.

"I wanted to tell you about something, something I've only shared with Uncle Tobias so far."

"Oh, what?"

"I got a job offer, but if I take it, I'm going to have to leave Sarasota."

"Piloting for the Kingsleys, I assume?"

"Yes."

"I liked the Kingsleys. They're a nice couple."

He couldn't read her expression. Why did her reaction mean something to him? Maybe it was because he wanted to continue getting to know her again, but leaving Sarasota after the new year would definitely complicate the matter.

"I'd live in southern Connecticut, where they have a permanent home. They have a place here in Sarasota, but it's more like a get-away spot for them. Ted said he'd even pay for advanced training, if I'm interested in flying larger aircraft like for overseas flights."

"Oh, Silas, what an opportunity for you. But, Connecticut?" The light changed, and she hurried across. He lengthened his stride to keep up with her.

"I know. Matthew doesn't want to leave Sarasota, he told me not long ago. Yes, he's practically grown, but I don't like the idea of the three of us all over the place."

She slowed her stride. "Did you talk to him and Lena about the job offer?"

"Not yet."

"Well, I'm, ah, honored you chose to speak to me first, outside of your family."

"I couldn't tell my parents. Not just yet. They still want me back in Ohio. Moving back there isn't an option for me."

"So, have you prayed about it?"

"I have."

"What do you think the answer might be?"

"I . . . I don't know. Not a yes, or a no. Of course, I see reasons why and why not. But not one more than the other."

"Maybe the answer for now is to wait. When do you have to give him an answer?"

"On December twenty-third."

"Ah, so you still have time to decide."

He nodded. True. "You're right." They passed the Yoders' complex of stores, closed for the holiday, and continued along toward Pinecraft Park.

Right about now, Silas wanted pie. But pie meant sitting in the room with unspoken questions and glances exchanged by his family members at Uncle Tobias's house.

The shuffleboard courts had a quartet of players. No one played bocce on the expanse of park lawn today.

"This is the wedding site," Rochelle announced.

"Wedding site?"

"The park lawn. It's where Betsy and Thaddeus then Emma and Steven will be getting married on December thirtieth."

"Huh, not at the churches. A bit out of the ordinary."

"True."

Did she know about the tension between Lena, Emma, and Steven? Maybe she did. He wasn't about to bring it up. Better leave it unsaid, and hope things blew over.

"They wanted to share their day as much as possible. Which makes sense, not having to cook two reception meals. I've been drafted to help with cupcakes. We're making three hundred, with aqua or teal blue frosting. Emma's request."

"She definitely knows what she wants."

"On a good day, yes."

They ambled along the path winding past Phillippi Creek. A heron on the opposite bank spread its wings, then soared into the sky.

The afternoon light made Rochelle's face glow, erasing the years from her features.

No, the reason for his hesitation about Ted's job offer stood beside him. He didn't want to leave Sarasota, at least not so soon. And not without knowing where Rochelle stood.

Today, taking a walk, was literally another step telling him the door was open. Or, was he interpreting her politeness and kindness as interest?

Long ago, he never had a problem knowing what to say to her. Maybe it was the confidence of youth.

But now he stood beside her, after slogging through the weight of the past year. Some confidence. He'd been brave enough to take her flying, but only because of the Kingsleys. The look of bliss on her face as she told him what it was like to soar through the skies, well, he'd been buoyed along by her expression for days afterward.

He glanced around the park. The oblivious shuffleboard players kept up their game of skill, paying them no mind.

Silas reached for Rochelle's hand. She didn't pull away, but stood there, staring at his hand clasping hers.

"Rochelle . . ."

"Please, if you're thinking about leaving, don't . . ."

"I haven't decided I'm leaving. Not yet. I want to know if there's a reason you can think of for me to stay."

"I want you to stay . . . as long as you believe you should."

"No, do *you* want me to stay? Regardless of what I think? What do you want?"

"Silas, we've gotten to know each other again. I . . ."

"Don't think of me. Think of what you want. You always think of other people before yourself. You deserve the same consideration you give others."

Rochelle bit her lip. He knew he'd struck a chord, but he couldn't stop.

"Use your voice. Tell me you want me to stay."

"Silas . . ." Her voice caught, and she squeezed his hand. It took all his strength not to pull her into his arms. "I want you to stay. But I've learned in life, we don't always get what we want."

20

Rochelle sat up late Saturday night, trying to concentrate on the study guide in front of her. She yawned. If she didn't get to bed soon, she'd be yawning her head off at service in the morning.

But studies wouldn't wait, not anymore. After Thanksgiving weekend was over, the remainder of the semester would begin in earnest, and then final exams in two weeks.

She rubbed her forehead. Next semester, she'd limit herself to two classes and then pick up the third class in the summertime.

This was all Silas's fault. The walk on Thanksgiving after the meal, with Silas taking her hand.

Goodness, the moment had made her feel like a youth again. Of course, she had the wisdom of years to remind her hand-holding and a stomach doing flip-flops weren't the keys to a good relationship. Not as if she'd had experience with relationships over the years, save last fall. She shrugged off the memory and thanked God He had spared her further heartache.

She'd prayed for a husband in her most quiet moments over the years. If she couldn't have Silas as a result of her stubbornness, surely God could send someone else. She frowned about Daniel Troyer for the last time.

The cool night air drifted into the screened lanai and gently lifted the pages of the book. Staying indoors studying would have coaxed her to drift off to sleep.

Still, her mind wandered back around to Silas yet again.

He might be leaving Sarasota. This shouldn't surprise her. Most who came, visited, then left and went back to their "normal" lives back home. She tried to imagine what it must have been like for him, living in Africa for so long, then losing Belinda and trying to build a life without her.

He'd loved Belinda deeply. She could hear it in his voice, even mentioning her name. It had been a little more than a year. When was it appropriate to "move on"?

An older widow and widower had married last spring in their church, and everyone had rejoiced for both of them. Their engagement had been brief, yet no one doubted the couple's connection to each other.

Tonight, she'd remembered the couple as she stood beside Phillippi Creek while Silas held her hand.

Could she dive headfirst into the idea of loving Silas?

It wouldn't be hard. It hadn't been hard the first time.

However, things had crumbled when tough times came, losing her mother, and then losing John. Maybe their youth had been a factor in their relationship crumbling. And, on her part, she'd weighed Silas—unfairly—and found him lacking.

Soft footsteps in the kitchen made her look toward the doorway—Emma.

"I couldn't sleep," she said, her hair hanging in a braid past her waist.

"Ah." She knew better than to ask if Emma was all right. "All right" depended on the moment.

"But I'm awake because I'm excited. My *mamm* is coming on the Thursday bus, my *daed*, too. She'll have the dresses."

"Well, being excited is a good reason to be awake at this hour." Rochelle glanced at her book and notes. "I think upcoming final exams have me excited for a different reason."

"*Aenti* Chelle, I hope when I'm you're age, I'm like you," Emma blurted out. "You take such good care of people. You let me and Betsy stay here, and you didn't have to."

"We're family. And anyway, I have plenty of room."

A frown flickered across Emma's face. "I wish the whole family would come to the wedding. I asked *Mamm* again, tonight when she called, if they'd changed their minds. But no."

"They feel strongly you should have stayed in the church."

"I know. But I *am* part of the church. The Mennonite church."

"Yes, but to them, you know this . . . you leaving . . . was seen as an act of disobedience."

"The bishop didn't forbid it. But it took a lot of talking, for him to agree to *not* shunning me."

Rochelle knew about shunning. She'd seen it in action long ago, in Amish communities back home in Ohio. She remembered, dimly, the relationship between her parents and their extended family.

Pinecraft, though, and time, had likely insulated her from much of the harshness shunning involved in some districts. This, though, was the first time Emma had spoken of her own perspective.

"I'm sorry, Emma. Sometimes, no, many times there's no changing another person's mind, once it's made up."

"It's all right. I'm excited, *Mamm* and *Daed* will be here soon enough. And my friends will arrive right before Christmas."

"Not long now, is it? I love weddings and seeing the bride's face as she looks into her groom's eyes."

"It's a serious thing, I know. And about Steven, the other day, after we went fishing . . . he and I talked about it, and everything is okay."

"Good. Because," Rochelle said, closing her textbook, "I think it's time to start baking cupcakes. Four hundred will be a lot, you know, and with Christmas coming and finals and my schedule in general, I can't see me baking them within a week of the wedding. I'm planning to freeze them, and on the twenty-sixth, thaw them and then ice."

"*Yah*, it's a *gut* idea." Emma nodded. "*Danke* again."

Enough of studies for tonight. Rochelle put her study materials into a stack.

"I think a cup of tea is in order."

"I'll put the kettle on." Emma scurried into the kitchen.

Rochelle released a quiet sigh. Emma seemed to be back on track. Her choice hadn't been an easy one. Rochelle prayed the young woman had made the right decision.

❧

"Look, it works." Matthew sat astride his bicycle and started pedaling. The motor rumbled to life, and the bicycle shot down the driveway toward the street.

"Great job! Hang on, I'll join you," Silas called out. Matthew turned onto the street, heading toward Bahia Vista, then swung around and headed back for the driveway.

Silas grabbed one of Uncle Tobias's spare bicycles and joined Matthew, who delighted in zooming past his father.

"No fair, I don't have a motor." Silas kept pedaling. He hadn't bicycled in years, but like the old saying, it came right back to him.

They zipped along, waving at other villagers until they made a complete loop around the block, ending up back at Uncle Tobias's house.

Matthew's face glowed. He braked his bicycle and glanced at Silas. "What do you think?"

"I'm impressed."

"The motor kit was easy to put in. Uncle Tobias didn't even have to help me."

"Nope, I sure didn't," Uncle Tobias said as he left the workshop, wiping his hands on a rag. "Did you tell your dad what you've been up to?"

"It's a surprise."

"Oh, a surprise, is it?"

"I've made money from selling bikes I fixed up. I sold two, today."

Tobias nodded. "It was his idea. I hope you don't mind."

"Not at all." He needed to talk to Matthew and to Lena about the job offer. He and Belinda had always discussed things as a family.

He didn't realize how much he still found himself derailed since Belinda's death until he'd sat on the job proposal for almost a week.

Telling Rochelle was like holding up a mirror. He didn't like what he saw.

"You about ready to go, Son?" He tousled Matthew's hair.

"I wanted to have supper with Uncle Tobias and Aunt Fran."

"You know, you three are welcome anytime," Uncle Tobias said.

"Thanks, but we need to have a family meeting after supper."

"We haven't had a family meeting in . . . I don't remember." Matthew hopped off his bicycle. "But I like Aunt Fran's cooking better than yours."

Silas laughed. "Of course you do. How about some Village Pizza? I'll see if Lena can meet us there." Maybe if he plied them— Matthew—with pizza first, it would help him talk to both of them about their future.

"I'll buy the pop," Matthew said. "I have money now."

Silas shook hands with his uncle. "Thank you, again, Uncle Tobias."

"The pleasure is ours. See you tomorrow, Matthew?"

"Tomorrow!" he called out as they headed down the driveway.

Silas paused long enough to call Lena and ask her if Rochelle could drop her off at the pizza shop behind Big Olaf's.

They walked along the street. Silas could have driven from their home, but found walking the neighborhood kept him closer to it, instead of the vehicle separating him from everyone else.

"I've made almost two hundred dollars selling bikes." Matthew nearly strutted beside Silas.

"Two hundred?"

"Uh-huh. So Uncle Tobias let me buy a used motor from him, and I put it on my bicycle to go faster. And now, I've got money I can use to buy more used bikes, and fix them up."

"I didn't know." How had he missed this? Matthew was growing up. Of course he was. Maybe Silas had babied him, just a little, after losing Belinda.

"It's okay, isn't it?"

Of course, it was okay. Silas wasn't so sure he liked being left out. "You did a good thing. But son, don't ever be afraid to tell me about things like this. I never would have thought you'd be interested in anything like this."

"I'm saving up to get a good fishing rod and reel set, like Steven's."

The boy had put down his own roots in Sarasota, or so it sounded. Yet more and more, Silas was leaning toward accepting Ted Kingsley's offer. It meant stability, security. But then, he already had it here . . .

By the time they reached the pizza shop, Lena had arrived and was waiting for them on the patio outside. She held her book bag slung over one shoulder. She was talking to another young Mennonite woman, someone Silas had seen at church but couldn't place her name at the moment.

"Hi, Dad."

The young woman waved at Lena as she left, carrying a pizza box.

"Hi, how was your day?"

"Good. I'm tired. My brain is so full it hurts. I have a lot of study-ing to do tonight."

"So you don't mind having pizza?"

"Of course not." She stood, shifting her backpack to her other shoulder. She gave him a quick glance before they went inside the shop.

"I'll buy the pop, you just tell her what kind you want." Matthew stuck his chin out.

Silas ordered a large pepperoni special and while the young woman behind the counter boxed up the ready pizza, they helped themselves to bottles of pop from the glass-doored refrigerator by the door.

Once they settled at an outdoor table, Lena gave him another glance.

"Dad, is something wrong? I can tell by the look on your face."

"No, but I do have something to tell you both."

"Did someone die? Is it something bad?" Matthew frowned at his bottle of pop.

Lena said nothing, but passed out paper plates and napkins. She opened the pizza box and laid a slice on her plate.

"No, nobody's died. And, I don't think it's something bad, but it's important to me, and for the three of us." He pulled out a slice of pizza, oozing with cheese. "I have a job offer, a permanent one, not charters."

"That's great news, Dad." Lena nodded and took a bite. "You won't have to wonder if the rich family's going to keep hiring you or not. I know you want to go back on the mission field someday, but maybe later . . ."

"We can stay here, forever, if you work for that family?" Matthew asked.

"The job offer did come from Mr. Kingsley, but they don't live here in Florida year-round. They actually live in Connecticut most of the time. So, we'd have to move there."

"Connecticut." Lena frowned. "I'm not sure if I can even spell the word right. What's in Connecticut, anyway? Did you tell him yes?"

"He's giving me until the twenty-third to give him my decision."

"In less than two weeks." Lena sipped her soda. "So, what would this mean for all of us? Because I . . . I don't want to leave Florida. I love it here."

"I do, too. And we'd have to leave Uncle Tobias and Aunt Fran." Matthew scowled. He still hadn't put any pizza on his plate.

"When would we have to go?"

"Sometime not long after New Year's."

"Do we have to go?" Matthew pleaded.

Silas tried not to sigh. He knew this wasn't going to be easy, especially for Matthew.

"Your mother would want us to all be together. I believe we need to stay together." His family wouldn't fall apart. He only had the two of them.

"Dad, please don't take this the wrong way, but I'm going to be twenty next birthday. I'm not a child anymore. I'm raised. When you were gone on flights, I helped Mom a lot in the mission field." Lena's voice shook.

"I did, too." Matthew nodded. "Didn't you tell me I needed to help take care of them for you, when you were gone?"

Yes, he'd told Matthew to be "the man of the house" if he was gone on overnight flights. But, the idea had been figurative at the time.

"Neither of you are ready to be on your own, especially you, Matthew. I don't think you'd live by yourself; it's a ludicrous idea."

"I can live with Aunt Fran and Uncle Tobias. Aunt Fran is always telling me after school how much she loves having me there."

Silas expected resistance, but not this pulling away from him. "I couldn't ask them to let you live with them."

But Lena was right, especially about her. Ever since arriving in Sarasota, he'd seen evidence more and more his daughter wasn't a little girl.

"The world is a cruel, harsh place. It's lost, without God. There are people out there, in this city, and even coming through this neighborhood, who wouldn't think twice about pulling you away from God."

"Dad, I've seen a good piece of the world in college. We talked about college and its worldly distractions back in Ohio, when I told you I wanted to go." Lena shook her head. "I don't think you're as afraid of the world pulling us away from God as you are us growing apart from you."

The truth struck him in the heart.

But what was he going to do about it?

If he stayed here in Sarasota, he'd be passing up an opportunity that didn't come along often in a pilot's career, especially a missionary pilot.

If he left, he'd lose his children. And he'd have nothing left.

21

Rochelle checked the clock on her phone again. Twelve-thirty on the dot. The atmosphere at the Mennonite Tourist Church parking lot was nothing short of electric. Well, as electric as it could be among a cluster of Plain people.

The Ohio bus would be here, and riding in its steel underbelly the latest edition of *The Budget* newspaper, national edition. Hot off the presses from Sugarcreek, the newspaper held all the latest information submitted from scribes throughout the world of the Amish. Even from here in Pinecraft.

"I can't wait to see my *mamm.*" Emma craned her neck to see above a row of Amish men on tricycles, a futile effort since no one had seen the large travel bus yet.

Rochelle nodded. "The last time I spoke to her, she told me how much she was looking forward to coming."

They bumped elbows with a series of older women, some Mennonite and some Old Order, also waiting for the bus.

Arrivals were the most joyous times at the parking lot. Snowbirds came twice a week, sometimes more, and come January, buses would stop every day in the parking lot.

Rochelle smiled. She'd made the journey herself to Ohio last fall by bus for a wedding, and the sensation she felt of coming home as the bus turned onto Bahia Vista nearly overwhelmed her.

"You just never know who's going to step off the bus, do you?" a voice said beside her.

She knew the owner of the voice well. Imogene Brubaker, her trademark camera slung around her neck.

"Imogene, you're so right."

"I wonder how full the bus is. It should be here any moment now."

"Yes. Are you waiting for anyone in particular?"

"No. I'm waiting to see who shows up. It's part of the fun of waiting for the bus, seeing who comes off the bus. Or what." Imogene gave her a pointed look. "I haven't seen you here in a while."

Rochelle nodded. "It's been a while since I've met a bus. I've been busy with work and with classes."

"You need to take a vacation. Slow down, if you can."

"I've . . . I've been thinking of selling my business." This was the first time she'd admitted it aloud since telling Silas on the Atlanta trip.

"Oh?"

"Yes. I suppose I could start advertising or asking around. But then I don't want my clients to worry they won't be served."

"I can help you find someone, if you'd like."

Imogene, somehow, seemed to know everyone in Pinecraft and all the latest news, and knew who was related to whom, and kept it all straight.

"I suppose I'd need to figure out how much to charge. I have my client list, records, my workers, supplies, and tools." Rochelle shook her head. Maybe it would be easier to just close the business. But she had six women who considered working for Rochelle part of their livelihoods.

"Well, I'll start by listening to people, see if some younger snowbird might want to take the business over from you."

"I'm not even sure who to ask. It's not everyone who likes to clean for a living."

"Hiram Mast is a businessman. He might be able to give you some input."

Hiram owned several homes in Pinecraft, as well as a golf shop. The more liberal Mennonite had a good reputation in the village.

"I'd have never thought to ask him. I might call his office and make an appointment. Thanks, Imogene, for the suggestion."

"Not a problem."

A shout rang out. "The bus is here!"

Rochelle looked up to see the mammoth Pioneer Trails travel bus turning off Bahia Vista, then decelerating as the driver steered the bus onto the church parking lot behind the building.

The waiting crowd had made wide berth for the bus to take up the empty space. It halted, with a whoosh of brakes.

There was Leah Graber, waiting with a few of her friends. They made quite the sight in their cape dresses, black shoes, and sensible stockings, with starched white *kapps* gleaming in the sun.

One day, *she could end up like Leah, old and alone in her home.*

Stop it. Look at how happy she is.

Leah smiled at something one of her friends said, then squinted at the bus.

The door swung open.

Step by step, the passengers climbed down the steps, faces lighting expectantly as they surveyed the crowd.

Happy tears flowed as old friends embraced. Rochelle's throat caught.

Comings and goings happened in Pinecraft all winter long, but the reunions were the best part of all.

Her friends would come to Pinecraft over the years, but visits trickled off, and she was left with the year-rounders, most of whom were older.

Had she grown old before her time? Soon enough, she'd be waiting with the old ladies in a row, waiting for friends to climb from the bus. Catching up on news, giving an extra hug and kind word for those who'd lost a spouse.

"*Mamm!*" Emma angled herself around a clustered family and went up to an older woman wearing a navy blue dress and white apron.

She embraced the woman, who responded with a swift hug. Emma's father hung a few steps back, then moved forward to greet his younger daughter. A teenage boy tumbled off the bus behind them. Emma's brother, who had to be about sixteen or so.

A pair of men carrying a square folding table passed by Rochelle. Another man followed with a tall glass jar with a lid. Ah, *The Budget,* reported to contain news of Betsy's upcoming wedding ceremony with Thaddeus Zook.

Judging by Emma's smile, she didn't seem to mind in the least her sister had a publication in *The Budget* and she did not.

Emma had left her order to join the Mennonite church, being baptized there instead. Some districts would have shunned her for the action. Rochelle couldn't imagine the exuberant young woman being cut off from her family altogether.

Only in Pinecraft did it seem to work.

Rochelle joined the trio beside the luggage compartment. "Nora, so good to see you. And you as well, Mr. Yoder."

Emma and Betsy's *mamm* might be Nora to Rochelle, but their *daed* and his serious demeanor would always be Mr. Yoder to her.

"*Danke*, Rochelle Keim. I trust my daughters have behaved themselves with you?"

"Yes, sir, they have." She figured Emma could explain about her job change, or perhaps she already had. "Did you all have a good trip?"

"*Yah*, but it seems to get longer and longer every winter. And, this year . . ." Nora's voice trailed off with a pointed look from Mr. Yoder. He shook his head slowly and said nothing.

"I can hardly wait to see the dresses. I know they must be *wunderbar*."

Mother and daughter continued in German, while Rochelle scanned the crowd. Mr. Yoder headed for the table, where someone had stacked the latest edition of *The Budget*.

A few more passengers left the bus, with reunions to follow.

The driver pulled luggage, suitcases and backpacks, and plastic ice cream buckets containing *kapps* from under the bus.

A young beardless Amish man with auburn hair stood to the side. Someone else was scanning the crowd, like her. She'd seen this young man before . . .

"Emma." Rochelle rasped out her great-niece's name. No one heard it in the chatter and movement of locating luggage.

"Emma." Mr. Yoder returned, carrying a stack of newspapers. "I have the copies of *The Budget* for your sister, and anyone else who would like a copy of the wedding announcement."

" . . . we're baking cupcakes and freezing them ahead of time . . ." Emma's voice trailed off as she saw the auburn-haired young man.

"Eli. Eli Troyer?"

"*Ach, dochder*, you knew he would be coming, sometime this winter." Mr. Yoder's voice was low but firm.

Rochelle drew closer. "Emma, it's all right. I'd like to see the dresses, too. I know your *mamm* has worked hard on them, and I know you all will want to spend time together before the wedding."

She couldn't miss the longing in Eli's expression when he'd set eyes on Emma. Then when he realized she'd seen him gazing at his former fiancée, something like a shadow passed over his eyes.

Eli Troyer stepped over to a row of suitcases, picked up a small-ish rolling suitcase, then called out to a friend who'd stepped off the bus not minutes before.

Emma nodded. "*Yah,* I'll help get your luggage, and we can all head to *Aenti* Sarah's house."

"I have my van, parked just down the street," Rochelle offered.

"*Danke*, Rochelle, but if you don't mind, we'll walk." Nora smiled apologetically. "We've been cooped up for hours and hours on the bus, it will feel *gut* to stretch our legs."

"I'm going to walk with my parents, *Aenti* Chelle."

"Of course." She smiled at Emma. A quick glance toward Eli showed the young man heading off down the street, into the heart of the village.

No, you never knew who'd get off the bus in Pinecraft.

It was Saturday morning, and Silas had no flights and big plans to spend the day in the village with Matthew.

After the tense meal of pizza with Lena and Matthew a few days ago, he wanted to show them both, especially his son, that although things had rapidly changed in their family over the last year or so, the fact they were a family hadn't changed.

Someday, Matthew wouldn't want to spend time with Silas as much anymore. Now with the end of school for Christmas break less than two weeks away, this meant other visitors Matthew's age would be arriving in the village.

"Dad, I told Levi Miller we were going fishing, and he said his father said it was okay if he met up with us, too."

"Ah, does he have a fishing rod and tackle?"

"Yes, he does. He fishes a lot. Someday he wants to have a boat like Steven does."

"Well, sure. I can't guarantee we'll catch anything. It's just Phillippi Creek."

"It doesn't matter, Dad. It's fun enough to reel them in and let them go." Matthew pulled his bicycle from the garage. "Levi's meeting us at nine."

"Good."

Lena still slept, having stayed up late the night before studying, and was due to clean two houses in the afternoon.

"Too bad Lena won't come with us."

"Maybe sometime."

"Maybe."

Silas took his own bicycle from the garage. The gleaming burnt-orange single-speed bicycle was unlike anything he'd ever had before or imagined having. He'd never pictured himself feeling enthusiastic over having a bicycle, but there it was. Also, Matthew had given it to him, saying he'd bought it from Uncle Tobias, then fixed it up and repainted it.

"How's your bike, Dad?"

"Runs great. All it needs is a motor like yours."

"Yes, so you can catch up with me." Matthew laughed, then zoomed off down the street. "Race you there!"

"Watch for the light," Silas called out after him, shaking his head. He pedaled hard to keep up with his son. He found a chuckle coming out and let it go.

Silas caught up with Matthew at the light, and they continued between Big Olaf's and Yoder's and continued on their way to the park.

They waved to a pair of older men, chatting on a front porch, then whizzed by a young couple, strolling hand in hand, a brave display of public affection not often seen other places.

The basketball and shuffleboard courts came into view, but they passed those and continued along the side street, rounded the parking lot, and found a place to chain their bicycles in view of the creek.

"Levi should be here soon," Matthew said as he padlocked his bicycle. A few bicycles had come up missing—stolen—and one couldn't be too careful, especially with a motorized bicycle.

Voices drifted on the morning breeze. The bocce players, one of whom was Uncle Tobias, were already at it with the day's round of matches, distances measured with a tape measure to the inch.

They cast off their lines. Silas had no idea if they'd catch much of anything.

Not ten yards away, an elderly African American woman wearing a big floppy hat sat with her own fishing line in the water.

The sight transported him back to the work he and Belinda had done overseas, him piloting itinerant doctors and aid workers to remote villages, helping the people with water supply and medicine, Belinda helping local women start their own textile businesses to break the cycle of poverty.

The woman smiled at him, her grin bright. "Got some nibbles this morning, but nothing biting. But you never can tell."

"We're hoping we get something," he replied to her. "Or we make a trip to the fish market before supper."

She then leaned back and laughed, the brim of her hat flopping. "What a surefire way to make a catch."

"What are you using for bait?"

"Worms. Sometimes I use crawfish or minnows, when I can afford 'em. I got worms today."

A young man arrived by bicycle. "Matt."

"Levi, you made it." Matthew beamed. "We've just cast our lines. Nothing yet."

Just then, Silas felt a tug on his fishing rod. It could be the current, or something else. Like a log.

He pulled hard, and the something pulled back.

"You got something, Dad!"

"Yes, I can feel it." He cranked the handle to the reel. The fishing rod bowed. He reeled more.

A fish leapt into the air, gave an odd wiggle, then released from the line. Silas's pole snapped straight again.

"Lost it."

They continued in the same manner for a while, with Levi having an elusive fish, and their bait supplies dwindled. Silas also gave some bait to the older woman fishing nearby.

"Silas!" Uncle Tobias approached.

He'd never seen the man walk so briskly or in such a straight line. "Yes, Uncle Tobias?"

"It's Fran. She called me, not a moment ago. Lena's trying to reach you."

"I left my phone at the house."

"She's having some bad stomach pains. Fran went over to your place to check on her. She was upchucking and running a high fever. Wouldn't let Fran touch her stomach."

"I need to get home."

"What's wrong with her?" Matthew asked.

"Not sure." Silas had his suspicions.

"Go, be with her. I'll stay with the boys. Might even catch a few fish myself."

"Thank you, Uncle Tobias."

Silas hopped on his bicycle and sped back toward the house. Good thing they'd decided to bicycle instead of walk.

Lord God, touch my daughter, in Your mercy.

Helplessness had never been part of his vocabulary. Another time he'd felt so helpless; no, two times. Years ago, with the attack on John, and when hearing the news about Belinda . . .

He arrived home quickly enough, zipping around Fran's vehicle and stopping at the garage. He let the bike lean against the garage door and ran to the front door.

Aunt Fran opened the door. "Good, Tobias reached you."

"Dad!" Lena called out from where she lay on the sofa.

"Is anything helping?"

"No, it's not. I tried a heating pad, and some aspirin, but nothing's helping."

"We're going to the ER."

Lena didn't argue with him. She swung her legs over to the floor and tried sitting up, gasping with pain as she did so. "I think I can do it."

Silas and Fran helped her to her feet.

"We'll take my car. I'm blocking you," Aunt Fran said. "I'll call Pastor to get the prayer group on this, too."

"Yes, please."

They continued outside to Aunt Fran's vehicle, where Silas settled Lena in the back seat.

"Can you sit up?"

She nodded. "It hurts, but I can do it."

"We'll be there soon." As long as the traffic cooperates.

"I'll go as fast as I can, dear," Aunt Fran said to the rearview mirror.

Silas wondered if he ought to commandeer the driver's seat. "Aunt Fran, if you need me to drive . . ."

"No, I've got it." With a squeal of tires, she backed out onto the street. Then she shifted, and the car shot forward.

Lena moaned. "Oh, it hurts. It hurts so bad."

"Pull over, Aunt Fran. Call an ambulance."

22

Rochelle slid the first two pans of cupcakes into the oven just as her phone rang. She'd planned to bake four dozen cupcakes this morning, then visit her one Saturday cleaning client before spending the evening studying for exams.

She closed the oven door and went for the phone. Lena.

"Good morning, Lena."

"This is Silas."

"Oh, good morning."

"I'm sorry about the short notice, but Lena won't be able to take care of her clients this afternoon. I'm with her at the emergency room right now."

Emergency room? Rochelle sank onto the nearest kitchen chair.

"Tell her not to worry about them; I'll work it out. What's wrong?"

"I think it's appendicitis. She's getting examined now. They mentioned getting a CAT scan before doing surgery . . ."

"Okay. Do you need anything else? I'll make sure her clients are covered."

"No, I don't think so. But she wanted me to call you first."

"What a sweetie. Tell her thank you, and I'm praying for her."

"I will. And thanks for praying."

She made a call to one of her other cleaners who said she'd be glad to take today's clients, as Christmas was drawing closer and she could use the extra money.

Rochelle wanted to pack a bag and head to the emergency room. But it wasn't her place, and no one seemed to know if or when Lena would need surgery. Maybe it wasn't appendicitis at all.

Maybe Rochelle merely had the fidgets and wanted to distract herself from her thoughts by thinking about someone else. She took out another cake mix, then washed the mixing bowl and beaters, the sound of the running faucet loud in her ears.

The house felt still and quiet otherwise, with only her inside. Much like it had years ago, in the beginning. Some had questioned the wisdom of a young woman purchasing a three-bedroom house, but she'd been able to provide a place to stay for a trickle of extended family members throughout the years.

Everyone loved family who owned a house in Florida.

The timer! She'd forgotten to set it. She went over to the microwave, guessed at how much longer the cupcakes needed to bake, then punched in the numbers.

Rochelle pulled out her calendar. One more week, then finals. She'd already selected her classes for next semester. Only two this time. Then clinicals and exams next fall, and then, Lord willing, she'd be an RN.

After this semester, she'd realized how her heart truly wasn't in cleaning anymore.

Right now especially, her heart was at Sarasota Hospital. She was with Silas, waiting to hear news about Lena. He'd welcome her there if she showed up. Ever since Thanksgiving and their walk and talk, he hadn't been far from her mind.

She planned out her week ahead, and the following week, after which came Christmas week, the busiest in Pinecraft.

When the timer beeped, Rochelle knew exactly what she'd do.

She'd let these cupcakes cool, then visit her client early, and head to the hospital. She likely wouldn't be the only one there lending support.

Whatever came next, she had no idea.

❧

Not quite two hours later, she found her way into the emergency room, where Silas sat. He had a bottle of soda and half-eaten bag of chips on the end table. His face brightened when he saw her. His Aunt Fran stood, wearing a smile of her own.

"Oh, good, you're here," Frances Fry said. She gave Rochelle a warm hug. "I was hoping he'd ask you to come. Lena will be glad to know you're here, too."

Rochelle gave Silas a glance. "I . . . felt like I should be here."

"I'm glad you're here. Lena's getting a CAT scan now. They . . . they had a backlog of people waiting at Radiology."

"It's going to be all right, Silas." Frances moved back to the seat beside him, and then paused. "Here, Rochelle, take my seat. I . . . I need to head home, but I'll be back soon with Tobias and Matthew."

"Thanks," Silas said. "Thanks for taking me."

"No problem at all." Frances smiled. "It's what family is for. Now, I'll be back, lickety-split. Call, call, *call* me when you know something more."

Silas nodded, and Rochelle settled onto the cushioned chair, which shared an armrest with Silas's chair. He sat back and faced her.

"You didn't have to come. I know you have a lot to do . . . but I'm glad you did." He reached for her hand again. Another flashback of his warm strength, of walks on Ohio country roads. Then the present came into focus as she stared at their hands, older now.

"I wanted to be here for you and Lena."

A young medical assistant in blue scrubs emerged from a locked set of double doors. "Fry?"

"Here." Silas stood, pulling Rochelle along with him.

They met the young man at the doors. "Come on back. Your daughter's back in the examination bay."

Still holding his hand, Rochelle went, too, her heart thudding all the way.

The medical assistant pulled back a curtain. "Your parents are here."

Rochelle wanted to correct the man, but now wasn't the time. "Hey, Lena."

Lena smiled, her face pale. "Rochelle . . . you're here. I'm so glad. And Dad . . ."

"The doctor will come in a few minutes and go over the CT results with you."

"Thank you." Silas released Rochelle's hand and drew closer to his daughter's bedside. "How are you feeling?"

"I still hurt. They gave me something for nausea, so I feel a little woozy." Lena closed her eyes, and sighed. "I need to study. I have exams coming up."

"Worry about it later."

The curtain slid back and the doctor came in, carrying a folder. "I have the CT results back, Lena. You have a severely inflamed appendix, and it needs to come out."

"I suspected as much," said Silas.

"Someone will come by with consent forms, and your family is welcome to stay here with you until we take you to the OR."

"Okay." Lena's voice came out as a whisper. She glanced from Silas to Rochelle.

"The procedure is laparoscopic, so all you'll have are three small holes in your abdomen to heal up from. We'll discharge you home tomorrow, if all goes well."

"If all goes well . . ." Lena repeated.

The doctor left with more reassurances.

"These kinds of operations are routine," Rochelle said after the doctor had pulled the curtain closed and left them alone. "Technology is amazing. Years ago, you would have ended up with a long incision on your side, and weeks and weeks of recovery time."

"I've never had surgery before. I had stitches once, but it doesn't count."

"Why did you need stitches?" Maybe she could help distract Lena. Silas released Lena's hand, then sank onto a nearby chair beside the heart monitor.

"I fell. I was running after Matthew in the kitchen, while I was carrying a glass. Who knows what he'd done. Anyway, I dropped the glass, then fell. On the glass."

"Ouch." Rochelle shook her head.

"Yes, ouch." Silas half chuckled. "You screamed like someone was trying to tear your leg off."

"I was ten and dramatic." Lena laughed, then sucked in a breath. "Ow. You're both trying to distract me."

Rochelle darted a look at Silas. "Of course we are."

The curtain moved, and Marvin, their pastor, entered the emergency room bay. Excellent timing. Rochelle stepped aside to allow him a place beside Lena.

Silas moved closer and whispered to her. "I'm glad you're here."

And so was she.

⚘

Instead of pacing in the surgical waiting room after Lena had been taken back for surgery, Silas suggested they walk in the outdoor atrium. Fresh air and quiet. Time to pray and wait. Wait and pray. He held the light-up pager the woman at the desk had given him. Instead of calling his name, they'd use the pager to signal him if needed.

Pastor Marvin had led a simple yet heartfelt prayer. Silas could sense Lena relaxing during the prayer, her features appearing less tense. He'd apologized for leaving, but was also visiting another church member who'd had surgery the day before.

Today, the breeze warmed Silas's skin, the sun a reminder of why people flocked here every winter and some stayed. Like Rochelle, beside him.

He squeezed her hand, not caring if anyone saw.

"You like holding my hand." She grinned, and a dimple he hadn't seen in years bloomed in her cheek, then faded.

"It's been a long time. I'd forgotten . . ." He stopped himself. He hadn't exactly forgotten. He'd merely chosen not to remember.

"So, have you come any closer to deciding about the job offer?"

"I don't think I'm going to take it. My life is here now. My family might not think they need me. Despite Matthew's protests and Lena's nose in her studies most of the time, I'm going to stay around. There will be other opportunities."

"What about the mission field?"

They'd once had the same dream, yet Belinda had been the one to experience it with him.

He shrugged. "Maybe I'll be out there again, someday." But it wouldn't be the same, going it alone.

"I'm thinking of applying to the Overland Missions group. They need nurses, and I'm ready for a change."

To ask if she'd consider going with him would be to presume much, much more about their relationship, such as it was at this point.

Friends, and yet something more. Yet not a couple.

They continued along the brick walkway, covered with names of donors to the hospital. He led her to a secluded bench in the corner.

"I wonder how much longer it's going to take," she said as they sat down. "It's been, what, forty minutes or so now?"

"I think so." He tucked the pager into his pocket and settled onto the bench as close to Rochelle as he dared. Lena lay in an operating room, somewhere in the hospital, and right now all he could think of was Rochelle being near to him.

He'd been immature, years ago. She'd been wounded, grieving.

"Rochelle, may I kiss you?"

She leaned closer, turning her face toward him, and her eyelids fluttered closed.

He kissed her swiftly, not allowing himself to give her the kind of kiss he wanted to. When he opened his eyes, red shot to Rochelle's cheeks, and her gaze slid toward the brick pathway.

The pager then began to buzz.

"The surgery must be over." Rochelle scrambled to her feet.

They hurried back to the surgery desk and the receptionist.

"Mr. Fry." The woman stood, handing him the phone. "The surgical nurse needs to speak to you."

He glanced at Rochelle as he took the phone and set the pager on the counter. She frowned. If the surgery was over already, why hadn't the receptionist said so?

"This is Cynthia, the head nurse on your daughter's case. The surgeon is converting Lena's procedure to an open operation."

"Open operation?"

"Her appendix is too inflamed to remove laparoscopically," the nurse explained. "He doesn't want to risk rupturing her appendix on removal. So the procedure will take longer than planned. But he wanted me to let you know instead of keeping you waiting in the dark."

"I . . . I understand."

"What's your blood type, Mr. Fry, in the event your daughter needs blood products?"

"It's AB." Blood products?

"Thank you. We ask, just in case. You sit tight, and we'll have her in the recovery room as soon as we can. I'll let you know when he's finished closing her up."

"Thank you." He shook his head as he handed the phone back to the receptionist. "Could you reset the pager for me, please?"

After the receptionist reset the pager, he moved to the nearest set of chairs.

"What is it?" Rochelle touched his arm.

"It's going to take longer." He explained, and Rochelle sighed.

"We'll keep praying."

Another thirty minutes—how long could it take to make a bigger incision, anyway?—and the pager buzzed again.

Cynthia the nurse had called, this time with news making Silas's stomach curl over on itself.

"It's worse than we thought. Your daughter is anemic, and she's lost a lot of blood during this procedure. We're out of her blood type in the blood bank, and she's going to need a transfusion after all is said and done. We've put out a call for her blood type, because hers is O-negative and rare."

He didn't know much about blood types, but he knew even his own blood probably wouldn't help Lena.

"Is it because I'm not her biological father that I can't donate?"

"No, sir. She can only receive O-negative blood."

At Silas's words, Rochelle backpedaled and nearly stumbled over the chair.

All these years, it had never seemed to matter. Not to him, not to Belinda. And Rochelle knew . . . didn't she?

The nurse kept talking about screening his blood anyway, and if there were other family members or friends who might have O-negative blood, but he heard little of it.

"I'll . . . I'll ask around." He hung up the phone and turned to Rochelle. "I thought . . ."

23

$\mathcal{N}$ot now, Silas." Rochelle shook her head as she caught her balance. "Not now. I don't want to hear. Take care of Lena. She's what matters right now."

"But, we need to talk. I thought Belinda—"

"I'm going to get a coffee." She turned and left the waiting area and found her way to the main hospital corridor.

Silas and Belinda had let them all believe Lena was their child.

She well remembered the feeling when she heard, years ago, that Belinda had given birth to a little girl seven months after the wedding. No one said much about Lena coming early, but murmurs mentioned a "honeymoon baby."

Lena was John's child.

The realization tumbled into her head as the circumstances added up.

Did Lena know?

She referred to Silas as her father, and their interaction seemed natural, loving, like a father loves his daughter.

Rochelle recalled her own words to Vera, about love always believing the best of someone.

She would stay out of it. She'd help Lena, but as far as whatever she thought she and Silas had, she wasn't so sure it was meant to be.

He and Belinda had, in a sense, lied. Never denying his paternity, because nobody talked about such things, but they'd allowed people to believe Lena was his. Or, likely people knew, but didn't say anything except in private, behind closed doors. She'd been in Florida then, was working for Leah and building a life away from Ohio.

Rochelle shoved the knowledge into a corner of her mind and out of the way. She followed the signs to the cafeteria, purchased a coffee, and went to a quiet corner table.

It shouldn't matter.

The identity of Lena's father didn't change anything.

The young woman still needed a blood transfusion.

Silas still needed his family and friends to support him.

And Rochelle still loved him.

But surely Belinda would have told her, about the baby . . .

Except, after John's death many of those days and weeks were a blur, except for the final good-byes Rochelle had said to Belinda and Silas.

She kept her focus on the foam cup with its steaming brew in front of her.

The current circumstances almost made her laugh. This morning, her greatest source of stress had been getting four dozen cupcakes baked and cooled before going to see her cleaning clients.

She glanced up to see Silas approaching, then looked down again.

He took the chair across from her. "I talked to Aunt Fran, asked her to get the word out in the village to see if anyone might help. I'm not sure if any will."

"Or can. We don't seem to keep up on things like blood types, especially the Old Order folks." Certain aspects of medical treatments were still looked at as borderline heresy by some.

"I want to explain, about Lena."

"You don't have to." She took a sip of coffee. "I figured it out. You did a kind and selfless thing, stepping in on John's behalf, all those years ago."

"It wasn't an easy choice."

"No, I'm sure it wasn't." She reminded herself they were in a public place, and she had no business speaking to a man—married or otherwise—about someone else's indiscretion, or any indiscretion.

"I know you tried to be there for Belinda after she lost John."

"I did. But she pushed me away. So, I decided to wait until she was ready to talk to me."

"She told me you were pushing her."

Rochelle gave him a sharp look. "My best friend in the whole world was locking herself away from everyone. I couldn't let her do it. She needed to get out there, even if she didn't feel like it. I knew I'd done the same thing after losing Momma."

Silas shook his head. "Who were you to say she needed to? How did you know the time was right for her?"

Not much got Rochelle riled up. She couldn't remember the last time she'd been so frustrated, besides the time recently when Emma slacked off on cleaning Mrs. Gentile's house.

"If you don't recall, I lost my mother not three months before we lost John. I was still deep in grief. But I knew I couldn't stop going. I had to keep going, in spite of the changes I didn't want." She didn't add about her father selling the house, and her feeling uprooted from everything she'd known.

"I remember. I was there, too. But everybody grieves differently."

She felt a pang of guilt for unleashing on him like this, but didn't back off. "It might be true, but I won't apologize for loving my friend and trying to be there for her. Everyone figures after the funeral, life goes on. People forget quickly."

Silas quirked a slight smile at her. "Don't apologize. You were always the strong one. Belinda never seemed strong, not like you were, anyway. Oh, she was strong enough on the mission field. I knew . . . I knew going into our relationship, such as it was, part of her would always love John."

Rochelle nodded. But Silas had given up on her, on them.

Of course he had. She'd pushed him away.

Part of her wanted to look at this from the perspective of an outsider. This was ancient history and should have no bearing on the present. Stop living in the past, people liked to say.

The infernal pager began buzzing again.

"Her surgery should be over. They said this next page should be it." Silas picked up the pager and stood. "Will you come with me?"

She shook her head. "I'll . . . I'll give you two some time." She struggled with her unspoken question. "Does Lena . . . does she . . ."

"Does she know?" He nodded. "Belinda told her, when she was young. She knows about John. Hasn't spoken about him in years. But, she knows."

"Good."

⁓ℰ℈⁓

Light filtered through the blinds of Lena's hospital room. Silas stood at Lena's bedside. A soft beeping monitored her vital signs.

Aunt Fran and Uncle Tobias had arrived, along with Matthew and their pastor and his wife. The room felt snug with all the people, but no one shooed them away.

Lena's eyes fluttered open. "Dad . . . I . . ." She moved slightly. "Ow. How did the surgery go?"

"It went. They had to open you up more than planned at first, but they say you're doing well now." He wouldn't mention about the blood-level scare, not just yet.

"I feel like my head's floating." Her words came out in a soft, low tone.

"The nurse said it's the anesthesia." She'd been out cold, or so he assumed, when he first entered her hospital room and the nurses were getting her settled. The head nurse had given Silas the latest update and said someone would be by to try Lena on some pudding for supper.

"Did . . . did you talk to Rochelle, about my clients?"

"I did, and she made sure they were taken care of."

"Good." She glanced at Matthew. "Hey there. Did you catch a lot of fish this morning?"

"A few." Matthew hung back. "We had a lot of bites, though. Levi met us there." For all he'd seen as a youngster overseas, they hadn't spent much time in hospitals, especially where their own health matters were concerned.

"Sounds fun."

"We wanted to check on Lena, and pray with all of you," said Pastor Marvin.

"Thank you," Silas said. He realized again the infinite weariness a sudden crisis brought on. Or, maybe it was this kind of a crisis. He'd had other things come up when in the field. But it felt a lot different when trouble circled close to home.

The last time he'd been in a hospital was the night Belinda died. She was one of the few who'd survived the collision initially, but all attempts to stabilize her upon arrival at the hospital failed. He didn't like hospitals much.

But here, with his closest family and pastor assembled in the room with Lena, this hospital was a place of healing. And for it, he thanked God.

"Let us pray," Pastor Marvin said, as they bowed their heads. "Our Heavenly Father, we come to you with thanks and praise for Lena, for guiding the surgeon's hands, and giving doctors the skills and wisdom to treat her. Give Lena, Silas, and Matthew peace as she heals, and we continue to trust our lives to Your care. Amen."

"Amen." The only one missing right now was Rochelle. He should have insisted she join them, to not worry about giving them space.

Aunt Frances spoke up first. "When you're ready, come to the house and get something to eat. Unless you plan to eat here?"

"Go ahead, Dad. You don't have to stay here with me. I'm tired, I won't be good company."

"I'll stay for a while." His cleared his throat. "We were worried, earlier."

"I'm sorry I've ruined everyone's day."

"No, you didn't. Not at all."

"I still got to go fishing," Matthew said. "Next time, I want you to come, too."

"I just might." Lena's eyes opened wider. "My exams. I have exams coming up. Can I go back to class this week?"

"One thing at a time." Silas touched Lena's forehead. "For the rest of the day today, you need to focus on getting better."

"I know." She tried to reach for the container of ice water with a straw on the tray table.

"Here." Silas picked it up and handed it to her. From the time she took her first toddling steps, she would always tell him and Belinda, "I can do it myself."

"Son, how are you going to get home?" Uncle Tobias asked.

"Ah, I hadn't thought about it." Which, he hadn't. He could stay here tonight. But already, Lena's eyelids drooped as she sipped her water.

"We can wait for you. We don't mind."

"We have room to give Matthew and Frances a ride home, if need be," Pastor said.

"Thank you, Pastor." Aunt Frances drew closer to Lena. "If you need anything, I'll be here lickety-split, and then first thing in the morning."

24

Rochelle prepared a casserole to take over to the Frys', a chicken casserole recipe passed around the family, and one of *Aenti* Sarah's specialties. Silas probably wouldn't cook, and she didn't blame him.

His refrigerator would likely brim with the help of the neighborhood. Anytime a need or crisis came up, the villagers would pitch in.

She'd already offered to give Lena any help she needed in preparing for exams. The young woman had come home from the hospital on Sunday afternoon and was comfortably propped up on pillows in the living room.

Rochelle tucked the still-warm casserole into an insulated bag, then carried it out to her bicycle. The casserole took up most of the basket.

As she headed off across the village, she zigzagged on her bicycle through the streets on her way to the Frys.

A cluster of villagers stood on Leah Graber's porch. A familiar face caught her eye and the person flagged her down.

"Rochelle Keim." Imogene Brubaker motioned for Rochelle to stop.

Good thing she'd tucked the casserole into the insulated carrier. She pedaled up the driveway and stopped behind the closest tricycle.

"Hi, Imogene." She looked past Imogene's shoulder at the group on the porch. "What happened?"

"Leah . . . Leah Graber passed away this morning."

"Oh no . . . I saw her, recently, waiting for the bus, the same day I saw you." Rochelle placed her hand on her chest. "I didn't know she'd been ill." The woman wasn't one of the younger retirees in Pinecraft. She'd been in her sixties, at least, when Rochelle first moved to the village.

"I don't know either, but evidently she passed sometime in her sleep."

Rochelle walked with Imogene to the porch. A woman she recognized as one of Leah's daughters already wore her Sunday best, as did a few of the others.

"Rochelle, is it?" The woman approached her. "You used to work for my mother."

"You're right. Rochelle Keim. And yes, your mother taught me everything I know about running a cleaning business."

"She . . . she thought a lot of you." Her blue eyes glimmered with tears. "Matter of fact, at Thanksgiving she mentioned you came to see her."

Rochelle nodded. "Yes. I'd been busy and been meaning to stop by. I'm glad I made the time."

"Well, as I said, she always thought a lot of you. Thank you for remembering her. People get so busy now." She took a tissue from her pocket and dabbed at her eyes. "It happens to all of us. We try to remember to visit with each other as often as we can."

"I'm sorry. I know you'll miss her."

"She lived a long, full life." She glanced toward the front door. "I'm not sure what we'll do with the house. We don't live here year-round."

"You could always rent it out."

"Maybe. My grandfather built this home. It's one of the oldest in the village. It would be a shame not to keep it in the family."

"I hope you can. It's a sweet house. And I like the parrots in the backyard." Rochelle smiled at the memory.

"Well, one thing at a time, I suppose. Thank you again for stopping."

"Of course. I'll be praying for your family."

Rochelle left and continued on her way. So it went with Pinecraft. Although Leah Graber had gone on to her eternal reward, she would be deeply missed by those still here on the earthly shores.

Rochelle pedaled along toward the Frys' rental home and the sound of a horse's neigh behind her nearly jolted her off her bicycle.

Tobias Fry grinned from the front seat of his horseless buggy, where Fran sat beside him. "Good afternoon, Rochelle."

She had to chuckle at their amusement. "Hello there."

"You heading to visit our great-niece and family?"

"I most certainly am."

"Race you there?"

"Ha. You'll leave me in the dust."

"See you there!" With another blast from the neighing horse horn, Tobias and Frances shot past her.

The sound made her smile again. She wasn't sure who took more joy in the village, the young children visiting and seeing the beach for the first time, or the older men like Tobias, tinkering with the vehicles and gizmos others in the Plain world could only dream about.

A few minutes more and she arrived at the Frys' and found a spot to padlock her bicycle in the carport. The side door leading to the kitchen was open to the carport, and laughter drifted outside.

". . . so good to be home, even though I was only gone for one night," Rochelle heard Lena saying as she carried the casserole to the side door.

"Come on in, Rochelle, we're sort of spread out here between the kitchen and the living room," Frances said. "Oh, sorry, Silas. It's not my house."

"No worries, Aunt Fran. I don't mind."

Rochelle pulled the screen door open and stepped inside, balancing the casserole on one arm. "I know you probably have gobs of food, but I wanted to make something."

"Thanks," Silas said, leading the way to the counter. "You can put it here. Smells delicious."

"One of *Aenti* Sarah's recipes," she explained.

"Well, we were just popping by to say hello and see Lena, but Tobias needs to get back to the shop." Frances plucked at her husband's elbow.

"I do?"

"Yes. You do." She gave him a look, at which Rochelle tried not to chuckle. She'd hoped the elder Frys would stay as a sort of buffer between her and Silas.

She still hadn't quite processed the shock over learning about Lena's true father. But then, she'd always seen Belinda in Lena. But not Silas. Not that it mattered. Yet, no matter how much anyone said the past didn't have a bearing on the present, sometimes it did.

The couple said another good-bye to Lena before heading out.

Rochelle went to the living room and smiled at Lena. "How are you?"

"I'm sore, but I'm glad to be home." She shifted on the couch and adjusted the crocheted afghan covering her.

"I know you're probably thinking about finals, so if you need me to pick up any work from your professors, I don't mind."

"Thanks." Lena glanced from her father, to Rochelle, then back to her father again.

Silas cleared his throat. "Ah, I need to make a phone call. The airport manager called about a possible flight. I'll be right back."

Rochelle didn't want to sigh with relief, but instead took a seat on the nearest chair. "I've found someone to take your clients until you can go back. Vera Byler's daughter, Patience, was looking for work."

"Good." Lena glanced past Rochelle toward the kitchen. "So, what's going on with you and my dad?"

"Um, what exactly do you mean by 'going on'?"

"I know he cares for you. I know you and he were . . . together before he and my mother married. But there's something now, something new between you."

"It's . . . it's something we need to work through. Or, I do." She wasn't about to tell Lena it involved her. Kids often paid for their parents' actions. Not always. But this didn't seem to affect Lena.

"Well, I hope you do. I haven't seen him this happy since before my mother passed away."

But they weren't "together," were they?

"I'm just glad they found a donor for your blood transfusion."

"I knew they had to do a transfusion. But a donor?" Lena wore a quizzical expression.

Silas entered the room at that moment, and Rochelle sucked in a breath.

"What are you talking about?" he asked, glancing at Rochelle.

"Dad, why did I need a blood donor? Why couldn't you donate blood for me? We studied this in Intro to Hematology. You're my dad, you can be a donor . . ."

<hr />

"My blood type isn't compatible with yours. I'm AB. I couldn't father a child with O-negative blood." Silas clenched his jaw. Lena seemed as if she didn't know. But Belinda had told him, long ago, she'd told Lena.

"But . . . but that means . . . how can you *not* be my father?" Lena turned pale. "But you've . . . you've always been here, for as long as I can remember."

Silas paced the room, then stopped, sitting gently on the end of the couch. "Your father was my best friend, and his name was John Hershberger. He died before you were born."

Lena shook her head. "No . . . no."

Rochelle shot Silas a look. "You told me Belinda talked to her, and she knew. All I did was mention the transfusion, and—"

"You shouldn't have said anything."

"Someone *not* saying anything all those years ago is the reason we're in this situation right now." She turned her attention to Lena. "Oh, Lena . . ."

"Leave me alone. Please." Tears streamed down Lena's cheeks. "Just please, leave me alone."

Silas continued. She had to know about John. Why hadn't Belinda said something? "I don't know why your mother didn't say anything. She . . . told me she had. I was gone, for almost a week, when you were six. I told her before I left on my flight, you needed to know. You were old enough to know the kind of man your father was and how honored I was to step in when he couldn't."

"I thought . . . I thought you loved my mother."

"I did."

Rochelle stood. "I'm sorry. I should go." She moved to the kitchen with Silas on her heels.

"Rochelle."

She stopped at the kitchen table. "I tried to help. I was only making conversation. I'm sorry."

"You didn't mean for this to happen."

"Of course not." And then, the dam she'd used to hold back everything over the years broke.

He pulled her into his arms. "It's not your fault. It's Belinda's. She told me she'd talked to her. I should have been there. Should have insisted we did this as a family. But the moment I got back from my trip, Lena came and hugged me, told me how happy she was God had given me to her as a daddy and I'd come home safe. How was I supposed to know Belinda didn't talk to her?"

She leaned against him, and he allowed himself to touch her hair, the silken strands pulled back into a bun and covered. Just then, he knew beyond a doubt he loved her. Maybe he always had and he'd locked it away into a corner of his heart and made himself forget.

All because of their stubbornness and youth.

Maybe now their youth was gone and in spite of the stubbornness remaining, they could build on the foundation of their old love, something he'd buried long ago.

Rochelle said nothing, but kept her face buried in his shirt. He kissed the top of her head.

Then he pulled back and kissed her firmly on the lips. Her arms tightened around him as she responded.

"Stop." Rochelle wiggled away and took a few steps. "I need to go. I . . . I need to go."

25

*E*mma and Betsy chattered away in German with their mother, while Frances knelt at Rochelle's hem. The five of them filled Frances's sewing room.

"I love the shade of blue." Rochelle had slipped the dress on and the texture of the fabric felt terribly fancy, even for her. She knew the girls must think the cloth extravagant.

How did the dresses, especially Betsy's, pass muster for the weddings? Not so much Emma's, whose Mennonite ceremony was a few shades less plain than Betsy's. But Betsy, belonging to the Old Order Church, had certainly taken a few risks with the pleats and trim on her wedding dress.

Nora Yoder nodded at something one of them said.

Rochelle's German, patchy at best, enabled her to understand *dress* and something about changes needing to be made.

Betsy nodded. Emma frowned.

"The new bishop," Nora said, raising her hands. "It's a bit more difficult now, knowing the expectations."

Rochelle liked being Plain, but didn't see the harm in a few pleats and a ruffled row. Pride could surface in many other ways besides a person's clothing.

"So what will you do?" Rochelle asked.

Nora shrugged. "Make the changes to the dress."

"It's not fair. It's only one day, only one dress—Betsy's." Emma shook her head.

"It's the way it's done at home. You know this, *dochder*."

"Well, knowing it doesn't mean I have to like it."

"Changing my dress a little bit doesn't matter much to me." Betsy smiled, staring out the window. "I'm marrying Thaddeus, at last. Our marriage is a miracle for which I'm thankful."

Emma fell silent.

"I think it's a beautiful miracle," Rochelle said. "And to have the weddings Christmas week is perfect. Everyone, or almost everyone, will be here in the village anyway."

"Hold still, and I'll get your hem tacked up so I can finish it." Fran fastened the last pin. "There. This should do it. I'll have this hemmed in no time."

"Thanks, Fran."

"Lena was asking about you yesterday." Fran glanced upward.

"How is she doing? I haven't been by since . . . since the day she got home from the hospital." Not quite a week, and Lena already had her exams straightened out. She wouldn't return until the spring semester and would take her exams remotely in the comfort of her home, with their pastor's wife, Bea, serving as proctor.

"Sore, but getting around a little more every day."

She wanted to ask about Silas, but didn't. She missed him. Somehow, after the fiasco of Lena finding out about John, Rochelle had found plenty of reasons to stay out of the picture. It still stung when she recalled her role in the fiasco.

"Okay, step down. Betsy's turn now." Frances waved Rochelle off the low stool. "Never mind, Betsy. I just need to see your sleeves to take out the ribbon pleats."

Betsy moved to where Rochelle had once stood.

"I'll get changed." The sooner she got done here, the sooner she could continue studying for her final exam. One more, and the semester would be over.

Rochelle picked up her day dress from a nearby chair and headed for the Frys' bathroom. Oh, how she missed Silas. She missed Lena and Matthew. She forced them from her mind, for now. Time would come when she couldn't avoid them. They'd be in church on Sunday, occupying the same row as usual. As would she.

Rochelle put her dress back on, taking care not to rumple the dress she'd wear for the upcoming wedding. Next week, already. But so much to do in the meantime, and clients with extra requests for cleaning before their own company rolled into town.

One thing at a time, she reminded herself as she left the bathroom. She entered the sewing room to see Fran pinning up the hem of Emma's dress.

"Eli Troyer was out and about with his family," Nora said.

"Well, he hasn't spoken to me, and I am relieved he hasn't." Emma stuck her chin out.

"He moped for months. Finally seemed to snap out of whatever it was when he began walking home with Miriam's younger sister."

Emma darted a glance at her mother. "Hannah? Why, she's not old enough to go to youth group."

"Why, yes, she is." Nora's voice held a singsong tone. "I'm happy for both of them."

"Well, I am, too."

Rochelle wasn't quite certain she believed Emma. Did she see a flicker of jealousy? But then, Emma had broken things off with Eli last winter. Rochelle had been there for the rocky road after Emma essentially left her Order and joined the Mennonite church.

She herself knew the taste of jealousy, especially when she'd heard of Silas and Belinda's wedding.

But she'd pushed Silas away while her friendship with Belinda had crumbled in their mutual grief.

"Fran, I need to leave now. Thank you for your help with the hem."

"Of course. I'll bring the dress with me on Sunday."

"I'll see you then."

"Bye, *Aenti* Chelle." Betsy, still wearing her starry-eyed expression, came out of her reverie enough to tell her good-bye.

Nora followed Rochelle into the hallway. "Rochelle, could I have a moment?"

"Yes. What is it?"

The older woman frowned. "I'm worried, about Emma. Not so much Betsy, but Emma. Since we've been here, I've noticed how much she has changed. And with the new bishop, her father and I feel . . . pressured."

"How so?"

"Ah, I don't want to pull you into it. I'm afraid her father and I will have consequences for these weddings."

"Doesn't your bishop understand your family has spent months planning this day for Betsy and Emma?"

"He does. He also said something about our family being a bad 'example' because of our 'extravagance.'" Nora's shoulders slumped.

"I'm so sorry. Surely he knows having two weddings in one day will save everyone much trouble and expense."

"He doesn't see it the same way we do." Nora hung her head. "We've been told we're 'flaunting' our wealth."

Rochelle shook her head. "But your husband's company employs a goodly number of workers, even some of them from among your district."

"For some reason, it doesn't seem to matter to him."

"Bide your time, Nora. One more week or so, and the weddings will be done." She touched Nora's arm. "I'll be praying about the situation."

"Thank you. And if you get the chance, perhaps you could speak with Emma. For some reason, *mudders* don't know much about their *dochders'* fears and doubts. Maybe Emma's *aenti* will."

"I'll be glad to find an opportunity to talk to her. But, what about your more immediate family? Surely there's someone closer, someone Amish. I don't mind, at all, but . . ."

"I love my family, but I'm afraid one or more of them might misunderstand a young woman's normal doubts and speak to the bishop."

Rochelle nodded slowly. "I see. Well, I'll try to speak with her. But don't worry. I'm sure everything will come out all right, God willing."

"*Ya, Gotte* willing."

Whatever came next, she had no idea.

Silas knew he had his answer for Mr. Kingsley, and it was a simple matter to pick up the phone and gently refuse the man's offer of permanent employment. Part of him felt like a fool for turning down the opportunity, but he called Ted and informed him of the decision before leaving the airport parking lot.

"I understand," Ted said. "I imagine you'll be taking to the skies in another part of the world someday?"

"Someday. I hope to return to missions work. But right now, I believe my place is here, closer to my family. They've had so many changes in the past year of their lives. I know they're grown, but it's best for me to stay in Florida."

"Well, I admire your decision. With our child's surgeries, I've had to do my own soul-searching. It's not easy, but necessary. But keep in touch. Before you head off on your next venture, let me know. I'll give you my financial support."

"Thank you, sir."

Silas ended the call, knowing deep inside he'd made the right decision.

He arrived back in the village after his latest charter, another simple day trip to Miami and back for a Sarasota businessman. A quick hop, then home again.

A vehicle Silas didn't recognize sat parked in front of the house. He pulled up into the driveway and stopped the engine.

Laughter rang out from the backyard. Lena. He hadn't heard her laugh in such a way since before her surgery. He rounded the corner to see Lena propped up on a chair, with Matthew and Steven cleaning fish.

"Hello, Mr. Fry." Steven's grin was white in his tan face. "I got a good catch today so I thought I'd bring you all some fish. The least I could do was clean them for you, too."

"Ah, thank you, Steven." He glanced at Lena, whose face glowed a faint shade of pink. "How are you feeling, Lena? I thought I heard your laugh when I came around the corner."

"Much better. See? I said you didn't have anything to worry about, leaving me for the day."

Until now, he didn't worry so much about her being alone as worrying about the status of things with the young man with tousled blond hair scaling a fish.

"So, Steven, your big day is coming soon." He sank onto the nearest empty lawn chair.

"Yes, sir. It is. Finally."

"Finally?"

"I love Emma, but anytime we're together, all I hear is more about the wedding. My new suit is ready, and my shirt. All we have to do is get ready and show up."

Of course, Steven had no clue about all the wedding details so important to a woman.

"A little more than a week, you'll be done. So, where do you plan to live?"

"I've rented one side of a duplex from my Uncle Henry Hostetler. Our part of the house has two bedrooms, one bathroom, and we share the backyard with Uncle Henry. He's getting older, so the family will be glad to have us living next door to him." More scraping of the fish before he deftly sliced it open and removed the guts.

"Good for you. Have you lived there long?"

"I just got my things moved from my parents' house. They wanted me to wait until Christmas, but I didn't."

"I understand what you mean." Silas had to smile at the young man's words. He reminded Silas of himself at the same age, always ready to push ahead for what he wanted.

Nobody thought a young Mennonite man would grow up to fly planes, but he did. The life Steven had chosen for himself, however, wasn't so much different from his Plain counterparts who lived inland and farmed. Steven, instead, worked the Gulf waters.

Lena's expression of admiration nudged him, though. She'd never shown an interest in a young man before, though a few had noticed her during their time in Ohio. Instead, she'd seemed oblivious of the attention. Until now.

He caught her glance, and she frowned, staring down at the blanket on her lap.

"I don't mind frying these for you, if you'd like fish tonight."

"Sounds good to me." Truthfully, he'd considered sending Matthew over to Village Pizza to buy supper. "I think we have some leftovers in the refrigerator to go with it."

At the realization Steven would stay for supper, Lena beamed.

"What about Emma?" Silas had to ask.

"She's getting her dress fitted, and some of her friends are arriving tonight. They're going to play volleyball at the park." Steven shrugged. "I don't want to sit there and watch a bunch of giggling girls play volleyball."

"Some boys play volleyball, too," Matthew interjected. "Levi's going tonight, and some of the other kids. May I go, too, Dad?"

"Yes, of course." He had no plans for the evening, and Lena wasn't in any shape to be bicycling or riding over to the park to sit on some bleachers, or even benches if there was a concert in the park.

"Sunday night, they're having a Christmas singing," Lena said. He heard the longing in her voice.

"Well, maybe we can go, if you're up to it."

"I'd like to." And she smiled at Steven.

26

*A*n evening breeze swirled through the pavilion in Pinecraft Park, and Rochelle shivered. A few around her did so as well. She tugged her cardigan a bit tighter. She should have taken out her winter jacket, kept in the front closest for only the rarest of chilly evenings in Florida.

Tonight, in spite of the wintry air, the music warmed her heart. A visiting group of Mennonites from Indiana played guitars, and one kept time with a pair of sticks; another playing a harmonica.

Christmas hymns swelled up from the group. When they didn't all sing together, the musicians sang some unfamiliar, newer songs about the Savior's birth.

Nights like tonight made any troubles shrink to their proper size when compared to God's love. Rochelle was reminded of the miracle of Christmas, the lavish gift of grace.

She scanned the crowd. Not an empty seat remained in the pavilion, where a makeshift stage had been set up along with some tent walls to block out some of the cold. Some brought their own lawn chairs and others occupied a few picnic tables.

A sea of head coverings, a wide variety, mostly white, dotted the room along with a few men's hats and ballcaps.

She shivered.

"James Stoltzfus has a coffeepot set up in the back," whispered Betsy, sitting beside Thaddeus without a sliver of open night air between them. "I think he has hot water for cocoa, too."

Rochelle nodded. Coffee sounded good, so she made her way to the rear of the pavilion, to a picnic table with one half covered with two large metal containers and a stack of cups.

"Coffee, please," she said to James. She tucked a donation into the plastic jar stuffed with dollar bills, marked "Pinecraft Park Fund."

He nodded, then filled a cup for her. "We've got cream and sugar and fixings on the end."

"Thanks." She glanced toward the nearest pillar of the pavilion. Silas Fry leaned against it. He caught her eye and smiled at her.

If it was nearly Christmas, and tonight was full of grace, she figured she'd seize the opportunity to talk to him. Her heart swelled. How she'd missed him.

She doctored her coffee, then approached Silas. "It's a beautiful evening."

"Even more so now."

She felt a warm flush creep across her face. "How . . . how are you?"

"I'm well." His gaze swept the area. "Would you like to go for a short walk?"

"Yes, yes, I would." They stepped out into the darkness, and Silas reached for her free hand. Now, it didn't feel as cold.

"I've missed you," they both said at once, then laughed.

"You go first." Silas squeezed her hand. They strolled toward the path winding beside the creek.

"The other day, when I told Lena . . . I'm sorry. It was meant for you to tell her."

"Don't apologize. You love her, and you were concerned. And I thought Belinda had years ago. Which wasn't true. Lena's hurting, she's healing up inside and out. But it's not your fault."

Rochelle nodded. "Sometimes, we try to help people, and our good intentions cause more harm than good."

"The truth helps." Silas stopped. They looked toward the pavilion, where glowing rectangles of light illuminated the crowd inside. Nearby, the empty shuffleboard courts provided plenty of shadow.

"Ye shall know the truth, and the truth shall set you free," Rochelle quoted.

"Belinda had a hard time with the truth." Silas turned to face her. "She avoided it. I think if she ignored the fact John was Lena's father, to her it helped her feel less guilty about marrying me."

"Ah. I see." But she didn't see. "When I heard you two had married . . . and then Lena came . . . it felt like . . . I don't know."

"Like I'd forgotten you so quickly?"

Rochelle nodded. A hot tear on her cheek surprised her.

Silas reached out and swept the tear away. "I love you, Rochelle Keim. Don't cry."

He pulled her to him and she dropped the foam cup of coffee on the pavement. This kiss wasn't the sweet peck on the lips he'd stolen in the hospital courtyard, but the kind of kiss reminding her of what they once had.

Here in the dark, people might still see—

She pulled back, trying not to gasp, her heart hammering away in her chest, her knees wobbly. "What are we going to do, Silas?"

"I'm going to love you as long as you'll have me." And then, he kissed her again.

A shout rang out from the volleyball court, a stone's throw away. Someone whistled. They'd been seen by the young people. Rochelle squatted down, scrambling to pick up the cup she'd dropped.

"Silas Fry, you're nothing but trouble." A thought troubled her. "But, your job with the Kingsleys?"

"I turned it down. I'm staying here."

They slipped through a space of lawn between the shuffleboard court and the sandy volleyball area where rotating teams of young people were still hitting the ball back and forth.

"There's Emma and Steven." Silas nodded toward the rear of the bleachers.

Emma's arms moved in vivid gestures. She shook her head. Then Steven said something, at which she nodded in response, then stumbled off down the street, away from the park.

"Uh-oh." Rochelle frowned. "I wonder what's going on."

"Nothing good, I'd guess."

"I should probably—" Rochelle began.

"Go ahead, see what it is. I'll see you at church in the morning." He gave her hand another squeeze, which made her stomach flutter.

Rochelle followed Emma from the park. In the streetlights, the back of Emma's head covering looked like a white bouncing blob above her shoulders.

"Emma," Rochelle called out. She glanced back at the volleyball court. The young people still played, just as they had all evening.

Emma stood, motionless, staring down at the rows of tricycles gleaming in the light filtering through the Spanish moss. Then she frowned before heading away from the park, but not in the same direction as Steven.

"Emma," Rochelle called again. The young woman didn't turn around, nor did her pace slow. Rochelle broke into a trot and kept it up until she caught up with Emma.

"I don't want to talk about it," Emma said. But her pace slowed.

"Okay." They continued at a stroll now. Rochelle shivered. She wanted the warmth of Silas's arms.

The sounds of voices, raised in song, drifted to the street. A neighborhood singing, for those who didn't want to venture to the park.

"One of my favorite songs," Emma said. She paused at the mailbox. "We sing it . . . back home."

"Pretty soon, your home will be here in Sarasota, permanently."

She wanted to reassure Emma things would work out just fine. However, she'd had her own dream of a wedding and life had taught her reassurances didn't carry much weight sometimes.

"It doesn't seem possible. I thought . . ." Emma shrugged and fell silent. The song ended. Someone began a peppy number on a banjo.

The music made Rochelle want to tap her foot, in contrast to the seriousness of the conversation. She resumed walking, and Emma did, too.

"What did you think, Emma?"

"I imagined I'd be preparing for a wedding to Eli Troyer. But I'm here, planning a wedding in Pinecraft to Steven. I left my Order, joined your church. Just like Jacob Miller did for Natalie."

"Yes. Sometimes things don't turn out like we imagined."

"You were in love once. Did you ever wish you could make things different? Not as if *Gotte* would change the past for us."

Rochelle laughed softly. "I've wished for it several times. But I've also prayed for God to see to my future."

"Steven and I had a disagreement tonight. It's childish. Almost like a pair of *kinner* arguing over who's right."

Rochelle didn't venture to ask why the disagreement began, but she had a sneaking suspicion it had something to do with the regular presence of Lena Fry in their lives since summertime. The day of the fishing trip had reminded Rochelle of another such fishing trip two years earlier, when Jacob Miller, Betsy, and Natalie Bennett were all on Steven's boat for hours.

"Well, I hope you can work things out, and resolve whatever is wrong."

"I hope so. Oh, *Aenti* Chelle, I thought coming here would feel like a vacation, all the time." Emma frowned. "And I'm sorry I wasn't helpful with your business. I made people angry at you, but it was because of me."

"Pinecraft might be for vacations, but Emma, real life happens here. We have to work, just like anywhere else. It's not singings and volleyball and fish fries every night." Rochelle did her best to keep her tone gentle. But Emma had such an unrealistic viewpoint about life sometimes.

"I know, and I'm sorry."

Two more blocks, and they'd arrive at the house.

"You're forgiven." She slipped her arm around Emma's shoulders and gave her a half-hug. "Sometimes, when we have a disagreement with someone, we just need to swallow our pride and make things right. I wish I'd done so in the past. My stubbornness caused me to miss out on something wonderful." No bitterness, no more pangs of regret.

She wasn't the same young woman anymore, nor did she want to be. Since she'd started rekindling her old dreams, she'd started to see possibilities before her, because of God's goodness.

"I'll talk to him, in the morning, as soon as I can." They turned the corner onto Rochelle's street. She glimpsed her van in the driveway.

"Good. Sometimes a good night's sleep is a remedy for a lot of problems."

"And swallowing pride, too."

"Yes, and swallowing pride, too." At last, Rochelle felt like she'd gotten through to Emma. Maybe Emma and Steven courting had helped transform Emma from the doted-upon youngest in the family to a woman realizing the world was ripe for someone to serve in it, and her concerns mustn't come before the concerns of others.

Despite her resolve to believe she wasn't the same person she was not quite twenty years ago, her former stubbornness had indeed cost her more than she'd imagined she'd have to pay.

⚜

Christmas, three days away, and Silas hadn't found the right gift for Rochelle. He'd racked his brain, but everything he'd come up with didn't seem right.

He wasn't handy with woodworking, so something crafted was out. He couldn't think of anything she needed.

Aunt Fran bustled through the house, insisting she'd help clean it while banishing a still-sore Lena to the easy chair. Despite Silas's protests, he did appreciate the help.

"So, what's on your mind?" she asked him.

"A gift for Rochelle. I haven't found the right gift. And I don't want to get her nothing for Christmas. I know it's a little late to think of shopping, and I'm not good at making things myself. I have no idea what to get for a woman." He shook his head. All those years with Belinda, and Christmas gifts usually were simple things for the children. The two of them would enjoy a walk on the beach and hunting for shells.

"I have an idea. Several of them. I've been making some items for the Haiti Benefit Auction in January, so why don't you come over and pick something out?"

"Thanks. When?"

"How about now? It'll only take a few moments. My work is almost done here, anyway."

"Okay then." He headed for the front room. "Lena, I'm going over to Aunt Fran's. I'm getting a Christmas gift for Rochelle."

"Good. Because I know she found a gift for you." Lena's voice had a singsong tone.

She'd gotten a gift for him?

Silas and Frances headed the few blocks to her and Uncle Tobias's home, and she parked in the driveway, allowing room for bicyclists to get in and out of the yard.

"Like I said," she continued, leading him to her sewing room, "I have a whole pile of things. Woven rugs, quilted pillows, crocheted dishrags."

Crocheted dishrags. If he gave Rochelle a gift like that . . . no, she wouldn't be hurt. But he wanted it to be something special.

Then he saw it. A square quilted wall hanging, the image of a pink hibiscus flower arranged in a four-pointed star pattern, with four smaller pink blooms inside it, and a seafoam green border.

"This is the one." He touched the fabric, the stitches hand-quilted. Fresh, pretty, tropical Florida. And Rochelle would love it.

"It's one of my favorites. I had a hard time deciding if I should keep it for myself, but at the auction, it would sell for a good cause. You can hang it on the wall, or use as a small table cover, or put it on a rack."

Not useful or practical, but it looked pretty.

"How much do you want for it?"

"Nothing. I can't charge family for this."

"Well, I'll donate to the Haiti fund."

"I think it's a good deal." She folded up the wall hanging, then tucked it into a plastic bag. "I might have a box, if you don't."

"I probably don't. I was just going to use wrapping paper." He figured the paper would get torn up and thrown out anyway.

"Here, use this one."

"Thanks, Aunt Fran."

"Now, we need to hurry."

"Hurry?"

"Your parents are coming on the twelve-thirty bus."

"They are?" He thought they weren't traveling for Christmas this year, since they'd already visited at Thanksgiving.

"Last-minute decision. If we hurry, we can get to the parking lot and find a good space to wait. Your uncle will be honking the horn on the buggy any moment."

A faint whinnying sound drifted into the house.

"Told you he'd honk."

Silas shook his head and picked up the bag. "I'll leave this here while we go to meet the bus."

Then they shot off in the horseless buggy, zooming along Pinecraft streets, crossing Bahia Vista, and coming to a stop near the church parking lot. A throng of people waited for the bus, and soon a cluster surrounded the buggy, with men asking Uncle Tobias plenty of questions about the cart, and how he'd transformed it into a buggy and how he'd set the horn up.

Not until the bus arrived and Silas saw his parents emerge from the bus did he realize how much he'd missed them.

"Dad. Mom." He enveloped them each in a hug. "I've missed you."

"We saw you but a few weeks ago," Mom replied with a gleam in her eye.

"I know, but it was all so fast."

"When Lena had her emergency surgery, we knew we had to come." His father clapped him on the back.

They'd never hugged much as a family. But his father's love shone out from his eyes.

"I'm glad you did, Dad."

"Let's get those bags rounded up." Uncle Tobias hopped down from the front seat of the buggy. "We can stick them all the way in the back, with Silas."

"We only brought one." His mother smiled, then yawned. "Oh, such a long trip. I'm trying to talk your father into living here year-round, what with Tobias and Frances here, and now you and the children."

"One thing at a time," his father said.

He and his parents crammed onto the rear seat of the buggy after he secured their suitcase on the back, with the aid of an elastic cord.

"I understand you've been spending more time with Rochelle Keim since Thanksgiving," his mother began.

"Yes, I have."

"So what say you? Another wedding in the future? Pinecraft will have two of them in less than a week."

"I . . . I don't know yet." Ever since the revelation had come out about Lena, things had seemed to click into place for them both. The old had gone; the new had come.

"It's a big decision, Patricia." His father's voice held an old familiar tone, and it made Silas smile in spite of his mother's grilling.

"He decided pretty quickly the last time."

"*Patricia.*"

"Well, it's true."

Silas held onto the edge of the buggy. Trapped inside, until they arrived at Tobias and Fran's, he couldn't leap from the buggy.

"Mom, you're right. I did decide quickly to marry last time."

"All because of John . . ."

"You're right. It was because of John." And a lot more, but he'd been around the whole story many times. Tonight, he'd have to tell them the story of their granddaughter. "Next time around, I'm going to take my time."

He wouldn't rush into marriage, not with Rochelle.

27

Christmas morning came, and with it a delicious carry-in brunch at Rochelle's house, filled wall to wall with visiting Yoders, along with Jolene and her family.

Before they ate, they sang a hymn together, and Jolene's husband said a prayer. Gifts would be exchanged later at everyone's own home, after the annual Pinecraft Christmas parade.

"I can't wait until the parade," said Rochelle's niece Winnie, home for college break.

"Me either." No matter how old Rochelle got, she knew she'd never tire of the annual tradition on Christmas afternoon.

This year the parade began at Der Dutchman's parking lot, then wound through the village streets.

Rochelle's phone buzzed on the kitchen counter.

A message from Silas: *Meet me at the park after the parade? I have a gift for you.*

She'd tucked her gift for Silas away, wrapped it in dark blue paper covered with snowflakes. A little out of place for Florida, and he'd laugh at the paper. She wasn't sure when she'd give him the gift, but after the parade seemed as good a time as any.

I'll see you there. I have something for you, too.

Rochelle was doubly glad she'd purchased the plaque for Silas, even though it was purchased on impulse at the time.

She tucked her phone into her pocket.

The minutes dragged by while the family dispersed, some to play games and others to sit on the lanai and visit. For the Yoders, Rochelle knew it was a few treasured moments of peace before the wedding hubbub began in earnest.

Rochelle lost two rounds of dominoes in a row. She chalked it up to distraction.

"Chelle, you look as dreamy-eyed as a young girl in love," Jolene teased.

She didn't respond to her sister, but Emma and Betsy exchanged glances.

Thankfully, neither of them mentioned anything about Silas in front of her sister and brother-in-law. She wasn't ready to share what had happened. She also wasn't sure about giving her heart to him again, not just yet. More opinions from family and well-meaning friends could muddy the waters.

What she needed was some clarity.

Instead, Rochelle studied Emma's expression, cheerful and upbeat about Christmas, the family celebration, and the parade to come. Her mood had seemed better with the family near for Christmas.

Nora and Jedediah Yoder visited on the lanai with the quieter, more conservative branch of the family. Truly, Rochelle was mildly surprised they'd all agreed to gather on Christmas Day, especially after Nora's words about the new bishop in the Yoders' district.

Maybe the family had prepared themselves for the consequences to follow the weddings. Maybe Rochelle's former houseguest from last winter, *Aenti* Sarah, had insisted they agree to the gathering.

Whatever the reason, Rochelle loved having the house full.

"It's time," Rochelle's brother-in-law announced.

They gathered their chairs and blankets, piled their three-wheeler baskets high, and stuffed Rochelle's van as well as Jolene's vehicle.

Thousands would come and line the parade route, from Old Order plain folks, ladies with their black stockings and sturdy plain shoes, to the most liberal Mennonites, women with short hair and wearing capri pants.

The expected crowd was exactly why the caravan hurried along to the nearest street corner on the parade route, found a place to park, then set up the chairs and blankets.

Rochelle knew her home was closest to the parade route, so naturally her home would be the logical place for the family to congregate. She smiled. It didn't matter. They were all together, at least for today.

Children across the street, a stairstepped bevy of little ones all clad in sky blue, the girls in dresses the same shade as the boys' shirts, waved their plastic bags, since many of the parade participants would throw candy to the children along the parade route.

"Can't wait to see the tractors. I heard Herb Stutzman brought a new one this year," said Jolene's husband.

Anyone and everyone could participate in the parade. Rumor had it Otis Beachy was driving his brand-spankin'-new motorized recliner, and to steer you had to hold on to the recliner lever.

Trucks, riding lawnmowers, a solar-powered buggy, and more began to roll through, with cheering and clapping for the vehicles riding by.

Even Betsy and Emma's father sat up and took notice of the gigantic green tractor that looked out of place in the heart of the city, but was enough to turn certain gentlemen green with envy at its owner.

A familiar horseless buggy glided into view. The Frys, Tobias and Frances, with Tobias honking the neighing horn, to the delight of the Amish children across the street.

"Rochelle!" Frances called out, waving.

Rochelle returned the wave and gave Frances a smile. "Merry Christmas!"

"Join us, I need help throwing candy." The buggy glided to a stop, making the parade progress pause for a moment.

She glanced at Jolene. "Here's my keys, if I don't wind up back here by the time the parade's over with." She darted into the street and hopped onto the rear seat of the buggy.

She hit the cushioned seat with an *oomph*, and the buggy resumed its forward movement.

"Here." Frances handed Rochelle a bag of wrapped candies and chocolates. "My arm is tired from throwing."

Rochelle tossed candy, first from one side of the buggy, then the other. Children of all ages scrambled for the candies, which they tucked into bags and squealed over. She laughed at their joy.

Santa even rode in this parade, somewhere in the lineup. She wasn't sure how far back, but even Pinecraft had a Santa Claus in full costume who waved and smiled and ho-ho-hoed. Funny. None of the people she knew acknowledged Santa as part of their Christmas celebrations.

Yet Rochelle knew Santa Claus lurked back there, somewhere, in the parade line behind them.

"You know I have an ulterior motive for calling you aboard the buggy." Frances looked over her shoulder, her eyes twinkling.

"I didn't suspect one." Rochelle grinned and tossed another handful of candy to a trio of children in shorts and T-shirts. Her first time participating in the parade, and she didn't know why she hadn't before. She could have had someone throw candy from her van while she drove it in the parade line.

"We're to drop you off at Pinecraft Park. Silas is there with Matthew and Lena."

The horse's neigh rang out yet again, and Frances darted a look at her husband. "Tobias, must you every five seconds?"

"It's for the children."

"And old men," she said.

"All right, I'll do it every ten seconds, then."

Rochelle laughed at the older couple and tossed more candy at the children by the edge of the street.

She caught sight of a familiar face. Emma, in the crowd, standing with a cluster of Old Order Amish. Rochelle didn't recall her being at the family gathering, and wasn't sure when she'd disappeared after brunch.

Emma spoke intently with another young woman Rochelle didn't know. Emma frowned, nodded.

Rochelle looked away and focused on a group of young children, their faces aglow as they saw the candy in her hand.

෨

Silas had never seen such a spectacle passing through Pinecraft's streets, not since he was a small boy. He, Matthew, and Lena gathered along Fry Street, close to the entrance to Pinecraft Park. Lena sat comfortably at the edge of the street, while Matthew perched on his electric bicycle. Silas had his own chair beside Lena.

One parade "float" featured a tractor pulling a small flatbed trailer, where a bluegrass band played and sang Christmas songs. Another man drove a "solar buggy," a horseless buggy in the customary black, with solar panels attached flush to the buggy's roof.

"Dad, did you see the buggy?" Matthew's voice held open admiration. "I should ask Uncle Tobias about it. I wonder how it works."

Silas wasn't sure how solar-powered technology worked, either. "I have no idea myself, Son."

The gentleman waved at them as he passed.

Another odd-looking vehicle passed, with a pair of large wheels that bore flashing green lights on the rims, almost as tall as Silas. The driver rode on a seat between the pair of wheels, as did his companion.

The contraption paused, then the driver spun the vehicle in one direction, then another.

"Would you look at *that*." Matthew tugged on Silas's arm.

"Just think, you might have missed seeing it if you'd ridden with Uncle Tobias."

The procession continued, and children nearby scrambled for candy someone had thrown from another vehicle in the parade.

Then came another participant, a local man known for his smoked meats and savory foods he sold throughout the village. A large smoker trailed behind his truck.

Anyone and everyone, it seemed, who wanted to join the lineup on Christmas Day could.

Silas realized this Christmas was so much better than last year's.

Last year they'd somehow made it through the blur of contemplation, services, hymns, and visits among the family.

Their loved ones, it seemed, weren't always sure of what to say or do, with it being the first Christmas without Belinda.

This year, he'd thought of Christmases past, but this year he felt a glimmer of hope. God hadn't forgotten them. He could still hope and pray for direction, clarity, healing.

"There's Uncle Tobias and Aunt Fran—and they have Rochelle with them!" Matthew pointed.

The horn neighed at them, and a few other onlookers cheered.

What made Silas want to cheer was the smile Rochelle gave him. He'd brought her gift, tucked into a box securely strapped to the basket Matthew had on his electric bicycle.

The buggy paused, with Rochelle slipping from the back seat. "Thank you!" she called out to Uncle Tobias and Aunt Fran before they continued along their way.

She met Silas at the side of the street. "I had a ride here. Isn't the parade wonderful?" She sounded and looked not much older than Lena.

"Yes, it is. I'd always heard about the parade. This is my first."

"The first of many more?"

"I hope so."

She glanced toward the box in Matthew's bicycle basket.

Silas unstrapped it. "Yes, this is what I told you about." He grinned at her. "Care to take a short walk?"

"Oh, but I'll miss seeing Santa Claus in the parade." She pouted.

It took but a second for him to realize she was joking. "Suit yourself." He walked off in the direction of the pavilion.

"Hey, where are you going?"

He heard footsteps behind him.

"Never mind. You don't want to miss Santa."

"It doesn't matter." She caught up with him. "Anyway, I didn't bring your gift with me."

"Huh." He stopped at the far side of the pavilion. "So, I guess I'll have to stop by later to pick it up."

"You . . . you can." Rochelle kept her hands clasped lightly in front of her, but he could tell it took her self-control not to pluck the gift from his hands.

"Merry Christmas, Rochelle." He extended the box toward her. "I hope you like it."

"I'm sure I will."

She set the box on a picnic table and gently lifted the upper half of the box, then peeled back the layers of tissue paper. Silas was glad he'd used tissue paper, at Aunt Fran's suggestion.

Rochelle sucked in a breath. "Oh, it's beautiful." She pulled the wall hanging out, unfolding it as she did so.

"Ah, it's handmade, of course. I'm not sure who did it. My aunt might know."

"The stitching. It's so detailed. And the colors. So beautiful. I know exactly where I'll hang this. Thank you, thank you."

"I'm glad you like it. Merry Christmas."

"Merry Christmas, Silas." She took a step toward him, as if she wanted to hug him, but then stopped as if she thought better of the idea. "I . . . Come by later, you, and Lena and Matthew. The family will likely be at the house, or some of them might. I think there will be some games, too. And food, always plenty of food."

"I'd . . . we'd very much like to." He let himself reach for her hand and squeezed it.

28

Rochelle thought much of the family would go their separate ways after the parade dispersed. She'd been a poor hostess, running off and jumping into the Frys' horseless buggy and riding in the parade.

The Frys found her at the park, then dropped her off at the house, where Jolene and most of the crew waited for her return.

"There you are," Jolene said when Rochelle walked into the house. "We're playing games and I think *Aenti* Sarah is reheating some of the food."

Rochelle clutched the box containing the wall hanging and nodded. "Good. Silas and his kids are on their way. They'll be here in an hour or so."

"Uh-huh," Jolene said, eyeing the box.

"See what he gave me?" Rochelle slipped the top from the box.

"Lovely, absolutely lovely. And I've never seen this pattern before. And tiny, tiny stitches."

At the words *pattern* and *stitches* the rest of the female members of the Keim and Yoder clans gathered around to see the wall hanging—Nora, Betsy, Emma, along with *Aenti* Sarah.

The women lapsed naturally into German, exclaiming over the unique combination of appliques.

"*Gut* work, *gut* work," Nora said, nodding.

"I agree. I'm going to hang it on my bedroom wall."

"Sweet gift from a sweetheart." *Aenti* Sarah touched the fabric.

The women all giggled, and Rochelle's face flamed.

"So much better for you than someone like Daniel Troyer." Emma's voice stilled the giggles.

"Yes. Much better." Rochelle slid the tissue paper over the wall hanging. A faint pang of regret nipped at her heart. No, she hadn't quite "fallen hard" for Daniel Troyer, a man who wasn't all he seemed. Not as hard as she'd let herself fall for Silas.

"I'll put this in the bedroom, out of the way." She smiled at them as she put the top back on the box.

Once she emerged from the bedroom, she heard familiar voices in the kitchen. Silas, Lena, and Matthew.

They all extended Christmas greetings to one another, and Betsy took out two whole pies, freshly made in her shop the day before.

Steven approached Emma straightaway, and Emma seemed back to her chipper self unlike the brooding intensity Rochelle had seen during the parade.

"So, where's my gift?" Silas asked.

"Aren't you brash?" She hadn't teased anyone like this in, well, it had been a long time. And she realized she'd missed it. "Don't you want to visit and have dessert first?"

"Ah, I guess I can."

"I'm joking." One of the best parts of her and Silas had always been their laughter, the gentle banter kindling a burning glow inside her. "A minute, and I'll be right back."

"All right. I'll get a cup of coffee."

As Rochelle disappeared into her bedroom once again, she heard the doorbell ring.

Thank You, Lord, for a beautiful Christmas, with loved ones near as we celebrate together.

No one could purchase the simple joy and fervent peace of the day. Rochelle slid open the closet door and pulled Silas's gift from the shelf.

She headed back into the kitchen, where she discovered the Christmas crowd had swelled some more. Henry Hostetler, her distant cousin, along with a pair of men she didn't recognize. One of the men carried a guitar case, the other a rectangular case.

"Merry Christmas, Rochelle."

"Merry Christmas, Henry. So good to see you."

"We old widowers were out and about—me, Levi, and John. I told them Betsy Yoder's pies live here."

"Only until they're eaten." Rochelle smiled. "Please, stay for coffee and pie."

"Thank you." Henry glanced at the men. "Levi and John Bontrager, Rochelle Keim."

After introductions went all around, they discovered with the help of Imogene Brubaker the brothers were actually second cousins, once removed, to the Yoder family.

Rochelle didn't know how Imogene kept the branching family trees straight, but the woman could piece together family connections faster than Betsy could roll out a piecrust.

"Levi and John, I see you have instruments with you," Rochelle said. "Would you like to have a singing here? I don't have a carport, but we could gather on the lanai, and Steven and Matthew can light the torches in the backyard before it gets dark."

"We'd be honored," Levi said, nodding. Judging by the intonation of his voice, Rochelle guessed he was a baritone.

While the brothers tuned up their instruments, Levi his guitar and John his banjo, the family members maneuvered chairs onto the lanai and a few in the backyard.

Rochelle seized the moment to turn her attention back to Silas, who leaned against the counter as he sipped his coffee.

"Sorry. I've had a crowd all day." She still held his gift.

"Yes, you have. And you've loved every moment of it."

"You're right. This has been the best Christmas in . . . well, it's been a long time." And it wasn't because her home was filled with family in nearly every corner. It was because of the second chance set before her with Silas.

"You deserve it." He eyed the box.

"Okay, here you are." She smiled, holding the box out to him. "Merry Christmas, Silas."

He tore off the vivid paper, grinning as he did so. "I know it's not a plane. The box is too small."

Rochelle chuckled, then glanced toward the living room. The family had mostly piled onto the lanai. Someone said something, and a ripple of laughter came in response.

She knew her gift was a bit unusual. Funny, too, she'd given him something he could hang on his wall, also unusual.

Silas lifted the plaque from the box. He set the box on the counter. His eyes scanned the front of the plaque. His expression softened, his blink increasing.

"Wow. It's quite a poem. Different."

"I . . . I hope you like it."

"Ah, I do. Thank you. I'll treasure it, always." He nodded. "Thank you."

Rochelle knew it wasn't a gift of Scripture, and likely a few might think it bordering on blasphemy, as if someone could be so presumptuous as to touch the face of God. But she hoped Silas understood.

"I'm glad."

Silas glanced toward the group gathered on the lanai, then closed the distance between him and Rochelle, and gave her a swift kiss on the cheek. She touched her flaming cheeks.

"Do you want to go to the singing with me?"

His funny request made her laugh. "Yes, I'll get a cup of coffee first."

⋘⋙

Silas hummed all the way home after leaving Rochelle's. This Christmas had been better than he imagined.

Rochelle's gift, simple and different from anything he'd ever received, sat in its box between the van's front seats.

He wanted to tell her how much it truly meant to him, but the words wouldn't come, not in the way he wanted.

She'd always supported his flying, even when some didn't understand the compulsion and passion he felt for taking to the skies. Some called it foolhardy, others called it prideful. Even Belinda didn't completely understand.

Yet Rochelle always had, despite her former fear of flying.

Lena heaved a sigh, the sound one Silas hadn't heard from his daughter in months.

"What is it?"

She kept silent. "I'm just tired. It's been a long day, going to the parade, then to Aunt Fran and Uncle Tobias's for gifts, then over to Rochelle's and the singing."

"We could have left early, if you'd wanted to."

"No, it's all right."

"She's jealous of Emma and Steven," came Matthew's voice from behind Silas.

"I am *not*." Lena's voice held an edge.

"Matthew." Silas gave him a warning. Some things, even if they were obvious, didn't need to be said.

"You don't know what I'm thinking, so stop."

They arrived seconds later at the house, the porch light glowing. Tomorrow, they'd set the house in order before going over to Tobias and Fran's for a family day.

Silas reminded himself this was vacationland for people, and with Matthew and Lena both on Christmas break, they had a rare opportunity to have a vacation themselves.

He killed the engine after parking in the carport.

"What's that?" Matthew said, pointing to the side door of the house. The outer screen door was partly ajar, as if being propped open.

"I have no idea." Silas left the van, coming around to the other side to help Lena from the front seat.

"Thanks, Dad. I can do it."

"I wanted to be sure."

Lena smiled, her glance sliding over to the side door.

Someone had left a box, a wrapped present, between the doors. The tag simply read "Lena" and was otherwise unsigned.

"Someone left you a gift," Matthew said.

"Mister Obvious." Lena sighed, picking up the box, wincing as she bent to do so.

"Lena, you don't have to be rude to your brother." Silas couldn't help but talk to them as though they were much younger, Lena especially. What else could he do? Ignore her rudeness?

Something was a bit off about Lena, but she smoothed over her expression. "I'm sorry, Matthew. Dad, I don't know what's wrong with me." She gave a sob.

Silas patted her on the shoulder. "You're tired. When we get inside, you go ahead and get right to bed. Don't worry about setting an alarm clock. Sleep. Remember, the doctor said to sleep when you could."

He unlocked the door and they entered the chilly kitchen.

Lena shivered. "I guess you're right. I'm just tired." She studied the box in her hands.

"You going to open it?" Matthew craned his neck as if somehow he could see the contents of the box more easily, even though Lena hadn't peeled away the wrapping paper.

"Of course I am." She ripped away the paper and opened the flat rectangular box. Inside lay something made of fabric in shades of blue, varied as the Gulf waters. "Oh . . . it's beautiful. It's a head scarf."

"Who's it from? Is there a card or something in the box?"

"No. I don't think so." Lena emptied the box. "No. Nothing."

"Huh. Interesting." Silas didn't know what to make of it. A friend, stopping by this evening, with a gift for Lena? Or someone from outside the village?

"Maybe the neighbors saw someone come by today. I'll have to ask," Lena stated.

"Good idea."

Lena and Matthew went to their rooms, Matthew yawning something about being tired already and Lena not saying anything more, but clutching her Christmas gift. Silas went to the thermostat and flipped the switch for the heat.

What did someone say to a brooding, almost twenty-year-old young woman? Silas had tried, but this was one of those times he felt Belinda's loss the most keenly. Over the years, it had always been the four of them along with their missions team overseas.

As much as he'd felt more settled in Pinecraft than anywhere else over the past year, the sensation of the world being out of control bubbled to the surface again. Only while piloting did he feel the control.

He had a moment of quiet prayer in the kitchen before the children returned.

His foundation had been rocked to the core. No wonder Rochelle had such a wave of emotions and questions, losing her mother years ago and then witnessing John's brutal attack. Their peaceful lives were upended, changed forever.

They'd all fled, Belinda and he to Africa, Rochelle to Florida. Regardless of the circumstances and emotions driving a wedge between them years ago, now Silas wished he'd been more patient with Rochelle and less responsive to Belinda's cries for help.

Matthew entered the kitchen. "I'm going to bed, Dad. Did you have a good Christmas?"

"Yes, yes I did."

"Good. I hope you like the bicycle I got for you."

"I do. You did a good job on it."

"Thanks. Good night." Matthew grinned, still looking like a young boy before he left the room.

Maybe hindsight enabled people to see everything clearly.

God had still blessed him and Belinda with a son born of their love. For him, Silas would always be thankful.

As for Lena, the daughter of his heart if not of his flesh, he said one more prayer for guidance on how to help her. Maybe she was only enduring the effects of recuperating from major surgery, but Silas suspected something more lay beneath the surface.

Maybe Rochelle could help her. Not so she could report back to Silas, but be the listening ear and provide wise guidance to the young woman.

29

While the Amish branch of the family celebrated its second Christmas, or *Zwedde Grischtdaag*, for Rochelle the twenty-sixth was another workday. Several clients had special requests for day-after-Christmas cleaning, so she spent the day at three homes.

Betsy had left early in the morning to meet her family and Thaddeus. The young woman glowed with anticipation of her wedding day, in four more days on the thirtieth. Her anxiety over the weather dissipated when Rochelle shared the forecast with her: sunny skies, highs in the low eighties, chance of a late afternoon thunderstorm. By then, the sisters would be having their shared reception at the Tourist Church facilities and the rain could come if it wanted to.

She arrived home to an empty house—no sign of Emma—and made a cup of tea before opening her mail. Bills, end-of-the-year statements of accounts, a Christmas card arriving a day late, but no less appreciated.

She checked the cupcakes, covering the countertop and breakfast bar. She'd left them to thaw so she could frost them later, and they'd be served up at the wedding reception in a few days.

A knock sounded at the door, so Rochelle reluctantly got back on her feet to answer it.

Vera Byler and her daughter Patience stood on the front steps.

"Hello, Rochelle. May we come in?"

Rochelle braced herself, then chided herself for the reaction. But with Vera Byler, one never knew what would happen with the woman.

She glimpsed a wariness in the woman's eyes. Maybe Vera had learned a hard lesson from the words she'd used.

"Yes, please, come in. I've just put the kettle on for tea. Would you like a cup?"

"No, but some water would be fine."

So, she wasn't planning to linger. Rochelle opened the door for the pair and they followed her through the entry and front room, then into the kitchen.

Vera and Patience sat down at the table, almost in unison. Rochelle served them some ice water, then took out a mug for her tea.

"My, but you've made a lot of cupcakes," Vera observed.

"For Emma's wedding."

"Ah, so it's going to happen." Vera's eyebrows shot up.

"Yes, at last." Rochelle found the teabags. Of course, Vera and Patience hadn't stopped by to discuss the wedding. She waited for Vera to continue.

"The reason we're here is, well, we're interested in buying your business."

"You are?"

Rochelle hadn't expected this. Yes, she'd asked Imogene to help find someone, but with preparing for Christmas and closing her books for the year, looking for a buyer hadn't been high on her list of priorities.

"Yes." Patience finally found her voice. "Imogene Brubaker and I were talking recently, and she mentioned you wanted to sell your business. And I've liked pitching in, taking care of Lena Fry's clients," Patience said.

"I see." Rochelle glanced at Vera. Patience was old enough to be Rochelle's sister, but still followed in her mother's shadow.

"Her father and I discussed it, and we know Patience is a good worker. We believe she's equal to the job of running a cleaning business. After all, you're an old maid and you've been successful."

The kettle began to howl, and Rochelle let it make the screeching noise instead of the one she wanted to emit. Teabag in mug, she poured in hot water. She turned around and faced them.

"Yes, I'm thankful for how the business has gone all these years. It's had its ups and downs, but I have a file of happy clients and, I hope, equally happy workers."

"So, what are your terms? How much do you want for the business?"

"Well, I'm not quite sure yet. I'll have to talk to Phineas Beachy to draw up some papers and make you an offer."

"Good." Vera nodded.

Rochelle carried her mug of tea to the table. "I'm closing out the year's books this week, and it's been a good year. However, after this first semester of studies, I've decided for the last part of my training, it would be best if I could focus on my studies without the distraction of running a business."

"I understand." Vera glanced at Patience.

A loud clattering at the front of the house made them glance in that direction.

Betsy skittered to a stop, almost stumbling on her flip-flops. "Emma? Is Emma here?"

"No, I've been home about thirty minutes or so. I'm not sure where she is. I assumed she was with you and the rest of the family."

"No." Betsy shot down the hallway toward Emma's room. "*Aenti Chelle!*"

"What's wrong?" Rochelle sprang from her chair and headed down the hallway.

"It's true—Emma's *gone!*"

❧

They certainly made a sight at Siesta Key Beach, nearly two dozen Plain people spending the day at the shore. What had started out as a family outing somehow mushroomed into a Pinecraft expedition on the day after Christmas.

Silas sat on one of Uncle Tobias's beach chairs. He and Aunt Fran even made the bus ride to the beach, and they occupied another pair of beach chairs while Lena reclined on one they'd bought in Siesta Village.

Matthew and his friend Levi were knee-deep in the surf, trying to find sand dollars.

How Silas missed having Rochelle with them. He hadn't heard her mention the shore once during the nearly six months he'd been in Florida.

He had big news to share with her, something he'd known was coming up but hadn't thought much about. On Sunday, he would become an official member of the local Mennonite church. He had completed his time of proving, punctuated only by the murmurs of Vera Byler.

By finishing his proving, he was committing to the local church and all his commitment involved. He wasn't using the church for his personal gain, and he was making the statement that, yes, the Lord as well as his heart had him here in Pinecraft.

Rochelle had him here in Pinecraft, too, and had his heart.

Lena stirred on the chair beside his. She wore a pair of large sunglasses, the color similar to her vivid blue head covering. Some women in the church wore veils, some black, some white, others simple coverings of white lace. Nothing like this, though.

He might suggest she wear her white covering on Sundays and keep this one for days out like today.

He reminded himself of the idea he'd had last evening, to ask Rochelle to speak to Lena. Maybe this would be another area where Rochelle could help, if she was willing.

"Hey, Dad! I found some!" Matthew waved from where he stood in the surf. "Come try!"

Silas stood, rolling up his pant legs to the knee and adjusting his suspenders. "Here goes . . ." The Gulf waters were cool, but not so cool to make it uncomfortable.

At the beach the day after Christmas, much like in Mozambique. The waves smacked his legs, soaking him from the waist down.

"Do it like this, Dad!" Matthew leaned over, his arms mostly submerged in the water.

Silas rolled up his shirtsleeves as far as they would roll, then hunched over, reaching into the sand, feeling the pull of the water on his hands.

Wait. No, it was a piece of shell.

Then he stood up, stretched. Scrabbling for sand dollars was a young person's thing. His back complained, so he stretched again, then resumed scrounging on the sand.

There. A flat, round something. He lifted it up.

"You got one." Matthew splashed over in his direction.

"Yes, it's not broken, either." Silas glanced across the rippling water. Levi was back toward the shore, picking up shells and whatnot washed ashore. "I have something I'd like to ask you, Matthew. But it's important you don't talk to anyone about it, until I say it's okay."

"What is it? Am I in trouble?"

"No, not at all." Silas handed Matthew the sand dollar. "Here. For your collection. Anyway, what do you think of Miss Keim?"

"Uh, she's nice. Lena likes her a lot. I think she reminds Lena of Mom." He shrugged. "But she's quieter than Mom."

"What would you think if I asked her to marry me?"

"I don't know. But I like her, too. She's good at taking care of people."

"Yes, she is." He glanced at his son. "Well, what do you think?"

"Dad, it's not important what I think. I'm not marrying her. I'm not trying to be disrespectful. But you haven't been the same since Mom died. And since we've been here, and you've spent time with Miss Keim, you seem like my old dad. Except better." Matthew splashed a few steps away. "Maybe you should see what she thinks about it."

Out of the mouths of babes. Well, Matthew wasn't exactly an infant. But he was young, innocent.

Silas knew he needed to listen to the simple advice from his son. When the timing was right, he would see what Rochelle thought about the idea.

He glanced back toward the group. Someone was sitting in his chair. Steven Hostetler.

Silas sloshed in the direction of the row of beach chairs, the breeze chilling his body where his soaked garments stuck to him.

"Steven."

The young man bolted up from the chair. "Ah, hello, Mr. Fry."

The two shook hands, and Silas settled back onto his seat. Lena's cheeks flushed red.

"What brings you out to the beach today?"

"Just visiting like a good chunk of the village is." He bobbed his head, his focus bouncing from Silas to Lena.

A phone warbled. Steven pulled it from his pocket. "Excuse me." He frowned as he pushed a button. His features changed, his frown deepening.

"Yes. No, I didn't know. Yes, I'm at Siesta Beach right now, with the Frys . . . she *what*?"

Lena shifted in her beach chair, concern on her face.

He ended the call. "I . . . I need to go. I'm sorry."

Steven ran from the beach, sand flying up from his sneakers.

Silas watched until he disappeared from view, then studied his daughter's face. "What happened?"

Lena sighed. "Steven . . . Steven was the one who gave me the head scarf."

"What?"

"He apologized."

"Apologized?"

"He brought it over to the house, then changed his mind. But we'd already gotten home Christmas night, and it was too late for him to get it back."

Silas took his seat. "But he's marrying Emma Yoder in four days."

Lena leaned forward, wincing as she did so, burying her face in her hands. "I know."

Right now, Silas wanted Rochelle's input. "The gift wasn't proper. Not if he's marrying someone else."

"I know, Dad." She reached for the scarf.

"No, leave it on for now." He shook his head. "You can decide what to do with it later, after we get home."

Lena nodded. "Oh, Dad. I wasn't trying to cause any problems. He's so nice, and kind. He knows a lot about the ocean and animals, and we were talking because I was thinking of changing my studies."

Silas wasn't sure what to say, so kept silent.

"I . . . I think he likes me, Dad, more than he ought to. And, I like him, too."

Silas blew out a deep breath. Now what?

30

*R*ochelle rushed past Betsy and into Emma's room. Her bed was neatly made, the extra thermal blanket folded neatly at the foot.

She strode to the closet door and slid it open. Empty, except for hangers.

"Did she say she was leaving? Why would she go without saying anything?"

"Someone said . . . someone said they saw her boarding the bus today, the bus to Ohio." Betsy scurried from the doorway and back down the hall.

Rochelle went to the kitchen table for her phone. "I'm going to call her," she called out.

"Perhaps we should leave," Vera Byler said, standing as she did so. Patience followed suit.

"I'll let you know, Vera and Patience. I apologize for cutting our conversation short like this. But I promise, we'll speak about the business again soon."

"Please, let us know how Emma is," Patience said. "I like her, and I pray she's all right."

The two scurried from the house, and Rochelle pushed the button on her phone.

A ring sounded from the bedroom. "What on earth?"

She trotted back to the bedroom, where Emma's phone rang from its spot on the nightstand.

Why didn't the girl just *talk* to somebody? Why did she have to be so drastic?

Rochelle calmed herself as she returned to the kitchen. She could have used the same medicine to cure impulsivity at the same age.

Betsy's phone warbled. "*Mamm! Nein, mamm,* she's gone." She continued in German, shaking her head.

She looked up and frowned at Rochelle. "A moment, *mamm.*"

"Have they heard anything?"

"No, *Mamm* said she heard, too. They are on their way over here, *Mamm* and *Daed.*"

Rochelle sank onto the nearest kitchen chair. "But the wedding . . . Steven . . ."

Betsy's frown deepened and she continued speaking with her mother. She ended the call with a deep sigh, then set her phone on the table.

"Betsy, did Emma give any signs she was going to leave?"

"No, *Aenti* Chelle. At the Christmas parade, even, she was telling everyone how excited she was about the wedding."

"What a mess. And your *mamm* and *daed* even included a mention of them along with your wedding announcement in *The Budget.*"

Still, if Emma hadn't been sure, it was better for her not to marry at all than to marry with doubts.

The front door burst open. "Emma?" Steven's voice rang into the kitchen.

"She's not here, Steven," Rochelle said. "I'm sorry."

"Not here? Where did she go?" He paced the kitchen, his sandy hair askew, his face red.

"Back. Back to Ohio." Betsy's voice quavered. She shook her head.

"What? She told me . . . I should have known . . ." He continued pacing, tugging on his suspenders. "When Lena—" his voice cut off. "Never mind."

Rochelle glanced at Betsy, who stood and said, "I think I'll go see to my *kapps*," and headed off in the direction of the bedrooms.

Steven rubbed his forehead. "Aunt Chelle, she left. She's gone."

Rochelle nodded. The young man, in shock, took a seat.

"But we were supposed to get married. I don't . . . I don't understand. We had a disagreement, and then there was Lena." Then his brow furrowed.

"What about Lena?" Rochelle leaned forward on her chair.

"I like her, a lot. I love Emma, but Lena wasn't pressuring me. I felt so much . . . pressure with Emma. I don't know how to explain it." He groaned, then leaned his forehead on the table. He bolted upright. "Eli Troyer. He has something to do with this. I know. Ever since he got here in Pinecraft, I've seen him around."

"I don't think Eli would deliberately sabotage your and Emma's engagement. He respects your commitment. You do know Emma had been engaged to him, the end of the summer before this past summer."

Steven hopped up from the chair, the action knocking it over. The chair hit the tile floor with a crash.

"Aw, I'm sorry, Aunt Chelle, it was an accident."

"I know." She wanted to tell him what she'd told Betsy, about this perhaps being a blessing in disguise. He wouldn't believe it now, wouldn't understand, but one day, he would.

Steven set the chair upright. "May I get a glass of tea?"

"Yes, help yourself."

He stalked over to the cabinet, fished out a glass, then found the pitcher of tea.

No, if Rochelle was the kind of person to wager, she would be willing to wager Emma's doubts about Steven began to simmer when she quit Keim Cleaning. The young people's fishing trip set the simmer to a slow boil, followed by Eli's arrival, then the growing friendship with Lena.

When Steven and Emma had connected in the early months of the year, Emma had been giggly and charming. Lena connecting with Steven on the fishing trip had been direct and no-nonsense, with a charm all her own, the kind a young woman possessed and likely didn't realize.

Steven sat down again on the chair, gingerly this time. "Regardless of who's to blame, the wedding's off. If she's so unsure, I don't want to marry her."

"You're right. I suggested to her that if she were so unsure, she needed to talk to the man she loved. Not be stubborn or scared, and hide her feelings." *Like I did . . .*

"Well, she didn't talk to me." Steven took a big gulp of tea, then set the glass down. "I guess your suggestion backfired."

"Yes and no. I was only trying to help. What I guess is, we don't know what's going on inside someone's head sometimes."

Steven nodded. "Aunt Chelle, it's gonna be okay. You're a helper. It's what you do. And if you helped Emma and me avoid a big mistake, something we'd have to deal with the rest of our lives, then I'm glad you helped. Even if you didn't know what was going to happen."

Rochelle had to smile at the young man. A helper? Yes, she did like to help. "You're right, Steven, it's going to be okay. Like I told Emma, God is good at helping us unsnarl our messes. I'm sorry you're hurting, Emma was hurting."

However, she had a problem. She had four hundred cupcakes for a wedding that wouldn't take place after all. They covered the kitchen counter and all of her breakfast bar.

✑

With the tumult of the day winding down, Silas headed to Rochelle's home. He needed to speak to her and not put it off any longer. He knew Betsy would be there as well, so tongues wouldn't wag. However, if everything went as he hoped, the time for tongue wagging would be over for them.

Rochelle let him in. Her eyes looked tired, but she smiled at him. "I'm glad to see you."

"And I'm glad to see you." He followed her to the kitchen, where every horizontal surface was covered with unfrosted cupcakes. "This is a lot of cupcakes."

A Promise of Grace

"Yes, unfortunately, it is . . . they were to have been Emma's, for her wedding."

"It's why I'm here. How is Steven?"

"Angry. Hurt. Maybe a bit relieved, but I don't think he'll admit it yet." She shook her head and sighed. "Emma's gone back to Ohio. Eli Troyer, too. Her parents filled me in on the story."

"What happened to her?"

"Evidently, her parents told her they were being pressured, threatened to be put on the *banns* because of their 'extravagance' with the weddings according to their new bishop. Plus, the girl was simply homesick." Rochelle gestured toward the door outside. "Do you want to sit on the lanai?"

"Here is fine." He pulled an empty chair away from the table.

"Anyway, she liked Pinecraft because it's such a special place during the winter. Everyone's playing and vacationing. But she had a taste of Pinecraft during the rest of the year. We still have to work, just like everyone else. And Steven . . ." Rochelle sighed.

"Lena told me her side of the story. She likes Steven, but was always respectful of the fact he and Emma were getting married." Silas tried to choose his words carefully.

"Oh, I knew *something* was brewing with those two, but I didn't suspect they'd done anything improper." Rochelle sighed again. "Young people and the decisions they make sometimes."

"I'm glad the wedding is off, for both their sakes, if they're truly not ready."

"Me too." She scanned the room. "So, do you want to help me frost some cupcakes tonight? I suppose Betsy will have lots of extra desserts for her wedding." She laughed, softly.

Silas stood. He glanced at the cupcakes. "I can help you."

"I was half-joking."

"I'm serious. I'll help. Do you have frosting?"

"I'm going to make some. Betsy said she'd help me."

"Help you do what?" Betsy entered the kitchen. "Hi, Silas." She gave her aunt a grin.

"Make frosting."

"Of course, it'll take a moment to whip it up. Did you get enough powdered sugar?"

"Emma bought it, so I hope so." Rochelle went for the mixer.

Betsy waved her away. "No, go, spend a moment with your Silas."

Her Silas. He had to grin at Betsy's words. "Come, let's go to the backyard. I have something to ask you."

"Okay."

His heart pounded in his throat, the entire trip from the kitchen, out the door to the lanai, then out the screen door to the patch of lawn beside the creek.

Suddenly his palms were sweating worse than a youth's did. *You're a chicken, Silas Fry. Despite the arrogance of your youth, the confidence of a pilot, the experience of a mature man, deep down, you're a chicken when it comes to Rochelle Keim.*

"It's going to be a beautiful night," Rochelle said. "Look at the sunset."

He did. God had painted the twilight a vivid pinkish red, blending into purple and a deep blue where a single star glowed. The palm trees stood out in sharp contrast to the sky.

"Yes, it's a beautiful night already." He licked his lips. "There's something I want to ask you. I don't want to wait too long."

"What is it?"

"Rochelle Keim, I loved you when we were only youth. I was prideful, young, immature. I didn't give us a chance like I should have . . ." Part of his decision back then, he blamed on Belinda. "But now, being here again, I believe God's given us a second chance. I don't want to throw it away. Will you be my wife? Will you marry me?"

Astonishment swept across her face. Her mouth opened, but no words came out. "I . . . I . . ."

"Please . . . our stubbornness kept us apart before, but now . . ."

"I'm . . . can I have a moment, please?"

༄

Rochelle stumbled into her bedroom, ignoring Betsy's expression of concern as she darted through the kitchen.

Silas had proposed. At last. It was what she'd dreamed of years ago, a dream she'd let die.

But was now their time?

Yes, she cared for him, loved him. Did it mean they should build a life together?

The sting returned about Lena, John, and the story Belinda and Silas had kept from everyone.

She leaned on her dresser, where the box from Leah Graber rested, Leah's project box.

Open it.

The two words ricocheted inside her brain. Someone had hand-carved the box, a fine example of Amish workmanship.

She flipped open the lid. Some receipts, faded. A few empty envelopes, never used. Postage stamps. And an envelope, addressed to her, covered with stamps and multiple postmarks from overseas.

And the printing was Belinda's neat handwriting, the envelope postmarked eighteen years ago.

Her knees turned into noodles, but somehow she stumbled to the bed and peeled open the envelope.

Dear Rochelle,

I didn't have your address in Pinecraft, so I am writing to you at Leah Graber's because I know you have been working for her. I am writing this letter because I want you, of all people, to know the truth. As our little Lena plays in the sunshine after taking her first steps, I know I can't be silent anymore. Not to you. You, of all people, deserve to know.

Lena is really John's child.

Silas and I didn't want you to think the worst of us. Especially me.

You have and always will be my dearest friend in the world. But when I lost John and found out I was pregnant, I didn't know what to do. Silas promised to take care of me, and he has. Please forgive us. I hope you will, someday. Because of my pride and shame, I didn't care if you and Silas reconciled. For that, I will always be sorry.

With much love, always,
Belinda

Why hadn't Leah given her the envelope? Maybe it was being busy, forgetful.

Whatever the reason, it didn't matter now. Even if Leah had indeed given her the letter years ago, the contents of the letter wouldn't have changed the circumstances.

Rochelle clutched the letter to her chest. "Oh, Belinda, I forgive you. I'll always miss you. But someday, we'll get our reunion . . ."

And Silas was outside, waiting for her now. She put the letter on the bed and ran for the lanai. She passed Betsy again, the mixer whining and whirring as it whipped the buttercream.

He stood facing Phillippi Creek, his hands stuffed in his pockets. "Silas."

He turned in her direction, his face shadowed in the fading light. "Well?" he asked.

She went as easily into his arms as she'd done years ago. "Yes, yes, I'll marry you."

Not caring if the neighbors saw them, she let him kiss her thoroughly.

"I think we need to speak to Pastor Marvin, first thing in the morning," he said, after leaving her breathless.

"First thing in the morning?"

"We should find out if Betsy and Thaddeus mind sharing their wedding day with us."

"In four days?" So soon, and yet she'd waited years . . .

"After we speak to the pastor, we can get our marriage license."

"Come to think of it, your parents, our families, everyone is here already . . ." Some might say this happened too quickly, but others might agree it was a long time in coming.

He kissed her forehead. "Besides, you have hundreds of cupcakes in the kitchen needing to be put to good use."

"And I already have a new dress . . ."

"Then it's settled. We're getting married in four days." He swept her up into his arms and tried to spin her around.

Then he stumbled, and they both collapsed onto the lawn and burst out laughing.

"Did you hurt yourself?" She rolled over on her side. She'd landed on her hip, but the ground was soft.

"No." He leaned over and kissed her again.

"What on earth?" Betsy came running from the lanai. "I saw you out the kitchen window? Are you all right?"

"We're fine." Rochelle sat up, adjusting her *kapp*. "We're just fine now."

"So, Betsy, about your wedding day . . ."

31

"I never imagined this would be my wedding dress." Rochelle stood at the mirror. She adjusted her prayer covering, which looked a bit off-center at first. There. Its whiteness provided a fresh contrast to the vivid blue of the dress. If she liked the choice of fabric color the first time she'd seen it several months ago in Frances Fry's sewing room, she loved it now.

Truly, she didn't know if Pinecraft had ever seen such a nontraditional wedding day before. The order of services would not be any different, however. If only Daddy and Momma could have been here. At last, their daughter and Silas Fry, speaking vows before friends, family, and God above.

"You look beautiful." Lena stood in the doorway. Her own dress, a soft shade of lilac, brought out the sun-kissed tones of her skin.

A *daughter*. Not only was Rochelle marrying Silas, but she'd gain a daughter. And a son, too. Of course, they didn't need much raising.

"Thank you. So do you. You . . . you remind me so much of your mother at the same age."

"Chelle, do you mind if we . . . talk, for a few minutes?"

"Of course not. Come in, sit down." Rochelle motioned to the bed.

"I wish . . . I wish I had had the chance to know you before, that you and . . . my mother could have made things right between the two of you." Lena entered the room, closing the door behind her, and sank onto Rochelle's bed.

"Me too. But after she and your father married, I couldn't help it. I knew I needed to stay away from them. It hurt too much." As Rochelle spoke the words, they didn't sting like they might have once. "I knew I couldn't have a life in Ohio. And then, I heard you'd come along."

"Sorry." Lena half-smiled.

Rochelle had to smile, too. "Anyway, it's in the past. I'm not replacing your mother. No one could." Rochelle perched on a free spot on the corner of the bed.

"Oh, I know. But it will be good to have another woman I can talk to." Lena sat down beside her. "Speaking of talking, I'm sorry for not talking to you until now. I was angry about my mother. The letter shows she tried to tell the truth, but . . ."

"It was a lot for me to take in, too. I can't imagine how it was for you, and for your brother also. But I promise, I'll be here for you, and for Matthew."

"Thank you." Lena frowned, then smoothed her dress. "I wanted to say, I'm . . . I'm sorry for how I acted when I found out about Dad not being my, ah, real father. I felt ashamed. Then mad. I don't think I've ever been so mad in my whole life. Not since Mom died."

Rochelle nodded slowly. "I know. I was angry with your father and mother, too. I thought . . ." She stopped. She didn't want to share her thoughts, it hurt worse to know he and Belinda had created a child together, so soon. It had never occurred to her Lena wasn't Silas's daughter.

"My Dad broke your heart."

Rochelle nodded again. "Part of it was my fault. I was angry then, blaming him for John's death . . . your father's death. It hurt, I have to admit, when I learned about the lie. Besides, Belinda—your mom—and your dad were married. Silas and I talked about this, if we'd only not been so stubborn."

"Matthew wouldn't be here. I can't imagine not having my little brother around." Lena shivered. "We can all sure mess things up sometimes, can't we?"

"God works well at untying our snags."

"But some snags can't be fixed."

"Maybe some snags aren't meant to be fixed, but transformed, into something beautiful instead." She studied the young girl's face. "What is it?"

"I feel bad about Emma leaving like she did. I wasn't looking to meet Steven. I didn't think . . ." Lena bit her lip. "I wasn't trying to cause trouble."

"Oh, my dear. You didn't cause any trouble, not at all. In fact, I feel as if I was the one who had something to do with Emma leaving Pinecraft and going back to Ohio."

"You did? How?"

"Emma was mulling over her dilemma, after Eli arrived in Pinecraft. I told her if she didn't have a conversation she needed to have with the man she loved, then it would be a mistake."

"And she thought you meant Eli."

"She'd always loved Eli. But she was scared, unsure of herself. I think she wanted what Betsy had found, here. But her heart truly wasn't in Pinecraft." Rochelle shook her head at the recollection of Emma's clients firing her. "She was never meant to keep other people's houses or wait tables."

Lena released a pent-up breath. "Well, I'm happy for her. And me. And you, too."

Another soft rap at the door. "Is the bride ready to meet her groom?" Jolene's soft voice sounded a bit muffled. "It's time to leave for the ceremony. Nearly everyone's arrived."

The day-long, back-to-back wedding ceremonies were the talk of Pinecraft. They had set up chairs, as many as would fit on the green lawn near the park, at the base of a tree dripping with Spanish moss. First, Silas and Rochelle would wed and their guests would disperse so the wedding guests for Betsy and Thaddeus could assemble, and their ceremony would take place. After both ceremonies were completed, the entire entourage would make their way to the Tourist Church hall, where everyone would enjoy a grand feast together.

"I'm ready." A lump swelled in Rochelle's throat. She would not, could not, cry. Today was not a day for tears, or mourning. She'd had enough of those days. Today was a day of a promise fulfilled, a long-dormant longing granted.

"Let's go," Lena said as she stood with a smile on her face.

Rochelle stood, ready to leave her bedroom for the last time as Rochelle Keim. Lena surprised her with a quick hug.

Not far from the banks of Phillippi Creek, Silas Fry married Rochelle Keim. At last. At long last.

Their wedding party was a simple one, with Rochelle's sister standing as her matron of honor, and his father standing up for him.

As the sound of voices raised in song drifted away, Silas turned to face her.

"Well, it's you and me."

Her face radiated joy along with the late morning sun. "Yes, it is."

Then the well-wishers descended upon them, and the naysayers were likely home, boycotting the day. But he'd lost Belinda more than a year ago, had mourned her. What happened in the last several months between him and Rochelle . . .

Grace. Restoration. Another chance.

She clutched his hand, and he pulled her closer beside him. No more worrying about who might see what or say what.

"Mr. Fry." Rochelle blushed, appearing to him as if twenty years hadn't passed between them.

The small crowd milled around, most of the wedding guests leaving their seats to make room for Betsy and Thaddeus's guests. Some kept their seats; they were friends or family to both couples.

"We've run out of chairs," Rochelle observed.

"Yes."

"Let's stand in the back. I don't mind if you don't." She smiled at him, and he wondered how he would get through the hours of another wedding, then the feast to follow for both him and his bride, along with Thaddeus and Betsy.

"We're already in the perfect honeymoon spot," he said aloud.

At this, Rochelle's color deepened even more. "Silas Fry."

"What?" He grinned at her. "We're married. People know it. And they won't let us forget they know it."

She shook her head. "Honestly."

"Newlyweds, and you're already attending your first wedding as husband and wife." Henry Hostetler approached, looking as formal as Sunday in his black trousers and white shirt. He pumped Silas's hand, following up with a half-hug for Rochelle. "I'm pleased as punch you two tied the knot. At last. I was wondering how long it would take."

"Not long, it turns out." Rochelle punctuated her sentence with a laugh.

"Well, I knew something was brewing the day of the fish fry." He winked at them.

"Back then?" Rochelle asked.

"Are we all going to take a wedding trip together?" Matthew asked beside Silas.

"No." Silas tousled his son's hair. "Rochelle and I are going to a beach cottage for three days, and then it's back to work for all of us and back to school for you."

Three days, alone in a cottage, with her *husband* . . . Rochelle's heart pounded. "Maybe when school lets out for the summer, we can all make a trip to Ohio."

"The wedding's going to start," Silas said, his voice soft and low.

A few more guests took up the last few seats on the lawn. Rochelle felt tears prick the back of her eyes when she saw Thaddeus take his place, his attendants walking with him. Two empty chairs waited before the bishop, one chair for Thaddeus, the other for Betsy.

Then came Betsy, her face glowing as she entered, her attendants ahead of her. The other women sat, and Betsy joined Thaddeus as they went to speak to the bishop and church leaders.

How much joy Rochelle wanted for both of them. So blessed the two were, to have found each other.

Her heart hurt for Nora Yoder, knowing her daughter had left them to return to Ohio. But likely Nora rejoiced, because Emma had made her own choice at last. Emma had phoned her mother from the shanty; she was back home in her old room.

Steven was nowhere to be found at the ceremony. Rochelle suspected he was somewhere helping prepare fish for the wedding meal to follow in the late afternoon.

He'd heal up and would be blessed with a wife at the right time.

Would she be Lena, the daughter of Rochelle's heart? No one knew. In the meantime, he had his beloved boat and charters.

Lena moved closer to Rochelle, slipping her arm around Rochelle's.

"You had a beautiful wedding," she whispered.

"I thought so."

"Thank you for making my dad so happy."

Rochelle nodded. "He has made me happy, too."

They fell silent as the wedding continued. The streets surrounding the park swelled with people, wanting to catch a glimpse of the bride and groom.

A wedding in Pinecraft didn't often happen.

Rochelle never imagined hers would happen here. But so it did. She glanced up at Silas, her husband, and squeezed his hand.

Epilogue

*O*ne year later

Rochelle's hands trembled as she handed the house key to Betsy. "Here. I know you'll take good care of the place."

"You have our promise we will."

"And the freezer in the garage, it's quit working, and I haven't figured out what to do with it—"

"We'll dispose of it properly." Betsy glanced past Rochelle's shoulder. "*Aenti* Chelle."

The women embraced, and Rochelle willed the tears away.

"I'll write. Maybe I'll even call. Let me know as soon as you can, when the baby, he or she, arrives." Rochelle smiled down at the first signs of new life growing inside her niece.

Betsy nodded as Thaddeus stood at her side. "We will."

"Rochelle . . ." The sound of her name on Silas's tongue sent a happy shiver down her spine. "We need to leave now if we're to make our connecting flight."

"I know, I know. I didn't think it would be so . . . so hard."

"Thaddeus." Silas shook hands with Thaddeus.

"We'll be praying for you, brother."

"Thank you." Silas's smile was warm as he gazed at Rochelle. "Before we say good-bye a dozen more times, we must go."

"We'll see you again, God willing."

"*Gotte* willing." Betsy waved as Rochelle and Silas drove away.

The lump in Rochelle's throat swelled as Silas maneuvered the car through Pinecraft's streets. The last few weekends of the winter season still made the village's population feel a bit crowded.

Someone—one of the Lapp brothers—was attaching a flier to a corner light pole on Fry Street.

Even from the van windows, Rochelle read the notice someone had painstakingly written in precise black lettering on a plain piece of paper: SINGING TONIGHT AND HAYSTACK SUPPER, PINECRAFT PARK.

She would miss everything about this dear place. Nellie Bontrager, pedaling her three-wheeled cycle, waved, then slowed down to meet up with a trio of women chatting on the opposite street corner.

"I know you're a little sad." Silas reached across the space between them and squeezed her hand.

"I'm happy, too, you know. About you and me. Overseas. How much good we can both do. I feel like I'm waking up from a dream, but oh, what a sweet dream it's been. And yet, it didn't have you." She'd had a ton of convincing to do—convincing herself she wasn't taking up where Belinda left off, and she wasn't trying to make Silas's dream her own, just so she could have him.

"I loved Belinda, but she wasn't you."

"We won't go down the road again. It's time to go forward." She tried not to look wistfully at the palm trees.

Pinecraft had helped her grow up, by encouraging her to spread her wings and run her own business, yet stay true to her Plain faith. Silas coming to Pinecraft had taught her about grace, truly forgiving. Surely, some in the village might talk about their "hasty" betrothal and swift wedding beside Betsy and Thaddeus. However, the seed had lain dormant for decades.

"Pinecraft will always be here."

"I know. We're only leaving for a year, but it feels like it'll be longer."

They now arrived at the Bahia Vista traffic light and Big Olaf's Ice Cream parlor. Rochelle wanted to ask Silas to stop the van so they could get one more taste before leaving.

Instead, she kept silent and allowed her last glimpses of the village, of the Plain people—her people—walking its sunny streets, to etch themselves into her memory.

Glossary

Ach—oh

Aenti—aunt

Bruder—brother

Daadi—grandfather

Daed—father

Danki—thank you

Dochder—daughter

Englisch—non-Amish

Gotte's wille—God's will

Gut—good

Kaffi—coffee

Kapp—prayer covering

Kind—child

Kinner—children

Mamm—mom

Mammi—grandma

Mudder—mother

Nein—no

Onkel—uncle

Ordnung—set of rules for Amish living

Rumspringa—running around; time before an Amish young person has officially joined the church, provides a bridge between childhood and adulthood

Ya—yes

Group Discussion Guide

1. Who was your favorite character in *A Promise of Grace*? Explain why this character appealed to you?
2. Both Rochelle and Belinda experienced deep grief as young women. What can you do to help a grieving friend?
3. Silas is finding it hard to let go of his maturing children. What would you suggest to him to make the transition easier?
4. Rochelle decides to go back to school and finish her nursing studies. If you had the chance to go back to school, what would you study?
5. One of Rochelle's gifts is hospitality. What are some of your favorite at-home activities to enjoy with family and friends?
6. If you could give Emma (or Betsy) some pre-wedding advice, what would it be?
7. Silas feels conflicted about an ideal job opportunity. Have you ever had to make a difficult choice when it comes to a job?
8. Rochelle's advice to Emma backfires—or so she thinks. Talk about a time you gave a friend or family member a bit of advice and it didn't turn out like you expected.
9. Both Rochelle and Silas realized they still feel the effects of past hurts. What do you do when you discover you still need to work on extending grace to someone who's hurt you?
10. What was your favorite scene in *A Promise of Grace*? Why did that scene stand out for you?

Want to learn more about author
Lynette Sowell and check out other great
fiction from Abingdon Press?

Check out
www.AbingdonFiction.com
to read interviews with your favorite authors, find tips
for starting a reading group, and stay posted on what
new titles are on the horizon. It's a place to connect
with other fiction readers or post a
comment about this book.

Be sure to visit Lynette online!

https://www.facebook.com/lynettesowellauthor

We hope you enjoyed Lynette Sowell's *A Promise of Grace*. If you haven't read the first two books in the Seasons in Pinecraft series, please check out *A Season of Change* and *A Path Made Plain*. Here's a sample from *A Season of Change*.

1

We're having ice cream at Christmas time, Daed?" Zeke Miller trotted alongside his father on the pavement, trying to keep up with Jacob's pace. The boy would definitely sleep well tonight; he'd barely stopped since he'd gotten off the Pioneer Trails bus and tumbled into the Florida sunshine.

"Yes, we are. It's hard to imagine, isn't it? We're definitely a long way from home." Jacob rubbed the top of his son's head. At only five, Zeke didn't comprehend the idea of ice cream in winter. His sister, Rebecca, a dozen paces ahead of them, pranced alongside her cousins. The sound of the children's giggles drifted on the air.

Jacob slowed his steps to match Zeke's five-year-old stride. Their figures made long shadows as they strode toward Big Olaf's Ice Cream Parlor. The December twilight came early, even in Sarasota.

To Jacob, the words *Christmas* and *ice cream* didn't belong in the same sentence. And he certainly never thought he would be entertaining the children's eager pleas to ride the bus to the *beach* on Christmas Day. But, here they were, nestled in Sarasota's winter haven called Pinecraft.

"We're here, we're here!" Rebecca giggled, and stumbled. "*Ach.*" She stopped long enough to stick her foot back into the pink plastic flip-flops, a gift from her cousin Maybelle.

Jacob shook his head over his daughter wearing the sandals, but a smile tugged at the corners of his mouth anyway. As soon as they'd all climbed off the immense travel bus and stepped onto the parking lot of Pinecraft's Mennonite Tourist Church, the surroundings seemed to draw them in. The children burst with energy after being stuck on a bus for two days, save for a stop here and there to stretch their legs or pick up more passengers. The more distance between Ohio, the more passengers on the bus.

At first the novelty of riding on a mechanized vehicle had the children enthralled with the speed they traveled and the levers that brought the seats forward and backward, but eventually even Rebecca fidgeted and squirmed in her seat. Bored, as all the children soon became.

Jacob sympathized, but instead of running like a child would, he stared at his surroundings, the rows of homes both large and small, the orange and grapefruit trees in front yards. And the palm trees, of course.

He'd never had the opportunity to visit Florida, even after his grandparents bought a home here in Pinecraft. He hadn't seen the practicality of cramming himself on a bus and traveling hundreds of miles only to do the same two weeks later. Finally, however, desperation had won out over practicality.

He'd only seen photos of palm trees, only heard about members of his Order using tricycles for transportation instead of horse and buggy. No room for horses in a city. His own grandfather rode an adult-size tricycle with a large basket, peddling fruit for sale to tourists.

Zeke's grin lit his face and he pulled his hand from Jacob's grasp, trotted ahead to catch up with his sister and cousins.

Here, hundreds of miles from Ohio's fields and the cabinet factory where Jacob worked, his children laughed like they hadn't in six months. This made him smile, too, though his heart still hurt.

Hannah, gone so soon. When they were younger, they'd exchanged glances across the room on Sundays until he found the nerve to talk to her at a singing. Then they married when he was but twenty-three and she eighteen. They'd both vowed to embrace their Order and planned to be married as long as the Lord allowed. Which had turned out to be a mere eight years.

Hannah's third pregnancy had been much harder than the first two, and even modern technology hadn't saved her when the midwife urged him to allow the *Englisch* physicians to stabilize her at an *Englisch* hospital. The *boppli*, another son they'd named Samuel, had come too early. No one could have warned Jacob how difficult it was to carry a double load of grief. Their days together were finished on this earth, but Jacob found himself asking, *Why?*

He caught sight of his brother waiting for him at the sidewalk's edge. "The Yoders are arriving on the last bus before Christmas," Ephraim said.

The loaded statement snapped Jacob out of his pondering. A good thing. He was moving on, as he should. But he could still feel the emptiness in his bed every night Hannah wasn't there. Even though *Mammi* had given him the twin air mattress to sleep on while visiting in Florida, Jacob's memories and the children's chatter in the living room kept him awake at night. In his grandparents' snug home, filled with Millers in every nook and cranny, Jacob's lone state set him apart.

"That's what *Daadi* said after supper tonight." Jacob knew where Ephraim's small talk was headed, straight to Betsy.

"Betsy Yoder is coming with her parents, too." Ephraim glanced his way. "She told Katie at our last Sunday meeting they'll be here just in time for Christmas."

"It will be nice to see her and her family." Jacob tugged on his suspenders. Not too much farther, and they'd be at the Bahia Vista stoplight. A hint of a chill drifted on the breeze, waving the fronds of a nearby palm tree.

"Nice? Is that all you can say, it'll be 'nice' to see Betsy?"

"She's a nice girl. Smart, pretty, and she bakes really *gut* pie. She'll make someone a *gut* wife someday. A little on the tall side, though." Jacob paused, and Ephraim did as well. "Happy now?"

"You need to talk to her, not just hang back in the corner like you're a mute."

"I'm not ready to talk to her. Not yet."

"Don't wait too long. She likes you, and she told Katie so. She's wondering why you keep staring at her and never saying anything."

"Like I said, I'm not ready. I don't know if I ever will be. I'm grateful to you and Katie for everything you've done for me, especially Katie helping with the children. I can do my own mending. Rebecca has become a good little housekeeper." Jacob felt his neck growing hotter with every footstep closer to the ice cream shop.

"I know that. And Katie and I are glad to help you. But it's time. Your children need a mother, and you a helpmate."

"Stop pushing me, Ephraim. I know what you're trying to say." Jacob continued the few steps to the street corner and the Bahia Vista stoplight. He didn't want the children to try to cross the busy street alone. They weren't used to watching out for traffic, not like this, anyway. They would make a few trips into town back in Ohio, but the town was far smaller than Sarasota and its infinite worldliness. The traffic, the constant reach of everything not-Plain into his Plain world. He didn't always understand how Plain people could live in the middle of it all. Life in Ohio felt much more in control.

Right. He almost laughed. Nothing had been in control since Hannah had left him. Left them all.

Ephraim kept silent, and Jacob knew he'd probably aggravated his brother.

God knew he'd accepted Hannah's death, and little Samuel's as well. The wounds inside him had scabbed over. Every so often, though, the pain would resurface and catch him when he wasn't paying attention, like the one time he'd cut his hand with a band saw when he was distracted at the cabinet shop. He couldn't help but pick at the scab as it healed.

He expelled a sigh before continuing. "Ephraim, I promise, after we leave Pinecraft, once we're home again, I'll go on. I don't know if it'll be with Betsy Yoder, but I'll think about it." Jacob figured he'd give his brother a shred of a promise. But he couldn't explain to Ephraim the restlessness he felt. His world was the same after losing Hannah and Samuel. His job at the cabinet factory, his home with the rooms Hannah had kept so spotless and filled with joy. Yet, his whole world had changed with the hole Hannah had left. If only an ice cream cone could help him forget his grief for a few minutes.

In sharp contrast to the tropical colors around them, their group stuck out like proverbial sore thumbs as they stood at the traffic lights and waited. Cars crisscrossed at the intersection. Big Olaf's ice cream parlor lay just across the street from them at the light.

Jacob sucked in a breath. He still hadn't grown accustomed to the traffic that zoomed through the heart of the Pinecraft neighborhood, and almost wished he had stayed back at the house with *Mammi* Rachel.

He wasn't scared of honking traffic, and ignored the pointing and stares as they crossed the street—tourists, *Mammi* assured him. The locals didn't mind the novelty of seeing the Amish and accepted the village as part of the city.

Jacob didn't want the children to see his reluctance to venture to the edge of the block. Everything in Florida was so . . . different from Ohio. Yes, different. That was the best word. But he could understand loving the scent of the ocean, the warmth during winter time when all far away to the north was quickly freezing over.

The children scurried into Big Olaf's and Jacob followed as they gathered at the ice cream shop counter, Zeke and Rebecca with their cousins, clutching their money as they decided what ice cream they wanted. True to form, Rebecca changed her mind at least three times before choosing her flavor. That would have earned her a gentle scolding from Hannah. The thought made Jacob smile.

"I thought you wanted a cone," Jacob said as Rebecca turned to face him with a dish of vanilla ice cream, covered with chocolate sauce and nuts.

"I did. But then I decided I wanted to take my time while I eat. You can't take your time eating ice cream cones, you know," she replied and grinned at him, the blue of her eyes matching the fading blue of the evening sky. Hannah's eyes.

Jacob tugged on one of her braids. "Truthful girl, you are."

They all turned to leave. Even Ephraim and Katie had ordered ice cream. But not for him. Jacob shared his son's disbelief at the idea of eating ice cream at Christmas. And walking in shirtsleeves to the corner ice cream shop.

They carefully crossed the road and began to meander back into the neighborhood and safety.

"I forgot a spoon!" Rebecca exclaimed and whirled back toward Big Olaf's. "I'll be right back."

"Mind the road," Jacob called out. "Wait, I'll walk with you." He strode back toward Rebecca and the corner.

"Oh, *Daed*, I'm not a baby. I can watch for the light and look for cars." Rebecca's long skirt swished a few inches above her ankles. Not too many years from now, she'd be putting her hair up under her prayer covering. Jacob wasn't ready for that.

Just six paces behind her, Jacob saw the light turn. Rebecca kept her focus on the ice cream in the dish and then glanced up at Big Olaf's across the street.

She stepped into the crosswalk. A dark sedan took the corner. Cars moved so, so quickly.

Jacob's throat clenched. He darted forward. "Rebecca!"

She froze and looked back at him, then at the car.

The thud wrenched a shout from Jacob.

Rebecca's scream stung his ears.

He reached the corner as Rebecca's dish of ice cream landed on the warm asphalt.

❧

A compound femur fracture, a hematoma on the brain, a concussion. But no internal injuries. Jacob found one thing to be thankful for, besides the fact that Rebecca now breathed peacefully, sedated because of her injuries, in the intensive care unit.

How close they'd come to losing her two days ago.

The driver of the car, a young Mennonite woman returning home after visiting her grandparents, had dissolved into a heap on the pavement, sobbing upon leaving the driver's seat.

On Christmas break from college in Virginia, she'd borrowed her parents' vehicle and had been hurrying home to get ready for a date. She looked more *Englisch* than anything in her shorts, T-shirt, and flip-flops, but knew enough *Deutsch* to speak to him and the family after the accident.

She hadn't seen Rebecca, who'd been walking with the light while the young woman turned. Children moved so quickly. The police weren't going to press charges. Jacob didn't think pressing charges would serve any purpose. This young woman deserved grace, and was suffering enough for one mistake.

Jacob sat up a little straighter in the cushioned chair in the intensive care unit. It had been his fault, really. He should have watched Rebecca more closely, should have kept her nearer to him, insisted she stop and wait for him to cross the street with her. He should have been firmer.

"She's always been the more willful one of your children," Ephraim observed.

"*Ach*, it's true. Hannah always knew . . ." Yes, Hannah had always known how to handle Rebecca. Gotte*, what am I going to do now?*

"You'll have to stay in Pinecraft, far longer than Christmas."

"A long time." But he had a job in Ohio, and had to support his family. Yet, he wouldn't leave his daughter. Not here. Not alone, her body broken and her brain swollen, although she'd be with family.

No, he would stay here in Sarasota for as long as it took for Rebecca to get well again.

But Sarasota had turned out to be a far, far more dangerous place than he'd ever imagined. He had a nagging feeling Sarasota held more dangers for them still.

❧

"Natalie, dear, I wish you'd change your mind and join us for Christmas dinner," said Grace Montgomery. "You shouldn't have eaten alone. Come for pie, or something."

Natalie Bennett held her cell phone close to her ear, but not too close. She stood in the lobby of Sarasota General Hospital.

"Too late, I'm already at the hospital. But thanks for inviting me." She tried not to smudge her clown makeup. She hadn't brought her emergency makeup kit to fix any damage to the face she'd taken great care to paint not quite an hour ago.

"At least come for dessert later, please?" Even over the phone, Grace's sound of longing and gentle insistence couldn't be missed.

"All right, I will." A few passersby glanced Natalie's way and smiled at her getup. "I forgot to give you and Todd your gift the other night at the office party."

"Sweetie, you didn't have to get us anything."

"I know. But I wanted to." She glanced around. "Hey, I'll call you later. People are probably wondering who Bubbles the Clown is talking to on the phone."

"Just come on over once you're through."

"You've got it. Merry Christmas." Natalie ended the call and slipped the phone into her tote bag, full of tricks and novelties for the children she'd soon visit. She also toted a mesh bag stuffed with oranges from the tree in her apartment complex's yard. The kids would love them. Right. Who was she kidding? She should have brought chocolate bars. Being in the hospital at Christmas was as much fun as getting socks for a present. An orange probably wouldn't help soothe things like chocolate.

Part of her wished she'd told Grace, her boss, mentor, and friend, about her lack of Christmas plans, but then she didn't want the sympathy. Maybe Grace wouldn't have felt too sorry for her. Grace, like most people attached to the circus world, knew the traveling life quite well. Holidays and roots weren't the same for them. Natalie knew full well. She couldn't miss what she'd never had, could she?

A Christmas tree had sprouted in the main lobby of the hospital, and its twenty-foot artificial glory twinkled like a beacon against anyone who dared say that Christmas had forgotten the sick and injured children of Sarasota. A Chanukah menorah glowed on the fireplace mantel in the seating area.

Natalie headed for the elevator and braced herself for the atmosphere awaiting her in the ward. If they lived in a perfect world, no one would be in the hospital at Christmas. No one would be sick. They'd all have their Norman Rockwell scenes around dining room tables, and moms and dads would yawn over their ham or turkey after staying up late putting together toys. Kids would giggle around Christmas trees and then pass out like the little boy in *A Christmas Story*, clutching his zeppelin. But not these kids in the pediatrics wing.

Natalie was used to nontraditional Christmases, and some of the children she was about to visit were, too. Chronic illness and severe injuries didn't take holidays.

But Christmas, Natalie had learned over the years, could come anywhere. Natalie didn't put up a tree or send cards, although she was fond of the Christmas music classics. Dad always played them when they were on the road with the Circus Du Monde. He and Mom would dance to "Rockin' Around the Christmas Tree" on Christmas night, wherever they were, and then Dad would hit the makeshift dance floor with Natalie.

Then they'd turn out all the lights and light one candle as Dad read the Christmas story from a Gideon Bible he'd swiped from a hotel somewhere. She never understood how the baby Jesus story related to dancing around a Christmas tree. Even now, the side-by-side secular and religious traditions sometimes didn't mesh well to her. But she discovered she loved the Christmas Eve candlelight service at church. It was there for the first time, three Christmases ago, the realization that God really loved *her*—Natalie Anne Bennett—hit her with full force. She'd spent the last two years figuring out what that meant, and how she ought to respond with her life.

Which meant she didn't need the Christmas tree or dozens of presents. What she needed was right here, hallways of children and their families waiting for a little joy. It was her way to give back in one of the best ways she knew.

Her throat caught at her own Christmas memories, and she took a deep breath as she pushed the button for the elevator. Bittersweet emotions didn't fit with what she was about to do. Clowns weren't supposed to be bittersweet.

Natalie took the elevator to the main pediatrics floor and checked in at the reception desk with the charge nurse who today wore a Santa cap. Multicolored twinkle lights flashed along the aqua blue counter.

"Hey, Miss Fran. Merry Christmas." She made her best clown's face for the nurse and held up an orange from her bag.

"Merry Christmas to you, too, Natalie." With a big smile on her dark face, the woman rounded the counter and gave Natalie a hug that threatened to crack her ribs. Natalie was careful not to get makeup on the nurse's scrubs. "Why are you here today? You should be with friends or family."

"Same reason as you," Natalie replied. "For the kids."

"Ha, you're not gettin' paid double time today." Fran chuckled as she took the orange, returning to the other side of the counter. She tucked the orange next to a stack of files beside a computer monitor. "Course, I'm not missing out, either. My Tonya's going to have the ham done by the time I get off tonight. And sweet potato soufflé, just like I taught her to make it."

"Sounds yummy. So, who do we have that needs a little cheer? Anything special I should know?"

"We have a new patient, just moved to the floor from ICU. 304. I think she could use some extra cheering up today. You might want to start with her and her family." An alert chime sounded at a console behind the counter. "Gotta run, sweet pea. See you in a bit."

Natalie called out, "See you," as Fran hit overdrive toward the room with a light flashing above the door. Natalie made her way to room 304.

People in less-than-festive clothing, women in long dresses, plain primary colors, wearing white head coverings, and a few men with beards, dark trousers, and some in matching dark vests, clustered inside the sitting room. Amish, waiting their turn to visit someone. She made a clown's smile at them all and waved as she passed them in her rainbow-striped clown suit and flaming red wig with long braids.

Natalie entered the hospital room with brisk steps and skidded to a stop. The little girl, the new patient Fran mentioned, lay on the bed, whispering something to her bearded father, who touched her head gently. Her right leg was in traction and a monitor flashed the girl's vital signs. Poor kid. Natalie definitely should have brought a chocolate bar.

Her father looked in Natalie's direction and stiffened. He stood. His blue eyes looked troubled. And like the people in the waiting room, he wore the classic dark pants of the Amish with a white shirt and suspenders.

"Hello." Natalie tried to stay in character. "I'm Bubbles the Clown, and I wanted to visit and cheer you up today, and wish you a Merry Christmas." She almost let her words falter at seeing the expression on the father's face. Did the Amish even celebrate Christmas? She probably ought to focus more on entertaining the little girl and forget mentioning the holiday anymore.

The father was tall, with sandy brown hair and beard, blue eyes, and a dark expression. The beard lent some age to his face, but Natalie figured he might be about her age, or maybe about thirty or so. A young woman next to him wore a dark blue dress with a white apron. She whispered to the man who stood beside the girl's father. Brothers, Natalie guessed, by the shape of their noses and eyes.

One bearded man in the corner wore dark trousers and a tropical print shirt, along with suspenders. Now *that* was something you didn't see every day. She tried not to stare at him, like the rest of them stared at her.

"Jacob," said the older brother. "It won't hurt for the children to laugh for a few minutes. Come on in, Miss, uh, Bubbles."

A small boy sat in the chair in the corner, his skinny legs tucked under his chin. "Can you juggle?" He had a bit of a singsong tone to his voice, with almost a German accent. He reminded her of a mouse, with his guarded expression and a hint of mischief in his round brown eyes. His thick brown hair sprouted a bowl cut that ended at his ears.

"Yes, I can," Natalie replied. She set her tie-dyed tote bag on the floor and snatched out three small rubber balls. "It's not so hard. See? Start with one ball."

The boy sat up straighter, then shifted to the edge of the cushioned seat. His eyes followed the journey as Natalie circulated the balls from one hand, to the air, then to the other hand.

"I wish I could do that," came a quiet voice from the bed. The little girl, older than her brother, shifted on the mattress. Pain shadowed her blue eyes.

"What's your name?"

"Rebecca."

"Well, Rebecca, I bet you could learn, quick as anything, after you get better." Natalie stopped the balls, ending up with two in her left hand and one in her right. "It takes practice, but if you stick with it, you'll likely be better than I am someday."

"Thank you for coming to visit today," said the young woman in the blue dress. She didn't seem much older than Natalie.

"My name's Katie Miller, and this is my husband Ephraim, and my brother-in-law Jacob. It's nice of you to visit on a holiday." Katie offered her hand, which Natalie shook.

"I'm Zeke," came a little voice from the chair. The little tyke with the big eyes and long legs smiled at her.

"Hi, Zeke, and Katie, and all the Miller family. It's nice to meet you, although I'm sorry it's here in the hospital, especially on Christmas Day," Natalie replied. Katie. That had been her mother's name. But by the time Natalie had come around, she'd gone by Kat for several years.

"*Gotte* has a purpose in our being here," Jacob Miller said, and stroked his daughter's head. "I'm thankful He spared her life."

Natalie nodded. This wasn't her usual cheer-me-up visit. The kids had smiled at the juggling. "I brought you a present." She went to fetch her bag of oranges.

"How did you know to bring me a present, if you didn't know I was going to be here?" asked Rebecca.

"I knew some special kids would be here, and they should get oranges from the tree in my yard." Natalie drew two oranges out of the bag, and set the bag on the bed near Rebecca's feet. She gave the fruit a quick juggle, then presented one to Zeke and one to Rebecca.

"My *mammi* and *daadi* have grapefruit trees in their yard," said Rebecca. Her small hands massaged the pebbly surface of the orange. "But I like oranges better."

"Say thank you," reminded their father.

"Thank you." Rebecca smiled at Jacob, then Natalie.

What a tightly knit family. Natalie found she couldn't keep in character today. What was it about this family? She knew part of the answer lay at home, in a box her father had shipped to her just in time for Christmas. Too bad FedEx was so efficient. The box could have arrived after Christmas, and it would have been fine with her.

The orange slipped from Rebecca's grasp, tumbling onto the blanket. Rebecca's hands shook in a frenzy. Her head snapped back, her limbs stiffened. The vital signs monitor went crazy with beeps and alarms.

"Fran!" Natalie darted from the room and onto the floor. "She's seizing!"

The nurse was already flying around the desk, her bulky form moving with uncanny speed. Natalie had seen this before. She darted to the side to let Fran in. Another nurse dialed a pager.

The Millers joined Natalie in the hallway, and little Zeke was already sobbing. "My 'Becca."

Natalie squatted and touched his shoulder. "She's exactly where she needs to be right now, sweetie. She's being taken care of." Although she could make no promises for what lay ahead for the little girl.

"You're right," said Jacob Miller. He pulled Zeke closer to him. "We must find the others and let them know. We were taking turns, visiting her today."

The family filed toward the waiting room and left Rebecca to the doctor's care. Jacob, however, cast a worried glance at his daughter, then at Natalie. His look of sorrow pierced her heart.

Katie Miller glanced at Natalie. "We are going to go pray for Rebecca. Will you join us?"

Natalie nodded. "Of course." She ought to go to another room, and let this family do what they felt they must. But she followed them anyway.

When she entered the waiting room, the television set was off and the dark-clothed people were standing. A few of the women, about her age, wore pastel-colored dresses.

She bowed her head as they did, and one of the older men began to speak in another language. German, or Dutch, she figured. She didn't know the words, but felt the power and sincerity behind them.

Dear God, please guide the doctors. Take care of little Rebecca. I don't know what's wrong with her, but You do. Work through these gifted people who are caring for her now, Natalie prayed silently.

A warm, small hand slipped into hers and squeezed. Zeke Miller looked up at her with his mouse-eyes. Natalie squeezed back.